INTERSTELLAR FLIGHT MAGAZINE BEST OF YEAR 5

INTERSTELLAR FLIGHT PRESS ANTHOLOGIES

EDITED BY

HOLLY LYN WALRATH

INTERSTELLAR FLIGHT MAGAZINE BEST OF YEAR 5

Cover Image by Yaroslav Gerzhedovich/iStock Photo

Edited by Holly Lyn Walrath.

Published by Interstellar Flight Press

Houston, Texas.

www.interstellarflightpress.com

ISBN (eBook): 978-1-953736-43-7

ISBN (Paperback): 978-1-953736-42-0

CONTENTS

REVIEWS

INTERVIEWS

EDITORS NOTE

HOLLY LYN WALRATH

Each year, this anthology grows in its page count as the list of contributors to Interstellar Flight Magazine grows. As far as online SFF magazines go, IFP doesn't get a huge ton of recognition because as a whole, nonfiction is a little-recognized form of writing. There are few categories dedicated to essays in major awards (with the exception of the Bram Stoker Awards, which an IFP author has won in the nonfiction category in the past). Still very few magazines and journals dedicate large swaths of pages to nonfiction, and it is often as an afterthought. Nonfiction doesn't qualify writers for admission to major writing organizations in SFF like SFWA. Once, an author went on a tangent learning that we didn't pay "pro" rates—but then withdrew that rant realizing we only published nonfiction. (There is no pro rate for SFF nonfiction.)

And yet, every year we get contacted by filmmakers, book authors, and gamemakers who thank us for the work we do. For *getting it*. For recognizing that a character was coded as queer. For giving a book that received very little reviews some love. For making space for works that often don't get attention, such as speculative poetry.

The only rhyme or reason that dictates what IPF takes for our magazine is pretty much up to our authors. This magazine like most community organized publications, beyond the sales of the print anthology, is not a money-making venture. But the space it makes for new and underrecognized voices is why I keep up with it every year.

From science fiction to fantasy to horror, our little online magazine publishes interviews, reviews, and essays related to speculative works of media, from film to comics to video games to books. The majority of the essays we publish also provide a new perspective on underrepresented voices in some way.

I see the magazine as being about crossways. In this anthology, we have a co-authored personal essay on gaming as an escape from reality for teens. You can enjoy reading long essays on the greats in horror like Edgar Allen Poe, Shirley Jackson, and Stephen King. Readers can find their next film to stream or a cult classic to revisit from a new point of view. We uplift other small presses and celebrate works that challenge the status quo.

In short, if you love anything speculative, this anthology is for you. We hope you enjoy and consider sending us your own ideas. We are always open for submissions—and better yet, always open for a conversation.

ORIGINAL ARTICLES

THE NEVER-ENDING TEDIUM OF SURVIVAL: A LONG-FORM ESSAY ON THE FINAL GIRLS WHO STRUGGLE TO STAY ALIVE AGAIN AND AGAIN AND AGAIN

ANDREA BLYTHE

Horror movie franchises are often recognized by their iconic villains—Michael Myers, Freddy Krueger, Jason Voorhees, Ghostface, Pinhead, and many other often-masked and often-men baddies who are easily recognizable as a Halloween costume. However, they are not always the core of the series; more often, the heart and soul of a horror franchise is its survivor—the Final Girl (or Guy), who finds herself hunted all over again in the next film, who must learn to survive and survive again as she continuously stares down the ever-looming presence of the monster in the dark.

Bearing the wounds and scars granted by their roles as would-be-victims turned fighters, these Final Girls find themselves perpetually trapped in a limbo of trauma, dragging themselves through the mud and blood in the hopes of coming through the other side alive. This article will present an overview of a number of survivors, who have each appeared in at least three films within their franchise—and who each have their own journeys of coming to terms with their dark worlds.

Before I go any further, a heads up that I'm going to be talking about the endings for multiple films in each franchise discussed —so, **SPOILERS AHEAD**.

Sidney Prescott, Scream

When *Scream* came out in 1996, it reinvigorated the horror genre—particularly slashers—through its self-referential humor and declaration of the rules of surviving a horror movie (something that's been widely talked about before). The film also introduced audiences to Sidney Prescott (Neve Campbell), who became an iconic scream queen, joining a long list of Final Girls and becoming one of the few to become the heart of their series. (Though technically, she is not the "final" survivor because a number of other side characters also survive the murder spree.)

When we meet Sidney in the first film, she is already haunted by her mother's murder a year before. Because of the trauma of finding her mother's mutilated body, she has closed herself off—particularly from her boyfriend Billy (Skeet Ulrich). Though she is trying to move on, the sudden, brutal murder of a classmate dredges up the past. She is confronted by reporter Gale Weathers (Courteney Cox), who claims that Sidney accused the wrong man of murdering her mother all those years before, falsely sending him to prison. In addition, she is violently attacked by Ghostface (as the costumed killer is dubbed) in her own home, further exacerbating her trauma and making her uncertain who she can fully trust.

After suspecting and accusing her boyfriend of being the murderer, she eventually comes back around to wanting to trust him as there seems to be little evidence against him. Talked into it by her best friend Tatum (Rose McGowan), Sidney joins her friends at a house party under the assumption that she will be safe with so many people around. She meets with Billy during the party, and talking leads to intimacy. Almost as a way of making up for her previous accusations and distrust, they have sex (a violation of rule number one of surviving a horror movie), but afterward, Sidney is clearly uncomfortable with her decision since she is still unsure of him.

Ghostface attacks, forcing Sidney to both fight and flee. Several chase sequences later—with Ghostface either attempting or successfully killing off a number of characters—it is revealed that Sidney's gut feeling was accurate because Billy and Stuart (Matthew Lillard) were, in fact, the killers. Not only that, but they also murdered her mother the year before. And now they intend to kill her and blame the murders on her father.

Just in time, Gale arrives wielding a gun (which, unfortunately, has the safety on), and Sidney uses this distraction to slip away. Rather than just fleeing for safety, Sidney channels her terror into rage, using the voice box against the two killers and even donning the Ghostface costume when she drives the tip of an umbrella into Billy's stomach. Together, Sidney and Gale successfully kill the killers—preventing them from doing further harm to anyone else.

As the credits roll, the feeling is triumphant. The murders are over, Sidney has survived, and so have a number of her friends, including Gale, Deputy Dwight

'Dewey' Riley (David Arquette), and Randy (Jamie Kennedy), and they can all move on with their lives—or so it seems.

We don't see the full effect surviving these murders has on Sidney until the second film, *Scream 2* (1997). Now, in university, she is trying to move on with her life. She has new friends, a boyfriend, and the starring role of Cassandra in a college production of *Agamemnon*. Despite her attempts to reshape her life, the trauma is clearly present, as one friend points out to Sidney, telling her she needs to come out of her "self-induced isolation."

This is difficult to do, however, because the past will not stay dead. First, Gale Weathers digs up the past by bringing Cotton Weary (Liev Schreiber), the man Sidney wrongly accused and sent to prison, for a face-to-face interview with Sidney in a surprise confrontation. He wants public vindication (quite fairly), but Sidney just wants to be left alone.

Then, a new round of brutal murders begins to occur, with Ghostface killing the people close to Sidney—a confirmation of all her fears. Her response upon learning about the first murder is simple, "I knew this wasn't over." Naturally, she spins back into distrusting most of the people around her, particularly her boyfriend, which is understandable considering her past experience.

In the final confrontation with the killers, she once again triumphs with the help of Gale, Dewey, and Cotton. As the slew of cops and ambulances swoop in to clean up the mess, she takes a moment to give Cotton the vindication he desires by pointing the media to him as the hero.

Unlike the first film, this final moment does not feel triumphant. Her boyfriend and college friends are all dead. Her trauma is not resolved. As Sidney walks away from everyone and everything she knows, the camera zooms into a high aerial view, revealing that she is truly going into the world alone.

This isolation continues into the start of *Scream 3* (2000), with Sidney living in an undisclosed location surrounded by a security fence in the middle of nowhere. She lives under a false name and locks up her door every time she returns home, clicking in place a series of strong deadbolts and locks. The only person who knows how to contact her is Dewey, and the only person she meets in person is her father, who questions her isolation, stating, "It's as if you don't exist." To which she responds, "That's the idea." The never-ending string of violence has made it seem safer to erase herself from the world than to exist within it.

But Ghostface wants to eliminate her on his own terms and begins to leave a string of bodies in Hollywood in an attempt to draw her out. In Sidney's absence, Gale and Dewey are left to investigate the truth. The investigation leads to information about Sidney's mom, who lived in Hollywood when she was younger, and there are hints about the killer's connection to her mother.

Eventually, Sidney realizes that she can't avoid the past forever and comes out of hiding. She joins her friends in the search for the killer, who she discovers is actually Roman Bridger (Scott Foley), her older half-brother, who was born and abandoned when their mother was younger and then later rejected when he found his mother as an adult. Sidney has the life that he always wanted—and he reveals that he is the architect of everything that happened, instigating the murder of Sidney's mother and all the killings that came after in an act of revenge.

When he is ultimately defeated and killed, it feels like the closing of a circle. The past can finally rest, and Sidney and her fellow survivors can live their lives. This is symbolized in the closing scene. Sidney returns home, but this time, she is not alone. Surrounded by the laughter of friends, she glances back to see the front door has been left unlocked and stands open. She looks at the open door and smiles, finally allowing herself to be open to the world—a satisfying conclusion to her story.

But the franchise lives on, and, therefore, Sidney cannot be left in peace.

When *Scream 4* (2011) begins, Sidney is in a good place. She has written a memoir, *Out of Darkness*, in which she shares her experiences of surviving multiple killing sprees and finding her way back into the world. She returns to Woodsboro as part of her book tour and is staying with family, including her niece Jill Roberts (played by Emma Roberts). Almost immediately, everything goes wrong, with a new Ghostface appearing to threaten Sidney's family. Although this killer is mostly focused on Jill and her friends, a new generation of teenagers to terrorize.

In the end, the killings are not focused on past tragedies but on the question of who gets to wear the crown of Final Girl. Jill herself has instigated the killings and has been murdering all her friends with the aim of becoming the sole survivor. "I don't need friends, I need fans," she tells Sidney in the final showdown before killing her accomplice, telling him, "What the media really loves, baby, is a sole survivor."

Jill stabs Sidney in the gut, who collapses onto the floor unconscious. Then, Jill proceeds to enact a series of injuries upon herself, such as stabbing herself in the shoulder, slamming her face into a picture frame, and falling backward onto a glass table before collapsing beside Sidney, mimicking her position exactly. Two Final Girls side by side—with only one left alive.When Jill is in the hospital, she is confident of her victory and ready to claim her place as the final survivor—*except,* it turns out Sidney has survived the attack (always the fighter) and is in surgery. The true final showdown occurs in the hospital, with Jill ultimately being defeated. Sidney lies on the floor exhausted and glances over at her fallen niece and says one final quip, "You forgot the first rule of remakes, Jill: Don't fuck with the originals."

In the fifth film in 2022 (confusingly titled just *Scream*), Sidney plays a more minor role since a new group of teenagers in Woodsboro act as the focus of the killings, with sisters Sam (Melissa Barrera) and Tara Carpenter (Jenna Ortega) at the center. When the killings start to take place, these teens look to Dewey for answers, and he sends a message to Sidney and Gale that the killings have started again.

Sidney is pushing a stroller when the call arrives, a sign that she has not lapsed into her previous isolation but has begun to build a family life with Mark (presumably the same Mark from *Scream 3*). Nevertheless, she returns to Woodsboro, along with Gale, to help put an end to this new Ghostface. They are quickly met with tragedy, however, when Dewey is killed. Heading into the final showdown, they jointly decide that, if they survive, neither of them will write a book about this or speak to the media in the hopes that the story will die and the cycle of killings will stop.

Although they are helpful in stopping the two Ghostface killers, it is ultimately Sam and Tara who deliver the final blows, with the duo taking over the role of the Final Girls of the franchise. Afterward, Sam, who has looked to Sidney almost as a mentor, asks if she's going to be okay. Sidney knows all too well what likely lies ahead for Sam and simply says, "Eventually."

Scream (2022) really feels like a passing of the torch, with new survivors taking up the mantle of the franchise. And when *Scream VI* (2023) rolls around a year later, Sidney stays clear of the killings, opting instead to take her husband and children away into hiding. She is—it would seem—finally free of the burden of facing death.

Addendum: Gale Weathers and Dwight 'Dewey' Riley

Although Sidney is the heart of the Scream series and more comfortably falls into the classic Final Girl trope, it seems wrong not to discuss Gale and Dewey. Their journey is less about dealing with their trauma as survivors and more about their relationship to each other, with Gale in particular being caught between her personal drive for success as a reporter and her attraction and eventual love for Dewey and her friends.

Starting out, Gale is a sharp-witted and highly determined reporter who is solely focused on getting the story and who will ruthlessly run over anyone in her drive to become famous, while Dewey is an innocent and a little bit dopey deputy sheriff with no great ambition beyond doing his job. Despite their differences, they have a near-instant attraction to each other.

Over the next several films, their relationship bounces back and forth as Gale's ambition has a tendency to drive a wedge between them. However, she grows as the series progresses. While her ambition and passion for investigative reporting never really goes away, she begins to see the people around her as more important. This growth allows for Gale and Dewey to fully commit to each other, with them being (mostly) happily married in *Scream 4*.

However, the fifth film reveals that there has been a turn in their relationship. Dewey is broken down and living in a filthy trailer due to his guilt at leaving Gale without a word after he didn't know how to deal with her success. On her return after the start of the murders, she's angry at him for not contacting her sooner. There is no sign of the old Gale here—no cameras, no recording devices, just concern for the people she loves.

She is eventually left bereft when Dewey is murdered after their reconciliation. The loss causes her to return to some of her callous steamrolling ways in *Scream VI*, writing a book about the new Woodsboro murders despite her promise not to do so and shoving a microphone in Sam and Tara's face only to get clocked by Tara (in an echo of the first film). However, when faced with the possible deaths of those around her, she turns off the cameras and steps up to help. When she's separated from the group and left on her own, she is attacked in her penthouse. Despite using her wits to fight off the killer, she is stabbed. Before passing out, she says to Sam, "Tell Sidney he didn't get me," hoping to keep Sidney out of danger.

Although she's not seen again after this, it's revealed that Gale survived her wounds. It will be interesting to see if she will return in subsequent films, unable to keep away because, as Tara states, she's afraid that without Ghostface, she'll just fade away. Or maybe she take all the lessons she's learned and finally move on with her life. Time will tell.

Ellen Ripley, Alien

In *Alien* (1979), the crew of the spaceship *Nostromo* are awoken from hyper-sleep by the ship's computer systems in response to a signal in the void. Obligated to respond and investigate the signal (otherwise, they won't get paid), the crew lands on a strange planet and discovers leathery eggs that release a face-hugger that wraps itself around the head of a crew member named Kane (John Hurt).

From the start, Ellen Ripley (Sigourney Weaver), acting as warrant officer on the crew, is intelligent and practical in her responses to the emergency situation. When Captain Dallas (Tom Skerritt) attempts to return to the ship with the contaminated crew member, Ripley keeps the doors locked, noting that quarantine protocol requires 24 hours for contamination. As she explains later, "By breaking quarantine, we risk everybody's life."

However, her decision is overridden, and the crewmembers return to the ship, where the alien creature (xenomorph) grows inside Kane and eventually bursts from his chest, running loose through the ship. What happens next is no less than a massacre as the xenomorph kills each crew member one by one.

Throughout these events, Ripley keeps her wits about her, presenting an outward calm even if she's internally terrified. She even takes the lead when Dallas is killed, creating the plan most likely to keep them all alive. Despite her best efforts, however, everyone except for the cat is lost. Ripley is left to face the alien alone and manages to self-destruct the ship while escaping in a shuttle. Before she can slip into hyper-sleep with the cat, however, the alien reveals itself, having snuck aboard the shuttle. Using quick thinking, she dons a space suit and ejects the creature into space, finally burning it up with the ship's engines.

Exhausted and alone, she gives one final report to the computer, flatly reading off the names of the crew—too exhausted and worn down to express her feelings about the loss. "This is Ripley," she concludes, "last survivor of the *Nostromo*, signing off."

When her escape pod is found 57 years later in *Aliens* (1986), she is questioned about the events that led up to the destruction of the ship (with the company worried about the cost). Much to her frustration, no one believes her when she tells them about the xenomorph, and she is painted by the company as mentally unstable. According to them, a terraforming colony has been living on the planet the *Nostromo* visited with no problems.

But when it's revealed that the colony has gone silent, Ripley is asked is join a group of US Colonial Marines sent to the plant to investigate. At first, she refuses. But she continues to be bombarded by nightmares since her return, which brings her to a decision: if the team intends to destroy the alien creatures, then she is willing to participate. She wants to wipe them out so they are no longer a threat to humanity.

Arriving at the planet, she takes up her advisory roles, explaining what these creatures are and the danger they present. "Just one of those things managed to wipe out my entire crew in just 24 hours," she explains, but the marines are hardened and unimpressed by her warnings, certain they can handle anything thrown their way.

It is quickly proven that they cannot, however, when they stumble upon a nest of eggs and are attacked by a large number of xenomorphs. The majority of the marines are killed within minutes. In the face of this threat, Ripley once again keeps her cool and quickly comes up with solutions to address each new challenge. When the team first enters the facility, Ripley is the one who remembers that if the team fires their weapons, they could rupture the cooling system. When the team falls into trouble, she takes control of a transport to rescue them. When they find a small child survivor called Newt (Carrie Henn), she approaches her with calm and compassion. When the aliens drag the child away to be implanted, Ripley rescues her from the heart of the nest and dons an exoskeleton (described in the film script as "medieval armor with the power of a bulldozer") to fight the Alien Queen in a kind of hand-to-hand combat.

Through Ripley's actions, she is once again able to escape from the plant, but this time she is not alone. With her are fellow survivors Newt, Corporal Hicks (Michael Biehn), and Bishop (Lance Henriksen). They slip into hyper-sleep, hopeful of returning home—only to have that hope immediately ripped away from them in the subsequent *Alien 3* (1992).

The third film is the bleakest in the franchise. It opens with their ship crash landing on the planet Fiorina 161, with Ripley being the only survivor of the crash. Immediately, she is suspicious of how the crash happened, and evidence of acidic xenomorph blood leads her to witness the brutal and traumatizing autopsy of Newt to verify that the girl had not been infected with an alien parasite. Although Newt was not infected, Ripley is nevertheless convinced that an alien must have survived. She investigates by waking the android Bishop and learns that an alien did indeed make it onto the planet—not that she can convince anyone to believe her.

When the creature bursts into the medical facility, it kills two men and knocks Ripley against the wall. Having nothing to fight back with, she is helpless as the alien leans in close, teeth and double mouths inches from her face—but it doesn't kill her (as pictured at the start of this section). This moment leads Ripley to the terrifying revelation that she is carrying a parasite for an Alien Queen.

Ever practical, Ripley uses this apparent immunity from attack to help the prisoners fight against the alien creatures. Together, they trick it into a pit and pour molten metal onto it, then drop water upon the creature to quickly cool it, causing it to explode.

Shortly after, a rescue team from the Weyland-Yutani Corporation arrives. They tell Ripley that they can safely remove the alien from her body, but she knows that nothing good can come from giving the corporation access to research the alien. So, she opts out, instead jumping into the pit of molten metal, letting herself and the Alien Queen inside her burn up to nothing.

Technically, this is the end of Ellen Ripley's story—as we know her.

Two centuries after her death, the corporation manages to successfully clone Ripley and the Alien Queen from a sample of blood drawn on the prison planet. Due to the way the alien species incubate within the host, their DNA has become crossed. Therefore, during the cloning process, Ripley 8 (as the clone is called) became a little bit alien, and the new Alien Queen a little bit human. Ripley 8 is stronger, faster, and has slightly acidic blood. Although she contains some of her memories of being Ripley, she is not the same. She is colder, a bit disconnected from her humanity, but she does side with the humans on the ship. She warns the scientists that the Queen will eventually escape and kill them—which they don't believe, thinking they have everything under-control.

The Alien Queen does indeed escape and begins breeding more aliens, including a terrifying human-alien crossbreed. Ultimately, Ripley and a small part of the crew destroy the aliens and escape, making it back to Earth. When asked what she plans to do now, Ripley 8 answers, "I don't know. I'm a stranger here myself." Although she is not the same Ripley, we have come to know and love, she at least has an opportunity to shape a life for herself without the constant threat of alien attack.

Alice, Resident Evil

Only loosely based on the popular survival horror game franchise, the Resident Evil films that first kicked off in 2002 are ranked among the highest-grossing horror movie franchises of all time. While the movies borrow a few key elements, such as the evil Umbrella Corporation and the exposure of the T-Virus that causes the dead to rise along with other even more deadly mutations, they chart their own path in terms of overall narrative—first, with the notable introduction of the lead character Alice (played by Milla Jovovich).

At the start of 2002's *Resident Evil*, Alice awakens on the floor of a shower with no memory of who she is or what has happened. The mansion in which she finds herself provides few clues, but the commando team that crashes through the windows informs her that she is an operative of the Umbrella Corporation and that her amnesia is a temporary effect of defenses unleashed when the Red Queen, an artificial intelligence system, locked down the secret underground research facility known as the Hive and killed everyone inside.

Dragged along with the team, Alice and the commandos are confronted by two enemies—the Red Queen and the hundreds of zombies loose within the facility. The fight quickly becomes desperate, and members of the commando team meet a series of gruesome deaths. In the struggle to survive, Alice begins to regain knowledge of her hand-to-hand combat and weapons skills, as well as memories of her desire to take down the Umbrella Corporation.

Though Alice and one other survivor make it out of the Hive (mostly) intact, their relief is short-lived. A team of Umbrella Corporation men in hazmat suits burst into the room, taking them both captive. Later, Alice wakes on an examination table with a tangle of tubes and wires protruding from her body. When she inevitably escapes outside, she is confronted with the aftermath of these events. She grabs a shotgun out of an abandoned cop car and—in one of my personal favorite horror endings—the camera zooms out, revealing a city utterly wrought with destruction.

The first movie is certainly the strongest. After this point, the narrative grows increasingly convoluted as the series goes on. Having been experimented on by the Umbrella Corporation, Alice begins to display an expanding array of powerful abilities, including increased speed and strength, the ability to heal, and telekinesis, which are then taken away from her at the start of the fourth movie (*Afterlife*, 2010)—not that it in any way stops her from being a badass that can survive a plane exploding into a mountain and other impossibilities—but not to worry, her humbling is short-lived because her abilities are then returned to her at the end of the next movie (*Retribution,* 2012), but not really because for some reason she doesn't seem to have the full extent of her powers in the sixth and final flick (*The Final Chapter,* 2016).

Meanwhile, throughout all of this, the Umbrella Corporation allows Alice to escape their research facility for some reason, only to desperately try to hunt her down and get her back again—and despite the fact that they've managed to nearly annihilate humanity, they really want to continue their research and experimentation projects because reasons, I guess? These movies not only have zombies and mutated monsters, but they also have clones and mind control and underground city simulations—and let's face it, it's a lot.

Don't get me wrong, I love the Resident Evil series for all the muchness that it contains. These movies are full of slick and stylish action set pieces with giant explosions, boss fights with giant and seemingly unstoppable monsters, lots of gore, and plenty of jump scares. They are, for the most part, fun.

However, at no point do they even pretend to evoke any deep emotional context for any of the characters. Alice constantly watches her comrades and companions meet horrifying deaths at the hands and teeth of the undead—but the movies are too busy moving from action sequence to exposition to action sequence to allow her (or anyone else) space to contemplate these losses. Nor is she given a moment to come to terms with seeing her friends resurrected as enemy clones before immediately entering into a gunfight with them.

Alice is a badass action hero through and through. She is a creature of blazing guns, acrobatic leaps, and quick quips. She doesn't have time for trauma or even feelings, really. She fights and survives and moves forward to the next battle. In the final moments of the last film, Alice rides a motorcycle down a desolate road while the zombies and other infected slowly begin to die around her thanks to an airborne anti-virus. As a flying mutation swoops down behind her, she smiles at the battles ahead and the work to be done.

Ash Williams, Evil Dead

The Evil Dead was instrumental in popularizing the cabin in the woods horror sub-genre due to its success at the box office when it was released in 1981. The story follows a common formula—a group of young people decide to vacation at a creepy cabin in the woods and accidentally awaken something evil that leads to their deaths—in this case, playing the recording of a strange professor reading from the Necronomicon Ex-Mortis, a book with the power to raise the dead.

Among the group of young adults introduced in this first movie is Ashley 'Ash' J. Williams (Bruce Campbell). At the time, it was not obvious that Ash would become the iconic horror icon that he is today. His character is not terribly interesting, though he is sweet with his girlfriend Linda (Betsy Baker). He also jumps to the aid of his other friends. When Cheryl (Ellen Sandweiss) demands to leave after being attacked by the trees in the woods, he agrees to take her back into town, regardless of his personal misgivings about her story (though his efforts are in vain because the bridge has been washed out).

However, once the situation begins to escalate and his friends are possessed by evil spirits/demons, Ash becomes somewhat useless. For example, he is the only one who listens to the recording further and learns that the only way to stop the dead is dismemberment—a fact he shares with no one. He also freezes up and fails to take action, even when it could save a friend's life. Some of this inaction is understandable since these are people he cares about, and his hesitation is less about fear than about being unable to bring himself to chop up his friends with an axe.

One by one, his friends and girlfriend are claimed by the deadites (as they will be called in the second movie), and Ash is left alone to be continually tormented by the dead. Eventually, he has no choice but to take action, shooting, chopping, and fighting against his former companions turned deadites. As the night goes on, the camera tilt becomes more significant, reflecting his degrading mental state.

Finally, he manages to burn the book, and the deadites begin to rapidly decay. As the sun rises, he exits the cabin, lifting his arms to the brightening sky. He believes for a moment that he has made it through—only for something to come flying out of the woods, and we see Ash screaming into the camera (the implication being his death).

There is some debate as the whether *Evil Dead II* (1987) is actually a sequel or a requel (though Campbell himself has called it a requel). The beginning of *Evil Dead II* quickly recaps the first movie with some factual differences. Most notably, it only shows Ash and his girlfriend traveling to the cabin, awakening the dead, and Ash left fighting the dead. (My personal headcanon is that the first movie is how events actually played out, while the second movie is how Ash *tells it* since it shows him being more decisive).

The story continues with Ash being briefly possessed, with the possession seeming to burn off in the sunlight. Once again, he attempts to leave, only to find himself trapped by the collapsed bridge and being forced to return to the cabin. Upon returning, he begins to disassociate. He stares into his own reflection repeating, "I'm fine... I'm fine," only to have his reflection reach through and grab him by the head, stating, "I don't think so. We just cut up our girlfriend with a chainsaw."

At this point, his girlfriend resurrects and reassembles herself. She violently attacks him, and her detached head bites his hand—which causes his hand to become infected. His own hand turns against him and tries to kill him. In desperation, he does the only thing he can think of—grabbing the chainsaw and removing his own hand. Covered in blood and gore, he begins to laugh maniacally while the head of a deer and other objects within the room laugh along with him. It's not entirely clear whether this laughter of the objects around him is all in his own head or if it is the deadites finding new ways to torment him.

The laughter is cut abruptly short when he hears a sudden noise and—without hesitation—fires his shotgun at the door. It is not, as he assumes, more of the dead but another group of people who stand on the other side. They take one look at this wild-eyed man with a shotgun, and the evidence of blood and destruction spread around the cabin and, understandably, assume that Ash must have murdered the former occupants, Prof. Knowby (the voice of John Peakes on the recording) and his wife Henrietta (played by Lou Hancock when she's herself and Ted Raimi when she's possessed).

So, they lock him in the basement, where another deadite in the form of Henrietta awakens, and when she attacks, they release Ash, who attempts (and fails) to save them. More chaos, blood, gore, and death ensue—with all of the group except Ash and Annie Knowby (Sarah Berry) being killed. Together, the two final survivors attempt to use pages from the *Necronomicon* to open a portal to expel the deadites and send them through time and space.

Although Annie dies in the process, the spell works, and the evil is sucked away. The only problem is that the portal sucks up Ash as well, casting him into the spiraling vortex.

In *Army of Darkness* (1992), Ash finds himself trapped in the 1300s. Confused for a member of an opposing army, he is treated as a prisoner of war and cast into a pit to his death. When he manages to defeat the two deadites housed within the pit using his chainsaw and shotgun, he gains the respect of the local people—who call him The Promised One, the one who recovers the Book of the Dead and saves them all.

At this point, however, Ash is entirely cold to the concerns of others. Shutting down his emotions in the wake of ongoing trauma, he reverts to being quippy, arrogant, selfish, and cowardly. He doesn't care about anyone else, and it is only when they promise that going on this quest will make it possible to send him back to his own time that he agrees to go on the journey.

He builds himself a magical robotic prosthesis for his missing hand, arms himself with his trusty chainsaw and shotgun, and heads on his way—experiencing a number of hilarious challenges, including an army of tiny Ashes that emerge from the broken mirror and his doppelganger that he kills with a shotgun and buries alive (or undead, rather).

When he reaches the cemetery that houses the Book of the Dead, he flubs the process of saying the three words required to safely remove the book—mostly because he could not be bothered to remember the words correctly when the wise men told them to him back in the village. This act awakens the army of the dead, and Ash rides back to the village, demanding to be returned to his own time, despite the fact that his oblivious actions have doomed all of these people to death.

It is only when Sheila (Embeth Davidtz), a woman he'd grown close to, is kidnapped by the deadites that Ash is willing to take action. He brews his own gunpowder, turns his car (which traveled to the past with him) into a vehicle of destruction, and teaches the people how to fight. The day is won, and he returns to his own time, despite the peoples' pleas for him to stay and become their king—at least according to Ash's version of the story that he is telling to his coworkers at S-Mart. His story is proven to be true (ish, since I expect he would gloss over the uglier bits of the story) when a deadite bursts into the store, and he kills it with one of the shotguns on display.

Now, I have a confession to make. I have not yet watched the TV series *Ash vs Evil Dead*, which aired across three seasons from 2015 to 2018. It's one of an ever-growing list of shows that I mean to get to at some point. So, I'm going to have to lean on others a bit to give insight into how the TV series allowed Ash to go from being a caricature, as presented in the movies, to a more fully developed character with an emotional arc and growth. As Tom Reimann at *Collider* explains:

It's not until Ash vs. Evil Dead *that we get to see the man in context—how he interacts with regular people in a regular environment. And it is both my favorite interpretation of Ash, and the only version of Ash that can truly be considered a fully defined character. It's not that he begins the series descended even further into the realm of self-parody, having gradually transformed into the biggest, saddest loser. (Ok, it's not just that.) It's the fact that, for the first time, we're given a clear picture of who Ash is as a person. He's kind of an idiot. He drinks too much and makes terrible life decisions. He's blunderingly offensive, but not mean-spirited. His lifelong dream is to retire in Jacksonville, Florida. And he has history—a hometown full of old friends and acquaintances who all think he's a cool guy, or a bum, or a possible murderer, or some combination of the three.*

Thomas Mariani delves deeper into the character's arc in *Ash vs Evil Dead*, describing how the character kicks off the series in complacency, still leaning into his selfishness and living a bachelor lifestyle. Because Ash knows that evil can return at any moment, Mariani notes, he doesn't get close to anyone or make any attempts to build a life for himself. However, as the show goes on, he slowly begins to build a found family and make a connection with his daughter—and it is these connections with others that help him to grow, take responsibility, and stand up against evil, ultimately sending "his daughter and surrogate kids away to face evil on his own." As the author explains:

He willingly sends his stability away in favor of facing what could be a fatal fight. Ash fully accepts his role in the universe and fights off evil with blunt force and earnest sincerity amongst the silliness... Ultimately, it's Ash knowing that he now has to fight off evil in a world where they have the advantage... and he accepts it with a willing spirit. Especially with the promise of doing so with his little patchwork family. He rides off into the sunset on his beloved 1973 Delta Oldsmobile Delta 88 like a cowboy on his loyal steed. A fantastic way of sending off the character of Ash.

As much as the Evil Dead franchise is about the undead and demons and wacky, gore-dripping monsters, it is also about the trauma and guilt of survival and the toll that can take on a person. And if we include the series, then it is also about coming through that trauma and forming connections again—while *also* fighting against wacky, gore-dripping monsters.

Sarah Connor, The Terminator

Understanding the narrative of the Terminator series can be a befuddling business due to the twisty time travel elements at the center of its universe, with characters jumping from the future to drastically alter the past—grandfather paradox be damned. Sarah Connor's journey is carried through four properties (three films and a TV show), essentially representing three separate timelines (as I understand it).

The first timeline includes *The Terminator* (1984) and *Terminator 2: Judgment Day* (1991), in which the character is played by Linda Hamilton. In *Terminator 3: Rise of the Machines* (2003), it is revealed that Sarah died from leukemia prior to the start of the film, and the franchise follows her son, John Connor, and his journey toward becoming the savior of humanity.

The second timeline includes the first two films and then proceeds with *Terminator: The Sarah Connor Chronicles*, a TV series that ran from 2008–2009, starring Lena Headey as the titular character. Since I haven't seen the show, I can't comment properly on it.

The third and arguably final timeline (though no franchise ever really stays dead) also includes the first two films and brings Linda Hamilton back as Sarah in *Terminator: Dark Fate* (2019)—and this is the timeline I'm going to focus on for this discussion.

The Terminator fits within the tropes of the slasher genre. A series of young women are violently murdered one by one—all named Sarah Connor—and the final surviving Sarah goes on the run from an unstoppable and impossible-to-defeat killer. When Sarah learns of the serial killings via the news, she enters a local bar to wait for the police, hoping to find safety in a crowded and public place. But two men find her first. One opens fire, spraying bullets across the club, and the other drags her outside to safety.

He gets her into a car and begins to explain the situation. He is Kyle Reese (Michael Biehn), who has traveled from the future to protect her from a T-800 Terminator (Arnold Schwarzenegger), a cyborg killing machine sent from the year 2049 to kill her. Why? Because she will give birth to a man, John Connor, leader of the future resistance movement, who will be instrumental in stopping the machines from destroying all of humanity.

It is a wild story, one that Sarah is hesitant to believe. She is just a waitress, a nobody. She can barely remember to pay her phone bill, let alone become a warrior or mother of the future. And when they are both picked up by the police shortly thereafter, she quickly accepts the psychologist's explanation that Reese is delusional. Because despite witnessing what the Terminator is capable of doing, placing her trust in the police and authority figures feels safer.

However, her complacency and safety are short-lived, because the Terminator finds them. As it proceeds to slaughter the police officers, Sarah and Reese manage to escape and once again find themselves on the run. As she dresses his wounds, Reese reveals that the reason he wanted to take this mission, with no hope of returning to his own time, was because he wanted to meet Sarah, who he describes as "the legend," the woman who taught John to fight, organize, and prepare for the coming war with machines when he was a kid. Their conversation leads to a deeper trust, and they have an intimate moment (the point at which her future son John is conceived).

As the Terminator closes in, we start to see the first signs of Sarah's strength and determination. She breaks into a factory to aid their escape, orders Reese to keep moving (sounding like a soldier herself), and she keeps fighting even after Reese dies in his attempt to destroy the Terminator. Injured and alone, she is able to crawl through a pressing machine, luring the terminator inside, and then uses the machine to crush and destroy the cyborg.

In the end, a now-pregnant Sarah heads to Mexico to go into hiding. A young boy tells her (in Spanish) to be careful because a storm is coming. She answers, "I know," indicating that she is now prepared to face the future.

Sarah Connor's evolution in *Judgement Day* is dramatic. Our first view of her is in a mental hospital, locked in a room with the bed overturned so that she can use it as a bar for pull-ups. She is physically ripped and intellectually intense—and it is revealed that she has been institutionalized for trying to blow up a computer factory (presumably in an attempt to stop the future from happening). Dr. Silberman (Earl Boen) notes that she has attempted to escape multiple times and exhibits violent behavior, including stabbing him in the knee with a pen.

When she learns that her son John has been attacked, she immediately enacts another escape attempt. She feigns disassociation and snags a paper clip, using it to escape her restraints and her cell. She attacks a guard and takes Dr. Silberman hostage using a needle full of drain cleaner. When he claims that she's not a killer, she answers, "You're already dead, Silberman. Everybody dies. You know I believe it, so don't fuck with me!" She has become so wrapped up in the horrors of the future that she can't even see the people around her as people—even her own son. When he comes to rescue her, she berates him for risking his own life. His role as a future hero is more important than this moment of human connection.

Her ongoing trauma is presented in a few ways. Outwardly, she's tough, strong, and capable. Inwardly, she's terrified. We see this in the way she panics upon seeing T-800 for the first time. She falls backward, feet slipping beneath her. She screams, all intelligent calculation gone, and runs straight into the arms of the guards attempting to catch her. "He'll kill us all!" she screams as they slam her to the floor, and she's shocked and shaking when John appears, explaining that it's okay, this T-800 will not kill them. She quickly puts her fear aside and returns to action once she's on solid ground, with an understanding of who her real enemy is, the T-1000 (Robert Patrick).

Later, when they stop to supply themselves with weapons, Sarah dreams. In her nightmare, she sees a version of herself—young, innocent, and playing with her son in a park—when suddenly everything is burned to ash in the wake of the nuclear explosion to come. She wakes with a jolt and stares down at the phrase "No fate" carved into a picnic bench.

Sarah has no intention of letting the future play out as planned, no intention of allowing the future to continue to come for her son. Without a word, she leaves her son with the Terminator and hunts down Miles Dyson (Joe Morton), the leader of the project that will create Skynet, the artificial intelligence that will attempt to destroy humanity. She takes aim with a sniper rifle and fires but misses. Then immediately pulls out a secondary weapon and stalks into the house with all the resolve and relentlessness of a Terminator.

As she points her weapon at Dyson, however, his wife and son get in the way. Up close, she sees their fear, his fear, and she hesitates, suddenly afraid of what she's become. Moments later, John and the Terminator burst into the room. She's grateful and slightly awed that her son came to stop her from killing Dyson, and she admires his compassion. For the first time since the start of the movie, she tells John, "I love you."

When Dyson learns about the future to come, he agrees to help them by destroying his research and the cybernetic arm and chip found after the first T-800 attacked Sarah in the 80s. They manage to get into the facility and obtain the items, but Dyson dies in the process, the building is destroyed, and the T-1000 is once again on their tail. They escape into a molten metal manufacturing plant and manage to drop the T-1000 into the molten metal, along with the other items. In order to fully stop the future, all evidence has to be destroyed, including the T-800, and Sarah holds onto her son in his grief as they watch the terminator slide down in the molten metal and disappear.

With Dyson dead and all cybernetic machines destroyed, Sarah finally looks to the future with hope—but as with every franchise, that hope is soon destroyed.

At the start of *Dark Fate*, Sarah reveals that their actions did successfully stop Judgement Day from occurring, but she couldn't save her son. Another T-800, a Terminator from a future that never happened, successfully assassinates John Connor, leaving Sarah bereft—but not idle.

For decades, she has been receiving text messages with precise GPS coordinates for the location of a time portal opening with something coming from the future. So she gathers her weapons, heads to the location, and kills whatever comes through. "I hunt Terminators," she explains. "And I drink till I pass out."

On her most recent mission, she helps save the life of Dani Ramos (Natalia Reyes) alongside Grace (Mackenzie Davis), an augmented human sent to protect Dani. Although Sarah and John were able to stop Skynet, a new robotic threat called Legion, a program designed for cyber warfare, rises to take its place and will begin its own campaign to destroy humanity in the future. (In a franchise, even if the enemy is defeated, another one will always rise in its place, bigger and more powerful than before, not allowing its characters to rest.)

When she learns that Dani has been targeted the way she was decades before, Sarah doesn't hesitate to offer her help, feeling connected to Dani because she's been through the same thing. However, she misunderstands the reason as to why Dani is being targeted. Caught up in her own past, Sarah rants about how Dani will be the mother of some man who will one day save the world. "Fine, she concludes. "Let someone else be Mother Mary for a while."

However, later, Grace reveals the truth. Dani is not the mother of the future, but rather, she is the future. She will become the person who will bring people together and lead them to fight back against the machines. "She's John," Sarah says, and in that small moment, it hits her—the loss of her son and a renewed compassion for Dani, a new future leader, who she has been fighting to protect and guide, just as she once did for John. Additional evidence that she is meant to become a mentor to Dani is when Grace states, "You taught me there was no fate but what we make for ourselves," the phrase that Sarah repeated to herself over the years, a phrase that she likely would have taught to Dani and that Dani would later teach to Grace.

As they search for a way to defeat the REV-9 (Gabriel Luna) that's hunting them, the group decides to find the person who has been sending Sarah text messages. If they can predict when something from the future comes through, then maybe they can help stop the machine. It turns out to be the T-800 that killed Sarah's son, now living as a human named Carl, having grown a conscience in the absence of new orders.

Sarah reacts the way you would expect a traumatized and heavily armed person would under these circumstances: He grabs a gun and immediately attempts to kill him. After some conversation, Sarah agrees with Grace and Dani that they need his help in defeating the REV-9, though Sarah promises to kill him as soon as the mission is done. As a soldier, however, Sarah grows to respect Carl as they fight side by side, and we see a level of acceptance and forgiveness when she calls him by his chosen name during the fight.

After a number of epic battles, the team manages to defeat the REV-9, though it takes everything they have, and both Grace and Carl are lost along the way. Only Sarah and Dani are left, and they watch a young Grace play in a playground, unaware of the future to come. "I won't let her die for me again," says Dani, and Sarah replies, "Then, you need to be ready."

Sarah has lost so much throughout her life, but she has never given up fighting. Although Skynet was destroyed, another enemy rose in its place because, as Sarah puts it, humanity never seems to learn. In the face of a new threat, she could collapse in despair and defeat. But Sarah is a soldier and a fighter, and she has no intention of quitting. The future will come, whether she's prepared or not—so she is going to be prepared, and she is going to make sure that Dani is prepared, too.

Laurie Strode, Halloween

Halloween (1978) helped define the slasher movie sub-genre. It introduces Laurie Strode (played by iconic scream queen Jamie Lee Curtis) as the first Final Girl and essentially develops the horror movie survival "rules" (don't have sex, don't drink or do drugs, etc.) that are emulated in other slashers and later described satirically in *Scream*.

On Halloween night in small town Haddonfield, Laurie and her friends are getting ready to babysit a couple of kids who live in the same neighborhood—unaware that Michael Meyers (Tony Moran), a man known in the community for having killed his own sister and parents when he was a child, has escaped a mental hospital. All throughout the day, Laurie notices a man in a mask watching her in the distance. He doesn't seem to be doing anything; just watches her and then disappears shortly after. Although it's weird and creepy, she doesn't become fully spooked. After all, it's Halloween, and it's not unusual to see men in masks wandering around, pulling pranks.

When evening falls, Laurie and her friend Annie (Nancy Kyes) go to their respective babysitting gigs. While Laurie seems to be taking it seriously, playing games and keeping an eye on Tommy (Brian Andrews), Annie seems more interested in having time with her boyfriend. It's not long before Annie brings the kid she's babysitting, Lindsey Wallace (Kyle Richards), over to Laurie to watch so that she can make out with her boyfriend in peace.

As the night goes on, Annie and the other teens are brutally murdered by Michael. When she doesn't hear anything from Annie, Laurie becomes worried. She leaves the two kids at Tommy's to go check on her friend. At the neighbor's, she discovers the corpses of her friends displayed throughout the house and is attacked by Michael, who has locked all the entrances and exits to trap her.

Despite a tumble down the stairs, she manages to escape the house and runs screaming down the street. She bangs on doors, but no one will let her in—not until she reaches Tommy's house and the kids let her back in. Ushering the two kids inside but soon realizes that the man has also followed her into the house. She tells the two kids to hide and also hides in a closet herself, but he finds her and bursts through the closet door. She fights him off with coat hangers (the only weapon she has on hand because she foolishly threw the knife away) and manages to stab him in the eye. He collapses backward and appears dead.

Laurie sends the kids to the neighbors, telling them to call the police. She then slides down to the ground and sits, expression blank. In her shock, she doesn't notice Michael rising behind her. He attempts to stab her again, but she fights back. In their struggle, she pulls the white mask from his face—which forces him to stop and put the mask back on. The pause is long enough for Dr. Loomis (Donald Pleasence), a psychiatrist who has been hunting Michael all night long, to arrive. Loomis is able to shoot Michael in the chest six times, causing him to fall out the window.

Shaking and terrified, Laurie says, "It was the boogeyman," referring to Tommy's warning of the boogeyman coming to get them earlier in the movie. Loomis turns to her and answers, "As a matter of fact, it was."

Halloween II (1981) kicks off immediately after the events of the first movie. Laurie is carted off to the hospital on a stretcher to receive care for her injuries. When the doctor says they'll need to put her under to patch her up, she begs the doctors not to give her, afraid of being so vulnerable and helpless, but they ignore her. They stitch her up and leave her in a recovery room to heal.

Laurie lays in her hospital bed, silently trying to make sense of what's happened to her. She is occasionally comforted by a kind and cute EMT named Jimmy (Lance Guest), who informs her that Michael Meyers was the killer. She recognizes the name from local lore, and she's shocked and horrified. "Why me?" she asks, "I mean, why *me*?"

While in bed, she also has dreams of the past. In one, a woman turns to a young Laurie and states bluntly, "I am not your mother." These dreams are connected to the investigation being conducted by Loomis and Sheriff Leigh Brackett (Charles Cyphers), who discover that Michael is not targeting Laurie randomly. After Michael killed his sister and parents and was sent away to a mental hospital when he was a child, Laurie was adopted by the Strodes, and her records were sealed. He is hunting her because she is his sister.

Unaware of this information—or that Michael is already in the hospital and killing nurses, security guards, and everyone he finds—Laurie becomes uncomfortable with waiting. She abandons her hospital bed, barely able to move due to her injuries and the lingering drugs in her system. Nevertheless, she wanders down the hallways until she finds an empty room in which to hide. She attempts to use the phone, but it is disconnected. So, she resumes wandering the halls, slightly dazed, which is when she stumbles into Michael.

She flees, escaping into the basement and then outside while Michael chases her. In the parking lot, she discovers that all of the tires on the cars have been slashed. She climbs into one of the useless cars and curls up into a ball on the floor of the footwell. When she sees Loomis and the sheriff entering the hospital, she runs to them—and is let inside just as Michael is about to reach her.

The sheriff is killed quickly, leaving Laurie and Loomis with nothing to do but run. Finding themselves cornered, Loomis gives Laurie a gun, which she uses to shoot Michael in each eye, blinding him. As he swings the butcher knife wildly around the room, they open valves to fill the room with flammable gas. Loomis tells Laurie to run, and when she's out of the room, he ignites the gas, causing an explosion that consumes both Michael and himself.

Laurie watches Michael stumbles out of the flames and collapses in a burning heap. She has survived the night, but as she is transferred to another hospital, we can see by the flat expression on her face that she will be dealing with the trauma for years to come.

Curtis leaves the franchise after the second film, and Laurie Strode is only mentioned briefly in *Halloween 4: The Return of Michael Myers* (1988), when it is noted that Laurie died in a car accident prior to the start of the movie—and her daughter Jamie Lloyd (Danielle Harris) has taken up the role of Final Girl.

However, *Halloween H20: 20 Years Later* (1998), the seventh film in the series, brings Curtis back to reprise the role of Laurie. This film ignores the daughter (who no longer exists) and reveals that Laurie faked her death in a car accident and changed her name in order to stay hidden from her homicidal brother.

Two decades later, Laurie is the headmistress of a private school. She bears a lot of scars—both physical (the scar on her arm where she was cut by Michael) and internal (nightmares, anxiety, and a penchant for drinking). She even has occasional hallucinations, seeing Michael in reflections or out of the corner of her eye—images that vanish as soon as she turns her head. With it being Halloween, she is especially jumpy to the extent that even her boyfriend, Will Brennan (Adam Arkin), a guidance counselor at the school, notices and asks her about it. She admits to him that she has tried a number of ways to deal with and process her past—such as self-help, aroma therapy, and meditation—but it hasn't worked.

Another element of her trauma is the overprotectiveness of her son John (Josh Hartnett), who she can barely let out of her sight. Since he is 17 and wants to forge his own path, this causes tension between them, which devolves into a fight when she catches him sneaking out of the closed campus. John retaliates, stating, "If you want to stay handcuffed to your dead brother, that's fine, but you're not dragging me along." The fight jars her enough that she agrees to let him go on the school camping trip, a concession to make peace with her son and a reflection of her desire to not live in fear. However, he betrays her trust by secretly hiding out in the school with some friends.

When Laurie tells Will the whole story about her past, he asks her why Michael would wait so long to finally come after her. He means this to be comforting, but it is at this moment that Laurie makes the connection—her son has just turned 17, the same age she was when Michael first tried to kill her. She immediately panics and tries to get ahold of her son—quickly realizing that he has skipped the camping trip, so he must still be on campus.

Laurie and Will manage to find John and his girlfriend Molly (Michelle Williams) just in time. They are both injured but alive. And Laurie comes face to face with her monster for the first time in two decades.

Although she suffers the loss of Will, Laurie manages to get John and Molly safely out of the school—but she turns back, closing the gate behind her, essentially locking herself in with Michael. The moment echoes a lesson that Laurie taught earlier that day, in which they discussed Frankenstein having to take responsibility for his own monster. Laurie now intends to do the same and put an end to Michael.

Laurie confronts Michael with an axe and hacks into his shoulder, only to get sliced in the arm herself (the same arm with her original scar). He chases her through the building, and she evades, finally getting ahold of two kitchen knives and using them to hack and slice at him until he falls backward through a window. Although the police arrive and put him in a body bag, she is not convinced that he is truly gone. She steals the ambulance that holds his body bag and crashes the vehicle, causing it to tumble down a hill and pinning Michael between the ambulance and a tree. Unable to move, he reaches for her —and she uses an axe to remove his head, finishing him off.

Unfortunately, the satisfaction of this ending is immediately negated by the opening of the subsequent movie, *Halloween: Resurrection* (2002). Laurie is locked away in a mental hospital, apparently catatonic since the events of *H20.* Two nurses discussing her condition reveal that the man Laurie killed was actually an EMT; Michael crushed his vocal cords and put him in the mask so that an innocent man was killed instead of him. Therefore, her catatonic state is due to guilt.

But wait—Laurie has actually been faking this whole time, waiting for Michael to come for her. She sees him standing outside and sets a trap, leading him up onto the roof, where she catches him in a snare. As he dangles over the edge of the roof, she confronts him, stating, "You failed Michael, and you want to know why? I'm not afraid of you. But what about you? Are you afraid of me? Are you afraid to die, Michael?" But before she can bring herself to cut the rope and send him plummeting to his death, she wants to make sure that she has the right person this time. So, she reaches to remove his mask—only for him to regain control of the knife, stab her, and drop her to her death instead. A brutally unsatisfying turn of events.

Now, let's do a reset.

Another twenty years later, Curtis once again returns to the role of Laurie Strode in *Halloween* (2018), which is more or less a direct sequel to the first film in 1978. As a result, it removes all reference to Michael and Laurie being siblings, as stated in *Halloween II*, or anything else referenced in the other sequels.

The Laurie of this film is old, hardened, and still traumatized by the attack that happened four decades ago. She lives in a house of locks and traps, does target practice with firearms, and regularly cleans her guns to make sure they're operational. She is well prepared for Michael's return, but her life is a mess. She is an alcoholic, has had two divorces, and her daughter Karen (Judy Greer) was taken away from her by the state when she was young. As a result, her relationship with her family is rocky. Her daughter explains how Laurie's trauma was passed on to her and that she is still unraveling the experience of living in lockdown and being taught paranoia and fear throughout her childhood, which is why she has distanced herself from her mother.

However, Laurie's relationship with her granddaughter Allyson (Andi Matichak) is slightly better. With it being Halloween, she goes to Allyson's school and watches her through a window (an echo of the way Michael once watched her). She gives her granddaughter $3,000 in cash and attempts to convince her to leave town. Instead, Allyson confronts her about her inability to let go of the past and how all her preparations cost Laurie her family. Laurie simply responds, "If the way I raised your mother means she hates me, but that she's prepared for the horrors of this world, then I'm okay with that."

Unable to help herself, she drives to the mental hospital where Michael is housed and watches as he is loaded onto a bus for transport to another facility. The sight of him causes her to have a panic attack, and she is still upset when she goes to the celebratory dinner for Allyson making the honor society. Although she tries to remain calm, it is all too much for her, and she breaks down at the table and leaves—returning home to barricade herself inside.

Later that night, she watches the news and learns that the bus that was carrying Michael has crashed. She immediately arms herself, locks up her home, and goes to retrieve her family and bring them to safety. However, she's hostile about Karen and her husband's lack of defenses as soon she enters, and, since they don't believe her about Michael's escape, they kick her out of the house. Laurie then goes looking for Allyson, who is out partying for Halloween.

After a series of murders later, Karen and Allyson begin to realize that Laurie was right about Michael's escape. Both separately make their way to Laurie's house, and they join her for a final showdown. While putting Karen in a safe room in the basement, Laurie confesses, "I was wrong to raise you the way I did. But I can protect you." She then locks her daughter in and proceeds to clear the house, searching each room before locking it down.

In her confrontation with Michael, Laurie receives a gut wound. But together, the three women are able to use their wits, along with guns and knives, to trap him in the basement and set the house aflame around him. They escape on the back of a pickup truck, believing they have defeated him—but by now, we know how this goes.

As Laurie and her family are rushed off to the hospital in *Halloween Kills* (2021), they see the firefighters arrive to put out the fire. They shout at them to let the house burn, but by then, they are too far away. At the hospital, Laurie is immediately rushed into surgery for her wounds, and she is left to recover from her injuries while townspeople turn into a mob to hunt down Michael. As a result, Laurie doesn't have much to do in this movie except talk about the past with Officer Hawkins (Will Patton) and wax poetic about the nature of evil and how Michael feeds into the fear of the town.

In the end, Karen joins the mob and leads Michael into a trap, where he is beaten and stabbed by an angry crowd of people. Karen joins in, stabbing him in his upper back and delivering what she believes to be the final blow. However, he almost immediately gets up and slaughters most of the mob, as well as finding and murdering Karen. When Laurie calls Karen to check on her, she is greeted with Michael's breathing. Enraged at the death of her daughter, she promises, "I'm coming for you, Michael."

Halloween Ends (2022) jumps ahead several years. After the massacre in 2018, Michael Meyers disappeared, leaving the town of Haddonfield bearing the scars of that night and unable to heal. As a result, Laurie explains that the people have become infected, thus falling "into grief, blame, and paranoia."

However, in the four years since she last saw her monster, Laurie is doing her best to improve herself. To honor her daughter, she explains, "I made a promise not to let fear rule my life anymore." She has made a home with her granddaughter Allyson, a regular home instead of a trap full of baked goods instead of weapons. We also learn that she has given up drinking, gone to therapy, and is writing a memoir to process her experiences. She wants Allyson to be happy and encourages her to get out and have fun. Gone is the overprotection, the paranoia.

Laurie almost seems like a different person—the polar opposite of who she was before. But as the movie continues, we see the cracks in her façade as a happy little homemaker. The people of the town, it turns out, blame her for the massacre, claiming that it was her fault for antagonizing and stirring Michael Meyers up into a frenzy. When she's confronted with this as she's leaving the grocery store, her mask slips, and we see some of the lingering depression that lies underneath her mask.

Despite Laurie's attempts to make the home as open and loving as possible, Allyson still feels trapped by her grandmother. She confesses to Corey (Rohan Campbell), a boy haunted by his own past (having accidentally killed the boy he was babysitting), that she feels like she can't escape Haddonfield and the past like she wants. She is afraid that, if she does, her grandmother will relapse to her old ways.

Initially, Laurie encourages Allyson's relationship with Corey, but she quickly becomes suspicious of him when she looks into his eyes one day and sees the same coldness she once saw in Michael. And she is unaware of how right she is about him. He has secretly been meeting with a wounded Michael Meyers and learning how to kill from him—has, in fact, killed several people who were antagonizing and bullying him in town with Michael's help. Some of Laurie's hard-edged nature comes out when she Corey and demands that he stay away from her granddaughter. He responds in turn that if he can't have Allyson, no one can.

This confrontation comes to a head when Laurie tries to warn her granddaughter away from him. However, Allyson is exhausted and tired of everything, and she only grows angry at the suggestion. She has found common ground and happiness with Corey. In her frustration, Allyson blames Laurie for the deaths of her friends (echoing the blame of the people in town) and announces that she's leaving with Corey that night.

Alone and upset, Laurie starts drinking again. Her attempt at building a happy life is falling apart. She unlocks a gun from the safe—and for a moment, it seems as if she is going to kill herself. But it is really just a trick for Corey, who has come to make sure that she is dead. They fight and Laurie shoots him, but Corey's final act is to stab himself in the neck to make Allyson believe that Laurie killed him in cold blood. When Allyson comes looking for Corey, she is horrified at what she sees, furious at her grandmother, and runs away.

Despite her despair, Laurie notices that the back door is open and immediately goes into defensive mode. She sets up a noise trap, drawing Michael into the kitchen, where they get into a gnarly fight. He slams her face into a clock and attempts to shove her hand into a garbage disposal, but she is able to fight him off. She pins both of his hands with knives to the butcher block. "I've run from you," she tells him. "I have chased you. I have tried to contain you. I have tried to forgive you. I thought maybe you were the boogeyman. No, you're just a man about to stop breathing."

She cuts his throat, and when Allyson returns again, they slice his wrists open. He's dead at last but "not dead enough," according to Laurie. They form a nighttime procession of townspeople, who take his body to the scrapyard and publicly dispose of his body in a metal shredder—proving once and for all that Michael can never come back. The town puts up no memorial or tombstone for him in the hope that memories will fade and the town can finally heal.

In the end, Allyson packs up and drives out of town, a smile on her face to finally be free, while Laurie writes the final chapter of her book. "I've said goodbye to my boogeyman, but the truth is evil doesn't die," she writes. "It changes shape." An oddly pessimistic closing to her book.

Nevertheless, rather than retreat inside and wallow alone, she sits on her porch chatting with Hawkins about cherry blossoms, which generally symbolize rebirth, renewal, and new beginnings. She is still traumatized and will still have to deal with her feelings of guilt and grief, but she is willing to consider the future.

A Splattering of Final Thoughts

When diving into my favorite horror franchises, I can't help but have a dual-edged experience. On the one hand, I love to see my favorite characters return to the scary stories I love and watch them smartly struggle against seemingly impossible odds and still come out on top. On the other hand, it would be so much better for these Final Girls if we would just leave them alone.

After all, as long as they continue to be on screen and present within the film, they are subject to the horrors and the looming presence of death that abide there. They cannot escape the cycle of fear and trauma to which they are subjected.

It is rare for the the survivor to kill the killer and remove them from the fictional universe, good and for all, since the franchise always needs to go on. Even if they do, the villain can always be resurrected as someone or something else. The only other way to break free, it would seem, is to either die or to pass the curse of survival onto the next generation of Final Girls, who must struggle through their own horrors.

And yet, despite the ongoing trauma, the act of surviving a horror franchise is itself a form of privilege when you consider that all the Final Girls (and Guy) mentioned here are white, straight, and cis-gendered. They fall into a set of particular expectations of who is allowed to survive at the end of the film and return for the next one.

We are starting to see a shift in this regard, as a number of new horror films are pushing the boundaries of what it means to be the Final Girl. Alexa Woods (Sanaa Lathan) not only becomes the sole survivor in *Aliens vs. Predator* (2004) but also gains the respect of the Predator she fights alongside. In the *Fear Street* trilogy (released on Netflix in 2021), lesbian couple Deena (Kiana Madeira) and Samantha (Olivia Scott Welch) are able to pool their strength and skills together to fight off a centuries-old curse. And Tess (Georgina Campbell) manages to claw her way out of a horrifying AirBNB experience in *Barbarian* (2022). This is just a small fraction of the films that are redefining the image of the Final Girl, and horror novels are also actively examining this trope.

Notably, these break-the-mold survivors tend to be the stars of a single film or two. They rarely get an opportunity to continue on as the center point of the horror franchise—an important exception being Sam and Tara taking up the mantle from Sidney as the ongoing survivors of the Scream series.

On the flip side, the villain/killer of most major franchises tend to be male—Michael Myers, Freddy Krueger, Jason Voorhees, and Pinhead. Ghostface is recognizable as the villain but is essentially genderless, as the killer can be of any gender under the mask. Likewise, since the Deadites are possessed humans, they can also be any gender but lack a single instantly recognizable visage. However, there are virtually no women killers who have been granted a place as the central villain of their own franchise. In the Western horror world, the only exception I'm aware of is Tiffany (Jennifer Tilly), who appears in four films—*Bride of Chucky* (1998), *Seed of Chucky* (2004), *Curse of Chucky* (2013), and *Cult of Chucky* (2017).

Female horror villains do appear more regularly in Asian cinema, however. For example, Sadako Yamamura in the Ring franchise, played by various actresses across eight Japanese films, and Kayako Saeki in the Ju-On franchise, also played by multiple actresses across seven Japanese films and four American adaptations. These women also appear in a crossover film, *Sadako vs. Kayako*, released in 2016.

The different portrayals of women in Asian horror are largely due to cultural differences, as explained by Ren Zelen at *Horror DNA*, who points out that "women in Asian horror have the better deal regarding roles offering depth and personality." To further expand on this, she notes that these portrayals of women in horror are often counter to the restrictive cultural expectations of women in real life:

Confucian ideals of womanhood have been pervasive in Asia for almost two thousand years. Since the Han Dynasty, parables about the selfless wife and humble daughter-in-law became embedded in education in China and the surrounding regions. Unsurprisingly then, East Asia also generated a system of stories depicting women seeking revenge after they have been victimised because they have not abided by these norms—women who have been maligned simply because of their biological qualities.

Asian horror cinema has proved to be the perfect medium through which this restrictive image of femininity can be challenged. What could be further from the Confucian feminine ideal than a woman who terrifies men by grotesque physical deformity, biological otherness, supernatural potency or violent rage?

To close, I'll simply say that there is room in the horror genre for a variety of stories from a multitude of perspectives and for new, innovative storytelling, and we are seeing more and more of that in horror films, novels, and games that are being released. Of course, not every horror film transforms into a larger franchise—some because they don't need to be (a single story is enough on its own) and others because they don't manage to achieve that combination of luck and marketing that launches a multitude of sequels. It's not always possible to foresee—or control—what will become a successful franchise. Either way, I'm looking forward to seeing what kinds of Final Girls, villains, and monsters will come forth in the future.

THE SEGA SAGA AS TOLD BY A KID TRYING TO ESCAPE: A PERSONAL ESSAY

SALENA CASHA AND MAHAILEY OLIVER

You blow into the cartridge, a big bad wolf. From the moment the blue logo sings its way onto the screen, reality slips away. You forget–about homework, drama, your incessant inner monologue telling you to be *enough*, but not *too much*.

You know how to Up-Down-Left-Right-A-Start your way to the levels that you want–and you'd be lying if you said it was anything other than the Casino level. Is this the beginning of your craving for instant gratification? Perhaps. You collect the rings, that *ring! ring! ring!* sending your developing mind into a dopamine landfill. And the sound when you earn a hundred rings? Get a new life stocked? *Dun-da-da-dun-dun-dun-da!* Music to your ears. Gold, in all its forms, solves everything, doesn't it?

Who knew that you would grow up to chase paychecks the same way? Without the sound effects, the *pings*, the *rings*, the *dun-da-da*s affirming your monetary ascension, that dopamine hit just isn't quite the same. Doesn't quite feel like life is stocking up at all, does it?

You always go for Tails because he can fly and you can't. To be fair, you haven't tried and probably shouldn't, and also, your mom would totally kill you first, so you let him be airborne for you on the screen hooked up to the console in your parents' room. Collecting twirling golden halos. Sliding through checkpoints with a *ping* that makes you forget your hand is cramping around the controller, makes you forget that even though Amy Rose is a character option, you hardly ever go for her. She's a tomboy who'll tell your fortune and has a temper, hammer and all, but people call her 'girly,' 'bossy,' 'erratic,' things you tire of hearing about yourself in real life, so you set her to the side. It's important, you tell yourself, to always be more than someone's girlfriend, even in the Sonic world.

In college, you'll watch boys play Final Fantasy—mostly because they would never trust you to level up—but here, at your parents' home on the TV in their bedroom, you're the one in control, the main character. With people watching. Mostly, just your sister, sometimes, your friend and her brother. No matter where or when you are after this moment, your hands will always itch for the toggles, the feel of plastic slick with sweat.

Reasons why *Sonic the Hedgehog* commands your time:

- You're born with special powers
- You're normal compared to all the other characters because everyone is different in here
- Instead of having to work for it in your lifeguarding/babysitting/tutoring life, gold is just lying around
- You can track your progress clearly through the world and always know where you stand, even at the beginning
- You get to start over
- And over
- And over
- And somehow, you can still win and make it through and recharge your heart and forget the pain of jumping off that cliff or losing all your rings.

Starting from zero isn't starting from zero here. Not really. It doesn't mean anything, and, in that way, it teaches you to get back up and try again. And again. And again.

When you tire of Tails, you start playing as Knuckles–he's an echidna, which sounds like a kid, which you are, but there's something else about him. He glides so much farther than Tails can fly; he's like a superhero you didn't know you needed. But, you also know that he was Robotnik's henchman, and for some reason, that makes you feel like you're on the inside–Knuckles knows paths through levels that Sonic and Tails could never fathom.

You like being on the inside, even if it's all in your imagination.

Isn't everything better there, anyway? Still, sometimes, you remember–even now in your quarter-life crisis–how good those escapist fantasies were. Maybe you dust off that old console, blow into the cartridge that's older than you are, and pull a couch cushion onto the floor. You hit "Start" on the console, see that logo zip across the screen, and all of a sudden, none of it matters anymore–your bills, your deadlines, your incessant self-judgment and criticism. None of it matters. Nothing except *which character you choose to play*.

UFOS AND THE LINK TO ANCIENT INDIAN LITERATURE: A DEEP DIVE INTO FASCINATING FUTURISTIC TECHNOLOGY FROM THE PAST, WITH BRISHTI GUHA AND INDRANI GUHA

BRISHTI GUHA AND INDRANI GUHA

In recent years, the Pentagon and NASA have acknowledged that UFOs (or UAPs, unidentified aerial phenomena, as they are currently called)—are real rather than being simply figments of science fiction enthusiasts' imaginations. Luis Elizondo, who headed the Pentagon's investigation into unexplained aerial phenomena, highlighted the unusual features of UFOs that he had gleaned from many years of probes into accounts of strange airborne objects seen by pilots and naval officers. We describe some of these below.

Unlike the aircraft we are used to, UFOs don't have wings or even visible rotors, or windows. They tend to be either tubular or oval, like mints, though they are not necessarily tiny; pilots have reported them to be about 40 feet long. Not only can they be airborne without wings, but they can move and accelerate at unusually high speeds. They can change direction at gravity-defying velocities. They can react to approaching (US) aircraft or submarines by retreating a distance of 60 miles within a few seconds. They can also descend rapidly from a height of 80,000 feet—at speeds roughly 30 times the speed of sound—and position themselves, motionless, above the sea. They have a striking ability to stay absolutely still, which is unlike anything the aircraft known to us are capable of; the UFOs stayed in place even when buffeted by strong winds and atmospheric currents. They can go underwater as well, where they have been detected moving at roughly twice the speed of nuclear submarines. So they are capable of traversing different types of media —air, water, and land surfaces. They also display a wide variety of movements. Observers have seen them rotating, hovering, receding, and moving from side to side like ping pong balls. No matter how covertly they are approached, they can sense the movement of other craft and react by rapidly moving away. They are also good at "cloaking" or maintaining "low visibility." They are difficult to detect through advanced radar technology, and by the naked eye, alike: at times, all that observers can see is the haze or glow surrounding them.

The Pentagon made these revelations to the public very recently. But more than a century ago, during WWI, a manual in Sanskrit had come to light with instructions for making flightworthy craft with an uncanny similarity to the UFOs we've just described. The manual mentioned twelve "spectacular" movements that the craft would be able to perform. These included rotating, moving sideways, staying motionless midair, receding (moving backward), and sudden and rapid descent—all of which military pilots have observed UFOs perform, according to the information released by the Pentagon.

The manual describes specific craft, like the *Tripura* (three-part) craft, which can move on land, in the air, on the surface of the sea, and underwater—just as UFOs could traverse multiple media and switch between them. The craft had retractable wheels which could fold up when it was underwater; a separate set of wheels was used for the ground.

The Pentagon had also pinpointed low visibility and ready ability to evade detection as a key feature of UFOs. Cloaking, or invisibility, is mentioned in detail in the Sanskrit manual. There is mention of elaborate chemical remedies for making the outer part of the craft look like the sky so that it would be extremely hard to detect by enemy vessels. There are also details about how to camouflage the aircraft using machines and mirrors installed within.

Pilots inside the craft could even use a special device to view the scene on the ground beneath them, which would be projected on a screen. They could also use devices to view the movements of enemy aircraft and could even use a "sound capturing device" to listen to conversations carried on inside other airborne or sea-borne vehicles. This allowed them to behave much like the UFOs Elizondo described, enabling them to respond to and even anticipate the movements of other craft.

Some of the models of aircraft described in the book were tested in 2017 by Travis Taylor, an aerospace engineer at the University of California, Irvine. Performing a wind tunnel experiment, Taylor found that the model was flightworthy [1]. The model he tested was tubular (like many of the UFOs mentioned by Elizondo, such as those witnessed in the 2004 US Nimitz incident) and lacked wings or rotors. It was capable of lift and stayed motionless in the air, exhibiting remarkable stability even when buffeted by strong winds created during the experiment. This also harmonizes well with Elizondo's descriptions of UFOs which displayed anti-gravity lift without visible means of propulsion; many accounts also remarked on their ability to stay stable even in the presence of strong destabilizing forces. In fact, the video on the experiment also discusses the possibility that the models in the book were actually models of spaceships.

The possibility that UFOs were present in the ancient world was mentioned by Elizondo himself [2]. He mentioned an ancient Roman scroll, at least 2,000 years old, where Roman soldiers mention mysterious objects, shaped like flaming shields, in the sky. These objects followed the soldiers from battlefield to battlefield, remaining airborne all the while. There have also been mentions [3] of mysterious discoid flying shields that alarmed elephants during Alexander the Great's fourth century BC battle with the Indian king Porus. This made the elephants stampede in panic and worked to the Indians' advantage by creating alarm and confusion among the Greek ranks. After this spooky experience, the Greeks refused to continue their invasion of India.

This brings us to parallels with UFOs in ancient Indian literature. Ancient Indians had legends about a godly race we considered hugely superior to our own in terms of power, longevity, and technology. These beings rode self-propelled flightworthy vehicles that—unlike more typical "chariots" common to various countries' myths—were not yoked by birds or animals. The vehicles could not only fly in the air but could also traverse multiple media—water, land, and air.

Some of these vehicles were owned by the Ashwins—a pair of twins repeatedly mentioned in the *Rigveda*, the oldest oral literature of India. The Ashwins, who belonged to this powerful race of beings, served as healers and emergency rescue workers. The *Rigveda* is full of accounts of the Ashwins rescuing stranded or trapped people in dramatic ways; they then provided them with emergency care and immediate transport to a safe location. For instance, one of their rescue missions involved saving a man called Bhujyu, who had been betrayed by his father, injured, and tossed into the ocean from a ship.

The Ashwins saved him using an "animated vessel" that could go deep into the ocean, but which then—after retrieving Bhujyu from the ocean's depths—proceeded to "traverse the air" so that the waves did not touch the craft. Other Rigvedic accounts [4] of rescues by the Ashwins all involve difficult terrain—they had to save people lost in deserts, people who had fallen into mountain pits, or who had been buried under trees in inaccessible forests. The Ashwins made part of their journeys by air, but their craft were equally capable of traversing treacherous land terrain, or of moving on the surface of water, or of diving deep into oceans. This reminds us of the ability of modern-day UFOs to negotiate multiple media.

The *Rigveda*—which mentions the Ashwins—was initially memorized and handed down as oral canon, although it was later written down. Its original date of composition is estimated to have begun before or during the early Indus-Saraswati valley phase (fourth millennium BC); see Shrikant Talageri (2000, 2009)[5]. The oral tradition in ancient India continued into times when books were actually being written down. As India was subject to frequent foreign invasions, and as ancient manuscripts were written on perishable materials like palm leaves, written material would often be stolen, lost, plundered, or destroyed—providing an incentive to preserve the oral tradition through the centuries. The biggest repository of ancient manuscripts was a library in Nalanda, ancient India's most famous university (considered by historians to be the world's oldest residential university, established during the early fifth century). Tragically, at the end of the twelfth century, the library at Nalanda, with its tens of thousands of manuscripts, was burned down by Bakhtiyar Khilji, a Turkic invader, along with the rest of the university. Throughout all this time, people had been studying and writing about this mysterious flightworthy craft (we know this because many other early writings are referred to in the Sanskrit manual mentioned at the beginning of this essay). But, because of the large-scale destruction of old texts, only two such texts have survived.

The first of these is the *Samaranganasutradhara* of King Bhoja. Bhoja was a major historical figure, an eleventh-century king who reigned from 1010 to 1055 in central India. He was celebrated as a scholar king, a polymath, and a prolific author. Chapter 31 of the *Samaranganasutradhara* (which, in general, is about mechanical inventions and architecture) focuses on Bhoja's and his engineers' attempts to build flight-worthy vehicles. According to the book, these machines were built of light wood, bird-shaped, and powered by boiling vats of liquid mercury. According to the book, they were capable of ascent and descent and flying long distances.

The second is the Sanskrit manual—named the *Vaimanika Shastra*—mentioned in the beginning of this essay. This second book is particularly striking for the similarity of the properties of its craft with the features exhibited by UFOs. The history behind the book is complicated. It was dictated by Pandit Subbaraya Shastry (1866–1940), apparently during 1918–23. At the time that Subbaraya made the contents of the book known, India was under British rule. The British immediately put Subbaraya in jail, where he remained till his dying day. Thus, the general public never got to have any interaction with him. He, however, claimed to have received knowledge of the contents of the book from his guru, a wandering ascetic, who in turn had passed on ancient lore transmitted orally from generation to generation. The person credited as the originator was an ancient wise man, an Indian sage named Bharadwaja, who, along with his descendants, composed many of the hymns of the *Rigveda.* Bharadwaja, perhaps, was intrigued enough by the fascinating vessels being flown by the Ashwins to conduct extensive research into their possibilities. In addition, Bharadwaja also had the opportunity to experiment with a flight vehicle since his adoptive parents, who belonged to the godly race mentioned in the *Rigveda*, possessed one.

We must remember that the technology conceived of in this text—and remarkable for its parallels with UFOs, modern and ancient—was, going by these accounts, 5,000 years old. The materials and ingredients used were those that were available in ancient India (and perhaps in other parts of the ancient world) 5,000 years ago and might seem strange and unfamiliar now. In what directions did this technology subsequently evolve? Did it improve in terms of craft speed or maneuverability? Were the materials and ingredients used upgraded? The answers to these questions elude us so far. Until then, we are left with an intriguing mosaic of clues, which suggest that at least some ancient humans were not only familiar with UFOs, but even, perhaps, had a hand in developing them.

[1] The YouTube video of the experiment is available at https://www.youtube.com/watch?v=zpKIj4-bmt0

[2] The YouTube video of Elizondo's talk is available at https://www.youtube.com/watch?v=4yX6ETCKyPo

[3] By Frank Edwards, a 1950s radio TV host and writer, in Stranger Than Science (1959, Lyle Stuart, NYC).

[4] For details, see "Aircraft in ancient Indian literature: flights of fancy or lost leaps of science?" by Brishti Guha and Indrani Guha, https://myvoice.opindia.com/2022/04/aircraft-in-ancient-indian-literature-flights-of-fancy-or-lost-leaps-of-science/, OpIndia April 22nd 2022.

[5] Talageri, S. (2000): *The Rigveda: A Historical Analysis*, Aditya Prakashan, Talageri, S. (2009) : *The Rigveda and the Avesta: the Final Evidence*, Aditya Prakashan.

THE LOTUS EATERS: A LONGFORM ESSAY ON ADDICTION IN THE WORKS OF EDGAR ALLEN POE, SHIRLEY JACKSON, AND STEPHEN KING

GRANT BUTLER

Tales of monsters and substance abuse have coexisted side by side since the dawn of Western literature. For ages, people everywhere have been captivated by stories filled with both horrors, whether it's *The Odyssey*, where Odysseus encounters both a group of people who indulge in a food that leaves the eater in a state of bliss reminiscent of a drug-induced haze and two horrifying sea monsters, or *The Wizard of Oz*, where the Wicked Witch of the West tries to cast a spell on Dorothy and her friends as they skip through a field of poppies, the flowers that produce opiates.

But while many authors may appreciate the connection between writing about the horrors of the human experience and the nature of addiction, Edgar Allan Poe, Shirley Jackson, and Stephen King exemplify it to a unique degree. Not only do the works of Poe, Jackson, and King chronicle the unique monsters haunting the American mind, but their work and lives chronicle the history of American addiction.

Edgar Allan Poe: Fighting the Darkness of Addiction

Edgar Allan Poe was an American original. Poe's tales of murder, the macabre, and the dark side of human nature made him a unique presence on the American literary scene at the time. No one had written tales that were uninhibited in their description of the darker side of human existence before. But Poe's work also depicted people attempting to fight that darkness. Poe famously wrote what is considered the first modern detective story, "The

Murders in the Rue Morgue", which featured Parisian C. Auguste Dupin trying to solve the murder of a woman and her daughter.

Poe's work often featured substance abuse as it could either mitigate or contribute to the darkness. Alcoholism plays a role in Poe's story "The Black Cat", just as the murderous narrator seeking revenge in "The Cask of Amontillado" is likely an alcoholic as well. But it's in "Ligeia" where Poe references both "the radiance of an opium dream" and "the excitement of my opium dreams." The narrator in "The Tell-Tale Heart" would have believably relied on laudanum or other opiates, as it was used to treat countless ailments.

Poe himself was no stranger to alcohol, he was famously intolerant and struggled to abstain from it throughout his life. Due to his unexplained death, theories abound about Poe's health. It has been suggested he may have had bipolar disorder. If this was the case, then it would make sense he may have indulged in alcohol to help cope with the disease during that era. Charles Baudelaire, Poe's French translator who admired his work and felt a kinship with the American author, was beyond candid about his own experience with substances from opium to hashish.

Poe's work was a watershed moment in American literature because it plumbed the darker side of what was lurking in the mind of his fellow Americans, because not only was Poe writing grim tales about human nature and what it could lead to, he was writing grim tales about human nature in the era where the American Civil War was steadily approaching. Poe himself had attended West Point and served in the military, so he may have had a better idea than many that a unique catastrophe was approaching.

He may not have lived to see the Civil War, but Poe's works certainly did. If anything, the unprecedented slaughter, death, and the chaotic aftermath may have contributed to his enduring popularity. The fact that Edgar Allan Poe's work invokes the macabre, death, and the occult would have a unique appeal during the Civil War and the period after because spiritualism flourished during the war and its aftermath, with First Lady Mary Todd Lincoln famously meeting with many spiritualists who claimed to be able to communicate with her dead son. And with that spiritualism and death also came addiction. All those grisly battlefield injuries required any number of gruesome treatments, to say nothing of the unsanitary conditions of camps, which caused disease to flourish. The treatments of the time to address these issues were limited, but there was one all-purpose treatment that was used to treat an array of disorders or symptoms including pain, headaches, gastrointestinal distress, and asthma. That was opium and its derivatives laudanum and morphine. Every soldier who was wounded during the Civil War or suffered from disease due to unsanitary conditions was at risk of developing an addiction to morphine or opium.

Poe's work and its themes of murder, grisly violence, death, sickness, the occult, and an undertone of addiction, summed up the American experience in the era that immediately followed his death. But as the 19th century rolled into the 20th, the United States of America would undergo unprecedented growth and change as it endured World War I, the Great Depression, World War II, and the beginning of what would be known as the Cold War. The image of America was of a shining, happy beacon to the rest of the world. The 1950s was an era associated with benign contentment. But like the rest of human history, there were unique horrors lurking in that era. One author who understood that better than most was Shirley Jackson.

Shirley Jackson: Demons of the Mind

The author of the widely known short story "The Lottery", Jackson wrote acclaimed books about paranoia and the other demons of the mind. Her novel *The Haunting of Hill House* is considered one of the best ghost stories ever written. What made Shirley Jackson unique is that in her stories, the elements of paranoia, suspense, tension, and fear are centered around the idea of the home and everything that entails, including motherhood. Paranoia forms a strong element in not just Shirley Jackson's work, but that of many writers who tell stories of monsters, both human and otherwise. But in Jackson's case, the paranoia is unique because the source of it is oftentimes quite literally where you live, in your own house. The fear was hiding in plain sight and could look extraordinarily boring at first glance.

Jackson's work is also unique in how it emphasizes not just paranoia, fear, and the monsters lurking in the human mind, but how that paranoia and fear could be a unique experience for women, particularly women of her era. Although Jackson was also interested in the experiences of the past, because in 1956 she published *The Witchcraft of Salem Village* about the Salem Witch Trials. This isn't surprising, since the story of the Witch Trials has all the paranoia, discussion of the supernatural, the horror lurking within small towns and in the home, and the role of women that Jackson wrote about frequently.

But what does Jackson's work tell us about addiction and substance abuse in her era? Jackson understood not just the monsters lurking within the human subconscious; she understood how they could happen, and most importantly, she understood how they were perceived and addressed. While it may seem like Shirley Jackson lived in an era not far removed from the present, it was a radically different environment in terms of medicine and how certain conditions were treated. It was the era when everyone on TV or in movies smoked on camera, the image of doctors was used regularly in ads for cigarettes, and warning labels on cigarettes weren't required by law until 1965.

But tobacco wasn't the only addictive substance that flowed freely. Amphetamines, now tightly regulated, were freely given to women specifically in the form of diet pills to lose weight. Since Jackson herself was no stranger to having her weight frequently criticized by her mother, it's not surprising she was one of many women to take diet pills. But the use of amphetamines was frequently used in combination with barbiturates. A highly potent and addictive sedative that depressed the entire nervous system, barbiturates were used to counter the effects of amphetamines or other stimulants. Jackson, like numerous others during this era, was given a combination of both drugs.

Shirley Jackson's experience with the pharmaceuticals of her era was also influenced by the fact that she was an outsider who struggled with marital troubles. How outsiders, particularly female outsiders, feel and cope with the experiences that come with it, is a huge theme that runs through her work. The women in Shirley Jackson's stories are the sort of women who would have been given any number of pharmaceuticals in abundance. Elizabeth in *The Bird's Nest* would've almost certainly been given any number of the era's pharmaceutical staples. That's because Jackson realized that the demons of the mind won't be confined to the mind. They eventually manifest themselves in one form or another.

Jackson died far too young, at the age of 48, due to heart failure. How much that era's attitude towards certain medications played a role is uncertain. According to Jackson's son Laurence Jackson Hyman, his mother never took anything not prescribed by their family doctor, she had some health issues before her death, and she often resented having to take anything at all. This makes sense, because attitudes towards prescribing medication in that era was drastically different from modern practices. In that time, sedatives were beyond easy to obtain. Aside from barbiturates, there were Quaaludes. Originally prescribed for housewives with insomnia and anxiety related issues, Quaaludes were very easy to get throughout the 1970s. It wasn't until 1983 that Congress moved to classify it as a Schedule I drug.

The fact that these pharmaceuticals were widely used by women was not a secret at the time. Shortly after Jackson's death, *The Rolling Stones* released the song "Mother's Little Helper," about an overextended housewife who "goes running for the shelter of Mother's Little Helper". Mother's Little Helper is a nickname for Valium, the most prescribed drug from 1969 to 1982.

In 1966, Jacqueline Susann published the novel *The Valley of the Dolls* in which aspiring starlets pop pills to sleep, wake up, and lose weight. By the time of Susann's death in 1974, it was the best-selling novel of all time. One of the actresses set to star in the film adaptation of *The Valley of the Dolls* was Judy Garland, the actress famous for playing Dorothy in *The Wizard of Oz*. Like Jackson, the incredibly gifted Garland also had a difficult relationship with her mother and was given a variety of pills to both give her energy and help her relax or sleep. Judy Garland lived one year less than Jackson, dying at the age of 47 from a barbiturate overdose.

But while Jackson died far too young, her work had a far bigger impact than her contemporaries could've realized. When understanding why she wasn't appreciated enough in her time, it's significant to note not only that Jackson was a woman writing in the 1940s, 1950s, and 1960s, she was a woman writing stories about ghosts and things lurking in the dark in the 1940s, 1950s, and 1960s. In that era, the term horror would've likely brought to mind a slew of B movies of varying quality. One reason the horror genre in general gradually started to become more respected and mainstream is because of Shirley Jackson.

There is a direct line of descent from the women in Shirley Jackson's stories to the two novels that arguably changed not just American horror but horror fiction in general. *Rosemary's Baby*; a story about a pregnant woman who becomes paranoid about what her husband and neighbors are up to, and *The Exorcist*; a novel about a woman who is forced to imagine the unthinkable after her young daughter starts acting in a strange and terrifying way, forever changed the concept of horror fiction. What made them stand out is that they were stories that used the ideas of the supernatural and the occult to tell a much bigger story about humanity and human frailty than had previously been done before. The theme of motherhood and the unique terrors it can bring, which is at the heart of both stories, was a concept Shirley Jackson introduced to readers. It's also easy to draw a line from the women in Shirley Jackson's stories to the story of a high school girl named Carrie White, an outsider who has a strained relationship with her mother and uses occult powers to get even with her cruel classmates.

Stephen King: Bigger, Bolder, and More Brutal

Published in 1974, *Carrie* was a watershed moment in both American literature and speculative fiction. It was radically different from how horror novels had been written before, both in style and in content. That's one reason its author, Stephen King, has had a career spanning approximately 50 years and counting. Poe and Jackson's work is still widely read today, and Jackson was successful enough to become the primary earner in her family. But in terms of sales and public recognition, King is in a league of his own, and a huge reason for that is the radically different time and environment King was writing in than Jackson, to say nothing of Poe.

Carrie wasn't just a book about an outcast girl with psychic powers; it was a book about an outcast girl with psychic powers in 1974. From the time Jackson's last novel was published in 1962, there had been the Kennedy assassination, which King would subsequently write about in *11/22/63*, the Civil Rights Movement, the Vietnam War, the assassinations of Bobby

Kennedy and Martin Luther King Jr., the Apollo 11 Moon landing, the official start of the War on Drugs, and Watergate, which Carrie was published right in the middle of. The United States was a radically different country from 1962, and the concepts of fear, terror, and dread were much closer at hand than they'd been in the past. It was a bigger, bolder, and more brutal era than before.

Unlike Poe or Jackson, King lived to see the official beginning of the War on Drugs and everything that came with it. There is no question that King's work is filled with the theme of addiction, and there are numerous examples of it, but *The Shining* is perhaps the one that hits closest to home for King personally. A story about a failed writer whose addictions affect his family in ways he could've never anticipated, it's intriguing that the Stephen King novel that's such a personal tale of addiction also references Edgar Allan Poe, with a lengthy quotation from "The Masque of the Red Death" serving as one of the book's opening epigraphs.

Readers can make the connection between Stephen King's personal history and his work because King has been beyond candid about his past struggle with addiction and its impact on his work. King has also admitted that he has practically no memory of writing *Cujo*. In addition to being a heavy drinker, King himself estimates that he was a heavy cocaine user from 1978 to 1986. *The Tommyknockers* is another particularly relevant example of King's personal battle with addiction. According to the author, that's the last book King wrote before he got help. King went on to say that while he thinks *The Tommyknockers* is "an awful book", he also thinks that "There's a really good book in here, underneath all the sort of spurious energy that cocaine provides, and I ought to go back."

The fact that King started using cocaine in 1978 is significant, because not only does the timeline of King's personal usage match precisely when the drug was becoming a widespread national problem, it means he began using that particular drug after he'd become successful. Cocaine has a long history of being a drug associated with wealth, power, and excess, so it's not surprising he started using it in 1978 because he could afford to do so. So not only did King's addictions influence his writing, his writing also influenced his addictions, which makes sense because King has said that for him, writing is like being a drug addict.

There is no doubt that had he not been a success, King would not have been able to afford the massive amount of cocaine he consumed. Nor is there any doubt had he always been sober, he would've written many things differently, for better or worse. But that's what made him Stephen King. The books and stories he wrote from the 70s through the 80s were what first endeared him to readers everywhere, but particularly to American readers. He was writing about the monsters in the American psyche from a unique perspective, and a big part of those monsters was addiction.

The 1970s was the era when the idea of drug abuse as a serious widespread problem came into the public consciousness like never before, and King could tap into those monsters from a deeply personal perspective. But not only could King tap into those monsters, he was willing to do it, openly take it wherever it led him, and make no apologies for it. That is what separates him not just from Poe or Jackson, but from many of his peers. Stephen King became Stephen King because he talked about many of the monsters haunting the American psyche in the late 20th century, and he did it in such a brutally unflinching way. Not just once, but over and over, and in a thousand different ways. The story "Quitters, Inc" is just one example of how King understood not just addiction, but how it impacted human behavior and could lead to a unique type of monster. The story is about a man named Dick Morrison, a smoker who stumbles upon a firm that has a highly successful rate at helping clients quit smoking, but through highly unusual and unorthodox measures.

But King's personal story with addiction wasn't over despite getting sober in the late 80s. On June 19, 1999, King was walking along a road in Maine when he was hit by a van. His lower leg was broken in nine places, the part of the leg below the right knee had been reduced to "so many marbles in a sock", and he sustained four broken ribs, injuries to the right hip and spine, and a scalp cut that required thirty stitches. After five surgical procedures to put his leg back together, King started the grueling process of physical therapy. Getting back to writing was an even greater obstacle, because as King put it, "How was I supposed to write when the most pressing thing in my world was how long until the next dose of Percocet? " But King did return to writing, and eventually what he was working on became the novel *Dreamcatcher*. King would later say about the book, "I don't like *Dreamcatcher* very much" because "I was using a lot of Oxycontin for pain. And I was pretty stoned when I wrote it, because of the Oxy, and that's another book that shows the drugs at work."

Without even knowing it, King had found himself face to face with a twenty-first-century type of addiction, which would also turn out to be a uniquely American twenty-first-century addiction problem. Bryan Smith, the driver who hit King, died of an accidental fentanyl overdose a year later in September of 2000. Smith would not be the last, as fentanyl has become the subject of national news since the time of King's accident. A powerful synthetic opioid, a tiny amount of fentanyl is all that's needed to trigger an overdose, which becomes especially likely when dealers mix fentanyl with heroin they are selling. Over 100 times more powerful than morphine and 50 times more powerful than heroin, fentanyl overtook heroin in 2016 for the opioid causing the most overdose deaths.

Nor would King be alone in having an encounter with OxyContin that he looked back on with distaste. Stephen King is known for telling stories of the horrors lurking behind small-town America, and small-town America would be getting a major horror as the 21st Century arrived in the form of the opioid epidemic. OxyContin, promoted as a safer and less addictive version of oxycodone, was the drug to use as part of an ongoing and ambitious effort at the time to treat pain. Purdue Pharma started selling the drug in 1996, and within two decades, the drug would be widely associated with its role in the opioid epidemic that has been estimated to have taken over one million lives by 2021. Florida, where King and his wife have a house and several of King's stories are set, was home to many walk-in clinics providing easy access to painkillers called "Pill Mills", and in 2010, 90 of the country's 100 top opioid prescribers were Florida doctors.

The works of Edgar Allan Poe, Shirley Jackson, and Stephen King aren't just groundbreaking in their depiction of the monsters and fears that haunt the human mind, their personal histories help explain the monsters they articulated and explored. Their works are not just about monsters, fears, or madness, but what haunts the mind and the implications it has. Nor are Poe, Jackson, and King just writing about addiction or addiction in their respective eras, they're writing about how fear and madness effects the mind and the unique types of horrors it can lead to, one of which can be addiction. Their works all show the unique horrors of their respective eras and tell us that not only do stories about monsters and fear go hand in hand with addiction, the two can be one and the same.

Shirley Jackson, in particular, wasn't just writing about monsters and fear; she about fear that spoke to the experience of American women in the middle of the 20th century. The nature of their experience with medicine is simply one part of that story. The reason her work has not only survived, but grown in popularity, is because she understood that experience and articulated it to readers in a way that was both timely and timeless, much like King or Poe. Together, all three authors were able to discuss numerous fears and terrors through telling stories, and drug use, legal or otherwise, was just one of those fears that played a unique role in haunting the minds of readers around the world. But while the fears they were able to articulate appealed to readers everywhere, there is no doubt they hit particularly close to home for American readers.

What makes Poe, Jackson, and King unique is that they are all American authors, and their respective battles with addiction tell the story of addiction in America. Their stories have been the stories of countless Americans, and taken together, their lives give us a glimpse into the American history of substance abuse and its implications. But why do three of the greatest writers of monsters, both human and otherwise, all share a personal connection to the history of American substance abuse? Perhaps it's because there are unique terrors that come with the American experience, and King, Poe, and Jackson understood that addiction was merely a symptom of that.

But one other thing that makes Stephen King stand out is that by now, he has been writing for longer than Jackson and Poe lived. Which makes him unique as not only has his work obviously changed since the beginning, he's lived long enough to see an evolution in the attitude not just towards horror and other types of fiction, but in what scares people and how it's represented. King has written long enough to see his writing about what was lurking in the underbelly of the American psyche come to the very forefront. *The Stand*, King's massive book about a deadly pandemic that threatens humanity, became far more realistic in 2020 than many would've ever thought possible. When comparing their lives and works, it's clear that Edgar Allan Poe wrote about monsters, Shirley Jackson wrote about where the monsters were really lurking regardless of appearances, and Stephen King wrote about how big the monsters were and how nasty they could be. But as time went on, King started to write about one additional thing: that the monsters, no matter what they were, weren't hiding anymore. The monsters are now right there for everyone to see, plain as day.

WHY DO WE KEEP INVENTING THE MAGICAL SCHOOL?: FROM T.H. WHITE TO URSULA K. LE GUIN, HOGWARTS ISN'T THE ONLY SCHOOL IN FANTASY

TANVI CHOWDHARY

"The magical school is a representation of agency that is otherwise unavailable to children."

Although the most well-known iteration of it, Hogwarts is far from the only magical school in existence. Prior to the most famous fantasy book in the world, Ursula Le Guin's work, *The Wizard of the Earthsea* (1968) featured the School of Roke: where the main character Ged receives most of his training. Le Guin herself has noted, "I didn't originate the idea of a school for wizards—if anybody did it was T.H. White, though he did it in single throwaway line and didn't develop it. I was the first to do that. Years later, Rowling took the idea and developed it along other lines" ("Art, Information, Theft, and Confusion: Part Two", Essay by Ursula K. Le Guin, 2010).

Over the course of fantasy writing, the concept of the school has loomed over narratives. *His Dark Materials* (2000) by Phillip Pullman pays homage to the real-life Oxford, while Daniel Abraham's *The Long Price Quartet* (2010) begins with a mountain academy that teaches poets how to magically manipulate and hold words. Terry Pratchett placed all his wizards in The Unseen Academy (*Unseen Academicals,* 2009), while the fantasy series Pellinor

(Croggon) has social order made up almost entirely of schools. More recently, Naomi Novik's *Scholomance* (2020, 2021) features a magical school with a far smaller survival rate than Hogwarts. Admittedly, some of these texts are not meant for children—however, the heroes of these stories are often younger, of school-going age. If the text is meant for children, the protagonists are often of the same age as their readers—which is perhaps what makes the existence of a magical school so interesting. In a world that opposes the rules of the real world, younger protagonists are still placed within the boundaries of a familiar institution: the school.

Schools are curious spaces for child readers—the experiment that is modern education is not much more than two hundred years old, and in that span, schools have been subject to various pedagogical debates. They have alternatively been spaces for the creation of national identity, spaces for radicalization, and spaces for knowledge production. Research by several scholars and historians has exposed the imperial fault lines of the school system: it is a structure with a long and storied colonial legacy. Its existence in the realm of the fantastical and the magical is an anomaly that needs to be examined more closely, especially since the mythologies that fairytales and fantasy borrow from are typically sourced in pre-Christian traditions that existed well before colonialism. Why, then, do so many magical schools exist anyway? In unfamiliar, fantastical worlds filled with magic, dragons, and fairies, we still feel compelled to imagine a magic school—complete with its own rules and regulations (which look eerily similar to the British schooling system, more often than not).

The critical component that is *magic* tells us, more often than not—what we want schooling *to be.* Hogwarts is painted as extraordinary, often in contrast to the world of the Dursleys. The school is framed as a space of refuge for Harry. In it, he is unique: he is magical, like the rest of the world of Hogwarts. Oppressed and lonely as Harry is in the Muggle world, Rowling constructs the school as a space of escape for him to find other extraordinary individuals like himself. Harry finds refuge from his aunt and uncle in this space—in fact, it is even physically described as different from the world of the Dursleys. Mrs. Dursley's ordered garden and structured kitchen are in stark contrast to the chaotic and whimsical world of Hogwarts—with its talking portraits, floating ghosts, and moving staircases.

It is easy to see that Rowling finds the space of this school essential—she describes it in varied, loving ways. She talks about the beautiful grounds, the fantastic Great Hall, and the excellent dinners at great length. Moreover, the emotional beats foregrounded in the book are entirely about Harry's happiness: after a full day of Christmas activities, Harry thinks, "It had been Harry's best Christmas day ever." Throughout the series, Harry regularly and consistently thinks of Hogwarts as home—a place where he is taken seriously, where he has magical agency, and where he is seen.

The magical school is a representation of agency that is otherwise unavailable to children. The protagonists of the genre are extraordinary people (such is the case in all the examples used at the beginning of the paper. In fact, a lot of the protagonists are tied to prophecies, making them even more special within the realm of their topsy-turvy world) and their world is unique, awe-inspiring, amazing.

The question we have to interrogate further is simple: **Why are schools such a prevalent space for extraordinary children to go?** Naturally, the school is an easy shorthand for younger readers to understand the strange world filled with magic—it provides a familiar and comfortable setting, necessitates the delivery of information given by teachers, and still manages to provide a significant amount of agency to the protagonists. Agency is imagined somewhere or the other through an institution's structure, one that legitimizes an alternative mode of guardianship—where parents are not the final arbiters but teachers. Moreover, the school provides an easy space for a cross between agency and guardianship.

It is telling that a majority of these texts make a fantastical world, providing child protagonists with agency above and beyond what the real world would give—and reinscribes it to the structure of the school. Particularly since this has interesting implications for *who* has agency within the space of the school. In the case of Harry Potter, the answer is obvious: children coded as upper middle class and white are the driving forces behind the story. It is obvious that Rowling has modeled her school on the British boarding school, which institutes children with English values and celebrates middle-class values. Some contend that this is a celebration for all things magical, yet it is telling that what is magical is often very conveniently rather British: Christmas dinners, house systems, uniforms, detentions, and sports competitions.

Rowling's school is an imagination of what she wants a school *to be,* regardless of whether or not real schools are quite like that. Experience and scholarship have taught us that schools are not the egalitarian spaces they are imagined to be. The rich variety of literature that focuses on the classroom would be impossible to summarise: in particular, post-colonial scholars have focussed on the many inequalities perpetrated by the imposition of the British schooling system.

When placed in this context, one cannot escape the underlying implication of Hogwarts: that to have extraordinary agency, one would have to be a rather brilliant student of the British curriculum, preferably with access to one of the elite boarding schools that foster and nurture this kind of magic. By framing education as one of the central ways through which the magic of childhood can be imagined, we do a great disservice to forms of childhood that do not rely on schooling at all. And if children in schools have access to grand magic, so should everyone else.

This tendency in Rowling's writing has been critiqued by both scholars and writers: Mimi Mondol's scathing indictment of Rowling's writing takes to task her tendency to focus on white protagonists. In writing, to critique the school system has become far more commonplace: *Among Others* by Jo Walton does not feature a magical school but a magical protagonist—and is fiercely critical of the British boarding school system through the eyes of its Welsh heroine. Work by Nnedi Orkafor closely examines some of the colonialist tropes of fantasy fiction, while Naomi Novik's *The Scholomance* was written directly as a response to the more colonial overtones of a boarding school structure.

As the most recent iteration of criticism against "“”Things Hogwarts Stands For," it is useful to look at *The Scholomance* and examine how our notions of the magical school have changed. Written twenty years after the first *Harry Potter,* Naomi Novik's *The Scholomance* explicitly critiques education systems that rely on foreign students. Unlike other magical schools, the Scholomance takes magical schools to their logical conclusion, providing none of the protagonists with mentors, teachers, or any form of guardianship. They are essentially trapped alone in a school where magical monsters are notoriously attracted to younger magic users. They have to teach themselves to fight—through the limited resources the school provides. They are encouraged to make allies instead of friends in an effort to gain whatever little advantage they can to survive the four years of schooling.

Novik is cynical about all the reasons for building a school: over the course of the text, we see students who are not affiliated with any enclave go to enormous lengths to be part of one: they perform dangerous tasks that would normally result in their death, neglect studies in an effort to perform chores for the students who are enclavers, study exhaustively to be valuable to enclaver students. Moreover, Novik is careful in depicting the enclaves themselves as having their own power dynamics: with the enclaves in England and America systematically having more power than the ones from the East and Middle East. This worldbuilding which carefully incorporates real-world imperialism, is a far cry from that of Rowling, who tends to ignore the existence of other countries and cultures. The imperialism expresses itself in what classes are preferable (English and Mandarin), in what spells are better, and how dormitories, buildings, and rooms are called their American or British equivalents. Novik's critique of the neo-imperial network that funds an international schooling system is not subtle: at one point, El remarks that being in an enclave would essentially mean the death of students who were *not.*

This is why the ending of the trilogy is of particular importance: the trajectory of the school goes up and then down again. At the end of the second book, El discovers that the school is attempting to orchestrate a sense of camaraderie amongst the students—forcing them to work together by providing bigger and bigger obstacles that they have to team up for. More tellingly, El finds evidence confirming her suspicions that the school is attempting to save all the children. The school leads her to an old newspaper that proudly proclaims that the school's fundamental purpose is protection.

The existence of the magical school is a complicated thing—it necessitates the existence of a colonial legacy that allowed schools to become part of our everyday. It further necessitates a complex relationship with the more untameable, the wilder—magic. Almost all magical schools are somewhere or the other problems because of this—they cannot help but be antithetical to what they are meant to provide students. The Scholomance is not a refuge; it is not a safe space; it provides so much agency to children—at the expense of their lives.

And yet, the school wishes to protect them.

In the third book, the school is resurrected once again after a series of complicated political machinations necessitate its reconstruction. And with it, it becomes clear that the school is still, intrinsically, a part of our cultural makeup. As an Indian, I can tell you that when schools were established in the colonies, they were universally spaces for the establishment of British supremacy. Yes, schools were never meant to be anything more than bastions of inequality—and yet, as any student would tell you, we would *like* our schools to do the job they were originally given. Even if the job was given cynically and disingenuously.

Magical schools, or schools in SFF, betray our very complicated relationship with childhood and schooling. Through SFF, we can see what we *want* our school to be. That El reconstructs the school, hoping to provide greater sanctuary, protection, and agency to the children that it shelters. Perhaps that is why we keep inventing the magical school: because we want our schools to be better.

FIVE HORROR MOVIES THAT REFLECT OUR TIMES: THE POWER OF A POWERFUL MESSAGE IN CONTEMPORARY HORROR

RYAN FAY

The horror genre is founded on political commentary. This trend goes back at least as far as Mary Wollstonecraft Shelley's *Frankenstein; or the Modern Prometheus*, dripping with anti-Enlightenment sentiment. Even something as trite as the Friday the 13th series still has a moral to it, weak as it may be.

Yes, there are plenty of horror films that have little to offer aside from cheap entertainment, and there's nothing wrong with simple pleasures. But when a horror film fails to present a decent message, it fails at the box office as well (if it even makes it there).

If you want to watch a horror movie that offers something a little more complex than Old Testament punishment and a "winners don't do drugs" PSA, here are five suggestions to get you through the Halloween season.

The Monster (2016)

This movie does not get anywhere near the attention it deserves. The story is raw and down-to-earth, refusing to shy away from the nastier side of reality, as a movie about addiction should be. A young mom is struggling with the emotions of having to drop her daughter off with her ex when her car breaks down on the side of a country road on a stormy night. Told through a series of flashbacks, we see the story of both parents' struggle with addiction and their desperate search for escape from the daughter's perspective and how it affects her life. Between flashbacks, we see the mother and daughter call for help as they are terrorized by a monster that feeds in the darkness and only recoils when exposed to light.

***Us* (2019)**

A young family on vacation encounters a group of strangers who are limited in their ability to communicate. This group turns out to be the family's doppelgängers...or are they? Doppelgängers are, in a sense, murky reflections of ourselves. We see enough of ourselves in them, but they are just different enough to be uncanny "others," often thought to be evil. A lot of the conflict in this film comes not from the doppelgängers but from the class warfare this film represents. When we see where the doppelgängers come from and how they live, it's like looking in a broken mirror; what you see may be warped, but you can still see yourself in it. Who is to say which is the doppelgänger and which is the "real" person? Would your own family be able to tell you from yours?

***Candyman* (2021)**

This is a must-see for hardcore horror fans, but it also offers a fascinating story for those newer to the genre. An artist just starting to make a name for himself becomes obsessed with an urban legend—the Candyman. As the story unfolds, the artist starts to lose himself to the legend until he becomes part of it in an encounter with the police. To get the full experience, watch the 1992 version of the same name, as the lesson about how stories get warped over time and their meanings change when people change the details to fit their narrative. With the rise of fake news, "alternative facts, and sensationalist journalism, this is one you won't want to miss.

***The Menu* (2022)**

A biting (pun intended) commentary on the food industry and social media pressure for every meal to be picturesque, every meal to be an experience. Most of the guests in the film represent people who think nothing of high-end fine dining, who take it for granted, and refuse to live in the moment they spent a small fortune on. The head chef, who comes off as cold and unflinching, manages to show Anya Taylor-Joy's character a degree of kindness before making his final dish, a deadly twist on the classic campfire treat: s'mores. There is so much pressure in fine dining, but sometimes these things are just...bullshit. Besides, nothing's better than a simple cheeseburger and fries to-go.

***M3GAN* (2022)**

The story of the model three generative android, or M3GAN, gives us a harrowing message about the need for limits on artificial intelligence, specifically machine learning. Yes, it has plenty of satirical moments, but it is a horror movie that never crosses over into horror-comedy. Ethical limits on AI usage is a conversation we should all be having—especially when it comes to art—and the need for legal penalties should AI be used in such a way as to harm others, intentionally or otherwise. Think about all the horrible things on the internet and what would happen if a titanium robot learned from all of those dark corners.

"FALLEN WOMEN" IN FANTASY: SEX WORK AS CHARACTERIZATION IN POPULAR FANTASY NOVELS AND THE COMPLICATIONS THEREIN

ALEX KINGSLEY

The fantasy genre is overwhelmingly male-dominated, so a good female character is hard to come by. Many writers, especially male writers, misunderstand the meaning of a "strong female character." What readers want is for the *characterization* to be strong, but what they think we're looking for is a woman who is tough, often hardened by a difficult past.

And that past almost generally involves a tragic history of sex work. Why is this a problem? Well, it's not—inherently. Sex work is a common profession, and a dangerous one, so it's not unheard of for someone to find themself hurt. But this trend implies two very dangerous things: that sexual assault is necessary for a woman to have a "tragic backstory," and that sex work is inherently traumatic.

If a fantasy world is a form of escapism, why insist on maintaining the harsh realities of sexual assault? And why must sexual assault be repeatedly used as a tool for characterization?

For a better understanding, let's look at one of the most popular contemporary fantasy series: *The Kingkiller Chronicles* by Patrick Rothfuss (DAW Books, 2007). If you Google "top fantasy books," *The Name of the Wind* (DAW Books, 2007) will almost always be a top hit. The series has everything a fantasy fan is looking for: a creative magic system, a quick-tongued orphan who plays the lute, a magic school with quirky professors—the whole package.

It also features Denna, a semi-sort-of femme fatale (it's heavily implied this femme will be fatal, but we're still waiting on a third novel), whose main character traits are being hot and always dating a different man, with the notable exception of our yearning protagonist. Denna is very evasive about her past, but due to some invasive espionage on the part of the main character, her history of sex work is uncovered.

This sort of "trauma reveal" is echoed again and again in speculative fiction—it's not just limited to fantasy.

In science fiction, William Gibson gives a similar moment to Molly in *Neuromancer* (Ace, 1984), the sexy cyborg who serves as a sidekick for the protagonist. In fact, her story is even worse. She sold herself as a "flesh puppet" to a sci-fi service that allowed her to be essentially unconscious during her encounters with clients.

This trend is not just limited to male writers, either. Leigh Bardugo gives a similar backstory to both of her female protagonists in the *Six of Crows* (Henry Holt and Co., 2015) duology, but Inej is the most egregious example. Inej was sold as a sex slave as a child, and her flight from her former mistress dominates most of her character. Another contemporary fantasy classic, *The Lies of Locke Lamora* (Bantam Spectra, 2006), hardly features any women at all, but the only woman who appears who is *not* brutally murdered is a prostitute.

Even Brandon Sanderson, who is generally sensitive to his female protagonists, uses the threat of sexual violence as a tool. In the *Mistborn* (Tor Books, 2006) books, we meet Vin, the daughter of a prostitute, working for a band of petty thieves who constantly threaten to sell her to a brothel. If you're a man in speculative fiction, you can have just about any profession you want, from wizard to thief to hacker to musician. If you're a woman, your options suddenly seem more limited.

At this point, the abundance of sex work in fantasy is clear, but let's take a moment to clarify the issue. There's prostitution in fantasy; what's the big deal? Here's the big deal: Many readers enjoy fantasy as a form of escapism. The possibility of sexual assault is, unfortunately, a reality that we are confronted with in real life repeatedly. Anyone socialized as a woman is raised to expect unwanted sexual advances and often receives them. So being inundated with sexual trauma stories in the genre that promises an escape from reality is akin to being slapped with a wet fish in perpetuity.

One could argue, however, that the best aspects of fantasy are those that reflect reality, so doesn't sex work have a place in fantasy? Sure, though, I'm not necessarily convinced that Patrick Rothfuss should be the one to espouse the difficulties of being a prostitute. Real-life sex workers face a lot of stigmas, and the idea that their line of work is somehow inherently wrong and violent makes that stigma far worse. This is not to discount the trauma that sex workers face but to highlight the many sex workers who enjoy the profession. To suggests that all sex work is dehumanizing serves to, in turn, dehumanize the very real people who exist in that line of work.

What should we be looking for from women in fantasy? Women who are defined not by the trauma that they've faced by virtue of being a woman but who are defined by—well, literally any other quality. Women who are evil, weird, disgusting, funny, tired, creepy, angry—the whole gamut. In fact, I'd like to take a moment to nod to speculative fiction writers who do this well. Terry Pratchett was ahead of his time, writing the incomparable Granny Weatherwax as early as the 1980s. Becky Chambers and Tasmyn Muir write a rich variety of female characters, from lizard aliens to necromancers.

Does this mean sex work has no place in speculative fiction? No, of course not. Speculative fiction can be about essentially anything. That being said, I would like to see authors take a bit more care in how they manage it instead of wielding the threat of sex work as the default weapon to use on any woman who has unwittingly committed the crime of existing in a fantasy novel.

HOW SCIENCE FICTION AND FANTASY CAN HELP AUTHORS AND READERS FIGHT BOOK BANNING: FAHRENHEIT 451 AND THE BOOK THIEF TEACH THE POWER OF READING

PRIYA SRIDHAR

"More than ever, we get reminders that we have to fight for books. It is much harder and demoralizing, but we can still fight for it. It's the end of 2022, and we get reminders that we have to keep fighting. For ourselves, but also for future authors."

When I pitched this story, I was worried about encountering irrelevance. Banned Books Week is one of my passions because I understand the need to allow kids to reach books that may not meet their parents' approval. It's not until September, though Cast of Wonders postponed their call on the theme to May. Good for me that I can take my fiction break and recharge by writing nonfiction for April, taking notes on writing books.

Then Texas happened. So did Oklahoma, with their declaration of war on the graphic novel *Maus* by Art Spiegelman (*Pantheon*, 1996), and my state Florida has followed. (Thanks, Florida.) Somehow the world became more complicated and frustrating, even though we managed to pull ourselves from the edge of a dictatorship. I have been disappointed in what Disney did and has done with the Don't Say Gay Bill and how the damage control will need to be potent to make up for the betrayal. I won't go into the fight between the mouse and the elephant, only the mouse is rolling in dough and has been for years.

(For the record, *Maus* is probably one of the most accessible books about the Holocaust because the cartoony style allows one to process the horrors better, all of which did happen in real life. It's much less intense than some of the memoirs that I read before *Maus* as a teen, such as the memoirs from Alicia Appleman-Jurman or Jane Yolen's fantastic fiction.)

More than ever, we get reminders that we have to fight for books. It is much harder and demoralizing, but we can still fight for it. It's the end of 2022, and we get reminders that we have to keep fighting. For ourselves, but also for future authors.

Why Is It Harder To Fight For Books?

The real reason? Frankly, a lot of us are tired. Marginalized people spent several years fighting against people who want to erase us. Whether or not we lack the white skin and blond hair or fall victim to the fundamentalist conservatism that wants to smite straightness, it is exhausting to have to point out consistently that we exist.

As a teen, I assumed that challenging banned books was easier than it was. You had to bring it to the attention of the masses, to the righteous fury of the pre-social media Internet. Authors would sometimes cheer on their blogs when their books received a censuring challenge because it meant that more kids would fight to read the books in question. Goodness knows I was once that teen—reading *Sandman* before I could process all of the sex and nudity and trying my best to get to the French Revolution portrayed Neil Gaiman-style.

Now I'm thirty-one, and I'm tired. Some books have had negative ramifications, like *American Dirt* stealing stories from immigrants, being generally racist, and somehow still being lauded. There have also been controversies that open holes in the meritocracy, like when Lani Sarem's not-YA book somehow ended up on the YA list for NYT. It was revealed that her publisher fixed her taking the spot by buying nonexistent copies of a book that wasn't even well-written, according to people who went through the manuscript chapter by chapter (Quartz). The indignities do happen when a book is terribly written or in poor taste.

We sometimes ask what's the point in arguing with people that stubbornly conclude that we are invisible or that somehow we don't exist. After all, you can drain your energy, while their response to being proven wrong may be to travel to a mall and shoot up people just trying to decide what LEGO to buy first. That's not even going into the trolls, the number of people that get sucked into QAnon and Fox News, and life in general. One wishes that social media would deplatform the lot, clearing the timeline for only good news from writer friends and videos of their pets.

Yet the need to fight is strong. We just need to recharge a little more, and maybe turn to the books that inspired us to fight in the first place. Perhaps a little bit of inspiration from those stories that accompanied puberty and existential crises would do the trick.

What Have Great Science Fiction And Fantasy Books Said About Censorship?

Note: This passage is heavy with spoilers for *Fahrenheit 451* (Ray Bradbury, 1953) and *The Book Thief* (Markus Zusak, 2005). You have been warned, and I recommend dearly that you read them both.

Fahrenheit 451 is about censorship, despite what Ray Bradbury may have claimed, may he rest in peace. The main character is a fireman that burns down books rather than stop blazes from affecting houses. He has never stopped to think about his job until his wife overdoses on sleeping pills despite having everything she wants, and an old lady refuses to leave her home library. Montag finds himself reaching for a book from the flames. He takes a moment to consider the *why*.

Ultimately, destruction begets more destruction, and no one wins. Case in point, there's the scene when Montag asks questions and reads poetry to his wife's friends. He thinks that he can inspire change, but sometimes sparks can grow out of control. The metallic hound hunts down Montag in the night after he burns down his own house and his fireman boss. In the end, he leaves a trail of flames and ashes, but stragglers in the woods welcome him. They explain that their way was to remember the stories, commit them, and wait for the fires to burn out. A nuclear bomb falls as if on schedule, and they wait for the dust to settle. Montag knows that his wife Mildred died in the fallout and mourns for what he lost in his quest to understand more about the world.

Fahrenheit 451 teaches that there is more than one way to save a book. You can read them aloud in an enclosed space and listen to the words, to let them sink into your soul. Or you can memorize the words that matter to you, assuming that you are as hyper-focused and obsessed as a person that can bring their passion inside of them and nurture it. Technology actually allows us to share more books; you can get review copies if you review books on your computer and tablet, and pass on your friends' stories via the power of email and direct messages.

What's more, it's important to let stories make you feel uncomfortable. Sure, there is value in deciding what is triggering. Readers do what they can to protect themselves emotionally, but that doesn't mean they condemn all books. In the case of Bradbury's story, Montag makes his wife's friends cry by reading poetry, and he drives them out of the house because they lambast him for making them feel sad.

We can also go further back in time while reaching into the future for the publication date. *The Book Thief* takes us to Nazi Germany, where a surly Death has to make more rounds than usual. Death takes all humans eventually, and somehow a little girl catches his interest. It's not her time to die, not for a long time. But after losing her parents and little brother in a short while, she steals an instruction manual from a gravedigger and rescues a book from a country-mandated blaze. Liesel doesn't know how to read. Her teacher shames her for a lack of literacy when she tries to hide it.

Liesel comes to realize, however, that words have power. They help her process the grief of her little brother dying in front of her, as well as the realization that she doesn't like what her country is doing to innocent people, like how the Fuhrer's orders led to her Communist mother being arrested or when a Jewish refugee named Max needs shelter from the soldiers that want to send him to a camp. Words can change her perspective.

Liesel, at one point, realizes that she needs to tell her story. So she holes up in her foster family's basement at night and starts scribbling with her pen. That action helps her survive the blitz from the Allies, which levels the entire street because the basement protects her from the debris. Death also picks up her book when he makes his rounds and marvels at it. It's the only object he has stolen for himself. He gives it back to Liesel when she dies peacefully as a grandmother in New York, bemused and grateful in her 90s that Death kept the copy of her story safe. Death reassures her that he read it many times and will always remember the little girl that stole books from the flames. He confirms that despite the great tragedies she suffered, Liesel had a good and fulfilling life. Those books literally saved her and gave her the chance to grow.

Books can teach us, like they taught Liesel, that our stories matter. We may be the only audience, but we still matter. If we find ways to remember them, eventually, others will listen. That's why we have to find reasons to tell them, to make sense of the absurdity in the world.

Quite ironically, both stories have received bans or challenges. The Apartheid South Africa government burned *Fahrenheit 451* along with other books in the 1970s, and the original publisher, Ballantine Books, released an edition that removed the swear words, changing two incidents. While *The Book Thief* hasn't received formal bans, sources like Book Binding cite challenges owing to the stark portrayal of war and Naziism as a corrupting influence.

What Can Authors Do?

The first is if you are in a place of privilege, do what you can to raise awareness. Not all authors have a strong social media presence or the ability to avoid trolls. If you do have that power, speak up! Post on social media, list videos with relevant information and show genuine support. We are seeing this happen in real-time, with Maggie Tokuda-Hall challenging Scholastic's attempts to erase Japanese internment camps from her latest release.

As we enter a new year and challenges from school boards installed by tyrannical governors and morality poses from those who don't understand, we have to keep reading. Check your local bookshop and see what is new, a story that may sadden you or make you upset. I know my shelf is pretty full.

I'M (NOT) WHAT I WRITE: THAT TIME I WENT VIRAL ON TWITTER FOR BEING A "SCARY" HORROR AUTHOR

ROBERT P. OTTONE

There's a handful of things that I've heard throughout my life as it relates to my writing that consistently make me cringe:

"Oh, you write horror? I don't read that stuff; I'm married *after all. That's enough horror for me."*

"You write scary stuff? Is it really *scary? Like* CSI*?"*

"You're the next Stephen King!"

"You excited for the new Saw *movie? You like that stuff, right?"*

That last one is valid; that's more somebody asking if I like a movie, I guess, but the others? Whenever someone finds out I write horror, there's at least some form of one of these pat answers that I find myself having to smile and fake-laugh at to kill the conversation. I'm not an anti-social edgelord, in fact, quite the opposite. I enjoy social situations. I'm not much of a loner, except when writing or plotting out my writing. I'm not a "coffee/cat/introvert"-type of author, though I do love coffee and cats.

Most importantly, I'm not a raving sociopath murderer who admits his crimes via the fiction he creates. I'm not some mask-wearing misanthrope who plunges kitchen knives into teens while melting into the shadows. I'm not some demonically-possessed purger of words driven by his desire to spew forth the most vile and salacious nonsense for the masses.

So when an outlet reached out to me asking if I'd be interested in doing an interview for their platform, I agreed. The interview was presented as "an unpublished author interviewing a published author." It's still surreal to think of myself as a "published author," something I imagine my high school English teachers (as well as my critique group members and MFA professors) can't believe either, but whatever, here I am. I've been very fortunate and very lucky, and I'll always be thankful for every opportunity along the way.

I'm also a teacher. That's my "real job," or whatever you want to say. So, between writing, running a small press, teaching seven classes (two of which are at night), and giving lectures on various true crime cases all over Long Island, I'm a pretty busy guy.

I took an hour out of my schedule to meet with the coordinator of the interview. He was charming, friendly, etc. Los Angeles-type dude. Used the term "for sure" a lot. The young writer who was slated to interview me never showed up. No big deal; I got the information on the interview, the format, and all that good stuff, and we chatted a little bit about my upcoming projects, and that was that.

A couple of weeks later, I receive a text from the coordinator asking me to take more time to do *another* meeting, this time with the interviewer in attendance. I informed him that I didn't have any time on the schedule, and that my week was locked up with meetings and writing commitments, but he wouldn't take no for an answer. He mentioned how the interviewer felt "uncomfortable" because I write horror. He then said this:

"It's more about her not being sure who she is interviewing. She's likely imagining you being some Freddy Krueger, rather than a normal person. Point of the quick call would be to see if we can get past that."

I stared at the text, knowing that I had a mountain of work ahead of me, not only for my real job but other writing commitments, lectures, and interviews. I didn't know how to respond. I'm not exactly shy about talking about myself. I've had the loveliest experience in the horror community and have been given opportunities to chat with multiple outlets, all of which are available online. Whether a written interview or on a podcast, I'm just a Google away.

The point is: It ain't hard to do your research and know that I'm more or less a painfully normal person.

My wife was angrier than I was at the audacity of the interviewer to request a second meeting when they didn't bother to show up to our first one. I admit, it did feel nice listening to my wife rant and rave about how unprofessional the interviewer was and how I'd be helping them out more than myself. I hadn't even thought of it that way, but there it was.

When I shared this story on Twitter, the response was huge. I didn't expect it to go as wide as it did, but the general consensus was that this interviewer was wrong to have these preconceived notions about a fellow author. I thought about how many people in the genre have likely dealt with this in their lives. Perfectly normal, nice people who, when someone hears they write horror, are met with disgust or a cringey joke is made about how marriage is the true horror story, or they may even fall back on a Stephen King reference. Not that there's anything wrong with Stephen King, but I think he'd be the first person to say, "Hey, there's other people in the genre worthy of attention."

Do people in the romance genre get looked at as lusty sexpots?

Do crime writers get looked at as amateur detectives? Criminals?

Do science fiction authors get looked at as scientists?

Why do horror people get looked at like we're the crazy ones? That we're the dangerous people to have at a party? That we're the weirdos?

Let me tell you, if you have me over for a party, you can count on a few things:

1) I will silently judge whatever liquor/wine selection you have on offer. Sometimes altogether too harshly. Then I'll most likely drink a bottle of red or whatever whiskey you have that's local.

2) I will tell your assembled group of guests about my weird run-ins with famous people during my time as a reporter. I may even regale you with the times I was physically threatened while tracking a serial killer.

3) I may sing.

Scary stuff, right? Maybe that last one, depending on how many flirtinis I've had, but truly, this concept of "horror writers are scary people" is such a lame cliché, it's bordering on idiotic. It's become the very concept we all get angry about when we watch a horror movie. When characters make the brilliant decision to split up. When the potential victim runs up the stairs instead of out the front door. When suddenly a driver forgets how to start a car.

How did this happen? Where did this stigma come from? You ever see that picture of Stephen King and Clive Barker with the cat from *Sleepwalkers*? Real scary, huh?

HP Lovecraft was a weird-looking dude, but he wasn't scary (other than his personal views).

Robert Aickman? Total dork obsessed with British waterways.

Shirley Jackson? Just plain cool.

Mary Shelley? Even cooler than Jackson.

Point is, we're not scary people. Some of us may take the whole "I write horror"-thing a little too far and have a Twitter picture of us screaming or being super cool and edgy or whatever, but show us a cat meme, and we will likely melt.

I think it's time for people to really get over their weird preconceived notions regarding horror authors. When will the time come that people will admit that it's okay to like horror literature? We shouldn't be making a big deal out of stores having "horror" sections when "Faith" and "Science Fiction" have had sections for decades.

There has to be a good answer somewhere. There has to be a reason why people don't accept horror and, by extension, horror writers as "normal." We see far worse things happening every day on social media, in the news, and all over the world. An individual losing body autonomy is scarier than anything anyone in the community could write. So why don't we have a reaction to that news the way we do to the people who write *fiction* when *fact* is so much more terrifying?

I wish I had answers. I really do. The people I know in the horror community are remarkably kind. Beautiful, supportive souls, all trying to tell great stories and be heard. That's not hyperbole.

None of them are "Freddy Kruegers." None of them are scary in the slightest bit. Socially awkward, some of them. Funny, most of them. But overall, they're just ... normal. Everyday people not afraid to write in the genre we all love.

So, if you're an outlet looking to interview a horror writer, just Google them. Don't make them jump through hoops. You know how hard it is to get a socially-awkward person to talk, to begin with? Make it easy on them. Hold their hand a bit.

I promise, we aren't going to waste our creativity on actually scaring or killing you.

We save that for the page.

IS IT FRANKENSTEIN'S CREATURE OR MONSTER? A RETROSPECTIVE ON TWO EARLY FRANKENSTEIN FILMS

RYAN FAY

It's that magical time of year. The leaves are changing, the air is growing crisper, apple cider doughnuts are going on sale, and the bugs are all going back to hell where they belong. As Halloween approaches and people look for the perfect costume, the same old argument is resurrected even though it should be long dead by now: is it Frankenstein's Monster or Frankenstein's Creature? In order to settle this debate once and for all, we will need to look at two movies: *Frankenstein* (1931) and *Bride of Frankenstein* (1935).

For the purposes of not swaying your opinion, I will refer to the Monster/Creature as "the Being," at least until the end of the argument. I want you to reflect on how people learn and the influences you have had in your own life. Who impacted your learning? Who taught you right from wrong? Who changed the way you think?

Let's take a quick look at the basis of the argument. In his analysis of monsters and what makes one worthy of the moniker, Stephen T. Asma writes, "One aspect of the monster seems to be the breakdown of intelligibility. An action or a person or a thing is monstrous when it can't be processed by our rationality, and also when we cannot readily relate to the emotional range involved" (10). This is why people often debate whether to call the result of Frankenstein's experiment "the Monster" or "the Creature." If we are to call the Being "the Monster," we are drawn to our lack of understanding of the Being's anatomy. Expressions of emotion, especially complex ones, humanizes the Being, shifting the argument more toward "the Creature," as it is more relatable.

First, let's look at the physical aspects of the Being. In creating the Being in *Frankenstein*, the body had been put together, save the final piece of the puzzle: the brain. Igor is sent to find a brain and watches a professor's lecture about the anatomy of the brain. We see one brain in a jar labeled normal and another in a jar labeled abnormal. The professor notes that the abnormal brain had similar "degenerate characteristics" as the cadaver before him, a man whose life had consisted of "brutality, violence, and murder." Igor attempts to steal the normal brain, drops it, and steals the abnormal one. It would be easy to say the abnormal brain is to blame for everything, but that does not give us the full picture. Would the normal brain have altered the Being's behavior? If we are to say it is nurture over nature and ignore the abnormal brain, what does this say of the Being's teacher in the film? And what exactly would make the Being a monster? Asma goes on to say, of the literary version of the Monster, that:

"Of course not all monsters are evil. ... Mary Shelley's creature in Frankenstein is perhaps the most famous of the gentle-hearted giants gone bad. It is the failure of Victor Frankenstein and society generally to provide a space for him in the human family that turns the creature into a monster. ... This novel gives us a glimpse into the subjective interior of the monster's life and gives us a tragic archetype of the misunderstood outcast" (11–12).

The literary version of the Being gives us a far more philosophical version than what we get in director James Whale's version, but Whale still shows us the Being's emotions. We have to look at *The Bride of Frankenstein*to get a complete picture of the Being because that is where Whale focuses on the Being's emotional maturation.

Now, let's look at how the Being learns and who influences the being. The Being does do some fundamental learning in the first movie. We see Doctor Frankenstein's attempts at teaching the Being to sit, stand, and interact with its environment—all of which the Being may well have figured out on its own given enough time—but it is the Being's emotion-driven responses, its instincts, that are largely on display. We see anger when the Being groans and flails after being rejected over his frightening appearance. The Being is also capable of joy, smiling, and laughing—the capacity for friendship—with little Maria as they throw flowers into a lake (before he throws her into the lake, after which it shows concern). The Being fears pain when Igor attacks it with a whip and a fear of fire when Igor re-engages with a torch. This teaches the Being to respond to fear and pain with violence, going on to hang Igor with the whip. We see the fear of fire again during the climactic windmill scene, but, despite the Being's screams, the fear may not be so much of the fire or of the second death it represents, but of suffering, of the feelings of being trapped and overwhelmed.

In the sequel, we see two primary teachers emerge: a blind monk with pure intentions and Dr. Pretorius. The Being stumbles upon a humble cottage in the woods, where it encounters the blind monk. This monk cannot reject the Being for its appearance and treats the Being as he would any regular person. While this is a nice moment for both characters, the monk sharing bread, wine, and cigars with the Being in a display of friendship, Dr. Pretorius puts his own nefarious twist on it. When the Being encounters Dr. Pretorius for the first time, they also share food and wine (and the Being unrolls and eats a cigar). By the end of their conversation, we see the Being take a turn toward the lecherous. The Being did not have much time with the monk, who could have taught the Being to act peacefully but ultimately was unable to protect it from the tortures of society. Pretorius has the time to teach the Being to get what it wants through threats and violence.

The crux of the matter comes down to the climactic ending of *The Bride of Frankenstein*. The Being threatens Doctor Frankenstein and kidnaps his fiancée until he agrees to make the Being a mate. While the Bride is undergoing her own awakening, raised high above the lab, kites waiting to be struck by lightning, the Being throws one of the hired goons off the roof of the lab to his death. When the Being killed Igor in the first movie, one could easily argue self-defense. Throwing this goon off the roof was a conscious decision that was entirely unnecessary. Once the Bride is unwrapped, dressed, and given her iconic shock wig, the Being grabs her hand. She shrieks and hisses at the Being, and in this rejection, the Being decides to blow up the lab with itself, the Bride, and Dr. Pretorius still inside of it, saying, "We belong dead," as a tear rolls down its face. Some may interpret this as part of the emotional maturation process, possibly saving the Bride from the suffering the Being had to face. The problem is that the Bride is not hideous like the Being; played by Elsa Lanchester, the Bride is actually beautiful despite her monstrous anatomy. The Bride may not have had the same issues as the Being, but the Being does not give her a chance to make her own decision.

After the events of *Frankenstein*, it is fair to say that there is room for debate about whether the Being should be called a monster. The Being seems to operate almost entirely on instinct, akin to the actions of an animal. After the events of The Bride of Frankenstein, there can be no doubt that the Being must be called a monster. The Being learned to act like men, to act monstrously and misogynistically like Dr. Pretorius, and never once showed remorse for its actions. That is why we must refer to the Being *not* as a Creature but as Frankenstein's Monster. Also, it's listed as "The Monster" in the credits of both movies.

Stephen T. Asma. *On Monsters: An Unnatural History of Our Worst Fears*. 1st edition. Oxford University Press. October 14, 2009. Pages 10–12.

THE MASH-UP MYTHOS: A PARENT'S GUIDE TO THE MONSTERS YOUR KIDS ARE OBSESSED WITH: KIDS HORROR FROM GAMING TO MEMES TO MCDONALD'S

PATRICK BARB

In the '80s and early '90s, our monsters sprang from the horror aisles of local video stores. With unassuming names like Jason, Freddy, or Chucky, these slashers enraptured Gen X'ers and trickled down to my generational cohort via elementary school compatriots with older siblings and/or lax parental supervision. These fright-flick phenoms enjoyed sanitized reincarnation via playground pretend. Characters responsible for mass murder on-screen were reborn as dolls, action figures, and comic book characters.

Given the popularity of these mask-wearing maniacs, it shouldn't come as a surprise that they'd be scrubbed clean for kids. Just as the Universal Monsters, like Wolf Man, Frankenstein's Monster, and Dracula, thrilled and chilled viewers in the '30s and '40s, only to be softened for Baby Boomers to witness their meetings with Abbott and Costello, popular horrors are always consumed by the never-ending hunger of the youth market.

Today, I'm a parent (my boys are eight and five years old at the time of publication), and I've noticed the same pattern repeating. Only this time, the things going bump in the night come from mascot survival horror games, creepypasta, and memes. This new terror pantheon is further filtered through online gaming content on platforms like YouTube, TikTok, and Roblox. It's hard to know where to put the legend "Here There Be Monsters" on today's virtual map, but I'm here to provide some vague direction and context.

Animatronic Bears and Jump Scares

Do you think this is a game?

When it comes to today's monsters, the answer is often: *Yes*. Or should I <jumps from around a darkened corner with adorably-large eyes turned sinister in this unsettling context, scaring you to death> say, "*YESSSSSS!!!!*"?

From online gaming markets to apps to websites and all digital points in between, the horror games of the twenty-first century veer away from casting villain roles with the traditional monsters of earlier franchises like *Resident Evil* (zombies), *Castlevania* (vampires), or *Altered Beast* (werewolves). Instead, new games shine the spotlight on cute and cuddly mascot killers. From kids' restaurants to carnivals and from toy factories to kindergarten classrooms, these settings transport players to places they *should* love, only to recast the seemingly friendly denizens of those worlds as rampaging monsters.

But don't worry, those big-eyed, cartoony menaces remain cute and cuddly. After all, there's still the merchandise sales to consider...

Five Nights at Freddy's

Created by Scott Cawthon and released on August 8, 2014, the video game *Five Nights at Freddy's* (or *FNAF*) is the Ur example of this particular strain of "cuddly killers on the loose in a kid-friendly space" trend. *FNAF*'s game story centers around a Chuck E. Cheese restaurant analog named Freddy Fazbear's Pizza, where the player must avoid the possessed animatronic mascots by solving various puzzles and navigating maze-like spaces in First-Person POV. The game's signature feature is its use of "jump scares," an oft-cited flaw in horror cinema that's become a feature in horror gaming. Mascots surprise the player, resulting in the POV character's death and an increased heart rate for the player at the controls.

While creator Cawthon's previous work consisted of Christian-oriented game development, it was his flirtation with the dark side that led to success. The series (currently consisting of nine games) attained popularity through Reddit posts, "Let's Play" videos, and spotlight features from content creators like The Game Theorists focusing on the series' "lore." A major motion picture adaptation is due from horror powerhouse Blumhouse in theatres and on Peacock on October 27, 2023.

From the looks of it, kids will be spending a whole lot more than five nights with Freddy.

(And isn't it interesting to see that the most slasher-ific of names has been reused for a monster of this new generation?)

Poppy Playtime

Just as John Carpenter and Debra Hill's Michael Myers inspired a slew of babysitter-slaying copycats, so too did *FNAF* pave the way for more mascot horror. The *FNAF* series has inspired a number of fan games, knock-offs, and more. One of the most successful mainstream imitators is the episodic horror video game *Poppy Playtime*.

Criticized as an *FNAF* clone, *Poppy Playtime* is set at an abandoned toy factory (subbing for the pizza restaurant) and features more puzzle-based challenges with jump scares committed by mutated toys.

While comparisons to its predecessor are apt, it's important to remember that Jason Voorhees has enjoyed as much success as (if not more than) his antecedent Michael Myers. Indeed, the stuffed animal versions, both licensed and knock-off, of the character Huggy Wuggy are some of the most in-demand for children. (For those wondering what this character looks like, picture *Sesame Street's* Grover with jagged white needle-like teeth in his mouth.)

Not only has the character managed to scare fans via gameplay and in toy form, but he's also achieved the dubious distinction of being a Satanic Panic-style urban legend campaign subject. Rumors about children hugging each other and whispering menacing threats inspired by their favorite character are prevalent across the internet.

Rainbow Friends

Rainbow Friends is a multiplayer game designed in and available via Roblox (more on that below) in which players assume the roles of kidnapped children in a creepy amusement park. Color-coded mascots (Blue, Green, Purple, Orange, etc.) are transformed into monsters, and now these bizarre giant-sized dolls stalk players.

Here, we see the edges of characters, as seen in franchises like *FNAF* and *Poppy Playtime*, filed down to create more palatable fright experiences for younger fans. The Rainbow Friends have a more Claymation-style appearance, favoring curves and drool over sharp angles and stitches.

Garten of BanBan

Garten of BanBan is another mascot survival horror game series with gameplay focused on navigating mazes and solving puzzles, all while avoiding primary-colored, kid-friendly antagonists. Here, the setting is a kindergarten (hence the *Garten* of the title) classroom with monster mascots akin to the wacky waving inflatable tube guys at used car dealerships. A relative newcomer, *BanBan* has broken through to young audiences in part because of an official Roblox re-creation.

Creepypasta-dot-exe

Whether it's urban legends told around campfires, scary stories accompanied by nightmare-inducing pen-and-ink illustrations, or digital tales shared on message boards and social media, the allure of forbidden, frightening knowledge is undeniable. While the creepypasta trend has a cross-generational appeal, following in the fright-steps of those "I heard it from a friend who heard it from his brother who heard…"-style schoolyard rumors, a number of digital urban legends appeal directly to the young.

Often, characters, settings, events, etc., relevant to a younger generation are given a macabre twist and become stars in scary stories spread online. For example, let's say you take an adorable, wisecracking blue hedgehog from a video game franchise and add a dash of cosmic horror and bloodshed…

Sonic.exe

Originating in a creepypasta posted by *JC-the-Hyena*, the malevolent X or Sonic.exe (from the story of the same name) has taken on a life of its own in the imaginations of young gamers and content creators. It's not too dissimilar to the way the character takes over the life of a hapless player who's made the unfortunate decision to play a bootleg ".exe" file unleashing this "evil" Sonic the Hedgehog.

The idea of the evil video game sprite has proven a highly influential one. While "exe" is simply a file extension designation, the attributes of blackened sclera, red pupils, and wickedness have become universal signifiers for video-game-inspired evil. In addition to Sonic.exe's infiltration into gaming platforms like Roblox, Minecraft, and Grand Theft Auto 5 via mods, the ".exe" designation has been applied to other child-friendly franchises like Toy Story.

While the evil Sonic is probably the most recognizable video game-based creepypasta character for younger generations, there's a treasure trove of terror found in gaming-related content. From the supposed ghost of the brother of *Minecraft*'s creator (who has no brother by the way) or the oft-rumored Sasquatch lurking in *Grand Theft Auto 5*, the notion that these sources of entertainment might contain a rogue force has proven rich territory for those interested in the nightmarish and macabre.

Don't Shake Grimace at 3 a.m.

Memes, those tiny idea units that infect the pop culture zeitgeist, are often carried both forward and back from the generational cohort in which they're spawned. Baby Boomers pick up trends from Millennials who in turn pick up trends and fads from Gen Z. And so, too, do younger generations benefit from trickle-down meme-onomics. How else would Millennials have received our first tastes of Gen X's favorite slashers?

Social media might seem a surprising source of monstrous inspiration, but much of this horror meme content draws from older traditions and superstitions. It's just the packaging and the applications that have changed.

3 a.m.

The "3 a.m." meme began as an internet challenge, in which content creators on platforms such as YouTube made videos of themselves committing or being the victims of pranks at that late-night/early morning hour. The trend extended to the gaming platform Roblox, which features a game called "Don't Call at 3 am" where players "call" and interact virtually with various creepy character bots.

This latter example speaks to the general creepy vibe that 3 a.m. has become synonymous with online. Content creators and game makers use it as shorthand, communicating to their audiences that bad things (i.e., monsters) are afoot. This superstitious treatment of 3 a.m. is nothing new, though. Traditionally, 3 a.m. is known as "the witching hour" or "the devil's hour." Online content referencing the hour is not so much breaking new ground, as it is resurrecting ancient beliefs.

Grimace Shake

Originally introduced in 1971 as *Evil Grimace,* a character in the McDonaldLand promotional campaign for the fast-food chain, the plump purple monster Grimace was perhaps most familiar to Gen Xers and elder Millennials until recently. However, the character—a giant, sentient taste bud (talk about body horror!)—gained meme infamy when McDonald's introduced a purple berry flavor shake to celebrate the mascot's birthday.

A TikTok trend emerged wherein people film themselves drinking the shake only for a jump-cut to reveal the shake-drinker "dead" with the purple berry cream splattered at the scene. McDonald's social media was quick to embrace this viral marketing via Gen Z humor, and the implied association between Grimace and death has filtered down to younger generations. References to the character treating him like the antagonists of those mascot horror games mentioned above have appeared in YouTube videos and Roblox games.

The Blox & Box of Horror

Sinister characters sourced from video games, creepypasta, and memes come together in a patchwork-quilt-style assembly because online spaces, whether for gaming, entertainment, socializing, or all three combined, tend to obliterate context. The flood of information my generation experienced at its onset is now simply a way of digital life for younger generations. Instead of trying to keep their heads above water, this latest generation of media consumers has grown metaphorical gills and swims through the deluge.

The Roblox gaming world offers a perfect environment for the cross-pollination of monsters from varying sources. In turn, YouTube, the massively popular video-sharing platform with content creators generating videos daily, allows fans to see new contexts created for characters via multiple evolving narratives. One can imagine these variations on myths about characters like Huggy Wuggy or Sonic.exe as similar to how different nations have contrasting elements in their tales of vampires, witches, etc.

Roblox

As noted above, Roblox is an online multiplayer game environment wherein players create their avatars, games, and "experiences" (i.e. multiplayer spaces with various functions, features, and challenges). Thanks to Roblox's lax enforcement of copyright laws, players often encounter any number of beloved monsters from games, creepypasta, and memes. Even when there are challenges to the legality of a property's inclusion, creators circumvent these by using parody names and off-brand color schemes.

That said, Roblox does play legitimate home to some popular modern monster franchises, including the Roblox-created *Rainbow Friends* and the Roblox remake of *Garten of BanBan*. Along with officially sanctioned options, players can fight, compete against, or otherwise interact with Grimace, Sonic.exe, and more. Roblox's open-world aspect puts players in control of the stories, allowing them to experience these fear-makers firsthand, resulting in bespoke horror experiences.

LankyBox

For monster lovers seeking a more curated fright experience, YouTube content creators have found success by drawing from Roblox and those creatures featured in the gaming environment for generating (churning out) daily doses of online material. A prime example of this approach is seen via the output of YouTube sensation LankyBox.

Justin Kroma and Adam McArthur, the personalities behind LankyBox, have been cited as some of the most influential gaming YouTubers currently producing content. They have over 160 million subscribers and their videos have over 33 billion total views.

The channel's content primarily consists of material spun off from Roblox gameplay. Whether they're featuring straightforward "Let's Play"-style videos, skits, or music parodies, LankyBox dips into the mega-popular horror well more often than not. They play horror games with the franchises mentioned previously, have in-world storylines involving 3 a.m., Sonic.exe (with .exe versions of the hosts featured), and utilize popular monster/horror media properties in SEO-friendly titles, sending their content to the top of search results.

While LankyBox is one of the most comprehensive sources for this new generation of horror content, there are many corners of YouTube catering to the monster-obsessed. Videos featuring fan-made crossovers between Rainbow Friends, BanBan, Sonic.exe, and more are the unlicensed equivalents of Frankenstein meeting the Wolfman or Freddy fighting Jason.

Defying corporate dictates and creator approvals, these emerging, oft-contradictory mythologies offer a million different pathways for the monster tale-teller or consumer. The need to both fear and befriend the monster is a universal *(heh)* and cross-generational trait. Taking a look at what your child loves to be scared by can open you up to new scare experiences.

And that's a good thing at any age.

THE NATURE OF FEAR: WHAT TRULY TERRIFIES US ARE THE HORRORS HAUNTING US FROM OUR CHILDHOOD

CHRISTINA SNG

I have a confession to make. It hit me today. Despite being a horror writer all my life, there are genres of horror I am afraid of.

They are the ones I quietly avoid, like Asian horror, the same horror I grew up with as a child, not through movies but through oral tradition. The ones your parents whispered about, the ones your relatives hissed in your ear, the ones your classmates told you in confidence, eyes wide with terror.

The rest resonated through my childhood: the faceless long-haired woman in a white dress, the ghosts in a banana tree, dead World War II POWs wandering through my house dragging their chains, the hanging nun swinging from a rope on classroom fans and her counterpart sitting on the fan blades looking down on you, the monsters pulling kids through school sewage pipes, and unforgettably, the headhunters who placed children's decapitated heads into the foundation of Sheares Bridge.

The setting of many of my terrors was school. Apart from the ghost nuns and sewage monsters, I'll never forget what a classmate told me during one of our round-robin ghost story sessions at the back of the school room. Her tale about the red-eyed man she encountered behind her bedroom door stayed with me, its visceral image burned into my young brain. I feared the backs of doors for decades afterward.

Home was no less frightening. Adults freely talked about ghosts and spirits wandering the world as if they were omnipresent. We children were never shielded from them as a potential source of fear and trauma. They were discussed over lunch and dinner with the same intensity as Aunty so-and-so's daughter getting married to a man she disapproved of.

My mother easily told of the time a ghost sat on her chest, waking her up, terrified, unable to sit up until the ghost went away. Her sister added how she often saw a shadow at the foot of her bed. She thought it was her husband, but when she turned, he was fast asleep beside her. Another aunt visited my childhood home once and never returned after seeing ghostly soldiers in the hallway.

In the afternoons, we never turned on the fluorescent lights. Instead, I sat alone in the sunlight to play, ever aware of the long shadows nearby that could easily hide monsters. At night, I kept my feet under the blankets as a child, far from the edge of the bed, worried the shadows beneath would pull me under.

As an adult, I don't avoid the supernatural because I dislike it. The truth is, I have a primal fear of it, despite not believing in spirits and spells. It's like my fear of clowns that seemingly had no origin, given I never watched Stephen King's *IT*, but I did watch the movie *Poltergeist* many times. Rewatching it now, I realize it was the clown scenes that subliminally scarred me, even as I forgot them.

This goes back to the effects of trauma in childhood that follow you through your entire life. Our childhoods were our maps of how we understood the world. Things we saw, things we could never unsee because they were etched into our growing minds, even if we forgot—this is how phobias and aversions are formed.

Our days as teens and young adults shape us further, as does the culture around us. The undercurrent of patriarchy, the quiet whispers of domestic abuse, the exclusivity of cliques, the discarding and condemnation of the fallen. These themes are rife in horror but resound so strongly in the lives around us.

I have no inclination to watch Asian horror. Movie posters of their offerings spark an existential dread when I see them. Intellectually, I know they're just another horror story like *Hereditary* or *Midsommar*, but that woman crawling out of the TV with long, disheveled hair and a haunted look on her face? It's too close to home. It's like looking in the mirror.

THE SMALL PRESS HORROR RENAISSANCE: SIX INDIE PRESSES PUBLISHING HORROR TO ADD TO YOUR TBR PILE

RYAN FAY

Just because an author signs a deal with a major publishing house doesn't guarantee their book will sell well. The problem with the ever-condensing Big Four (*Hachette Book Group, HarperCollins, Penguin Random House,* and *Macmillan*) is that they trade in quantity over quality. This isn't to say that these books are bad by any stretch, but it's hard to truly care about every single title a major corporate entity puts out when each imprint is forced to meet quotas.

This is where small indie presses come in. As a word nerd, nothing makes me happier than seeing all these books and magazines produced with genuine passion. The horror genre is experiencing a renaissance right now and it is truly reinvigorating. There are so many talented authors with gripping stories to tell that we would never have had the fortune to experience if not for these smaller presses. To cover every horror and gothic lit press that has emerged in the past few years would take too long, but if you're looking for a good book that will haunt you well after you've put it down, here are a few small presses to check out and book from each.

Bad Hand Books

From South Dakota comes Bad Hand Books, run by Doug Murano, who has won both a Bram Stoker Award and Shirley Jackson Award. Bad Hand has been an incredibly supportive presence in the horror lit social media scene.

Each story in The Hideous Book of Hidden Horrors will make you check your peripheries for those that lurk just beyond perception. Editor Doug Merano brings together an All-Star lineup of horror and dark fantasy writers, including Alan Baxter, Todd Keisling, Gabino Iglesias, Josh Malerman,

Cynthia Pelayo, Hailey Piper, and more. With this lineup, it's no surprise that this book earned The Shirley Jackson award.

Ghost Orchid

Ghost Orchid has been one of the more interesting presses I've been watching. Editor A. R. Ward built up her press through a microfiction series called Hundred Word Horror. Each book in the series is comprised of 100 stories and poems, each 100 words long.

One of my favorite things to do in the summer and fall is to take a walk through the woods around my house. Then I read Chlorophobia. It's been a while since my first reading, but sometimes, when I wake up in the middle of the night to get a glass of water, I'll look out the kitchen window and watch the trees for a while to make sure they don't move. Fifty authors come together to deliver an eco-terror anthology that made me hyper-aware of every falling leaf.

Hungry Shadow Press

Run by Brandon Applegate, Hungry Shadows is small but powerful. A labor of love and true passion for the genre, Applegate—a writer himself that I first learned about in Ghost Orchid's Hundred Word Horror: The Deep—puts forth stories that will change how you look at the same old stories.

Eric Raglin, Laurel Hightower, and Alex Woodroe are among the author in It Was All A Dream: An Anthology of Bad Horror Tropes Done Right, an anthology dedicated to classic tropes that we all love to hate. Each story takes a different trope and twists it into a better version of itself, capturing your interest to see how this once-predictable story will go.

Off Limits Press

Off Limits Press has put out banger after banger without a single miss in its 15-book catalog. This is one of the few presses I genuinely get excited about when I see a new book announced.

Through In Nightmares We're Alone, Greg Sisco gives us three unique stories that intertwine to give us one extensive story that unsettled me in the best way. A mother's unhealthy obsession with dolls. A misogynist con man that could never seem to settle and grow roots finally does...through his fingernails. A woman receiving messages from her late father's typewriter. Each story is gripping in its own right but when you see the threads all tying together, you just have to give it a chef's kiss.

Quill and Crow

If straight up horror isn't your thing, try Gothic stories instead. Run by Cassandra L. Thompson, an author herself, Quill and Crow leans hard into novels and anthologies that present a masterclass in setting the mood for the reader. In addition to stellar books, Quill and Crow offers shirts, candles, mugs, and jewelry with witchy vibes.

Easily one of my favorite anthologies of all time, Haunted is a Gothic story collection that made me feel compassion for the ghosts trapped in Victorian mansions. explores the different ways people are haunted. If you're looking for something more in-line with dark fantasy, Grimm & Dread: A Crow's Twist on Classic Tales is another fantastic choice.

Night Worms

While this one isn't a small press itself, it does help out the indie scene. Sadie Hartman and Ashley Sawyers work to bring you high quality book packages that worth far more than the price you pay. Each month has a unique theme, accompanied by amazing art work, that gets you two books and a loaded bag of stickers, teas, and other goodies. If you want to ensure that you're getting quality returns on your investment, trust Night Worms to deliver.

As previously mentioned, these are only six of the many small presses that are producing incredible work. It's safe to say that horror fans are eating well. Support your local indie presses by buying directly from them whenever you can, and long live the horror renaissance!

HORROR HOSTESSES WITH THE MOST-ESSES: LATE-NIGHT HORROR HOSTS FROM VAMPIRA TO ELVIRA

RYAN FAY

If you're a horror movie buff like me, you've seen most of the big-name stuff and spend a lot of time sifting through the various streaming services, looking for something decent. That's where horror hosts come in. Horror hosts have been introducing audiences to horror and B-movies that we may not have otherwise seen since the 1950s. There have been plenty of hosts, but it's the hostesses that have popularized the style of show that adds value to the movies being shown.

Vampira

Vampira was the first-ever horror host, starting in 1954 with WABC-TV. The idea was to add sex appeal to the lineup of late-night horror movies in order to capture the audience's attention. To create the character, Nurmi "combined elements of Snow White's Evil Queen, a comic strip dragon lady and under-the-counter bondage models. To exaggerate her already waspish waistline she strapped a flesh-wasting poultice of meat tenderizer to her midsection with a tightly-bound rubber inner tube" ("The Incredible but True Story of Maila 'Vampira' Nurmi"). What made her stand out most was her incredibly thin waist, her measurements having been "advertised as 38–17–36." Vampira would greet the audience with a scream and introduce movies like *Strangler of the Swamp*, *Return of the Ape Man*, and *White Zombie*. Though Vampira's reign only lasted a whopping eight months, and only broadcast in the Los Angeles area, the hostess remains an icon in horror culture.

Elvira

Although there was a host of hosts after Vampira that included Bob Wilkins, Count Gore de Vol, and Rod Serling, it was **Elvira**, Mistress of the Dark, who took the reigns in 1981. If Vampira was the one to introduce sex appeal to late-night horror, Elvira (played by Cassandra Peterson) took it to another level. In her book, *Yours Cruelly, Elvira*, Peterson writes about working with Robert Redding to design Elvira's costume. When they pitched the all-black, sexier costume to the management team at KHJ studios, "We were both a bit shocked that they didn't mind the plunging neckline that Robert had drawn. In fact, their only comment regarding changes to the costume was to ask that we make the slit on the leg a little higher." Elvira would go on to capture public interest for the next 30 years, expanding beyond the horror niche and into pop culture. Her show would feature the hostess interrupting B movies with quips and commentary, and prove so popular that Peterson would star in several Elvira movies, with a plethora of cameo appearances along the way.

Darcy the Mail Girl

Now with a plethora of streaming options, it can be a daunting task to find those diamonds in the rough. Thankfully, we have various podcasts and hosts around the internet, but none quite stack up against **Darcy the Mail Girl** from *The Last Drive-In with Joe Bob Briggs*. Technically, Joe Bob Briggs is the host, having previously hosted *MonsterVision*, and Darcy (played by Diana Prince) is the mail girl co-host. More than your typical mail girl, Darcy's passion for the genre shines through when she gets to introduce the audience to movies that may otherwise have gone overlooked. In an interview with Rue Morgue magazine, Prince said, "I think I'm kind of a feminist version of the Mail Girl, a different take on it. ... I very much consider myself a feminist. I'm having fun, and I actually get to speak about the movies—I think that's a big step in "Joe Bob world." I'd like to think I balance some of his more chauvinist tendencies..." (Thompson). Check out *The Last Drive-In with Joe Bob Briggs* on Shudder.

For as long as there are new horror movies being made, no matter the quality, horror hosts and hostesses will be there to help us find the diamonds in the rough.

Bibliography

Peterson, Cassandra. "How the Iconic Late-Night TV Character of Elvira Came to Be: Cassandra Peterson on Coming Up With the "Mistress of the Dark"." Literary Hub, 24 Sept. 2021, https://lithub.com/how-the-iconic-late-night-tv-character-of-elvira-came-to-be/. Accessed 30 Sept. 2023.

Peterson, Cassandra. *Yours Cruelly, Elvira: Memoirs of the Mistress of the Dark*. Hachette Books, 2023.

"The Incredible but True Story of Maila 'Vampira' Nurmi." Austin Film Society, www.austinfilm.org/2015/02/the-incredible-but-true-story-of-maila-vampira-nurmi/. Accessed 30 Sept. 2023.

Thompson, Rocco. "Darcy the Mail Girl on Cosplay, Feminism, and "The Last Drive-In"." Rue Morgue, 6 Oct. 2019, https://rue-morgue.com/darcy-the-mail-girl-on-cosplay-feminism-and-the-last-drive-in/. Accessed 30 Sept. 2023.

"Skal, David J. *The Monster Show: A Cultural History of Horror*. Farrar, Straus and Giroux, 2001."

DID RAY BRADBURY PREDICT THE SMART HOUSE IN "THE VELDT"? CAN THE HOUSE REPLACE US?

PRIYA SRIDHAR

"Nothing ever likes to die—even a room."—Ray Bradbury, The Veldt

---

Smart technology and the Internet of Things have dominated trends in the tech world. Refrigerators can now connect to smartphones and provide updates on when you need to buy more milk. Electronic doorbells can help you record package theft, harassment, or cute animal guests like deer in the spring. You can even set up baby or pet cams to watch your loved ones while you're at work or running errands, to make sure all is well at home.

We have the technology to make a safer world for parents and children. Yet there may be drawbacks, predicted way back in the 1960s. Ray Bradbury's tale explores a prototype of "The Smart House". Perhaps past fiction, dated by post-World War II values, can indicate what lies in store for the 2020s and 30s, respectively. "The Veldt" is a harbinger of what the virtual savannah promises for future smart houses.

What Is "The Veldt"?

"The Veldt" is one of Ray Bradbury's most popular- and creepiest- short stories. It first appeared as "The World the Children Made" in The Saturday Evening Post in 1950. It's about how two children, Peter and Wendy, come to resent their parents for being parents after receiving a virtual reality nursery that can give them anything they want, as long as they imagine the world. The parents in question, George and Lydia, become concerned when the kids summon the African savannah on a regular basis, with matching sounds and scents.

Seems odd? It does when you can summon magical lands with this virtual reality, and the kids want the hot plains with circling vultures. This savannah has lions constantly feeding, and the adults can't see which poor prey fell victim to the big cats. When George or Lydia try to change the nursery settings to something like Aladdin's Arabian nights, the lions keep staring at them while the humans sweat the savannah. They know the Playroom has safety settings to avoid this scenario. George is unsure of how the children were able to bypass the fail-safes and why they are acting as if everything is fine.

Not helping is that Peter and Wendy have become more rebellious. When Peter and Wendy don't receive permission to take a rocket to New York, the lions multiply within the playroom. George cannot make the big cats vanish with a command, though he certainly tries. Peter also says firmly that "Father" should never close the playroom, and that is not a request. George has to remind Peter who pays the bills in the house, but Peter does not care. He wants the Playroom, lions and all, and so does Wendy.

Much of the story posits the following question: has the Happylife house and Playroom replaced George and Lydia as parents? Lydia fears she has no purpose as a stay-at-home parent and senses George has lost his purpose as well. He brings in a psychologist friend, David McClean, who spells out that the whole family has become dependent on the house. He recommends that the family move out of the house, with the Playroom shut off, and the children visit his clinic every day for a year. The only problem is the kids beg for one more play session, and they lock the parents in the nursery. Cue the lions coming, and they are much hungrier for actual flesh and blood than they are for the virtual versions.

My middle school class read "The Veldt" in seventh grade. We grasped the horrific implications, and the story has stayed with me all these years. I've wondered how it predicted the Internet of Things and entitlement issues in wealthier generations.

Can The 2020s Smart House Replace The Human Owners?

Fortunately or unfortunately, no. We're not at the point where Smart Houses can replace a parent. If they could, home chores and bills would be much easier. Instead, we are at the point where smart house technology creeps into our lives and makes things convenient.

One difference is that you need an electronic connection to centralize all these devices. George has to switch off the various inventions one by one, which causes the children to panic. Smart technology, however, wants centralization and convenience.

Leisure And Maintenance

One interesting fact is that neither George nor Lydia have planned leisure time or hobbies. Nor do the kids; they often go to local carnivals and want to travel to New York on a whim. When Peter paints, he uses a machine. George drinks rather than play cards or reads books.

The Playroom doesn't just serve as a substitute parent but also is a substitute for imagination. All you have to do is state what you want, and the images come to life with matching scents and temperatures. There isn't a chance for the kids to build castles out of mud and sand or to hammer birdhouses and bee boxes into virtual trees.

The only time we see a hobby is regarding Peter's paintings. Peter doesn't want to paint his own images. Computers may learn how to draw for us. So far, however, all they can do is copy. As humans, we often struggle to draw a simple straight line, and then feel frustrated when others don't appreciate our scribbles. Many of us may wonder how we will ever achieve the perfection of a straight line, but we understand that computers are currently just helpful tools.

Basic Human Needs

Cooking comes up frequently in the short story, along with other house chores. Lydia expresses that, without chores and cooking, she lacks a purpose in the house. The kids do not love her the way they love the automatic toothbrush and bathtub back scrubber. Leaving for a few days on a "vacation" where she'd have to fry eggs and sweep the floor delights her. David McClean says that if the family keeps living in the house, they will forget their basic cooking skills and starve if a power outage happened: "You wouldn't know how to tap an egg."

I have to disagree with this point. Tapping an egg is not hard at all; perfecting the method is. While we do have devices like slow cookers and stoves with automatic timers, there isn't a case where we can make a command to a stove and receive a fresh-cooked meal. Humans still need to put in the work. We choose the frozen foods to put in the microwave or the ingredients for the slow cooker. If we forget the ketchup? At best, we can add it to a digital grocery list or a template.

The electric toothbrush also comes to mind as part of a daily dental routine. Peter sounds horrified when learning that if the family went away from the house for a month, he would have to tie his own shoes, brush his hair, and ensure his teeth are clean. His toothbrush would no longer remove the plaque or all the food particles. The plastic, basic version would have to do that.

Yet, in real life, an electric toothbrush still requires a human hand to angle it in the right places for a certain amount of time. My dentist can assert that claim because our teeth need brushing, flossing, and constant care. Again, the human has to put in the work.

Acquired Assistance With Virtual Reality

We also need accessories to bring VR to life. Such technology can include helmets or expensive computers, or television screens. Right now, we're not at the point where computers can consistently deliver odors as well through virtual walls. One could connect a diffuser to a smartphone to control it, but that is the extent.

Even with these tools, virtual reality cannot come to life and eat us yet. It can take up a lot of our time, causing eye strain, back pain, and empty wallets. Yet lions won't pop out of a virtual reality screen and decide we are meat. We are safe in that regard.

People can breathe a sigh of relief; smart houses cannot kill us yet for the crime of saying no to a child. The child or the person losing access to this technology would have to take action and commit the deed. While such a combined intent and action isn't a good thing, the smart house is not at the point where it could enable such a murder. Technology has limits.

What Did Ray Bradbury Not Predict?

While Bradbury showed that technology in the wrong hands can subvert its original purpose, he didn't understand that innovation went hand in hand with capitalism. Who is making money off this potentially dangerous technology? And why is there no regulation within this world?

We can answer the second question at least: lack of regulation in the tech world is disturbingly common. When we don't understand the potential for new inventions, for better or for worse, they can subvert the original purpose. As one example, Alfred Nobel invented dynamite for safer mining and became horrified when other nations used it as a weapon of war. The Wright Brothers wanted to revolutionize travel when taking to the skies, but Orville lamented how planes deployed bombs during World Wars rather than necessary supplies and transportation.

New inventions like social media have shown the hard way what happens when governments do not understand the potential for abuse or power plays. By the time that senators schedule a hearing about Facebook violating privacy or Amazon eavesdropping on customers, the damage is done. Society has to endure the impact.

Many businesses within and outside Silicon Valley benefit from the lack of regulation with smart technology. The consumer then suffers as a result, either due to a lack of privacy or faulty regulations. There have been reports of companies like Amazon utilizing Alexa devices to listen in on their customers and tailor ads based on these actions. Consumers were not given a choice to opt-in or opt-out of this eavesdropping, as highlighted by lawsuits concerning Google's home and Alexa. The primary purpose of using Alexa is to control temperature and music, not to disclose one's advertising preferences.

We don't see who profits off the Happylife home in the Veldt. Whichever company made it would either have installments on the amount of renovations that the system would gain. They also would need to have access to public domain settings like the fictionalized Aladdin or ones with colonial undertones like the Savannah.

That's another facet; technology in the West focuses on a white person as a target individual. Such a playroom can bring your dreams to life or someone else's worst nightmares. George doesn't consider that Aladdin was a fictional construction later added to One Thousand and One Nights.

What To Expect (And Fear From The Future)

One theme that remains relevant from "The Veldt" is the idea that technology may replace human connection. We have seen the little things like texting at the dinner table or streamers gaming for days on end. The pandemic hasn't helped, keeping most of us at home as we comprehend remote work and social distancing for several years.

We need to stay mindful that as parents or adults, behaviors we have may pass on to the next generation. Behavior, more than the way technology develops, will create a Peter or Wendy in the future that cannot understand the consequences of their actions.

Smart house technology, fortunately, cannot replace us. However, something in the future may, and we may get an ultimate Facebook congressional hearing, with more murder in the mix. To change that direction, we need to change our attitudes and focus on constantly putting in the work of human beings.

THE WITCH OF THE A&P: A HORROR AUTHOR LOOKS BACK ON CHILDHOOD TERRORS

PATRICK BARB

Have you ever read something so true, so genuine, you convince yourself there's no way it's *just* fiction and that some seed of reality's sprouted tendrils and buried its way through the printed page of supposed pretend?

The first time it happened to me was around 1985/86. I was three or four years old. It's a time of our development when the membrane between reality and fantasy is maybe at its thinnest. The book in question? The one that would seemingly leak its contents into my *real-world*, lived experiences?

Hansel & Gretel. More specifically, the 1980s Little GoldenBooks edition of the fairy tale. You know, the ones with gold(en) foil spines with pictures of tugboats and trains who could and puppies who poked on the back? That one.

This particular version—of the tale of two small children abandoned by their family due to financial strain who are then imprisoned and forced into indentured servitude by a cannibal in a candy house until they burn said cannibal alive—was told behind a cover I won't ever forget. The cherubic and *quite German* Hansel and Gretel sit huddled under a tree with green grass below them. There's even a bunny. This painted bucolic scene does little to justify the trembling terror on the visages of the Cabbage-Patch-Kid-faced titular heroes. Oh, sure, there's a fox in the background. But what's a fox anyway? Certainly, no wolf, I'll tell you that.

And most definitely *no witch*.

No, they saved the witch for the interior.

In writing this piece, I've conducted some internet sleuthing, trying to confirm what *my* witch in *my* edition of *Hansel & Gretel* looked like. I've had mixed results. Hunched-over old crones dressed in black or wearing shawls of blood red or monstrous purple. All potential contenders in the search results for "Witch Hansel & Gretel Goldenbook" But no witch stands out as "the one."

For the telling of my tale, I'll ask that you Google Image Search "Hansel & Gretel GoldenBooks witch" and find the image that calls to you, that crooks its long, bony finger in an appalling "come-hither" gesture. Once you've located it, let that stand as the witch I encountered in my bedtime reading. It's easier that way, offering you a chance to overlay whatever kickstarts *your* fear onto my tale.

Now, let's leave the woods and the candy house and go to a grocery store in small-town 1980s Virginia.

In particular, we're going to accompany young Patrick and his mother as they shop at the local A&P. This grocery chain existed from 1859 to 2015. Not a bad run, all things considered. In the early 1980s, the chain was ubiquitous enough to have made it to the small town in southeastern Virginia where I grew up. (And when I say *small town*, I mean it. Franklin, Virginia, had a population of 7,308 at the time of the 1980 census.) The most important thing to note here is that the A&P was there, and I was there, and my mom was there.

And the witch was there as well.

Filling in the blanks from a haze of personal history, I can guess that we walked in one set of sliding doors, grabbed a shopping cart into which I was placed, and then wound our way up and down the aisles filling the cart with whatever food or drink we needed back home.

But like our dear Bavarian *kinder* Hansel and Gretel making their way through a breadcrumb-less forest, it's less about the journey and more about reaching a final, potentially fatal destination.

And, hey, check-out lines *are* where they keep the impulse purchases. *Like candy.*

Remember, I was around three or four years old when all this happened. To say I'm an unreliable narrator is no great leap. As such, I'll pause now to turn the telling of the tale over to my mother and do my best to transcribe her narration of the encounter as told and re-told over some thirty-seven-plus years:

We were waiting in the check-out line with our groceries, and there was an old woman in front of us with her cart. You turned around in your seat and looked at her for a long time. Then, in the loudest voice possible (do three or four-year-olds have any other kind?), *you said, "Mommy, she looks just like the WITCH from Hansel & Gretel!"*

I love hearing that part of the story. As someone whose personality trends toward the introverted, hearing this unfettered exclamation coming from my mouth is pretty darn impressive. Of course, you might think, "But how awful to say such a thing about an old woman going about her business, retrieving groceries from the A&P."

But I'll let Mom continue:

She turned around and started to curse me out. I didn't know what to do. I couldn't go anywhere. You were crying. I started crying. It was awful.

Sure, it's not getting fattened up to be cannibalized, but it's not what I'd call a good time, either.

When we got home, I went to my room and threw *Hansel & Gretel* into my parent's closet. In subsequent years, whenever I'd encounter that tome, I'd always make sure it found its way back to exile. Not so much out of genuine fear, but more as ritualistic practice. In a sense, a feeling of betrayal wormed its way into my heart when it came to that particular book with those particular words and pictures.

As far as young-me was concerned, I'd encountered its wicked antagonist in the real world, absent the safety of being able to say "The End" and close the cover.

Was that old woman the witch from *Hansel & Gretel*? Did my encounter with her happen as my mother described?

Probably not. Maybe. Kind of. Sort of.

However, the notion that some bit of dark fairy-tale fantasy can worm its way from the page to my head to a real-world encounter speaks to a magic potent enough to crisscross realities. Reading and writing horror fiction is perhaps the natural by-product of this formative encounter. After all, with every story I read or scary movie I watch, I'm still looking for the witch again. I'm still challenging myself to face her again and to see how I'll respond, knowing everything I know. Will I break down and cry? Will I have my magic words at the ready? Or is chasing that sensation of reading fiction so compelling it feels like reality akin to being lost in the woods with the breadcrumbs all gone?

FROM SPOOKY LOVERS LOVERS TO AMANTES ESPELUZNANTES: ONE BOOK, TWO LANGUAGES: J. V. GACHS ON THE PROCESS OF PUBLISHING IN MULTIPLE LANGUAGES

J. V. GACHS

"Girl meets girl on a dating app.

Girl finds out her crush is a ghost."

That was the seed for a simple short story about a spooky first date in a graveyard. I fell in love so deeply with the characters of Ernestina and Avra that I just kept on writing and writing about them, and a flash story ended up becoming my novella *Spooky Lovers*, to be published by Interstellar Flight Press and the subject of this article.

Although my first language is Spanish, I chose to write this story in English. I'm what's called an ESL (English as a Second Language) writer. I live in Spain, even though I'm aware that some ESL writers live in English-speaking countries. I wonder if they get asked why they write in their second language as often as I do. My stories take place in Spain, my characters are Spanish, and the creature in my debut novel, a Xana, comes from my region's mythology, so why do I complicate my life by not writing in Spanish? Well, the answer is as simple as the seed for Spooky Lovers: out of necessity.

I learned through experience that writing in my mother tongue offered limited possibilities for publication if I wanted to pursue a career in horror, while in English, by the time I started drafting Spooky Lovers, I had sold multiple short stories, and I had already signed a contract for my debut novel *Epiphany* to be published by *Off Limits Press* (December, 2023).

Right before COVID hit, I started out writing in my first language, focused as I was on learning the craft and with little to no worry at all about the publishing industry. It didn't go unnoticed to me, even in those days, that most of the indie horror I was reading hadn't even been translated into Spanish. There were only a handful of short story magazines in Spain and even fewer dedicated to speculative fiction. Also, when I felt I was ready to start submitting my work for publication, I found hardly any information about the process in the Spanish market, while the resources available if I were writing in English were abundant and very useful. So, being bilingual, it wasn't a difficult decision to try my hand at translating my own stories. After a couple of tries, my first short story "Hubris' Nest" was accepted for publication by Luna Station Quarterly in their Issue 45. It proved to me that it was doable, so I kept going.

When my cuentos in Spanish languished without markets to be sent to, while the same stories got picked up by, mostly, US anthologies, I stopped bothering to write in both languages. I found other horror writers online to share experiences and critiques with, and I abandoned the idea of publishing in my own language altogether.

I wrote, revised, and polished Spooky Lovers in English, and I was fortunate enough that Guest Editor Lee Murray picked it up as part of IFP's horror novella series.

And that would be the whole story, one not so interesting about writing in your second language, if it wasn't for a Spanish press: *Dimensiones Ocultas.*

One thing I've learned in my writing journey is that a rejection is not a death sentence for a story, and it certainly isn't a rejection of you as a writer (even if they do sting sometimes). It was a rejection that led me to send my novella to Dimensiones Ocultas.

When DO announced a call for their first anthology, I was also starting out on my horror journey. I submitted a story that didn't get picked. Roberto Carrasco, *Dimensiones Ocultas* EiC, sent me a message afterward to tell me he had really enjoyed my story, though.

Two years passed, and he was scouting their 2024/25 publishing catalog. Roberto Carrasco texted me and asked if I had a novel or novella that could match their needs. Being familiar with their books, I was sure Spooky Lovers would be a good fit. The only problem was... I had written it in English.

I believe that when it comes to publishing, one should seize the opportunities when they present themselves, so instead of asking him to wait and rush a translation of Spooky Lovers, I explained to him what the situation was. Considering he's also a translator, he was kind enough to read my original manuscript and sent me the kindest acceptance message I've ever received. The contract was signed and as I write this, I find myself translating my own words from my second language to my first.

To be completely honest, I thought it would be easier... Spooky Lovers is sprinkled with humor and double meanings and innuendos that worked well in English. Finding ways to make them work in Spanish, too, makes me realize how difficult the job of a translator really is.

I consider myself lucky to be able to bring my characters to a wider audience by using the language skills I've cultivated in two different languages, but, at times, the imposter syndrome hits hard. Most writers I know suffer from it, if not all the time, then fairly often, and I've come to realize mine is more about worrying over typos and grammar mistakes in emails to presses and editors, social media promotion or writing an article about being an ESL writer with a book coming in two different languages. When I started communicating with *Dimensiones Ocultas*, it was the first time I had the chance to talk about contracts and publishing in my first language. I wondered, "Is this how English as a First Language writers feel all the time? This is *pan comido*! I can be anxious about the actual writing now!"

Being an ESL writer is both hard and rewarding, most of the time it feels like trying to run a marathon with your hands tied at your back. And then, it gives you these sweet opportunities and makes the effort worth it. I'm so thrilled to be able to present *Spooky Lovers* and *Amantes Espeluznantes* to readers that I can't wait for 2024's Spooky Season when you all will meet Ernestina and Avra and (hopefully) love them as much as I do.

REVIEWS

GREMLINS: SECRETLY A CINEMATIC MASTERPIECE?: ONE OF THE MOST POLARIZING HORROR FILMS IN EXISTENCE

ALEX KINGSLEY

Gremlins (1984) is one of the most polarizing films in existence. It's widely panned as a poorly made horror movie, but in some circles, it has gained cult classic status. At a glance, it looks like another "so bad it's good" situation a la *The Room*, and if one takes the movie at face value, sure, it seems hilariously bad. But when interpreted as a satire of horror tropes that makes a commentary on the treatment of POC in horror films—and in American media at large—and its relationship with consumer culture, the film takes on a very different light.

I hear your protests: "*Gremlins*? The movie about the little Furby guys? A satirical masterpiece? Impossible!" And sure, I understand your skepticism. As the popular meme points out, satire requires clarity of meaning lest it be confused with that which it seeks to mock. If a satire is not very obvious about what it's trying to parody, people will automatically assume that it *is* the exact thing it was trying to make fun of. I can't claim to know for certain whether or not *Gremlins* seeks to mock anything, but when I imagine it as a scathing critique of American consumer culture, it elevates the film from a fun romp.

Let's begin where the film begins: Rand Peltzer's voiceover narration informs us that he was looking for a Christmas present for his son while selling his inventions in Chinatown. Already, a few things are clear: Peltzer is an example of the American entrepreneurial spirit gone horribly awry. His inventions are all fatally flawed—and he knows it—but he fancies himself such a pioneer that he still peddles them everywhere he goes. We see him wander into the shop of an old Chinese man with mismatched eyes who smokes a pipe. This is where we stray into more morally ambiguous territory—while I prefer to imagine this is, in fact, a parody of the orientalism and Asian exotification so common in horror and speculative fiction in general, it is not quite over-the-top enough to be certain. Regardless, the messaging in the scene that follows is clear. Peltzer discovers the Mogwai, the little furry creature that will later spawn the titular gremlins, and decides he *must* have it, despite the fact the owner of the shop insists the Mogwai is not for sale because it is too much responsibility to take care of. Our good old-fashioned American businessman, however, is not used to being told no, so what does he do? He steals it.

Ah, a tale as old as time. A white man stealing from another culture because he simply *must* own the foreign curiosity that he discovered. And if history is any indication, the white man will not suffer the consequences of his folly.

Next, the movie leans further in the Christmas movie direction, directly referencing *It's A Wonderful Life* every chance it gets. But what does Christmas mean in the world of *Gremlins*? Not family or love or charity. It means money. The first shot we see of the winter wonderland is a young boy who's been forced to dress as a Christmas tree in order to promote his father's business. We meet Mrs. Deagle, the evil landlady who's named all her cats after international currencies. Lastly, we're introduced to Billy Peltzer, an aspiring artist who's stuck working in a bank, living with his parents because his passion isn't profitable enough to make a living. When Billy's father gives him the Mogwai as a gift, the creature and boy share a certain kinship—the Mogwai, nicknamed Gizmo, likes to sing while Billy draws. They are both artists living in a society that doesn't respect their work. Meanwhile, Billy's father is trying to come up with ways to capitalize on Gizmo, even considering selling the creature's offspring and branding them as "Peltzer's Pets."*

We're also introduced to Mr. Futterman, whose defining characteristic is xenophobia. Right from the start, he's complaining about cars with foreign parts, unlike reliable American-made machinery. In fact, Mr. Futterman is the first one to use the term "gremlins"—in describing his fear of foreigners.

This connection seems to imply that the gremlins who later appear in the movie represent these "foreigners," but I posit that this isn't the chase. I believe that the gremlins are actually a manifestation of white America's *fears* about what immigrants will do to the country. The gremlins exhibit all the behaviors that conservatives often claim outsiders show—making chaos, playing loud music, drinking, gambling, and, most importantly, reproducing. The biggest fear the characters have about these gremlins is that there will be more of them.

But do the gremlins really cause any harm? When Billy's mom first discovers them, they're making a mess—smashing plates and playing music. So what does she do? She mutilates one in a blender and explodes another in the microwave. She even does this all while shouting, "Not in my kitchen!" like the good American housewife she is. Shortly after, she is attacked by a gremlin hiding in the Christmas tree, seeking revenge for its gruesomely murdered brethren. I think a woman being attacked by her own Christmas tree is an excellent encapsulation of the entire film. Later, when Billy finds a whole movie theater full of gremlins cheerfully singing along to *Snow White*, he decides to trap them inside while he lights a fire and burns them to death. All they want to do is have a good time, and in return, they are brutally killed.

But most importantly: none of the events of the movie were even the gremlins' fault. This was all because one white man stole from a person of color to get his son a Christmas gift. The gremlins are everything Americans fear from immigrants, but the real issues come from unchecked greed and rampant consumerism.

Gremlins also uses the common horror trope of the moralization of death. For instance, many horror movies see teenagers who have premarital sex getting brutally murdered, thus warning children about the dangers of promiscuity. Who do the gremlins attack in this film? The racist man and the landlady.** A horror movie often passes judgment upon its victims by virtue of killing them, and in this film, the guilty parties are those who a) fear immigrants and b) champion capitalism.

If this analysis seems far-fetched, I get it. *Gremlins* is an unabashedly ridiculous movie and a children's movie too. You may be thinking to yourself, "It's not that deep." And sure, maybe it's not. But there are little easter eggs in this movie that indicate there was an extreme attention to detail in the writing of this film, which leads me to believe that none of this was unintentional. For example, early in the movie, Billy says hello to a Dr. Moreau, which seems like a nod to *The Island of Dr. Moreau,* one of the earliest literary examples of body horror. Later in the movie, *Invasion of the Body Snatchers* is playing in Billy's room, a movie that famously capitalized on the Red Scare to make Americans fear outsiders. The final confrontation even takes place in a shopping mall, the very symbol of American consumerism! While Billy and the final remaining gremlin have their showdown, advertisements play over the loudspeaker. With this level of specificity, I refuse to believe that the connections drawn above are a coincidence.

After the main action of the movie has drawn to a close and the final gremlin has been gruesomely disintegrated in a display of gnarly practical effects, the Unnamed Chinese Man from the shop (on IMDB, his character is only referred to as Grandfather) returns to reclaim Gizmo. When Peltzer introduces the man as the one who "sold" him Gizmo, the man says, "Sold! An interesting choice of words." Reminds me of all the artifacts the British museum "recovered," no? In the end, Gizmo returns to the man's shop, and the man delivers the most poignant line in the whole movie: "You do with

Mogwai what your society does with all of nature's gifts. You do not understand. You are not ready."

And yet, the film ends with commentary from Rand Peltzer, who caused all the problems, was not there for most of it, and judging by his epilogue, missed the entire point of the movie. He warns that gremlins could be anywhere—which is patently untrue because this whole thing only happened because of his own greed, entitlement, and irresponsibility. Then again, he wasn't present for the whole movie, so he doesn't realize that. And yet, despite all these points against him, the white man still gets to have the last word, and frame the narrative.

Typical.

*Ironically, this is essentially exactly what happened with the Furby, whose design was blatantly ripped from this film. There was a lawsuit and everything, and Hasbro ended up paying Warner Bros. for the rights to continue producing the horrifying toys.

**They also kill the science teacher who tried to "run some tests" on one of the gremlins, another trope that dates back all the way to the Transcendentalist movement: the scientist punished for playing god. I believe this trope is only here to poke fun at another horror trope: the black man dies first. Again, the film doesn't go quite over-the-top enough for it to feel satirical, so it's hard to tell if the film is critiquing the trope or fulfilling it.

UNDERWATER CIVILIZATIONS, ACTION AGAINST OPPRESSION, AND FRIENDSHIP: REVIEW OF WEIRD FISHES BY RAE MARIZ

ARCHITA MITTRA

Weird Fishes, a novella by Rae Mariz (*Stellaform Press,* 2022), is a strange and fascinating foray into marine civilizations with a careful ecological bent.

Set mostly underwater, the tale is populated chiefly by non-human protagonists (with their own unique histories and biological differences), although the presence of human activity and the threat of climate change is ubiquitous. Richly atmospheric and layered with metaphors, *Weird Fishes* unfolds a story of friendship, solidarity, and timely action against oppressive power structures, urging us to rethink our notions of collectivity and community in a greedy, capitalist world.

Much of the story follows the curious escapades of Ceph—a squid-like scientist with eight brains—who is convinced she belongs to the most advanced race on the planet. When she notices that the currents are slowing down (due to global warming), she is quick to investigate and embarks on an unforgettable voyage that takes her to the farthest reaches of the oceans, to sentient coral reefs, to the surface, and beyond.

Quite early on, Ceph befriends Iliokai (a seal-folk storyteller) in her travels, who reminds Ceph that just because she has stumbled upon terrestrial lifeforms doesn't mean she has "discovered" something new—humans and other beings have existed side-by-side for thousands of years. Ceph's sense of superiority over other creatures is clearly a self-construction that Iliokai gently corrects, making her realize that there are indeed different ways to imagine and perceive the world.

It is also a nod to how colonization has relied upon scientific and religious pretexts to justify the erasure of indigenous cultures, belief systems, and knowledge as part of their "civilizing" mission. Yet, unlike white colonizers, Ceph is an open-minded scientist, and her friendship with Iliokai forces her to question her own prejudices and labels.

But not all relationships depicted in the book are as enriching or wholesome. Later on, while attempting to stop a genocide, Ceph is brutally raped by a guard—a disturbing scene that nevertheless is a reminder of state-sponsored violence and the policing of female bodies to subdue activism. Of course, the violent aftershocks of colonization still reverberate among indigenous communities all over the world as they struggle to get their voices heard and their rights recognized and protected.

But Ceph's rape (and consequent fatal pregnancy) is also eerily relevant in the light of the recent anti-abortion legislation in the U.S. and other political movements happening all over the globe. At its heart, Mariz's evocative marine world functions as a metaphor for human societies at large, even as it suggests alternative ways to imagine and create a more inclusive, interdependent, and interconnected world.

The novella's strongest point is clearly the worldbuilding, as Mariz slowly builds up a rich visual language and vocabulary for the deep-sea ecosystem. From the squid-like creatures who can transition from female to male, to the ""whale riders" who surf the time gyres, singing songs as they travel between the past and the present, the author paints underwater life in lush and redolent strokes in an extremely convincing way. A particularly striking moment was when Ceph sees the sun for the first time and is confused by the idea of "binary thought"—as living in the deep sea, her kind has never divided the passage of time into "day" and "night". Even when the characters swear, the expletives are inflected with a marine idiom ('what the krill!') pointing to the pervasive influence of the living environment in shaping language, communication patterns, and cultures, and thus, the urgent need for its preservation.

In another example of lovely worldbuilding, Mariz invokes the idea of time travel as a safety net to preserve marine life, as seen in the following paragraph, which can even be read as a standalone piece of sea folklore:

'...They knew there were seven spots in the world's oceans where the currents curl in on themselves, that the center of these vortexes marked the entrance and exit points of an interdimensional network. Creatures of the sea had used these portals in time of need. When whaling practices threatened to eradicate humpbacks, they fled to a safer time, too smart to wait around to be hunted to extinction. Sometimes stray prehistoric sea creatures drifted from one era to another, doomed to spend their ancient lives trying to return to their

primordial homes. Ships lost at sea were more often than not lost in time.' (p. 44)

The initial chapters might be a bit disorienting as one slowly adjusts to the marine setting, but Mariz's prose is immersive and intuitive, following its own logic, such as when the corals speak in a united chorus or in the epilogue that is conveyed entirely through a transcript. Yet, the language of collectivity can also signal alienation and loneliness, especially in the case of Iliokai, who has been abandoned by her mother. While Ceph has siblings for support, Iliokai has always been alone, wandering the lonely sea with her songs. At one point, she remarks to herself:

"She wasn't a seal. She didn't live in a colony, rookery, herd, harem or bob. There were so many collective nouns to not feel included in." *(p. 65)*

Also woven into the text are the echoes and shadows of older fables and fairytales, be it "The Little Mermaid" by Hans Christian Andersen, various selkie myths, or even the Biblical image of Jonah being swallowed by a gigantic whale. This is important because while we've had several stories with their own renditions of marine life (even Disney's adaptation of *The Little Mermaid* had a slight environmental focus) most do not engage with the question of how a marine civilization can plausibly be like while retaining an anthropomorphic quality, which *Weird Fishes* manages to do in an engaging way.

These leitmotifs also add another intertextual layer to the narrative, coalescing together to deliver an urgent message about global warming. With multiple point-of-view chapters, *Weird Fishes* deftly tackles the ever-pressing concerns of climate change and the complicity of multinational capitalism and neo-colonization in furthering it, which perhaps can be countered by building networks of solidarity, empathy, and mutual aid across diverse cultures and taking swift political action.

This climate fiction story is both hopeful and heartbreaking, as the focus slowly shifts from Ceph and Iliokai's friendship to other thematic matters. I personally felt that while the novella form is succinct in conveying the author's message, it worked against the varied cast of characters and the relationships they forge with each other, which could have been better explored in a longer novel.

Ultimately, the love and care that blossoms between Ceph and Iliokai (which also serves as a kind of template for healthy and healing friendships that are required for building sustainable communities) needed a greater space to develop for it to have sufficient emotional depth and chemistry. While the marine ecosystem is vividly "shown," the backstories of the main characters are simply "told" or, in some cases, just hinted at, which can be frustrating for some readers (Iliokai muses, "Every scar is a story I'd rather not tell" in p. 48

even as the reader remains curious about her past). Thus, although this novella is enjoyable and enthralling enough to be finished in a single sitting, it may have been more memorable and captivating with greater details about the characters, a stronger plot, and a higher page count.

A smorgasbord of color and sensation and a celebration of cultural differences, *Weird Fishes* is a magical and exciting story that is sure to appeal to fans of climate fiction and anyone interested in the unique portrayal of a complex marine ecosystem, although readers are advised to heed the content warnings provided at the beginning of the book.

THE HORROR OF WOMEN'S PAIN: ON "THE RETRIEVALS," A TRUE CRIME PODCAST FROM THE NYT AND SERIAL PRODUCTIONS

HOLLY LYN WALRATH

"The women interviewed are part of around 200 women who were supposed to receive the drug Fentanyl as part of the egg retrieval process but instead received inactive saline. The result was a horrific, sometimes ongoing, experience of pain at the hands of one drug-addicted nurse."

Hospitals, Doctor's offices, and medical procedures are some of my most intimate places of fear. That's because I have dealt with chronic illness for most of my life, and as most chronically ill women have experienced, I've known the fear of being ignored, being put in pain without repercussion, and being disbelieved.

This fear is probably not helped by my True Crime obsession. I've become fascinated by stories about women's health and crime ever since I started making note of the variety of ways the US Healthcare system mistreats women. Examples include the common practice of women receiving pelvic exams without consent at hospitals; how drug studies often excluded women for years because they might be pregnant, resulting in different (and often ignored) side effects and dosing for women; how even crash test dummies in vehicle studies were calibrated to men's sizes for years; how the maternal mortality rate for women in the US is on the rise.

Women are routinely treated as if their health does not matter.

This is the center of the story behind "The Retrievals," a new podcast from the New York Times, Serial Productions, and Susan Burton. The podcast records the experiences of women undergoing fertility treatments at Yale Fertility Center in 2020–2021. The women interviewed are part of around 200 women who were supposed to receive the drug Fentanyl as part of the egg retrieval process but instead received inactive saline. The result was a horrific, sometimes ongoing, experience of pain at the hands of one drug-addicted nurse.

True crime is no stranger to the intersection of crime and healthcare. There is a history of doctors, nurses, and medical professionals carrying out heinous acts. "Criminal," the popular podcast hosted by Phoebe Judge, covered the Mayo Clinic outbreak of Hepatitis C in 2021 due to an employee using patients' syringes before they underwent painful procedures, exposing nearly 30,000 patients. The popular podcast "Dr. Death" covers the story of Dr. Christopher Duntsch, a Texas spine surgeon with many older women patients who underwent horrific torture and mangling that wasn't stopped by the Texas Medical Board. The case wasn't resolved until two other physicians reported Duntsch to the police.

The list of uncovered crimes is longer. In 2009, a technician at Rose Medical Center was found to be swapping dirty syringes with Fentanyl-filled ones, resulting in over 11 patients testing positive for Hepatitis C. In 2016 and 2018, at UT Southwestern's Clements Hospital, two nurses died of Fentanyl overdose after stealing it.

Despite all of this reporting and evidence—that Fentanyl is a substance that should be carefully monitored and yet, is clearly not being managed, to the detriment of patients' lives—the women at the heart of "The Retrievals" were still ignored by their doctors and nurses.

There's something particularly horrific about women's pain experiences in healthcare. From transvaginal ultrasounds to abortions to surgeries, women are often at a higher risk than men for medical malpractice and device-related negligence. Some studies even find that male practitioners are at a higher risk of malpractice claims, which is probably because medical practice is a male-dominated field. But it puts into perspective how women are often ignored by their doctors.

"The Retrievals" dials down to one specific procedure: egg retrievals in fertility treatment.

The women in "The Retrievals" were subjected to egg retrieval procedures without pain medication. A nurse, sometimes the nurse responsible for administering the medication, was stealing Fentanyl. Despite telling their doctors, nurses, and staff at the clinic of their severe pain, the women were told they were "anxious" or that their experience was "surprising," but not "alarming."

In a cruel twist, many of the women who undergo IVF are queer women who are trying to build a family in an already antagonistic world. One woman in "The Retrievals" was a cancer patient trying to preserve her eggs before undergoing further cancer treatments that would make her eggs unviable. One was an addiction researcher who presciently guessed what was happening behind the scenes. One was an attending trauma surgeon who had to visit her own hospital as a result of the procedure.

These were intelligent, highly educated women. Many worked at Yale. Yet over and over again, in over 200 cases, sometimes over multiple procedures, the women were ignored.

What kept entering my mind as I listened to their stories was the larger economic picture. Fertility practices have become a sort of venture capital focus as of late. Private equity firms are pouring money into practices in a market estimated at $8 billion dollars. Doctors at these clinics make anywhere from 200,000 to 400,000. Nurses make anywhere from 100,000 to 140,000. Women and their babies are seen as a cash cow.

IVF itself is a highly expensive process. Costs range from 15,000 to 30,000. Since IVF is often done out of pocket and not through insurance, the likelihood of foul play is higher. Other crimes perpetrated at IVF clinics in recent years include swapping the incorrect embryo, using embryos with cancer genes, incorrect destruction of eggs, and general fraud.

On the surface, it may seem like women not receiving pain medication is a crime without much harm. Sure, the women underwent a very painful procedure that should have been unpainful. But it's this kind of attitude that ignores the actual risks. Tampered vials and needles can put patients at a higher risk of infection. Pelvic abscesses are more common in IVF when the procedure is not done to high sterile standards. These abscesses can impact pregnancy. And, of course, there's always the risk of blood-borne illness like Hepatitis C.

"The Retrievals" is just five episodes, but it's a valuable addition to the growing call for change. The podcast is an empathetic, complex, and fascinating exploration of women's pain. And I, for one, hope these women get justice for the pain they endured. As of February, 2024, 83 patients were part of the lawsuits against Yale University.

A GUIDE TO BECOMING AN ELM TREE BLENDS GRIPPING FOLKLORE WITH SUBTLE BODY HORROR: IRISH HORROR FILM MESMERIZES WITH TALE OF OLD GODS

PATRICK BARB

In the black-and-white, Irish film offering for Fantastic Fest 2023, *A Guide to Becoming an Elm Tree* (Directed by Adam Mann and Skye Mann), the filmmakers and a superb duo of lead actors bring to life a mesmerizing tale of old gods defied, curses activated, and ancient wisdom used for selfish ends. All that, in a movie with a minuscule cast and extremely limited special effects. And yet, through performances, visuals, and a compelling storyline, this folk horror tale also manages to thrive as body horror. This understated approach demonstrates how one doesn't need makeup or digital effects to suggest sinister transformations. There's so much one can do with a leaf in a mouth and a whispered voice emerging from a tree.

The titular elm tree is described early on as "a gift from the gods." Gerry Wade plays John, the carpenter enlisted by grieving widower Padraig (played by James Healey-Meany, who alternates between pathos and menace in a manner reminiscent of actor Donal Logue) to help him build a coffin for his already dead and buried wife. John offers more than woodworking services, though. He's passing on ancient Celtic wisdom about the trees, including the elm which is used exclusively for coffin-building. It's Padraig who must build the coffin, chopping down the tree, sanding and smoothing the wood. This master-and-apprentice relationship hits the expected beats but does so in a natural and effective manner. Indeed, the film's use of silences in both two-header scenes and in moments where Padraig is alone proves a particularly engrossing choice. When the lush, moody score drops out, and we are left with ambient noise, whispers, and laughter alongside the faces of our leads, it's easy to believe in the supernatural as John presents it.

Indeed, the choice of black-and-white is an interesting one. With all the discussion of trees, from their appearance on the land where they provide shelter for birds and other creatures to their use by the humans sharing the land, either for the main woodworking craft of the film or to build barrels in which whisky is stored, it was at first surprising to see the verdant greens and browns left out of the picture in exchange for the high contrast of black-and-white. But as the story continues across the film's brief runtime (coming in around an hour and fifteen minutes), it soon becomes clear that an appreciation of nature is not the filmmakers' focus but rather the consequences of forsaking one's relationship with the land and those higher powers behind it.

As noted, there is a "Sorcerer's Apprentice" element to the narrative here. Padraig is the apprentice who uncovers forbidden knowledge, in this case, the existence of the Creann Na Mian (or "wish tree") said to grant one their heart's desire. Despite John's warnings that the granted wish will come with strings attached (as those things always do), Padraig grows obsessed with the notion of resurrecting his wife, whose death we're made to believe he may have played a more direct role in, rather than simply interring her in an elm wood coffin. Given the form she does take upon her return, there is a certain irony to be seen in his choice.

Having stolen John's books of ancient Celtic lore (books with paper made from trees no less) and utilizing the wish tree (with comparisons made to the Biblical tree of knowledge), Padraig finds himself succumbing to the consequences. These remarkably effective moments are played well by Healey-Meany, using coughing and a few well-placed elm leaves on the tongue to suggest a forthcoming transformation from man to tree. It's a welcome reminder in the days of CGI and incredible make-up effects that sometimes body horror can be just as effective when suggested rather than shown.

A GUIDE TO BECOMING AN ELM TREE is a haunting and mesmerizing film that imbues new life into two popular subgenres of horror while still maintaining a classic overall feel to the final result. The cast and filmmakers Adam and Skye Mann are to be commended for paying tribute to their roots while blossoming into something new and unforgettable.

WHY THERE SHOULD BE MORE FEAR STREET FILMS: NETFLIX'S HORROR FILM TRILOGY AND TEEN HORROR

CHLOE SMITH

If you were to ask me what my favorite horror trilogy was, my answer would be the *Fear Street* (2021) trilogy on Netflix. They're not just my favorite streaming service original series of horrors, but they're my favorite series of horror films, point blank. The question that's plagued me since the series ended, and as time has stretched on and on since then, is **why haven't there been more Fear Street films?**

The first three were fantastic. Not only do they offer ample twists and turns in all three installments—*Fear Street 1994*, *Fear Street 1978,* and *Fear Street 1666,* respectively—but the big twist revealed in the finale made the series amazing and allowed the audience to see the first two films in a completely new light.

But beyond that, the series is a great example of teen horror. I'd argue that a particular death near the end of the first film, *Fear Street 1994,* rivals the more gruesome deaths in its cinematic peer, the *Final Destination* film series. Beyond being terrifying, it was also incredibly impactful because by that time, we had grown to love, and really care about, the character that died (I won't name them so people who haven't seen the film aren't spoiled!)

The *Fear Street* trilogy of films follows Deena (Kiana Madeira) trying to win back her girlfriend Sam (Olivia Scott Welch) while escaping the killers in the often unfortunate Shadyside where they live. But when they start to unravel the folktale of Sarah Fier the witch and her killer curse on Shadyside, her search takes her back decades in her attempt to save Sam and her brother from resurrected murderers and find out what really happened to the revered Sarah Fier.

The Fear Street franchise effortlessly made us care about its core characters—and while the protagonist's, Deena's, story, and that of the killer's was arguably wrapped up by the end of the trilogy, her story could easily be picked back up again. Another killer could appear in Shadyside, and Deena could be tasked with taking them down, especially if it comes for her girlfriend, Sam, or her brother, Josh.

Actually, speaking of Josh, the series could easily continue with him as the main protagonist. The smart, nerdy, and sweet younger brother of Deena, Josh already proved his chops against killers in the initial trilogy, and I think the talented and charismatic Benjamin Flores Jr could easily carry another film, or series of films, in the same universe as the first trilogy.

And in a world where so much of cinema is a reboot of older franchises, wouldn't it be great to see more new ideas, and new franchises, particularly in horror? *Fear Street* has already proved it's a great setting for a horror series, so continuing it with a character we already know makes sense.

Even beyond the first trilogy, if the next installment was just set in the Fear Street universe with all-new characters, then it would still be a fantastic standalone or even a new series of horrors. Not only does the source material offer some interesting themes and characters to bounce off from—*Fear Street* was originally a horror book series for ages 12 and up by R.L Stine—but even beyond that, the setting of an American city in the 1990s packed full of history and rowdy teens is the perfect setting for a future horror film or two.

It certainly wouldn't be a vapid take on the teenage experience—as the first trilogy proved, the film is able to craft a nuanced and honest look at teenage life, whether it's break-ups, crushes, and financial struggles, and that's just before we get to the guts and gore and murder.

It also goes without saying that the series should continue because it clearly values positive representation, whether it's having a lesbian of color as its final girl and protagonist in Deena and giving her a complicated and heartwarming relationship with Sam throughout the trilogy. Even with the lesbian character that's killed (again, no spoilers, but it certainly isn't an example of the bury your gays trope) she is given the justice and character exploration that she deserves. It's obvious that beyond being an intriguing and terrifying horror series full of great pacing, twists, and representation, the *Fear Street* trilogy is also a great example of writing realistic and in-depth characters and relationships.

So, by the end of not just the first film in the series, but by the end of the trilogy itself, you care not just about the core characters in each film but also the characters they care about—and even the ones that they don't. The writers could certainly carry this forward to make us care about a brand new set of characters in the *Fear Street* universe, but if they are thinking of revisiting any past characters, I'd love to see Ziggy as an adult now she's free of the particular killer that plagued her and Shadyside in the trilogy.

However, while the films are incredible—and very much underrated—the series could even continue in another form. A *Fear Street* TV Series would be another great way to continue the series, and if the visual medium is not possible, an audio drama would work just as well—and some cameos from Deena and/or Sam would be a great inclusion, too.

In short, it doesn't really matter how the Fear Street series continues beyond the original film trilogy—all that matters is that it and it's potential is allowed to flourish in some capacity. (Netflix, if you ever read this, please don't stop the Fear Street series there! Thank you).

JOURNEYS THROUGH THE RADIANT CITADEL: A SPELLBINDING ANTHOLOGY OF THIRTEEN SHORT ADVENTURES SET IN THE DUNGEONS & DRAGONS UNIVERSE, ALL CONCEIVED AND WRITTEN BY PEOPLE OF COLOR

ARCHITA MITTRA

"The adventures detailed here offer a mixture of strategic combat, diplomacy, mystery-solving and even some political machinations—which are suitable for a variety of playstyles."

At the ripe age of eleven, after finishing *The Lord of the Rings*, I had only one fervent wish—for Middle Earth to be real. I longed to join the Fellowship of hobbits, humans, elves, and dwarves in their quest to destroy the One Ring, and along the way, fight orcs, cast powerful spells, chase my friends through sunlit forests, partake in some court intrigue and maybe even convince a few talking trees to go to war. Naturally, I did all of that—in my detailed daydreams, through boring math's classes and tedious bus rides, and lazy, golden afternoons. At that time, I hadn't even heard of *Dungeons & Dragons* or the table-top role-playing community, and neither did I have access to open-world video games.

Years later, while I was enrolled in university and around the time the first season of *Stranger Things* came out, my friends and I began talking about *Dungeons & Dragons* in earnest. This time, armed with illegal pdfs, hand-written character sheets, random buttons, and rusty bolts (to represent our adventurers and the monsters, respectively), and dice-simulating apps on our phones, we finally revisited those fantastical landscapes from our childhood. It was magical and thrilling, like unwrapping a present containing something you had always longed for but never expected to get. Yet, even though we never tired of the high fantasy locales of the Forgotten Realms, there was that curious sense of dissatisfaction with the Euro-centric medieval aesthetics and Tolkien-inspired settings. So, we experimented with homebrew campaigns, turning derelict houses and riverside ghats into surroundings to be explored and creatures from our local folklore into bosses to be defeated or negotiated with; although, as experiments, they never quite turned out perfect.

This is where *Journeys through the Radiant Citadel* comes in. The hardcover tome, with an enticingly gorgeous cover, is a spellbinding anthology of thirteen short adventures set in the *Dungeons & Dragons* universe, all conceived and written by people of color with Ajit A. George and F. Wesley Schneider serving as project leads. As a tabletop enthusiast from Kolkata, this is the book that I *wish* I had when I first began to play *D&D* with my friends, sitting in the green, evening-lit, mosquito-infested lawns of my campus while stray cats and dogs with glowing eyes passed us by. From ancient China to the riverine state of Bengal, these standalone campaigns straddle an eclectic variety of locations and are infused with lush worldbuilding, cultural signifiers, and thoughtful storytelling to ensure an immersive and memorable experience for players, both new and old. While the genres of fantasy and science-fiction have skyrocketed in popularity thanks to cinematic mega-franchises, these fantastical landscapes remain largely Tolkien-derivative or defined by their formulaic storytelling, with little room for cultural nuance or vibrancy beyond the tokenistic diversity casting. In this regard, *Journeys through the Radiant Citadel* breathes fresh life into the *D&D* universe in particular and mainstream Western fantasy, in general, and is quite an important work.

There's a lot to love about this book. The adventures detailed here offer a mixture of strategic combat, diplomacy, mystery-solving, and even some political machinations—which are suitable for a variety of playstyles. In my (albeit limited) experience with this role-playing game, I've noticed that people play *D&D* for different reasons—some approach battles like a military strategist, others enjoy the exploration of new worlds and picking up on clues, and then some prefer the slice-of-life and found family elements present in the narrative. All these options are available in the campaigns (to varying degrees), and each session can be customized further by the Dungeon Master. For instance, in both "Shadow of the Sun" and "The Nightsea's Succor," the players have the opportunity to join factions and influence local politics; their decisions, motivated by their own political ideologies, can lead to multiple endings, not unlike that of a choice-based video game. On the other hand, "Orchids of the Invisible Mountain" with its unique network of "Grassroads" and "Crystal Caves" will particularly delight those who enjoy an action-packed fight in every session.

At its heart, *Journeys through the Radiant Citadel* is also a jubilant celebration of cultural diversity and vivacity. Each short adventure is accompanied by pronunciation guides, along with prompts and questions to anchor the adventurers to the traditions, myths, and festivities of each locale; this allows players to encounter and explore cultures they do not belong to in a respectful and enriching way. Festivals are a big theme in the book, featured in several stories. In particular, "The Fiend of Hollow Mine," which reimagines the Mexican "Day of the Dead" celebration as "Night of the Remembered," has a small section where the players are invited to take part in the festivities and leave offerings at an "ofrenda"—a shared altar—to commune with ancestral spirits. Similarly, while meals at the inns of fantasy worlds often end up as some bland combination of cheese, broth or bread, the variety of cuisines depicted here will surely whet the players' tastebuds and are firmly rooted to the local environment. For instance, in the volcanic region of Etizalan, spicy dishes are a regional favorite, while a character traveling through the Tayyib Empire could order a plate of biryani. When hosting games at home, we often ended up ordering biryani or pizza from the nearby restaurants or had home-cooked food while our characters rather unimaginatively dined on some variant of porridge or stew accompanied by mead or wine. So, these small details about food, clothing, and religious practices make the worldbuilding seem more real and organic. And it also feels warm and welcoming to see recipes and superstitions from our childhood reflected in the fictional world.

The stories in this anthology have been designed for characters of various levels (from levels one to fourteen). Each tale can be enjoyed as a standalone adventure, or woven into the DM's own larger narrative (there are hooks to contextualize the setting in a wider universe, or connect it to the Radiant Citadel), or even played one after the other in a longer campaign, where the travelers discover different cities and level up on the way. Thus, the adventures are versatile, both in terms of playing options as well as theme. In "Salted Legacy," players explore a bristling, magical marketplace, sort the rivalry between two merchants, and partake in local competitions (dubbed the "Market Games"), which are quite ingeniously planned out and perfect for those who prefer a game-within-a-game instead of smaller battles sprinkled throughout the session. If you're in the mood for something a little dark, melancholy, and Gothic, try "Written in Blood," that is is set in a haunted farmhouse. In "Fiend of Hollow Mine," the darkness and desolation surrounding the mines, metalworks, and abandoned cenotes are brilliantly contrasted with the vibrant festivities in the main town of San Citlán. "Wages of Vice" is a story about repaying debts and questioning the success and prosperity of a region that is built upon privilege and treachery while the "Sins of Elders" follows a ghostly folk hero who seeks retribution for having been erased from history.

Thus, although the tone is mostly hopeful and optimistic, the stories thoughtfully engage with themes of colonialism, oppression, and rebuilding community alongside honoring ancestral wisdom, local legends, and histories. "Gold For Fools and Princes" is filled with memorable NPCs and allows the players a chance to befriend and inspire confidence in a shy prince while uncovering a conspiracy. "Trail of Destruction," set in the volcanic region of Tletepec, which is prone to earthquakes, is about appeasing ancient spirits to save the innocent townsfolk. "In the Mists of Manivarsha," which is set in my own homeland of Bengal, characters befriend boatmen, navigate dangerous swamps and mangroves (with their menacing "angul roots"), and convene with river spirits. I wryly smiled at the small section where the adventurers could haggle with the boatman Dukha for a cheaper fare. That detail (since, in India, there often isn't a fixed rate at local markets or for some forms of transport, and being able to "bargain" well is a valuable skill to have), along with the references to fish delicacies, cooking competitions, and boat-making is something that natives will find intensely familiar.

Further on, "Between Tangled Roots" features a minor interspecies relationship between a "Ninuno" (spirit) and a "bakunawa" (dragon), highlighting the stories' commitment towards queer normativity. "Shadow of the Sun," which takes place in a desert, has distinct Aladdin vibes, riddled with fun escapades and flying carpets, while "The Nightsea's Sucor" transports the players into a vividly-imagined underwater world. In "Buried Dynasty," a quest for immortality quickly turns sour as characters uncover unsavory secrets of the government. Finally, the concluding adventure, "Orchids of the Invisible Mountain," delves into surreal visions from powerful ancestral spirits and even more surreal landscapes for players to traverse through. In fact, both "Between Tangled Roots" and "Orchids of the Invisible Mountain" are deeply concerned with mysterious diseases corrupting the land and its inhabitants, alongside healing strategies to rebuild the community, while the other stories engage with inequalities of wealth and power, the formation of political factions and activism of various kinds—all of which are reflective of the turbulent times we inhabit, marred by political uncertainty, environmental threats, and socio-economic disparities as capitalism and neocolonial powers dominate.

Thus, one of the greatest triumphs of the book is each of the stories is firmly rooted in their distinctive settings, mutually influencing the other. While Tolkien drew inspiration for his Middle Earth from the English countryside, other storytellers in that tradition often used similar geographical locations as a template instead or kept the settings deliberately vague or generic. For example, the characters might meet at a tavern, get quest details from the city's mayor, visit a cave in the forest to fight goblins and rescue the kidnapped daughter, and so on—of course, there isn't anything intrinsically "wrong" with such an approach (and there are exceptions; settings and atmosphere play a huge role in Gothic fiction, for one), but it is a missed opportunity for the writer or the DM to create a more immersive world for the readers/players. But folklore and magic realist storytelling traditions are often tied to the environment that has shaped our earliest myths. The authors of these adventures recognize that and honor this, with details about the local flora and fauna and glimpses into the daily life of different NPCs—be it the "Bonesingers" who maintain and conserve the magic of the "Skybridges," or the "Trench of Lost Love" in the deep sea that conceals a devastating shipwreck, or the "Gate of Illumination" that is situated inside a volcanic tunnel.

While no adventure is set in Radiant Citadel itself, this new location on the Ethereal Plane offers a neat framing device for the stories and isn't unlike the "safe rooms" in video games where characters can recuperate in between adventures. Reclaimed by immigrants searching for refuge and structured as a utopia of sorts, the Radiant Citadel is a world of restorative justice and healing; it encapsulates the book's core themes of collaboration, empathy, and diversity and offers a vision of what a truly sustainable, egalitarian society might look like. From the descriptions of the wise Dawn Incarnates and the esoteric Auroral Diamond, the Radiant Citadel boasts of some stellar worldbuilding. In fact, it's hard to pick flaws with this book, but I do wish there had been an adventure set in the Citadel itself (although there are a few prompts to inspire DMs in their campaigns). Finally, each chapter introduces one unique creature with its own stat block to D&D's ever-expanding bestiary, while other beings take on attributes of familiar monsters with minor modifications, but it would have been better for the book to have included more such new creatures with stat blocks that are influenced by the mythological beasts of the authors' own cultures.

Thus, *Journeys through the Radiant Citadel* manages to be thoughtful and comforting at the same time. As a form of collaborative storytelling, tabletop role-playing games work on multiple levels—the DM and the players work together to create an immersive story; pre-built campaigns aid the DM in crafting a memorable, interactive world rich with detail; and finally, a book like this helps readers and players, irrespective of their background to imagine worlds that are culturally diverse. With their resemblance to real-world histories and myths, these adventures offer not just escapism but also question the status quo and remind us just how gloriously varied speculative fiction can be when one looks beyond the confines of mainstream Western fantasy. Although I haven't yet run a campaign based on the adventures outlined here, reading this volume filled me with creative inspiration and excitement—and I feel simultaneously happy and perhaps even a little jealous for all the people whom I will introduce to *D&D* via the Radiant Citadel. So, whether you're a seasoned tabletop enthusiast or a new player, this volume has something for everyone and more importantly, will help you imagine a brighter, more ecologically conscious, and sustainable future. As the first book of its kind to be thoroughly envisioned and written by authors of color in *D&D's* nearly fifty-year-old history, I just hope that there's more such content to look forward to.

Note: My review copy of *Journeys Through the Radiant Citadel* was donated by Desis & Dragons.

DINNER ON MARS GIVES FOOD FOR THOUGHT

LISA TIMPF

Imagine it's the year 2063, and the colonization of Mars has moved from the realm of dream to reality. Getting there has required the resolution of plenty of issues, not the least of which is, what's on the menu?

For those inquiring minds who have always wanted to know, in *Dinner on Mars: The Technologies That Will Feed the Red Planet and Transform Agriculture on Earth*, Lenore Newman and Evan Fraser provide some educated guesses. Newman is the Canada Research Chair in Food Security and the Environment at the University of the Fraser Valley, while Fraser is the Director of the Arrell Food Institute at the University of Guelph. Both have published books about food and food history. The duo has, in essence, "devoted [their] professional energy to developing strategies to sustainably feed the world's growing population."

Newman and Fraser discuss the challenges of growing food on Mars. And there are plenty of them. For example, the Red Planet gets only half of the solar energy enjoyed by Earth, while also being more prone to damaging radiation due to the thin atmosphere. Martian soil contains toxic compounds called perchlorates, which will require amelioration before the soil can be used in a growing system. There are lower atmospheric pressures, and in some cases, plants will need to be genetically modified in order to thrive on Mars. There simply won't be the space to grow the same amount of grass-based crops, like wheat and barley, that we have now on Earth.

But none of these issues are insurmountable. The future, it seems, lies in cyanobacterias and yeasts, in nanotechnology and vertical agriculture. Newman and Fraser bring the reader up to date with the current state of research, including cutting-edge stuff like an Icelandic company that is working with "genetically modified barley that is engineered to produce proteins normally only found in mammals."

Dinner on Mars is engagingly written. Though it contains a lot of facts, these are delivered in an interesting and even entertaining manner. The authors give us a sense of the kind of discussions they had as they were working on the book, and rather than just talking about research, they provide sensory details to ground us in the places they have visited and the people they have talked to as they gathered information. There's a conversational tone, albeit a professional one, and the injection of humor makes the read more enjoyable.

Besides providing the facts, the authors move past the research to paint a picture of what life on Mars might be like. Newman and Fraser believe that any colony established on Mars will need to cater to humans' emotional and psychological needs as well as their physical ones. Hence, they envision that plants will be "encouraged to grow in all sunlit places." Plants, they argue, "will be one of the workhorse technologies of Mars. They will feed the Martians, filter the air and water, and provide everything from food to medicine to oxygen to building materials."

In Chapter 10, titled "Ballrooms of Mars," Newman and Fraser describe their vision of what a typical "night out" might look like for the Mars colonists. This ability to convincingly depict the future comes naturally. Both authors are admitted science fiction fans who "love how good sci-fi provides a way of exploring how the future may unfold." They state that "The best science fiction offers a thought experiment about how humans might live under different conditions and, in doing so, gives us fresh ideas about our problems today."

Unlike Earth, "where everyone seems to be toiling 24–7," Newman and Fraser think people on Mars will be encouraged to enjoy their free time, enjoying music, homegrown restaurant fare, and dancing in their off hours. As for food, "healthy diet, a lack of motor vehicles, work-life balance, and regular exercise and social activity" just might be a recipe for Martians to enjoy better physical well-being than their Earthly counterparts.

What will dinner on Mars look like? The authors envision algae-based cellular bioreactors, vegetables grown using composted waste organics, synthesized caffeine, fresh salads, and 3-D printed chicken or fish, with proteins either grown in a bioreactor or derived from yeasts. There's also a possibility of fresh fish if aquaponic technology is employed on Mars.

Newman and Fraser don't just pull this stuff out of the air. Chapter by chapter, the authors build a case for why certain approaches will be necessary and how we will get there. In some cases, they delve into the history and background of specific developments. For example, in the chapter discussing the role that greenhouses are likely to play on Mars, they provide a brief history of greenhouses and how they have evolved through history.

Experiments in tissue farming, the role of artificial intelligence and technology in growing crops, aquaponics, and nanotechnology, as well as other topics, all get an airing in the course of the book.

There are some who may say, and have said, that the extravagant amount of money required to establish human habitation on Mars or the moon isn't worth the expense and that dollars would be better spent here on Earth addressing those issues. Newman and Fraser tackle this issue upfront. While pointing out that money not spent on traveling to Mars wouldn't necessarily find its way to addressing Earth's problems, they also argue that the effort of trying to establish Mars-worthy solutions will help us here on Earth.

Newman and Fraser position *Dinner on Mars* as a "thought experiment." After careful study, research, and discussion, the authors have "come to believe a Martian community can and will feed itself successfully, and, in doing so, will develop technologies that will revolutionize agriculture on Earth." That revolution, they argue, is necessary: "Our current system of farming that came out of the Green Revolution has run its course. It's too energy-intensive, too vulnerable to climate change, too polluting, too hard on the land, and, despite using all these tractors, still exploits human and animal labor . . . humanity needs a new system."

Establishing human habitation on Mars, they note, "will be easily one of the most complex problems in human history. It is composed of tens of thousands of supporting problems, branching down in layer upon layer, peppered with missing keystone technologies and processes that are possible but not yet practical." But the authors remain optimistic that one day, the effort will be made, and furthermore, that the systems being designed for Mars will, in turn, help us farm more efficiently and more sustainably here on Earth.

From the moment that I read the title and premise of *Dinner on Mars*, the book intrigued me. There are a number of reasons for this. I freely admit that since exposure to *Star Trek: The Original Series* in my formative years, I have always held a romantic affection for the idea that humanity might one day fly, and live, beyond Earth's boundaries. I spent my earliest years living next to a farm, so I come by my interest in agriculture honestly. I've tried my hand at growing a modest vegetable garden, which lends me a general interest in plants. Finally, as a writer of science fiction, the book appealed to me as a resource that might help me craft more realistic scenarios.

I'm happy to say that *Dinner on Mars* met, and exceeded, my expectations. As someone who is concerned about the environment here on Earth, I was reassured by the link that the authors made between the technologies being developed for Mars, and the various ways they might improve life on Earth.

Whether you're a prospective Martian colonist curious about what you might find on the menu once you get there, a science fiction fan intrigued by a thought experiment about how things might play out when humanity goes to the Red Planet, or an earth-bound human interested in the future of food production, *Dinner on Mars* serves up plenty of food for thought.

SALTBURN DRIPS SEXUALITY AND INTRIGUE: BARRY KEOGHAN, ROSAMUND PIKE DEVASTATE IN THIS DARK MASTERPIECE OF DESIRE

HOLLY LYN WALRATH

Premiering as one of the secret screenings at Fantastic Fest, *Saltburn*, directed by Emerald Fennel, a former actress who draws on her private school upbringing in England in this salacious miasma of a film.

Set at Oxford, Saltburn sets up Oliver Quick (Barry Keoghan) as the mousy, shy schoolboy who becomes entranced by the wealthy and charismatic Felix Catton (Jacob Elordi). With obvious nods to *The Talented Mr. Ripley*, Saltburn dives into a far more convincing portrayal of unrequired queer love —or does it?

There's so much to enjoy about this luscious film that I hesitate to even write about it. Director Emerald Fennel draws on queer iconography by harkening back to *The Rocky Horror Picture Show* in the most intimate, disturbing scenes that had audiences salivating.

There are some real gasp-out-loud moments here. Twists and turns lie at every corner as Oliver Quick navigates and destroys the world of the hyper-elite British upperclass. His acting here is some of the best I've seen all year. He gives a no-holds-barred, wildly convincing, deeply unhinged character empathy and charm in the best ways, leaving the viewer rooting for "Ollie" to the very bitter end.

Jacob Elordi is sweaty and swoonworthy as the object of desire—a manic pixie dreamboy. Rosamund Pike is a treasure and should be protected at all costs—

give her this kind of role for the rest of her life, please. Archie Uchena Madekwe is lovable and hateable all at once. And Alison Oliver is convincingly imperfect in all the best ways.

The film is drenched in the female gaze—which may be its undoing, given the subject manner and set-up. We're supposed to believe Oliver is really and truly in love.

As I overheard a few women bemoaning leaving the theater, the only real imperfection in the film is its failure to give its queer anti-hero the kind of confirmation of his sexuality that would cement the film as a queer cult classic. In this respect, the film plays it far too close to the vest in its reminiscence of *The Talented Mr. Ripley*. Instead, it's just too milquetoast, despite being hailed as "hedonistic" and "trippy".

Absolutely worth a watch, though—maybe two, or three.

QUEER REPRESENTATION IN SUPERMASSIVE GAMES: BAFTA-WINNING GAME STUDIO AND QUEER GAMER CULTURE

VANESSA MAKI

Discussions surrounding queerness in horror are nearly always about television or film. We endlessly discuss the complicated sapphic relationship in *Jennifer's Body*, the unapologetic queerness in the *Child's Play* franchise, *The Rocky Horror Picture Show* in general, many of the characters throughout the *American Horror Story* universe, etc. There's nothing wrong with having our regular discussions about such media. However, queerness in horror can be found all over the place. Including comics, novels, video games, and even more. Yes, queer characters do exist in horror games.

Experiencing video games with even queer-coded characters is nice for queer gamers. However, it's even more exciting to see people being explicitly queer. A game developer that's released some solid games with a wide variety of characters is BAFTA-winning *Supermassive Games.* Believe it or not, some of the best horror games that are choice-based have been released by a British game developer. Games like *Until Dawn*, *The Dark Pictures Anthology*, and *The Quarry* are part of the *Supermassive Games* catalog. Throughout each game, we are introduced to a number of characters, and some of them are explicitly or at least coded as queer.

Until Dawn doesn't have explicit queer representation, but you can absolutely headcanon a few folks that are clearly not cishet. The absolute hit *The Quarry* gives us a potential queer interracial relationship between Ryan (Justice Smith) and Dylan (Miles Robbins), and they outright flirt with one another and are even given the option to kiss. It would have been nice to see them actually be together and not just flirt. But it's a surprising option, as cishet romances are the focus more often than not.

The Dark Pictures Anthology is a different beast altogether, though. *Man of Medan* is another case of queer headcanons with characters like Fliss (Ayisha Issa), who gives bisexual energy, or Brad (Chris Sandiford). *Little Hope* is somewhat void of queerness, but you can headcanon Anthony (Will Poulter). I can't personally speak for *House of Ashes* because it's the only game I haven't played from the anthology. *The Devil in Me* gives us a little love story between sapphics of color with Jamie (Gloria Obianyo) and Erin (Nikki Patel). It's more fleshed out than Ryan and Dylan (I ship them, but I wish something came of it), and there's a sense of it working out. As long as they both survive until the end of the game, that is. If you can make it so the sapphics survive a night from hell, you get a rainbow cookie.

It may not seem like much or that I'm reaching as far as headcanons go. But if you can see yourself in characters that ping your gaydar, there's nothing wrong with that! Fandom is for speculation and discussions like this.

ANNE HATHAWAY SHINES IN EILEEN, A STORY OF UNREQUITED LOVE: STUCK IN MASSACHUSETTS IN THE 1960S

HOLLY LYN WALRATH

"I looked like a girl you'd expect to see on a city bus, reading some clothbound book from the library about plants or geography, perhaps wearing a net over my light brown hair. You might take me for a nursing student or a typist, note the nervous hands, a foot tapping, bitten lip. I looked like nothing special. It's easy for me to imaging this girl, young and mousy version of me, carrying an enormous leather purse or eating from a small package of peanuts, rolling each one between her gloved fingers, sucking in her cheeks, staring anxiously out the window."

So opens *Eileen*, the book by bestselling author Otessa Moshfegh. The film, which follows the book closely and was screenwritten by Moshfegh, follows the story of Eileen (Thomasin McKenzie, who most recently stole audience's hearts in *Last Night in Soho*), a lonely secretary with a paranoid, alcoholic father and a dead mother. Eileen works at a boy's prison and is chiefly ignored and underappreciated by everyone in her life, so she falls into grim, even deadly, fantasies.

I'm a sucker for "mousey girls who defy expectations," and Eileen sits squarely in that category. There are layers of invisibility in identity. Eileen is invisible as a woman—specifically, an unattractive, plain woman without any confidence. So when she meets Rebecca, a blonde bombshell of a woman (in the book, she's redheaded) who also is in a role of importance uncommon for the time as the prison's psychologist—can anyone blame Eileen for falling in love?

Thomasin McKenzie is winningly naive as Eileen, making her darkest moments seem kind of sweet and funny. Anne Hathaway does an excellent job of being the seductive, enchanting older woman who leads Eileen into a dark situation, only to become another person who underestimates her.

The film captures the interiority of the book without spending too much time on inner monologues. As Eileen's fantasies of murder and suicide become darker and darker, her relationship with Rebecca deepens. What the film manages so well is the audience's expectations—we know before Eileen does that Rebecca will never fulfill her innermost desires.

Curiously, the movie verges into far more interesting territory than the book by coding Eileen as queer. In the book, Eileen says of her sexuality: "Let me be clear about this: I was not a lesbian. But I was attracted to Rebecca, and I admired her. You could call it a crush." By making Eileen's sexuality coded queer and placing her as the unrequited lover, Eileen's motivations are far more intriguing. It's one thing to be a mousy girl in the 1960s with no personality; it's another to be queer and hide that personality for safety's sake.

Underutilized in the film is Eileen's eating disorder, which adds a layer of psychological intensity to her character. In the book, her character binges and purges. In the film, she merely has a sweet tooth.

Being a mess is kind of a shield for Eileen. As Moshfegh said about the character in an interview with the Guardian, "Eileen is a character that makes people uncomfortable. She is not going to, you know, cheer you up. But might it not be liberating to hear the thoughts of someone who is completely ignored by society?"

Eileen is worth a watch for its dry humor and unflinching portrayal of female sexuality in the 1960s.

FIVE NIGHTS AT FREDDY'S OFFERS A NEW GATEWAY TO HORROR: BUT MORE EXPERIENCED FRIGHT-FLICK FANS WILL WANT TO WAIT FOR A LEVEL-UP

PATRICK BARB

Released the weekend before Halloween in theaters and on the Peacock streaming platform, the Blumhouse-produced adaptation of popular horror video game franchise *Five Nights at Freddy's* (*Scottgames*, 2014) has already proven itself a dominant box-office presence. The film version (*Universal Pictures*, 2023) plays like a "Greatest Hits" of the game's mythos and mechanics. You've got your abandoned pizzeria, your menacing possessed animatronics, creepy corridors to explore, and even security-cam-footage shenanigans. Lead Josh Hutcherson as the father-figure older brother/night-time security guard Mike does an admirable job of bringing depth and pathos to the player-POV character from the games. However, one can't help but note a checklist-style delivery to both story and scares, a by-the-numbers approach that seems more concerned with appeasing the fanbase and setting up a film franchise than anything else.

Regardless of one's opinion of the directorial work of Emma Tammi or the screenwriting by Tammi, *FNAF* creator Scott Cawthon, and Seth Cuddeback, there's no denying that the team behind the film has much to celebrate. Over its opening weekend, the film raked in $ 80 million domestically and $ 130 million globally. That's the highest opening for a Blumhouse production since the 2018 *Halloween*. Among other achievements, the film was also the highest-grossing Halloween weekend release ever. Based on these numbers alone, one can be sure that a new horror film franchise has been brought to life.

Given the introductory nature of the film, both in terms of the *FNAF* world and storyline *and* as a primer for horror cinema in general, the likely continuance of the series should be viewed as a positive. The challenge with an adaptation of this type is two-fold. Filmmakers must provide entry points for the casual viewer/non-fan, while also giving die-hard enthusiasts the characters, moments, and plot twists that they expect/demand. Given the game franchise's popularity with children (see "The Mash-Up Mythos"), the PG-13 framework for the film is not surprising. Tonally, the film slots in perfectly for a pre-teen/early teen demographic. Plenty of jump-scares, flashes of gore/bloodshed, and some weirdness and dread for good measure. Like the game itself, the movie provides digestible frights.

However, with this horror-primer approach, hardcore horror fans may feel like they're in the presence of a bar-band cover band rather than seeing a sold-out stadium rock show. From the dream sequences used to relay backstory (and wouldn't it just figure that *dreams* would tie into a horror movie featuring a character named *Freddy*) to the sequences of awful adults getting their comeuppance to the lone protagonist struggling to keep his family together, the beats play out in a familiar fashion. Of course, the horror film-going audience is perhaps not the main target here.

In terms of converting the *FNAF game players* to filmgoers, this adaptation can be viewed as a success. The animatronic mascots of Freddy Fazbear and company look incredible. Visually stunning, the filmmakers get performances out of these creations that are funny, frightening, and even heartbreaking when required. As mentioned, the sequences featuring the security cam footage are also pulled off well. Given how much of a focus they receive in gameplay, it would be a shame to see them falter.

As Mike, Hutcherson delivers a solid performance. Having lost his brother to a kidnapper during childhood, Mike now raises his young sister, works in security and uses lucid dreaming methods in an attempt to remember who took his sibling. Desperate to retain custody of his sister Abby, Mike accepts a job at the abandoned pizza restaurant Freddy Fazbear's. On the job, he meets Vanessa, a local police officer with a seemingly unending supply of lore related to Freddy's. It's through her that Mike learns of the children who went missing from the restaurant in the 1980s (the same time as Mike's brother). For viewers unfamiliar with the *FNAF* storyline, Vanessa serves as exposition-giver supreme.

It's a lot to take in and the deluge of information can sometimes feel a tad overwhelming. There are also some leaps in logic on display that seem designed to get the narrative from point A to point Z. While the movie concludes rather satisfactorily, there is one final twist (introducing a major character from the game franchise, with a performance from an actor who excels in horror films) that feels more like the set-up for the sequels than anything else. This reviewer would gladly have watched much more of this main antagonist and less of the dream sequences.

Ultimately, *Five Nights at Freddy's* succeeds in what it sets out to do, transferring the success of the game franchise to the film world. However, one hopes that future installments in the film series will take more risks and level up along with fans.

ASHIN OF THE NORTH REVIEW: THE FINAL GIRL BRINGS THE FIRE

CHRISTINA SNG

One of the most compelling movies from Netflix, *Ashin of the North* (2021) is the ultimate revenge story with Ashin herself as the Final Girl. If you've watched the Korean TV series *Kingdom* already, you'll know Ashin (Jun Ji Hyun) as the archer in Season 2. This is her story.

The movie opens with cave markings of the resurrection flower. The etching reads, "This plant brings the dead back to life... but you must pay the price."

A deer eats it and turns, going rabid, racing like a zombie before infecting a tiger. The tiger attacks a group of Pajeowi Jurchens and Joseon soldiers in an open field and is only taken down by Joseon commander Min Chi-Rok (Park Byung-eun). There, Min Chi-Rok tells the Pajeowi Jurchens, led by Ai Da Gan (Koo Gyo-hwan), that Ashin's father Ta Hab (Kim Roi-ha) is the traitor responsible for the deaths of their people.

Ashin (Kim Si-ah) is seen as a child in the cave, reading the etchings. She returns home to her village Seongjeoyain to tell her father that there is a cure for her mother but he brushes it aside. Ashin goes back anyway to collect flowers to save her mother. The enraged Pajeowi Jurchens overrun Seongjeoyain and kill everyone. When Ashin returns, everyone is dead, hanging from the raftors. Even the children are not spared.

Devastated and with nowhere to go, Ashin goes to Min Chi-Rok to ask him to help her avenge her father. He places her in the pig sty and gives her a job of washing the soldiers' clothes and spying on the Jurchen camp. Ashin falls into the grueling routine and trains by herself in the forest daily. Soon, she becomes a sharpshooter.

We see Ashin as a grown woman, and the soldier eyes her differently now. When one of them tries to rape her, she holds him at knifepoint only to be asked what will the camp do if she kills him. She relents. Over time, he continues to beat and rape her regularly, as we see from her bruises.

Min Chi-Rok catches him one day and warns him never to do this again. He knows Ashin is important to him as a spy, but his indifference has allowed this abuse to happen without giving Ashin any assurances of her safety or that she could come to him if anything like this happened.

The moment is brushed aside almost immediately. Min Chi-Rok instructs Ashin to infiltrate the Pajeowi Jurchen camp and gather intel. Steadfastly, she sneaks in. There, she finds her father with his arms and legs amputated, numb from the years of abuse, begging to die. Ashin weeps, holding him all night and at dawn, frees him from his pain. She leaves the camp burning.

Trudging back to the Joseon camp where troops are marching out in pairs to deal with the war against the Japanese, Ashin notices the colorful arrows in the sheath of a high-ranking member of the Haewon Cho clan Cho Beom-Il. The arrows look exactly like one she found when her village was massacred. A realization dawns.

With most of the soldiers gone, she breaks into the records room to find documentation by Min Chi-Rok that her father was indeed framed by the Joseons. All the abuse she endured waiting for the Joseons to avenge her father while they were, in fact, the real perpetrators.

With a quiet, simmering rage, Ashin unleashes her revenge. She returns to the camp and infects one soldier. He stumbles toward the gates, undead, and proceeds to infect the rest of the camp.

Ashin stays on the rooftops, shooting those who try to escape. She lights them on fire and watches them burn. When the whole camp is overrun, she returns to collect her rapist, whom she tied up and gagged, and brings him home in a sack for her undead family to feast on.

In that scene, we see her grief and regret at what should have been—a peaceful life in her quiet village with the people she loved. But because of the actions of the Joseons and the Jurchens, that can never be.

She is not done, however. Ashin brings the resurrection flower to Lee Seung-hui (Kwon Bum-taek), the Royal physician at the border in Uiji, and tells him how it works. Her final scene closes with her shooting an arrow at Ai Da Gan and his small company of soldiers on horseback. We know she survives this because she appears in *Kingdom* Season 2.

Ashin of the North is a study in nuance and silence.

It does this well using color. There was a stark contrast in the gender diversity in her village and the male-only camp: the brightly litcolorful village with men and women in equal balance, faces smiling to see Ashin, versus dull-colored scenes of Ashin in the army camp, pushing the laundry cart with men throwing their clothes onto it, and worse.

Cho Beom-Il's colorful arrows, for me, signify he is a trickster in this story. He is a loose cannon Min Chi-Rok had to rein in and cover for. Ashin seeing his colorful arrow is the critical moment she realizes it was all a lie. The resurrection flower too, is a trickster. Its beautiful tone belies the horror it will unleash, its promise greater than its warning.

Yet Ashin knows, having used it on her family as a child. And for her, it is worth it and necessary. She remains silent as many abuse victims do, tricked so many times that she no longer trusts anyone and relies only on herself. As the men pile on atrocity after atrocity against her, her rage grows. Her fury at the end is well-earned and cathartic.

THE TOXIC AVENGER REBOOTS "TOXIC" HERO: THE TOXIC AVENGER PREMIERES AT FANTASTIC FEST STARRING PETER DINKLAGE, KEVIN BACON, AND ELIJAH WOOD

HOLLY LYN WALRATH

The word "toxic" has two connotations. One is in terms of toxic waste—an all-too-familiar reality of today's world struggling with climate change. The other is the idea of something that is psychologically "toxic"—a toxic relationship, a toxic workplace, a toxic culture.

The 2023 reboot of The Toxic Avenger, directed by Macon Blair, explores the line between these two definitions. The cult classic gets new life in a bonkers, gonzo slayfest of a good time.

The original Toxic Avenger came out in 1984 from Troma Entertainment. Troma was well known for making "exploitation films" that aimed to disrupt the sensibilities of any average filmgoer (or New York Times Reviewer) by catering to the prurient curiosity and gore obsession of teenagers. At the time, films were often sold to home video sellers before even making it to the big screen, building on the large group of people who loved to buy or rent weird videos at their local video store. They were also regularly syndicated for TV.

"Sex, comedy, and an acceptable level of violence" was the goal. The original film cost less than $1.5 million to make. As one article of the time put it, the film relied "heavily on raunchy language, gory details, and a bit of soft porn."

("Savage Movies Don't Bloody Investors in Troma's Schlock" by Patrick Reilly, Crains New York Business, 1986).

Troma's Toxic Avenger was a surprise hit. It even spawned a musical score: The Toxic Avenger: New Jersey's first superhero. After that, Troma began making films with bigger names. The original film addressed fears of suburbia: Petty criminals preying on little old ladies and kids, making its criminals easy targets.

The 2023 reboot stars Emmy Award winner Peter Dinklage as Winston Gooze, a step-dad struggling to make ends meet and connect with his son after his wife's death. He has to face off against a cast of goons led by Bob Garbinger (Kevin Bacon) as the head of an evil corporation polluting suburbia.

Dinklage is buried in head-to-toe makeup and costumery that is satisfyingly realistic and clearly draws on Troma's history of real-life, practical effects. The SFX here seem to be primarily in the slashing of brains with a magical, sludge-infused mop. It's giving Goonies, and I'm here for it.

A surprising entry is Elijah Wood's role as the mistreated brother of the big bad corporation exec, Fritz Garbinger. With makeup and mannerisms that are obvious nods to Tim Burton's Penguin, Wood plays the role charmingly sweet under the uncanny surface.

The film has a high kill count and is a cheerful gore-fest with a heartfelt ending and a tutu-wearing, mop-wielding hero. It's kitschy, silly fun, and a blast to watch. What isn't to love?

For me, the film missed an obvious opportunity to tie the Toxic Avenger's early climate change message (something people were only just understanding the devastation of in the 80s) to today's audiences. Taylour Paige is a powerhouse as The Toxic Avenger's co-lead, bringing much-needed variety to an otherwise heavily white cast. But the satire of the film struggles, peppering what should be a critique of the right with anti-woke culture jokes that aren't as funny as we're convinced they should be. After all, it isn't woke culture that's killing the planet.

The Toxic Avenger struggles in its jokes—some of which are delightfully perfect, while others rely on tired take-downs. At one point, Toxie turns to his black female sidekick and raises his fist in the black power sign, which she shakes her head at, and Toxie replaces it with a rock-on sign. In another, a clearly right-wing news pundit is told off after making the last of several boring jokes about the left. The film should be making fun of the movement that for years successfully convinced most of the world that climate change wasn't real. It's that connection that I was wishing for in the film.

Peter Dinklage has a unique ability to bring another layer of complexity to his roles. In the original Toxic Avenger, there's a scene where an Asian laundress is killed. The punchline goes, "No ticky, no washy." Of course, the actress, Norma Pratt, wasn't Asian. But she was a little person. While B movies often pushed against norms in delightful ways, they also were well-known for perpetuating harmful stereotypes. That history is complex. (If you want a deep dive into little people in Troma films, I hesitantly point you to Lloyd Kaufman's 2010 article on the topic). Dinklage's role here is reclaiming that space, which he repeatedly does in his films, most recently the surprise romantic musical *Cyrano* (2021).

Avenging the toxicity that kills the planet? Maybe. Avenging toxic culture? I'm not entirely sure. Either way, it's a gory, face-shredding crusade of fun.

HAUNTED HOUSE AND CURSED LAND: MOMBAUER'S THE HOUSE OF DROUGHT BLENDS GOTHIC AND FOLK HORROR IN TIMELY CLIMATE CHANGE NOVELLA

PATRICK BARB

> "Even while eschewing the typical white protagonists filling so many tales of dark and dreary Victorian mansions for a cross-generational line-up of Sri Lankans of various social castes, Mombauer's cover version of the gothic and haunted house tropes reveals the vitality of these elements by showcasing their universality."

In Dennis Mombauer's latest novella, *The House of Drought* from *Stelliform Press*, the ongoing climate crisis pitting contemporary human civilization against the natural world is given new life via a compelling horror showdown between two of its most popular subgenres: the gothic and folk horror.

Crossing generations, Mombauer's story traces the downfall of a grand (and very out-of-place) colonial mansion built on Sri Lankan farmland, overlapping the haunted-house tale with a mythical Earth-Mother figure connected to the land and its bounty, both in abundance and decline. As these forces face off across the years, it is the characters and readers who are caught in the middle, trying to make sense of the losses shared through time.

Family secrets, secret passages (even an entire secret house in this case), characters (often women) driven by the past to take action, these hallmarks of gothic horror fill the pages of *The House of Drought*. Even while eschewing the typical white protagonists filling so many tales of dark and dreary Victorian mansions for a cross-generational line-up of Sri Lankans of various social castes, Mombauer's cover version of the gothic and haunted house tropes reveals the vitality of these elements by showcasing their universality. Beginning with an uncle on the run from debt, hiding away in the abandoned mansion with his nieces and nephews, following those characters with an upper-class family featuring an academic and cold-hearted patriarch at its head, then circling back to the abandoned daughter of the indebted man who's now trying to find her place in the world, those living in or near the House of Drought all remain at odds with the home they try to make their own.

But even as the characters and readers delve into the secrets inside the house, Mombauer adds an extra layer of danger originating outside the home. From the book's first pages, this existential threat is given a spotlight. As with many folk horror tales, we see an outsider (in this case a German documentarian Bernhard and his cameraperson Julia making a documentary about the devastation to the farmlands as a result of climate change) who unearths secrets from the land, setting off a chain reaction that will lead to retribution. With this frame narrative established, Mombauer's journey back in time in three acts also spotlights the land itself as a force to be reckoned with in each POV character's life.

Those residents of the Dry House with children will find one or more of their offspring drawn to an archetypal folkloric figure in the "White Lady" or "Sap Mother," an Earth Goddess entity who appears to dole out comfort and nurturing to the young as swiftly as she delivers vengeance and punishment to those she holds responsible for the downfall of the habitat over which she presides. In one of the more devastating aspects of the narrative Mombauer crafts, we see how even the nurturing of the children has an element of consequence.

With these two forces of horror—the gothic and folk—set in seeming opposition to each other, it is the characters, all of them outsiders in a house, that is itself an outsider, who Mombauer uses to explore the effects of these subgenres' distinct tropes and motifs. Starting from the documentarian with a similar background to the author (himself a German living in Sri Lanka), Mombauer deftly moves between characters, wrestling with their relationships to the horrors of the changing landscape and to the colonial past that's left behind a visible scar in the form of the Dry House.

Never a polemic about climate change, the narrative covers this global threat as one consequence of many, resulting from the choices of Mombauer's featured characters and those who came before the story begins. Complex forces are at play both in the world of the book itself and also in the author's craft and execution. By starting each section at its climax, then easing readers back into the how and the why that lead the characters to those moments, his prose mirrors our current tumultuous relationship to the climate crisis.

We find ourselves over and over again in moments of terror and fear, followed by attempts to figure out why these things are happening and how we got to these moments.

In *The House of Drought*, the antagonistic forces go by many names: the Dry House/House of Drought or the Sap Mother/White Lady, colonialism, global warming, climate change, etc., etc. Mombauer's greatest strength is found in how he drills down to the core of these threats and reveals how they're all connected deep down inside.

BAD MIRACLES AND OTHER SPECTACULAR THINGS IN JORDAN PEELE'S NOPE: SURVIVING TRAUMA AND MEMORY

GRETCHEN ROCKWELL

> "Miracles are associated with witness—it's not enough to see a miracle; it must be shared. Even a bad miracle demands sharing, the effort to have others see what you have and share its burden with you. Trauma, too, demands a sharing, an attempt to have others recognize its burden and its effects."

Jordan Peele's *NOPE* (2022) is, ostensibly, a film about spectacle. From the opening quote from Nahum to the double spectacle in the film, the audience is presented with scenes that shock, horrify, and astound. As an audience, we participate in seeing—less witnessing than watching. (Witness requires intent, after all, rather than merely absorbing what is in front of you.) In this way, *NOPE* reminded me of John Carpenter's *Halloween* (1978), where viewer becomes voyeur.

In *NOPE*, viewers are captivated by the stark visuals and carefully crafted sense of foreboding, breathlessly unable to look away in the same way as rubbernecking at a car crash or train wreck. *NOPE*, with its emphasis on eyes and seeing, seems to be pushing the viewer to consider their own sight and desire to see the horrifying spectacle.

But *NOPE* struck me for another reason. One of the film's strongest images is of a blue shoe, balanced perfectly upright after an act of terrible violence. The character witnessing this, Jupe, imbues this image with the belief that he is protected and exceptional—an interpretation and action that leads to his later attempt to create and control a spectacle for profit. This attempt, of course, fails, but serves as a clue to a vital part of the film: trauma and memory.

The nonlinear storyline—the present intercut with Jupe's memories of his past trauma—is clearly triggered by images and out of sync with the present. Moving between these two moments shows memory's associative (or dissociative) properties, particularly traumatic memories and how they resurface unexpectedly and continue to shape the person they belong to.

OJ, the film's protagonist, asks, "What's a bad miracle?" at one point. Miracles are associated with witness—it's not enough to see a miracle; it must be shared. Even a bad miracle demands sharing, the effort to have others see what you have and share its burden with you. Trauma, too, demands a sharing, an attempt to have others recognize its burden and its effects.

A friend and I recently had to compare notes on a story we'd hidden from a third mutual friend. My friend, years ago, was sexually victimized by someone we knew—someone our mutual friend liked and trusted. We decided to not say anything at the time, which perhaps was the wrong choice. In retrospect, I'm glad my friend trusted me with the truth of the event so I could provide support and help take action.

Although I didn't see the event, I witnessed its truth. I, the non-victim, remember certain things about the aftermath. My friend remembers the traumatic act itself. Neither of us had the vocabulary or awareness to name it as trauma, but we used other language; we developed a code of shared glances and unspoken signals, becoming closer as a result. In some ways, this was miraculous. Just not a miracle we would've ever wished for.

My aunt once told me to seek out and confront my trauma while I was young, that it would become harder the older I got. Her death is something I'm only now starting to recognize as a traumatic moment, not just a memory. It was unexpected, sudden: a bad miracle. Our lives are full of these moments and so often, we can't help but remember them. Is it harder when we don't get to see things—as I did not get to see the funeral or witness my family's grief—or when we do?

Peele, I think, wrote the film to be mainly about spectacle, confronting our desire to look at something terrible and questioning that desire. But I think memory and trauma are inherently there too: the bad miracle of remembering something traumatic, the small details that stick in the mind and fester. *NOPE*'s focus on looking and seeing applies to trauma and memory, too.

We aren't always ready to face it, to look at it head-on, much less challenge its grip on us. It takes time and preparation to be able to look at it—witness it. OJ knows how to handle things best of all: avoid looking directly at something until you're ready to face it with courage—take the bad miracle and make something out of it that you can survive.

A GAME OF SHADOW AND BONES: NETFLIX'S YA FANTASY SHOW AND THE CHANGING ART OF BOOK ADAPTATIONS

HESPER LEVERET

"The makers of Shadow and Bone threw everything they could at the screen, and that might not be enough."

The finale of *Game of Thrones,* HBO's hugely popular fantasy TV drama, aired in May 2019. Since then, studios have been searching the shelves for books with the potential to become the next big fantasy hit. While there are lots of options, some of the choices taken by TV networks are a little unorthodox. HBO is producing a prequel series, *The House of the Dragon,* based on George R.R. Martin's 'history' book about his own fictional setting. Netflix is adapting The Witcher book series, making some fairly big changes to the story and recasting the main character as they go. Amazon Prime is making a reasonably faithful adaptation of The Wheel of Time series. They are also making The Rings of Power, which is based on the appendices to The Lord of the Rings, stretching out the material while compressing the timeline.

Then there's *Shadow and Bone*. It's another Netflix show—Season 2 was released in March 2023. It's based on the Grishaverse books by Leigh Bardugo, and it condenses two different series into a single show. The title and the main story come from her YA trilogy about Alina Starkov (played by Jessie Mei-Li), a young orphan who discovers she has unique magical powers. But the series also features characters and material from her *Six of Crows* duology about a gang of teenage thieves staging daring heists, even though while the two book series are set in the same world (the 'Grishaverse'), they take place in different physical locations and points in time.

Why have the writers taken this approach? Well, with *Game of Thrones,* the showrunners had the luxury of a full eight seasons of television, but with George R.R. Martin's book series still incomplete, they ran out of source material long before they reached the conclusion. The show's later seasons were much less critically well-received than the earlier seasons, and the finale was widely panned. Shadow and Bone has the opposite problem.

There's no shortage of material to work with: the Grishaverse includes a trilogy, two duologies, and a couple of short story collections. But, operating within the notoriously cancellation-happy Netflix system, where many shows get canned after only one or two seasons, the writers seem to have decided to fling everything at the screen at once.

The first season featured the events of the Shadow and Bone book, plus some events lifted from *Six of Crows,* plus an original storyline for the Crows characters to bring them into contact with the rest of the cast. This was all well-integrated and meant that viewers got to see fan-favorite characters such as Kaz (played by Freddy Carter) and Inej (played by Amita Suman) as well as Alina's story. And, of course, everyone's favorite sexy murder-wizard, the Darkling (played by Ben Barnes).

Then there's Season Two. The first few episodes speed-run both the second book in the original trilogy (*Siege and Storm*) and the second book in the Crows duology (*The Crooked Kingdom*). The later episodes spin off into unknown territory, mashing together some events from the trilogy's final book, (Ruin and Rising), with another original storyline for the Crows. And then the cliffhanger ending points towards events from another duology, King of Scars, as well as the central Ice Court heist from *Six of Crows* itself. Confused? You're not the only one. While Season One was well-paced, Season Two often feels rushed and breathless, with plot beats coming thick and fast and newly introduced characters such as Nikolai (played by Patrick Gibson) given insufficient development.

As of June 2023, the future of *Shadow and Bone* is in doubt, with neither a Season Three nor a potential spinoff show starring the Crows characters confirmed and the writers' strike ongoing. There are fan campaigns to save the show. But there's no guarantee we'll ever see Alina, or the Crows, on-screen again, especially as Netflix seems to be putting resources (including director Mairzee Almas, who worked on Shadow and Bone) on a spinoff from The Witcher starring... a gang of teenage thieves. Hmm.

Netflix is famously secretive, although there's some analysis of what might be going on behind the scenes. Ultimately, fantasy television might be popular, but it's also expensive to make. The makers of Shadow and Bone threw everything they could at the screen, and that might not be enough. Will we see more adaptations that take a similar approach? In the ever-changing landscape of television, it's anyone's guess what might be coming next.

BLACK MIRROR SEASON 6 AND THE POWER OF SITUATIONAL HORROR: WHAT WRITERS CAN LEARN ABOUT STORYTELLING FROM THE POPULAR NETFLIX SERIES

HOLLY LYN WALRATH

> "What is it about *Black Mirror* that captivates us? Personally, I believe it's the way it juxtaposes situational horror, scathing commentary on our technological society, and imaginative science fiction to create a truly captivating experience."

I've been a *Black Mirror* fan since about Season Two and the episode "Be Right Back," which hit on one of my greatest fears of losing a loved one to a car accident from texting. (I know that's really specific, but it's truly something I worry over every time my spouse leaves the house.) Another favorite episode of mine is the famously queer "San Junipero", which I sometimes comfort re-watch just for the heck of it.

Every *Black Mirror* season feels like a little gruesome gift wrapped up for fans just like me who crave the over-the-top, wildly imaginative, slippery-slope scenarios that hit far too close to home. So when Season Six dropped on Netflix, a part of me wondered if we even deserve it.

What is it about Black Mirror that captivates us? Personally, I believe it's the way it juxtaposes situational horror, scathing commentary on our technological society, and imaginative science fiction to create a truly captivating experience.

But the best reason to watch the show, even if you've never seen it, is how it manages situations in horror.

A situation is the set-up for a plot. It's not story—that's dependent on characters and emotions. The situation is well-known to viewers from years of *I Love Lucy, Seinfield*, and *How I Met Your Mother*, comedy sitcoms that exploit easy set-ups for laughs. Situational horror does the same thing, only with the goal of creating fear in the viewer.

The best situations explore the answers to "What If" questions. In Season Six of *Black Mirror*, a fantastic example of this is the episode "Joan is Awful," where an averagely terrible woman suddenly finds herself at the center of a new Streamberry (this world's version of Netflix) drama that she is living daily. *What if your life suddenly became a Netflix show?*

The set-up hits on all of *Black Mirror*'s favorite tropes: Joan is trapped by her use of over-reaching technology (she, like most of us, signed away her rights in the fine print agreement to join Streamberry as a customer, and her phone is responsible for tracking her every movement); ridiculously Meta themes (Netflix publishing a show that criticizes Netflix is pretty clever); the episode takes the situation to its absolute extreme, becoming more and more absurd as Joan tries to deal with her overnight stardom; and it's a great example of how creating a compelling situation can be the basis of a terrifying story.

The episode is bonkers, gruesome, and has a killer twist that you'll love trying to figure out. Annie Murphy plays Joan to a T, really embracing the "awfulness" of the character, and the delightful cameos by Salma Hayek, Michael Cera, and Himesh Patel are a treat.

Situation makes a great story. Audiences want a situation that feels fresh and asks the viewer to think through what they would do (or in this case, how they would survive) when placed into a complicated situation. It's how we manage our day-to-day lives, after all. We react to what happens to us, or else we make decisions that have unexpected repercussions.

When I teach writing classes, I often ask my writers to come up with ten tense situations. Think of the most intense, terrifying, complicated, and devastating scenario you can. Then write a story about it.

Every episode of Black Mirror Season Six chooses a tricky scenario and plays it out to the extreme. In Episode Two, a young man returns home to his sleepy Scottish town with the goal of filming a bland documentary, only to get roped back into a serial killer story with a personal twist. Episode Three explores the idea of body doubles as a way for astronauts to travel long distances in space. Episode Four puts a tabloid photographer smack-dab in the middle of a speculative nightmare. Episode Five forces a quiet sales assistant into a life-or-death series of terrible acts.

Each situation makes the viewer think—what will the twist be? How would I react in this situation? What's going to happen next? And further, the writers of Black Mirror have managed to tie each situation to its most terrifying emotional conclusion, making the viewer both cringe and feel at the same time.

And that is the secret to fantastic storytelling.

I don't know about you, but I'll probably be re-binging the show this weekend, to relive some of my favorite horrific experiences from the safety of my living room.

FINDING A PLACE IN THE MEDIEVAL: THINKING QUEERLY BY JES BATTIS JOUSTS WITH TRADITION

LISA TIMPF

"How do we ensure that wizards can create space for readers beyond privileged white, straight, and abled communities?"

Back in high school, I participated in the annual drama productions spearheaded by the English department. In 1977, the artistic director selected *Camelot* as that particular year's offering. As a not-yet-out young woman who enjoyed playing sports and abhorred wearing dresses, I was already aware that I didn't fit neatly into the gender role expectations of my era. Much as I enjoyed the Arthurian tales, I didn't see a place for myself in the land of Camelot either. There, it seemed that women were relegated to the roles of queen, enchantress, or member of the court. When the knights jousted for fun or in earnest, our job was to stand on the sidelines and cheer.

Fast forward forty-plus years, when I got my introduction to the scholarly text *Thinking Queerly* by Jes Battis (*De Gruyter,* 2021). Battis offers a different and more diverse way of looking at medieval and medievally-inspired writing. In so doing, they offer queer and neuro-divergent folks a glimpse of unexpected inclusiveness in texts that, at first glance, may seem uninviting.

Battis, an Associate Professor at the University of Regina's Faculty of Arts, is in a good position to pen a work of this nature. Their research interests include medieval literature and medievalism, eighteenth-century literature, LGBTQ2+ histories and cultures, fantasy and speculative fiction, and neurodiversity and disability studies, among other topics.

In the Acknowledgements, Battis states, "This is also a book about disability and neurodiversity across time." *Thinking Queerly* does indeed cover a swath of history, referencing various Arthurian texts, including *The Vulgate*, Robert de Boron's *Merlin*, Thomas Malory's *Morte Darthur,* and a fifteenth-century poem by Thomas Hoccleve, among others. But there are also observations about more recent fantasy and medievally-inspired books, movies, and television shows, including *Carry On, In Other Lands, Buffy the Vampire Slayer, Sabrina,* and the Harry Potter series. Even *Young Sheldon* gets a mention.

Though the book is heavy with references, and Battis backs up points made with examples or quotes from original works, the writing style remains professional but conversational. Battis also lightens the text with the injection of humor. For example, after relating a story about Diogenes and Alexander the Great, they observe, "Diogenes would have loved earbuds."

Wizardry and neurodiversity, queering the magical academy, and queer adolescence in Sir Gawain and the Green Knight are among the topics explored in *Thinking Queerly*. Battis also devotes a chapter to the often-maligned character Morgan le Fay, positing her as "an ancestor to the diverse and queer witches that have emerged in recent YA literature."

Battis discusses how medieval scholarly tradition has "been hostile to Black, Indigenous, and POC (person of color) scholars," as well as members of other diverse groups. This begs the question Battis poses in the book's introduction: "How do we ensure that wizards can create space for readers beyond privileged white, straight, and abled communities?"

Fortunately for members of those communities, Battis offers clues to help the reader find greater inclusiveness than may have been imagined if one knows where to look for it.

Though the image that often comes to mind for me when I think of the medieval period is a knight in armor, galloping off to clash with his cohorts in war or play, Battis notes that "medieval literature . . . presents a number of individuals who struggled to deal with a fast-paced world, and seemed to value a quiet, bookish life over the buzz of court or the violent energy of the battlefield."

In *Thinking Queerly,* the author generously shares their own experiences. Battis notes, "as someone on the spectrum, I have struggled with neurotypical communication. I can recall countless instances of being told to 'speak up,' or 'get to the point,' or 'make proper eye contact.' " Battis also admits a vested interest in the topic of study: "As a person with a complex diagnostic history, I'm invested in the capacity of disabled and neurodivergent people to define themselves, and how that capacity translates into literature."

Battis links their personal experience with the texts. Observing that Thomas

Hoccleve's poem "My Compleinte" describes a phenomenon very much like an anxiety attack. Battis writes:

I've certainly felt this way in crowded spaces, my feet restless, my already sketchy eye contact dissolving into quick glances while I fall into sensory overload. Hoccleve's speaker knows what they should be doing in this social situation, but they can't manage it: a feeling many of us can relate to.

Battis talks about the appeal they found in the image of Merlin as portrayed in a book about the King Arthur stories written by James Knowles and illustrated by Louis Rhead. One illustration of Merlin "communing with a crow" was particularly impactful:

The knights were always in action poses, or sidling up to damsels, but Merlin seemed still and self-contained. I knew, even at nine, that I was reading this book the wrong way. Like a medieval chivalry manual, the stories of King Arthur were designed to teach straight boys how to be knights; the same way that my piles of forgotten hockey cards were supposed to teach me how to be an NHL star. What I wanted to be was that solitary wizard, chilling with his bird.

The author's personal sharing lends a deeper authenticity to the work and makes their arguments more convincing.

Thinking Queerly is published by *De Gruyter Academic Publishing. De Gruyter,* a long-established publisher that can trace its roots back to 1749, puts out books and scholarly journals. Though it's been decades since my university student days in the late 1970s and early 1980s, I can still recall the way I grimaced when it came time to pay for the texts required for my courses. Reflecting the type of publication it is, *Thinking Queerly* commands a higher price than, say, a mass-market paperback. However, for those who can get their hands on a copy, it's an enjoyable read even if it's not on the curriculum of a course you happen to be taking—which is more than I can say for my first-year Calculus text.

I could take a stab at crafting a concluding paragraph, but I don't think I could say it any better than Battis in one of my favorite sections of *Thinking Queerly*:

A wizard, like Merlin, offers possibilities for readers who don't see a place for themselves at the Round Table. There is, in fact, a place, next to Merlin, who's just as distracted as we are, probably dreaming of stillness, or birdsong, or a room full of books, or texture like fur . . . run your fingers down the soft tail-feathers of Archimedes, Merlyn's owl familiar. Get lost in the mirrors of the enchanter's gown, reflecting an infinity of queer futures, halfway between earth and air.

DARK POETRY ABOUNDS IN WHERE THE DEVIL ROAMS: SET AT A CARNIVAL IN THE GREAT DEPRESSION, THE LATEST FROM THE ADAMS FAMILY IS A ROTTEN RIOT

HOLLY LYN WALRATH

If you're not familiar with the Adams Family (not THAT Addams family), they are made up of mother and father John Adams and Toby Poser, and their two daughters, Lulu and Zelda Adams—and they make horror movies. Together, the family not only acts in but writes, directs, produces, and sound designs movies. The films are self-funded, allowing the family team to make all the most important, integral decisions in making a film.

Coming off the success of *Hellbender* (2022), their latest is *Where the Devil Roams*—a movie about a family of carnies on a murder rampage through the Catskills, NY, during the 1930s depression.

The film opens as a vaudeville performer recites a deliciously dark poem that ends, "blood will thicken, the devil's pulse begins to quicken, while the body rots to dust and bones, there's a tear in the heart where the devil roams." This is just the first of beautiful word play in a film that utilizes dark poetry as its beating, bloody heart.

Eve (Zelda Adams) is traveling with her parents (John Adams and Toby Poser) to various carnivals when she becomes entranced with a man who seems to have the magical ability to reattach his fingers after cutting them off for the benefit of awed audiences.

Meanwhile, her mother and father are a disturbing duo that wreaks havoc wherever they go. When their killing spree inevitably goes terribly wrong, Eve has to pick up the pieces (literally) and spell them back together.

The spell? A dark poem.

Dark poetry has a long history in horror—dating back to Edgar Allen Poe and H.P. Lovecraft. But this is the first time I've seen it explored in a horror film, and as a dark poet, I was delighted. It captures effectively all of the thrall of dark poetry—which can dive into the most horrific of themes and often contains old-fashioned rhyme schemes.

Another poem referenced in the movie is Psalm 88, considered one of the darkest passages in the Bible:

> *Let my prayer come before thee: incline thine ear unto my cry;*
>
> *For my soul is full of troubles: and my life draweth nigh unto the grave.*
>
> *I am counted with them that go down into the pit: I am as a man that hath no strength:*
>
> *Free among the dead, like the slain that lie in the grave, whom thou rememberest no more: and they are cut off from thy hand.*
>
> *Thou hast laid me in the lowest pit, in darkness, in the deeps.*

The poems in this movie weave through and with the storyline, driving the characters to more and more terrible decisions. Added to this experience is the fact that the Adams write and sing their own music.

The Adams were influenced by classic horror like Frankenstein and Nosferatu. The film's cinematography is dark, moody, and grainy in the best of ways. It utilizes part black and white and part color scenes, which, as Zelda Adams said in the Q&A at Fantastic Fest, "shows the characters and their story are rotting."

The film was shot on location at their home and family friends' homes in the Catskills. They shot mostly in winter and in snow, and the film took about a year to make. I was surprised to learn that Zelda was a senior at the time, about to head off to college. "The film is also kind of about not wanting to let go of my parents", she said, which must be difficult in such a close-knit family.

Where the Devil Roams is intricate, weaving multiple themes and references throughout its narrative until everything comes together in the end. Artsy but gory, elevated but terrifying, the film is difficult not to fall in love with. Perfect for the fan of dark poetry!

THE ONLY WAY TO SURVIVE THE WORLD BURNING: REVIEW OF BRIDGING WORLDS: GLOBAL CONVERSATIONS ON CREATING PAN-AFRICAN SPECULATIVE LITERATURE IN A PANDEMIC

TAYLOR JONES

As promised by the subtitle "Global Conversations on Creating Pan-African Speculative Literature in a Pandemic," this short but pithy non-fiction collection edited by Oghenechovwe Donald Ekpeki is less a treatise and more a conversation. It makes room for a wide-ranging variety of essays. Some are personal stories of the pandemic; some are interviews on subjects ranging from the mundanity of the present to hopes for the future; and some delve into the details of how the pandemic affected publishing and the craft of writing.

The collection includes perspectives from people in multiple countries: Nigeria, Australia, Canada, the United States, and Russia, for example. The international perspectives on the pandemic alone make this a worthwhile read. For people interested in speculative fiction by writers from Africa and the African diaspora, it's a treasure trove of thoughts and analysis from those writers.

For example, Geoff Ryman and Wole Talabi offer thoughts on writing for Western markets vs. African markets and what it might take to grow a thriving speculative fiction community on the continent of Africa for African readers. Sheree Renée Thomas and Zelda Knight take on the experience of writing, editing, and publishing while Black in Western markets. Nigerian writer Edwin Okolo offers thoughts on how speculative fiction looks different when you "already live in a dystopia":

"To live in this kind of unending chaos is to be changed by it, to be numb to it, to be motivated by a desire to overcome it. This is why I feel somewhat slighted when I send in a speculative fiction story and I am told that it isn't magical enough, or that the human stories are too dark, or too grotesque to be believable. I live in a dystopia, a violent, uncertain world where the rules are in constant flux and we are always in motion, scheming, changing, evolving to escape the mass death that chases at our heels. There is no speculative yarn that can match the chaos of a Nigerian news week, no fictional dystopia that can best the schemers that rule my country."

The essays don't focus exclusively on writing and publishing. They also include personal stories of intense ups and downs. Nikhil Singh grieves for her unhoused neighbors and their suffering. Chimedum Ohaegbu had to attend his grandfather's funeral in Nigeria over Zoom. The people writing these essays lost friends and family to the virus, suffered from it themselves, or were locked into dystopian quarantine conditions.

In the midst of this upheaval, there was also joy: B. Sharise Moore recounts a series of triumphs brought on by pandemic-inspired clarity of vision. Milton Davis describes having to make a choice about, as Gandalf put it, "what to do with the time that is given to us" and deciding to take heart from the victories of the year. The pandemic forced creative thinking about gathering digitally, enabling people from all over to gather in new and unexpected ways: for example, the Voodoonauts Summer Workshop for Black SFF Writers co-founded "during a Zoom call in the summer of a pandemic" by Yvette Lisa Ndlovu and Shingai Njeri Kagunda.

The essays don't focus exclusively on the pandemic either: other events of 2020 can't be, and aren't, ignored. Particularly powerful for me, as a U.S. resident, were Sheree Renée Thomas' words on the extrajudicial killings of Black people by police in the United States:

"I work in the science fiction field, and we are always talking about futures. But in the real world, off the page, it's so very clear that neither judges nor juries, police nor politicians give a hot damn or a real thought about Black families or their futures... I mean, how many times have we seen judges use their discretion to help straight up guilty people have lighter or no sentences because they were

'concerned about their futures'? Whose future gets that kind of consideration? It sure the hell isn't us."

Despite the stark grief and the harsh realities of life in 2020, there's a lot of hope to be found here. If I had to pick one message I took away from "Bridging Worlds," I would say it is the healing potential of creative work, as exemplified by a quote from Toni Morrison that Nicole Givens Kurtz calls her "oxygen mask:"

"This is precisely the time when artists go to work. There is no time for despair, no place for self-pity, no need for silence, no room for fear. We speak, we write, we do language. That is how civilizations heal."

The healing power of words has limits in the face of a global pandemic, of course. Shingai Njeri Kagunda cautions that "when there is a gun or a knife or a virus that ravages worlds, words will not keep you alive." But she also describes how words can make life worth living:

"Afrofuturism is a praxis of radical faith. Storytelling makes possible the worlds that seem impossible given the limitations history has prescribed over black experience. I think the only way to survive the world burning is to build alternate ways of being alive, breathe into reality worlds of living possibility."

As adrienne maree brown says, "'I believe that all organizing is science fiction —that we are shaping the future we long for and have not yet experienced." Shaping the future takes not just action, but vision. Pan-African speculative fiction writers are giving us visions of both the future we want and the future we fear, which will help us chart a path forward together. That work needs to be structurally supported in publishing, now more than ever. "Bridging Worlds" offers timely and important thoughts on what that support could look like amidst the fires of the burning world.

STRANGE DARLING FLIPS SCRIPT ON SERIAL KILLER MOVIES: JT MOLLNER'S SECOND FEATURE FILM EXPLORES THE GENDER DYNAMICS OF MURDER

HOLLY LYN WALRATH

The description for the Strange Darling screening at Fantastic Fest was just one line: "One day in the twisted love life of a serial killer." So, of course, I had to see it.

What followed is a twisty, turny take on the cat-and-mouse thriller trope that is lusciously shot and seductive to the end. In one of the best performances I've seen since Pearl, Willa Fitzgerald plays a woman who meets a nice guy (Kyle Gallner) at a bar, and the two head to a hotel. But that's about as far as I can get in the plot without completely spoiling the fun of watching this unexpected exploration into gender, murder, and power.

Women live on a constant edge, always aware of violence creeping in from all sides. Women's desire is carefully managed by society. In most cases, the power play sex can be usually ends in violence against women. But women are rarely killers. That distinction lies with men, who, as of 1990 made up 85% of the serial killers in the US (Hunting Humans: An Encyclopedia of Modern Serial Killers). Yet whatever the gender, serial killers still fascinate us.

Horror that sharply manages the viewer's expectations has always been some of my favorite films. Mollner does a fantastic job of holding the viewer out on a plank, asking them to look down, and then kicking them overboard. The film is structured in six parts, but those parts do not necessarily come in order, creating a non-linear story that reveals its secrets in satisfying pieces.

Shot on 35mm film, *Strange Darling* shines in its cinematography, feeling somehow like a 70s slasher mixed with a contemporary arthouse flick vibe worthy of a studio like A24. The film utilizes slow zooms that are reminiscent of Kubrick's *The Shining* (1980), but they don't feel overwrought because the focus is female rage, a topic rarely explored in horror in nuanced ways. As Mollner called it, the "candy-coated" Anamorphic format (a term for shooting widescreen on 35mm film) results in some stunning sequences.

The film also shines in its soundtrack. The original music was created by indie rock artist Z Berg specifically for the film. Since most of the songs are unfamiliar to the viewer, they give the film an atmosphere that pales in comparison to most contemporary horror.

Both Willa Fitzgerald and Kyle Gallner provide truly outstanding performances, and the two have a chemistry that pulls the story along to where as a viewer, you can't wait for them to collide again and again as they bounce back and forth between kills.

Willa Fitzgerald is endlessly watchable. In some portions of the film, she is almost unrecognizable to other scenes, her face shifting to shift the viewer's expectations. The end scene is particularly moving, a long shot akin to the ending of *Pearl*. If this is the new trope for female leads in horror movies, I'm down.

This is one you'll want to go in without knowing much about and stick along for the bumpy, blood-filled ride. Someone get this film to the big screens, ASAP!

MIKE FLANAGAN'S HOUSE OF USHER STANDS ON A FIRM FOUNDATION: ALL THAT WE SEE OR SEEM...

R. THURSDAY

"Flanagan has turned the story from an American pastiche of classic British gothic literature—opulent but withering castles, thin-blooded aristocracy, waif-y women—to a uniquely Modern American gothic tale about wealth inequality, corrupt corporate powers, generational trauma, and the cost of ambition."

My friend says this new 'Usher' show looks like they've slammed together a bunch of Poe references as little winking references. In fairness, Mike Flanagan's newest Netflix offering, *The Fall of the House of Usher* (loosely inspired by the Edgar Allen Poe tale), indeed spills over the boundaries of the eponymous maybe-haunted-house story to include a great percentage of the Great Goth's prose (and poetry!). However, the references don't wink at the viewer so much as hiss from dark corners, writhe beneath floors, and chuckle from inside walls: they're structural and necessary for this modern inversion of decadence and despair.

Flanagan and company flip the familiar tale inside out: Instead of a long-historied "old blood" family fallen on hard times, waiting for the decrepit edifice that mocks them with former greatness before collapsing on them, the Ushers here (in the persons of Roderick and Madeline) start with almost nothing and build an empire...that then collapses on them. The "House" in *The Fall of the House of Usher* is not the building—though there certainly *is* a house, a peeling suburban structure of the 50s. Instead, the "House of Usher" is made of the family, a royal line that would cause any Westerosi dynasty to weep with envy.

In performing this twist, Flanagan has turned the story from an American pastiche of classic British gothic literature—opulent but withering castles, thin-blooded aristocracy, waif-y women—to a uniquely Modern American gothic tale about wealth inequality, corrupt corporate powers, generational trauma, and the cost of ambition.

The frame narrative revolves around Roderick Usher's "confession" to District Attorney August Dupin in the former's childhood home: Dupin has been trying to take the Ushers (a not particularly subtle sendup of the Sacklers) and their pharmaceutical company down for years. Now, all of Roderick's children are dead from seemingly unrelated events, and Roderick claims to know why. The show jumps between this present, Roderick and Madeline's childhood, the recent past, and moments between to build a compelling mystery: Are the Ushers victims of their own selfish natures and a genetic condition that causes dementia and hallucinations, or are they being exterminated by a vengeful specter for the sins of the father?

Viewers familiar with Flanagan's previous work will recognize the skewed angles, stillness, lighting, and occasional flash of horrific images. The sets, though not the crumbling eons-occupied manors one might expect, tell you a lot about the characters that live or work there: cold and performative, disdainfully wasteful, pragmatic, or boisterous. Similarly, the narrative offered by the wardrobe delighted me, especially as a person who finds "rich people" fashion incredibly dull: These people are so *extra*, I loved it. The foley work is incredible, especially for things that go...squish. And the music choices are bangers top to bottom (the show opens with "Brick in the Wall," the most ridiculous-that-this-works reference to "The Cask of Amontillado" I can possibly imagine).

But it's the characterizations the actors brought to a smart script that make the show work so well. Many of the actors have done a great deal of voiceover work, and it shows in the nuances of emotional spectrum: Bruce Greenwood, besides playing Admiral Pike in the Abrams' *Star Trek* movies, has voiced Batman in numerous DCEU films; Carl Lumbly's role as J'onn J'onzz in the animated *Justice League* cartoon was iconic, and of course, speaking of icons, there's Mark Freaking Hamill, leaning in to the gravel that forced him to retire from playing the Joker. The Usher kids are all fully realized characters and so recognizable that even knowing they are monsters, you find yourself liking them, or at least thinking, "I've definitely met that guy." The show never lets you forget that these are vicious, entitled people who profit from the suffering of others, yet they are never caricatures, which makes their (sometimes gory, often violent) deaths hit so much harder.

And at the center: Roderick, Madeline, Dupin, and...well, what I will call "the Mystery," played gloriously by Carla Gugino, slipping through different characterizations with graceful menace. I often wondered how the gentle, righteous Roderick seen in flashbacks had so morphed into the cool, anything-goes, power grabber of the present, while Madeline is a crackling example of how gender expectations make characteristics more or less villainous. Lumbly's Dupin is genuinely good without seeming naive, absolutely done with everyone's shit, and yet genuinely empathetic even to Roderick, despite their past.

As a horror show, there are plenty of the scares and squicks you'd expect (heads up that the most body horror heavy stuff is early on), and quite a bit of high-strung tension, but I was most surprised by what wasn't there: sexualized violence. I'd heard that Flanagan didn't include that in other shows, but it's so pervasive, especially horror involving queer people, that I didn't even realize I was holding my breath waiting for it until it never materialized. Don't get me wrong, there are *deeply problematic,* messy, unhealthy relationships, but never violence linked to sex, and never violence as a punishment for sexuality (rate or preference). And in case it wasn't clear enough, the Usher offspring are *incredibly* queer. Even the token "straights" are queer-coded (camp and possibly ace/poly, respectively). I joked that it was a diversity win: Finally, we've reached a place where queer people—independent of their queerness—can be shitty humans who don't deserve their partners, too!

The layering of stories—"Murder in the Rue Morgue" and "Tell-Tale Heart" was my favorite example—is clever and effective, and even when I wrote down what I thought would happen in advance, the show is so well done that it was worth knowing *how* it would play out. Besides the named tales in the episode titles, there are recurring motifs and more subtle nods: "The Cask of Amontillado"; "The Bells" and other poems; and my favorite, "The Facts in the Case of M. Valdemar", to name just a few.

So was my friend, right? Was this a cute mashup of references for pretentious goths to pick through? As a pretentious goth, I answer: no, with a tiniest whiff of yes. Folks familiar with Edgar's body of work will find their knowledge rewarded, but every pull is intentional and builds into a dark, sad story that any horror fan will likely find engaging and heartbreaking...even if that heart is thumping beneath the floor.

SOUTH KOREAN FILM SLEEP WEAVES SLEEP DISORDERS, MAGIC, & MARRIAGE IN HEARTFELT LOVE STORY: DEBUT FROM JASON YU EXPLORES HORRORS OF SLEEPWALKING

HOLLY LYN WALRATH

As someone with sleep paralysis, I'm fascinated (and justifiably creeped) by horror about sleepwalking. What most films don't capture is how easily lulled those around you are by the phenomenon. Most of the time, it barely impacts them. But for the few who have a terrifying story of sleepwalking gone wrong, it can haunt your life forever.

Jason Yu, South Korean director of *Sleep*— wanted to explore just that. "Everyone has a morbid tale of a sleepwalker," he told audiences at Fantastic Fest. "This was me wanting to make a fun genre film." And as a feature debut, the horror/love story does just that.

What makes *Sleep* so convincing is the two leads—Jung Yu-mi as Soo-jin

Lee Sun-kyun as Hyeon-soo—who portray a couple dealing with the husband's sleep disorder but refuse to give up. When Hyeon-soo starts to have more and more dangerous sleep behavior, the couple has to decide how to deal with it.

Hung on the wall of the couple's apartment is a sign that translates essentially to "everything together." And that's essentially marriage. There comes a point in every marriage where you can choose to stay or choose to go. Successful marriages stick it out, no matter how horrific things get—for better or worse. Soo-jin is, as some women may feel, a wife living with two men.

When the couple's baby is born, things reach a new height of urgency. The intimacy between the two actors entrances on screen. While movies about marriage can feel dull, *Sleep* manages to make every scene—no matter how sweet and silly— fascinating to watch. Director Jason Yu commented that the two actors were his first choices, "like winning the lotto twice." As Yu notes, "the easiest acting is conflict but pretending you've loved each other for years and years as a married couple is harder." This chemistry is no doubt helped by the fact that the two have been in four movies together so far.

The addition of South Korean myths and spirit magic give the film a necessary mystery and speculative element. It's horror elements—from loud jump scares at precise moments to having its lead actor eat raw meat (something that Yu was afraid to do because of how respected Lee Sun-kyun is) are just the right amount of unsettling.

My favorite part of the film was that it got sleep disorders right. So many of the scenes in the movie draw on real-life problems sleepwalkers face. Sleepwalking can be very scary in real-life, and it can also be hilarious. *Sleep* does a fantastic job of melding those two truths.

Sleep is a satisfying watch, blending South Korean speculative elements with the universal fear of sleepwalking. And the best part is, the ending is spot-on. As Jason Yu says, he believes in "the power of love to save the day." It's nice to see a film choose a positive message, while still giving some delightful scares.

THE CREATOR PROPS UP HYPER-OPTIMISM WITH GORGEOUS VISUALS: BUT DOES IT SUCCEED?: GARETH EDWARDS' NEW SF FLICK MAY LEAVE A BAD TASTE IN THE MOUTH OF THOSE WORRIED ABOUT AI

HOLLY LYN WALRATH

META debuted its chat AI in September of 2023, bringing AI to social media in an entirely new way. The database "books3" used to train AI recently had its list of books revealed, leading to loaded discussions online about AI and plagiarism. US funding for AI hit 3.3 billion in 2022 alone. These are just a few of the news items surrounding the controversial topic of AI—the center theme in Gareth Edwards' (*Rogue One*) new film.

It took Edwards seven years to make his first original film after the sleeper hit of *Rogue One,* which I don't think anyone expected to become the beloved classic it has. So, it's no surprise that the film's take on AI is going to be different, considering how much the landscape has changed.

The Creator is told in chapters and follows the story of Joshua (John David Washington), who is undercover in a war of humans vs. AI, searching for the Creator, the supposed architect of AI. While on a mission, his wife (Gemma Chan) disappears. Years later, Joshua is conscripted to find a secret weapon the Creator built that has the power to change the future. The weapon turns out to be a child (Madelein Yuna Voyles).

Most of the film takes place in the future Southeast Asia, which is a satisfying change of scenery when most sci-fi films take place in the US or UK. The setting lends itself to metaphor, giving the conflict of the film the opportunity to be compared to the Vietnam War. And like most Vietnam War films, the US soldiers are decidedly horrific in their actions.

There's no doubt that the film is a visual delight to watch. Production designer James Clyne (*Avatar, Solo, Star Trek 2009*) does a fantastic job dreaming up a believable cinematic universe that feels real. It's part *Blade Runner,* part *Apocalypse Now.*

The Creator was filmed in the same way as Gareth Edwards' first film, *Monsters*, reverse-engineered by shooting scenes without a set and letting production design work happen after the shooting was done. The film was shot using a Sony FX3 camera, which runs for just under $4k.

On a storytelling level, the film doesn't cover much new ground in terms of sci-fi tropes. The father and daughter escape plot works well to build emotional resonance. Gemma Chan makes a lovely love interest but is criminally underutilized (more on that later). Americans are bad. War is bad. Survival is violence.

What surprises is the story's optimism about AI, skating over any potential problems therein by envisioning AI who are cuddly teddy bears who just want to protect humans, be Buddhist monks, and live in peace. Humanity (well, the non-US Part) even rallies around the AI in the end.

This "AI is all-good" approach lands awkwardly in today's landscape. The film casts all of the AI as Asian characters, which will probably induce not a small amount of discomfort in viewers. In an interview with HeyUGuys on YouTube, Gareth Edwards talks about this choice:

"Originally, AI was used as a metaphor in science fiction for people who were different. It was more like a fairy tale. But then, when you research AI there are fascinating philosophical questions that come up that really start to worry you about them being real and turning them off and what if they don't do what you want. The movie became more about that. Now watching it...I was like, Oh my god, this is really on the money with what's happening right now in terms of this fear of AI, and is it bad, and should we get rid of it. I'm actually quite optimistic. I think we're going to have some bumps in the road but I think AI is going to be an incredible tool." (Gareth Edwards Interview, HeyUGuys)

This isn't to say the film's positive message is bad—it just comes across unclear —and that may be simply due to the current landscape surrounding AI. It was difficult to discern how to feel about the AI in the film. Without a K-2SO style robot for audiences to latch onto and love, the message gets muddled.

One last irk is that the film's emotional journey centers heavily on the death of Joshua's wife. Her death serves as a catalyst for the character, and it's a shame we don't get to see her have more agency. Most of the women in the film die, are villains, or are emotional pawns for the main male character.

The Creator is a delight to watch, but for me, it didn't live up to *Rogue One*. And I'm fine with that because I want more movies like this. Give me more sci-fi—of all kinds—with unique, diverse settings, and phenomenal visual design.

A SHADOW OF REINCARNATION IN A SOLARPUNK WORLD: REVIEW OF ANOTHER LIFE BY SARENA ULIBARRI

MEGAN WEGENKE

"Is it possible to trust any of the good you've tried to do, when you can't disentangle your own legacy from the worst excesses of a broken world?"

Another Life by Sarena Ulibarri, a novella from *Stelliform Press,* wastes little time in setting up a bold premise: How would your life change if you received absolute proof that you were the reincarnation of one of history's greatest monsters?

Ulibarri takes us to a post-industrial solarpunk world where people have banded together to adapt to climate change, then introduces a wilder sci-fi concept—absolute scientific proof of reincarnation. At first glance, those concepts might seem to have little to do with each other, but Ulibarri wields the idea of reincarnation like a scalpel taken to the root of utopia. In the process, the book's central question emerges, one that rings with plenty of relevance here in the 2020s: Is it possible to trust any of the good you've tried to do when you can't disentangle your own legacy from the worst excesses of a broken world?

The novella is set in a near future after the United States has been broken up by decades of climate disaster and corporate greed. The story follows Galacia Aguirre, a co-founder of Otra Vida, a self-sustaining commune built in a flooded Death Valley. Galacia is proud of the community she's helped to build and largely content with her life. She'd be happy to focus on day-to-day concerns, like her campaign for reelection as Otra Vida's conflict mediator.

But everything changes when one of Otra Vida's residents invents a process that can show people their past lives. Galacia learns that she's the reincarnation of Thomas Ramsey, the morally bankrupt tech billionaire whose actions ignited the destruction of the old world. As Galacia deals with external threats and desperately tries to keep the rest of Otra Vida from finding out about her past life, she struggles even harder to find answers about what this news means for her own understanding of herself.

Galacia's existential crisis following the Thomas Ramsey revelation forms the main spine of the plot, but as the book went on, I found myself echoing her desire to get back to everyday life in Otra Vida. The worldbuilding that Ulibarri puts into this scrappy, homemade community is well-textured, from its elaborate sunshades to its vertical farms. It feels like a plausible, lived-in future built on plenty of real ideas about eco-friendly and anticapitalist community building. A subplot about how the community is evolving—the founders who fought to establish it reluctantly ceding ground to a new generation that's never known another way of life—is one of the most emotionally compelling threads in the book.

In contrast, however, the "scientific proof of reincarnation" plot element is an awkward fit. In a story so concerned with how societies function, the concept of people being able to discover their past lives with all the simplicity of taking a DNA test feels like it should carry far more massive ramifications. A discovery like this would inspire skepticism, debate, and existential dread, challenging religious doctrines and people's fundamental senses of self. It's a narrative black hole, warping everyone's lives out of shape with its gravity—or it should be.

All of these implications are gestured at in dialogue but otherwise mostly left unexplored. As a result, the reincarnation comes off more as a narrative shortcut to the book's themes than as something organically a part of this world. How the people of Otra Vida react to this technology often feel a bit too easy, taking things at face value that should be wildly complicated in practice. (There are some especially notable missed opportunities here—there's a trans supporting character, for instance, but the book never really asks what having access to past lives might mean for his self-concept in particular.)

As Galacia struggles with the idea that she still "is" Thomas Ramsey, it becomes clear what the reincarnation plotline is doing. It's about reckoning with the guilt inherent in inheriting a poisoned legacy and asking whether escaping that shadow is possible. But I kept asking myself: was such a distractingly enormous what-if actually necessary for the story that *Another Life* is trying to tell? Or would the book still mostly work the same way if Galacia had turned out to secretly be Ramsey's daughter or an inheritor of his legacy in some other mundane way?

Although they're granted plenty of page space, *Another Life* is really not *about* Galacia and Ramsey in particular. Its themes are built on using them as shorthand for the triumphs and failures of their respective societies—the excesses of the old world versus the fragile hope of Otra Vida. In that respect, the book succeeds in telling a resonant story for our present, where climate destruction and corporate overreach offer plenty of reasons to ask if a better world is possible. The book works best when it's operating on this community-scale level, exploring the complications in a utopian community building itself out of the wreckage of an awful past.

Another Life picks a roundabout way to get to that destination and in the process, opens a lot of doors it's not actually planning to walk through. The result is ramshackle but well-intentioned: much like Otra Vida, it's prone to offshoots and false starts but eventually gets where it wants to go.

Although most of the book's characters treat the disclosure of past lives with deadly seriousness at first, they eventually conclude that a monstrous legacy is unimportant compared to what one chooses to do in the present. *Another Life*, similarly, is most vibrant when it's fully immersed in its own present, observing the quietly radical texture of life in Otra Vida. The more it gets tangled in questions of reincarnation, the more it loses its sense of easy confidence. I'd love to read more works from Ulibarri with this kind of setting if ideally in a mode less beholden to the past: *Another Life,* on many levels, makes the case that life is better lived facing forward.

THERE'S SOMETHING FAMILIAR ABOUT *THERE'S SOMETHING IN THE BARN*: NORWEGIAN HOLIDAY HORROR COMEDY IS *NATIONAL LAMPOON'S* MEETS *GREMLINS*

PATRICK BARB

Fantastic Fest-offering *There's Something in the Barn* is a Christmas movie. Let's get that out of the way first. The holiday season is a time associated with tradition, ritual, and observing customs—no matter how strange or outdated they might seem (honestly, *who's* still drinking that much milk and at night no less???). With this new holiday horror-comedy, writer Aleksander R. Kirkwood Brown, director Magnus Martens, and star/producer Martin Starr (of *Freaks and Geeks* and *Silicon Valley* fame) draw from a surprisingly deep well of past examples in this slice-of-a-slice subgenre, paying homage to what's come before while still managing to leave viewers with an enjoyable movie-watching experience all on its own. Not only does the form fit the traditional mode, but the thematic elements are intrinsically tied to questions on the nature of tradition: is it good? is it bad? will it leave you set on fire or stabbed through the eye with an icicle?

Playing against his usual sardonic type, Starr is Bill, the patriarch of an American family in the Griswold mold who have just inherited a home in the Norwegian countryside. With two kids (the younger son who's more open-minded to their new spacious living quarters and the teenage daughter frustrated by the fact that even her internet connection gets frozen in this middle-of-nowhere locale) and his new(er) wife (the kids' stepmom) who is a self-help guru promoting her "Happy-Vision" lifestyle brand (Amitra Acharia deftly handling a role that's not always a sympathetic one), Bill is desperate to find acceptance but finds it hard to break through with the local Norwegians who seem to view the family as your typical ignorant Americans bumbling about and screwing things up.

Of course, Bill and company don't do themselves any favors when they upset a moose or mangle the language. It soon seems clear that no matter how often Bill wears a woolen cap with the word NORWAY on it in big letters, he and his family won't ever fit in. Even without being blatantly obnoxious, their American mannerisms are simply too bold, too flashy, too much everything for the local populace. And that's especially true of the barn elf living in the old, dilapidated barn on the land that the family inherited.

Bill and his wife Carol (yes, it's a Christmas movie with a character named Carol) have plans to convert the old barn into a bed and breakfast. They're ignorant of the elf who calls the barn home and who would very much like to keep things exactly as they've always been. From a certain perspective, viewers are watching an attempted gentrification taking place, with the local community resisting efforts to have the shabby chic, farmhouse American one-size-fits-all decorating style imposed on them. Or, as the local sheriff tells the family when she rescues them from a would-be moose attack: "If you mess with nature, nature will come right back and punch you in your faces."

As it turns out, what's true for the natural world also holds for the supernatural world. Once son Lucas (Townes Bunner) meets the barn elf (Kiran Shah in a surprisingly layered and nuanced performance), the movie shifts from the more broadly comedic traditions of *National Lampoon's*, to a *Gremlins*-style Christmas horror-comedy. Lucas soon consults a local museum owner well-versed in the barn elf lore who lays out the rules for successful co-existence with the mythical being. "No loud noises, no bright lights, no changes." The rules and accompanying scenes where they are stressed and re-stressed, but fall on deaf ears, are very reminiscent of the way that rules for keeping a Mogwai in *Gremlins* are treated. Indeed, the family's barn elf forms an Amblin-style bond with Lucas, akin to E.T. or Gizmo with their young humans. The thing to remember here is that this tiny creature has already killed at least once and seems more than willing to kill again.

While Lucas makes tiny inroads with the creature, resulting in a shoveled driveway and chopped firewood for the family, no one else seems to take his assertions of the barn elf's existence seriously. The rules are soon flouted, not just by the Americans but also by Norwegians (who prove more than willing to let their guards down with the outsiders once copious amounts of alcohol are introduced to the equation). As the family strings up lights, throws a loud, noisy Christmas party, and re-decorates the barn, the elf's displeasure and thirst for vengeance grows. When bumbling Bill eats the peace-offering porridge that his son intended to share with the elf to smooth over relations, the time for negotiating comes to a swift end. Not only does the barn elf want revenge, but he's also willing to call in back-up from other elves to help him achieve that goal.

The final part of the movie has the family of four coming together, learning to accept and forgive each other, and fighting back against the elvish threat. If you're worried about spoilers here, don't be. Recall that this is a movie tied to tradition, and letting these familiar beats play out is yet another nod to that thematic element.

Interestingly enough, the overall message of the film does not seem to advocate for blindly following tradition in order to remain safe and secure. While the family's deviations from customs do move them into hot water, one gets the sense that this behavior isn't viewed as 100% bad. When the other elves begin drinking, breaking things, and playing their own loud music (and shooting a gun), the family's barn elf seems to find fault with this apparent hypocrisy from his fellow elves.

Is there a happy medium between tradition and change? The creators of THERE'S SOMETHING IN THE BARN sure seem to think so. Their film follows in the bloody snow-covered footsteps of other holiday horror-comedy fare while still providing something new and enjoyable for viewers.

INTERVIEWS

MOVING WITH A MONUMENT: ART, ARCHAEOLOGY, AND ARTIFICIAL INTELLIGENCE, RESEARCH QUESTIONS AND PROJECT BEGINNINGS

T.D. WALKER

INTERVIEW WITH ROBOTICIST DANIEL WILLIAMS AND MASTER CRAFTSPERSON JUSTIN GREEN, COLLABORATORS ON SACRFICE: CAN YOU TRUST A STONE? AT THE UNIVERSITY OF MELBOURNE.

More and more, we interact with artificial intelligence online. For good reason, most of us are wary of those interactions. We may wonder what will come of our data, our interactions, or our creations. We may wonder whether we can believe what information we receive from AI, given its issues with "hallucination" and biases. Now, imagine those interactions in physical space. Such concrete and corporeal engagement with AI raises more questions about our trust in technology. T.D. Walker spoke with roboticist Daniel Williams and master craftsperson Justin Green, collaborators on *SACRFICE: Can you trust a stone?* at the University of Melbourne.

Interstellar Flight Press: *SACRIFICE* is both art exhibit and research project, in which audience members interacted with a robot swarm of standing stones controlled by AI when it was exhibited at the Melbourne Science Gallery in 2022.

AI is so much in public discourse right now, and there is much debate about the ways in which we can and should interact with the

technologies based on AI. Why did you choose the immersive standing stones as a point of interaction with the audience? And why situate the piece in place, rather than in an online medium, which is where we're most used to interacting with AI-based technologies at present?

Daniel Williams and Justin Green: We have been guided by the idea that to understand the present, we must look to the past. The origins of this project lie in a formative series of meetings during 2020 involving our directors, Dr. Robert Walton and A/Prof Airlie Chapman, which sought to explore the potential for interdisciplinary research at the University of Melbourne. While that earlier research commission didn't get off the ground, the relationships that consequently developed between our respective research groups motivated further discussions. Robert was particularly fascinated by the protocols and performative elements inherent within interactive technologies, while Airlie's research group was looking for an opportunity to study human engagement with co-located robots. At the intersection of our interests, we saw an opening for novel research collaboration.

Having established that we wanted to study how people might interact with robots, we looked to other technologies that had a more established track record in public consciousness. Moving from the modern, emerging technologies entailed by robotics engineering as a discipline, we shifted our focus to the older philosophical concept of technē and how this has historically manifested in civilizations across the world. This prompted us to reach out to archeologist Dr. Aleksandra 'Aleks' Michałewicz, who guided us toward the phenomenon of monoliths. Throughout history, standing stones have been installed on all inhabited continents. Some of these monoliths are associated with traditions and rituals that have been passed down over generations; hence, it is quite straightforward to ask local people about their relationships with the monoliths. Unfortunately, other monoliths have been orphaned from the cultures that made them, hindering our efforts to accurately understand their origins. There has been speculation that standing stones may have played roles in the astronomical reckoning of time and in preserving the memory of historically significant figures. We were intrigued by how these two functions were fundamentally tied to the passage of time and helped earlier societies negotiate transient concepts of self and identity. With this ancient technology as a starting point, we deliberated about creating a participatory experience that would similarly elicit reflections on our definitions and perceptions of time and their interplay in defining a sense of self.

To maintain continuity with the experience of visiting standing stones while also transcending the monoliths' geographic dispersal, we discussed various potential settings for the experience. We settled on a gallery space as one that would not likely overwhelm participants (unlike our laboratory space) but would allow them to freely interact with the standing stones of their own accord. Given how central an embodied presence appears to have been when engaging with many monoliths around the world, we wanted to ensure that participants could feel tangibly and personally immersed in the interactions. The same level of engagement would not have been possible in a purely virtual format, however, we remain interested in integrating augmented and virtual reality into the experience.

IFP: Standing stones connect us to both the natural world and its cycles as well as to the people who observed and engaged deeply with it. It's hard not to feel awe in the presence of the stones as they are in their environments. That said, there might also be a sense of being removed or disconnected from the world and its cycles as we spend so much of our time engaged with technology.

Why did you choose the standing stone as the shape (or maybe the "face") of the robot swarm with which the audience would interact? And what were some of your considerations going in when you selected the stones represented in the exhibit?

DW & JG: From the beginning, we have been keenly aware of the unease that humans may feel in the presence of an entity whose behaviors they may not be able to understand or explain. For humanoid robots, this unease has been characterized by the 'uncanny valley' phenomenon; however, it has been studied less with robots of other forms. Since we envisioned bringing participants into contact with an autonomous swarm of robots, it was therefore important that we design an appearance that would not heighten any fears of automation. Considering the extensive and enduring relationships cultivated between standing stones and their custodial societies, we thought that giving the swarm agents a monolithic appearance would allow participants to feel more at ease and form quasi-social relationships with the swarm.

Through the use of "stonelike" shapes, we also hoped to employ the power of their monolithic appearance to transform participants' instinctual feelings of unease into a profound sense of awe. This transformative experience would provide us with a means to delve deeper into the phenomenological aspects of the interaction, exploring the intricate and complex nature of our collaboration with objects that may behave in unexpected ways. By embracing the concept of monolithic reckoning and time, we encourage the participants to explore new pathways for understanding and interacting with the AI and gain a deeper appreciation for how embracing an unfamiliar experience of space and time can allow us to collaborate in unexpected ways.

The process of gathering a swarm of standing stones itself was a transnational endeavor. Assisted by our colleague Tom Keep, Aleks contacted several peer researchers at overseas institutions who had documented standing stone sites in their respective countries. Drawing on state-of-the-art digital archeology techniques, Tom devised a simple procedure for collecting photographs of standing stones from different angles and then constructing the corresponding vectorized photogrammetric models. Then, our fabricator colleague Justin Green used these models to create lightweight carapaces through a combination of scenographic fabricating techniques. Finally, our theatrical practitioner colleagues Robert and Goran Đurić then assembled the final swarm by determining production quantities for each type of stone. Due to space constraints, we elected to have more smaller-sized stones while retaining a few of the medium-sized and human-sized stones to give the stone swarm a sense of mass.

IFP: In the abstract to your presentation on the project for the 2021 Computer Applications & Quantitative Methods in Archaeology, you write: "An interdisciplinary research project guided by archaeology, robotics, and theatre, SACRIFICE seeks to engage the public in an immersive performance art experience."

Your team includes researchers working in the fields of archaeology, robotics, AI, and art. In the CAA Australasia presentation, you note that part of this project was to investigate what the boundaries of academic disciplines are.

Why go with an interdisciplinary team, and what research questions did each field bring to the project? And how did those questions overlap?

DW & JG: We have found that staying within an academic discipline inherently constricts what we as practitioners can observe and analyze, simply because a discipline is by definition bound by common modes of thinking, domain vocabularies, and agreed methodologies. We recognized the limitations of prioritizing one mode of knowledge over all others, as illustrated by the idiom "if you're a hammer, all you see are nails", as well as the ancient Indian parable of the blind men and the elephant. SACRIFICE, being a multifaceted project, demanded a profound level of expertise and comprehension within a wide spectrum of domains. We firmly believe that constraining ourselves to a single discipline's viewpoint would inevitably restrict our capability to comprehensively accomplish the project. We wished to develop a more nuanced understanding of how people interact with robotic swarms by asking open-ended questions and then delving into our different disciplines to combine relevant prior knowledge. The team is sustained by a mutual curiosity and admiration for each other's work, the borrowing of language and concepts to augment one's own discipline, and an excitement about applying our expertise in an area outside of our disciplines' traditional purviews.

The overlaps between our respective areas would be considered marginal to more conventional topics of research in our disciplines. Nevertheless, we have found that these grey areas contain questions that have needed to be discussed. For example, the stone robots' appearances have been decided by reconciling the archeologists' photogrammetric data with the techniques and materials available to our fabricator. The dramatic structuring of the performance art experience has been formulated as a finite state machine (a theoretical construct originating in electrical engineering and computer science), with environmental cues and external prompts translated into code by the roboticists and fine-tuned by the theatrical practitioners. In addition, we have sought to analyze the dynamics of trust between human visitors and the stone-robot swarm using system block diagrams. Even though there may be potholes in between our respective disciplines, we have found ways to communicate the intuitions of our questions in order to solicit the perspectives of our colleagues.

IFP: One of the most contentious aspects of AI is whether or not we should trust the technology itself, the uses of the data it gathers, the output, and the uses of this output.

Certainly, in the world of literature where I'm situated, this is the case. We see writers submitting poems written by AI online, and editors are seeing an increase in submissions that are generated by or rely on AI, and readers are left wondering whether what they're reading comes from some human source or if it's just the resulting output from whatever data was used to feed the AI.

To a larger fear, there's also the question of negative outcomes from AI, ranging from social harms through reflected biases to physical harms through human/robot interactions.

Since trust was central to this project, how did you go in from the beginning thinking about trust? And how did the different fields address this?

DW & JG: It is true that we as a society have begun to worry about autonomous systems and growing dependency on these entities (cf. human-AI relations in the 2008 film 'Wall-E'). An unspoken assumption underlying this dependency is that it arises when a human works with an autonomous system to achieve an objective, but must delegate some of that power to the autonomous system due to necessity (e.g., autopilot takeover due to human fatigue). Echoing the notion of trust in social psychology, this delegation of power creates a trust dynamic between the trustor (the human) and the trustee (the autonomous system). In this project, we wanted to explore other types of scenarios in which there were no explicit task objectives. Would humans still treat an autonomous system like a trustee in more open-ended and less structured interactions?

To address this question, we needed to shift our focus from a result-oriented paradigm toward the process itself. In doing so, we found ourselves drawn to contemplative studies when considering the subjective experience of humans. We wanted to design interactions that would encourage perceptions of safety and trust in the autonomous system. We realized that we could not achieve this with robotics alone, so we returned to the idea that crafted stone embodies a universal expression of human ingenuity and asked whether we could associate the trust placed in ancient monoliths with robotics. The perceived conflicts and similarities between the two technologies—their respective forms (motionless, mobile), timescales (civilizational eras v nanoseconds), and purposes (calendrical, memorial, computational)—are foundational to this investigation. We, therefore, sought to push visitors into the liminal spaces raised by these issues in order to reckon with them. We have not prescribed how visitors are to respond to the experience, however we have intentionally sought to create a foil that can prompt reflections on the interconnectedness of modern society's industrialized relationship with time, a sense of loneliness due to time pressures, and atrophy of trust in one's social network. As an Australian-based project, we felt strongly that some of our stone representations should come from a local site of significance. Being based on Country cared for by the Kulin Nations, the project consulted with Elders of the Wurundjeri Nation. While in discussions with the Elders, we explained that the project was titled Sacrifice because the participants would be asked to sacrifice time in front of the stones before they could draw a response from them.

This both puzzled and amused the Elders. They explained to us that the giving of time to Country was not a sacrifice; it was both a necessity and a joy. Time spent on and with Country is repaid with knowledge and understanding of both ourselves and our surroundings. The stones are not a conduit for experience to pass through but a way of connecting ourselves directly to the land and all it brings. The project title 'Sacrifice' would suggest that this very process of reflection might require us to find a compromise with older modes of knowledge in order to find better ways of living.

Interstellar Flight Press: Let's talk now about the technical implementation of the *SACRIFICE*. Initially, the team had planned to create the stones through 3-D printing, but then decided to go with theatrical fabrication to make the stones more similar to the textures people would encounter on the original standing stones.

What did that fabrication process entail? And since you moved from a more hands-off method of creating the stones to a more hands-on

method that more closely paralleled the original stones' creations, did that change how you saw the stones? Or how you wanted the exhibit visitors to see the stones?

DW & JG: During testing, while Justin found it would be technically feasible to create highly accurate replicas of the original stones using three-dimensional printing, due to the scale of the stones, it was not only far more labor-intensive than fabricating them using traditional scenographic realisation techniques but also would be considerably heavier. Archeologically, it was also felt that block printing the stones could trivialise the intent and craftsmanship that produced each of these monoliths in their original form.

Our archaeological data suggests that the "rocklike" appearance has a profound effect on people. This design characteristic can be intuitively felt and recognized without needing direct contact with the surface of the stone. Therefore, our design mandate is to fabricate the stone in a way that clearly highlights these intuitive design characteristics.

Parallel to this aesthetic consideration were the practical needs of the robots themselves. As it was always our intent to represent a megalithic experience; providing this size whilst facilitating the weight and stability requirements of the drones mandated a strong subframe and skin that would provide a rigid surface for our rocklike finish but was also light enough to allow the drone the free and full movement required to fulfil their algorithmic paths.

Through testing, Justin established that the best solution was a substrate of cardboard covered with paper-mâché clay, from which the stones would derive their rigidity. To achieve our "rocklike" appearance, each piece, or carapace, was treated with specific scenic techniques to match its geological and archaeological characteristics. Expanding foams were used for igneous surfaces, and sand and particulars were added to the clay to create sedimentary layers, while resin and texture mediums created smooth, polished surfaces. Upon completion, our largest stone stood approximately 2.5 meters tall and weighed just over 8kgs.

In such an intensely interactive piece, the tactile nature of the stones needed to match or exceed the expectations projected by their appearance. Here the calcium carbonate, a key component of paper-mâché clay, brought our making process full circle as our rock carapaces were literally made of limestone. Not only did this allow us to recreate the aesthetic characteristics of a "rocklike" appearance, but it also provided an excellent platform to build a similar response to the tactile nature of our carapaces.

To further the audience's engagement with the stones, the participants were gifted a real stone to handle and carry with them into the space. From a realisation perspective, this served two purposes; firstly, the stones were of a size and heft, not be easily held in one hand for long periods, thus limiting the amount of time they would maintain contact with our carapaces. Secondly, the stones served as a tactile reminder of the qualities they should expect upon touching our carapaces. By choosing rocks with a similar “feel” to our carapaces, we were able to prime the participant’s response to the stones, allowing them to accept our stones for what they appeared to be and move wholly forward into the archaeological and theatrical elements of the performance.

IFP: How did you integrate the fabricated stones with the robots that enable the stones’ movements? What challenges did you face when bringing these two pieces together?

How did you integrate both the technical elements with your research questions across the team’s various academic disciplines?

DW & JG: There were certainly challenges in bringing the two components together, both mechanical and electrical. First, we made sure to standardize the mechanical coupling between the robots’ frames and the structures underlying each shell. This was another advantage to using a scenographic build method as it allowed us to incorporate a generic baseplate into each carapace and then sculpt freely, with the confidence that each base was engineered to fit our drones regardless of the carapace shape. Second, we drilled recesses into the shells to create attachment points for motion capture markers. For the sake of rapid prototyping, we initially used plastic marker beads, however, due to unreliable lighting conditions interfering with their detection we decided to install infrared LEDs as active markers. Of course, there have been numerous iterations of debugging communications between the motion capture system, the software controller for the swarm and the headphones worn by visitors, however, this has created a minimal working example with which we have been able to work. We have really only scratched the surface when it comes to studying changes in the swarm’s form (including size, number, appearance, and behavior) and how they impact visitors’ impressions of the gallery experience.

IFP: In your video presentation for the CAA Australasia Digital Archaeology Conference, you outline how you would study trust through visitors’ interactions with the stones by surveys as well as cameras that follow where visitors moved in relation to the stones and where they focused their gaze while in the exhibit.

What was your process for implementing this? How did you analyze the data that you gathered? And were there particular challenges in gathering that data?

DW & JG: The temporary installation of a system of motion capture cameras in the gallery space allowed us to track the positions and orientations of objects in the space. By placing markers on both the stone shells and the visitor's headphones, we were able to relay their positions back to a data-logging computer. In addition to this physical data, we asked visitors to complete pre- and post-experience surveys in order to ascertain visitors' familiarity with robot swarms, their general level of trust in technology, and their mental state. When formulating the survey questions, we sought to get as much detail from respondents while reducing the time overhead to get more visitors through the exhibit in the limited hours available to us. The data that we were able to collect has allowed us to profile how visitor engagement responds to variations in the stone-robots' behaviors, however, in future work we are interested in modeling the relationship between macro-level swarm behaviors and visitors' innate levels of trust in the swarm over time.

IFP: Trust is something you mention not only in terms of the individual humans interacting directly with the robot stone swarm but also with the people worldwide with which you collaborated. *SACRIFICE* includes standing sites from culturally-significant sites around the world.

I'd like to go back to the concerns with AI incorporating creators' work without their consent. Even though the stones your team used were carefully chosen for the project with consent, there's still that association with the uses of cultural artifacts integrated with technologies.

With so many issues about unethical use of art, literature, and artifacts part of the larger conversation around the creation and consumption of art, what questions do you think we should ask about AI-generated or AI-enhanced cultural objects? How does trust work not only with originating cultures but with the broader audience outside those cultures? And how did you address that cultural sense of trust while working on *SACRIFICE*?

DW & JG: It is important to point out that technology and objects of cultural significance are not mutually exclusive and the ethical problems with AI-generated or AI-enhanced art predate the advent of specific AI technologies as they are closely bound to longstanding problems with plagiarism, cultural appropriation, and representation in artistic depiction. With respect to our project, there were many potential issues that we contemplated.

Our consultations with Wurundjeri Elders about using stones from the local area prompted us to consider the specific cultural considerations our stones. Among the Kulin Nations, by accepting Wominjeka (an invitation to come with purpose), you make dhumbali (promise/commitment) to Bundjil and the land of that Kulin Nation. The first dhumbali, is to obey the ngarn-ga (understandings) of Bundjil. The second dhumbali, is to not harm the bubups (children). The third is not to harm the biik biik (land) and wurneet (waterways) of Bundjil. The stones are a part of Country. They are a fundamental part of the biik biik. By replicating them outside of Country, we remove them from the land, in essence we are taking them out of Country and that could harm biik biik, breaking the laws of Bundjil. Whilst the Elders were happy for us to use stones from Kulin land, to keep with Bundjil's law they would need to be altered so they ceased to be part of Country.

This led us to consider the practice of deliberate imperfection. Just as the Kulin people pay respect to Bundjil the creator, Catholic stone masons, Quaker cabinet makers and Amish quilters' all use the inclusion of a deliberate mistake to convey human fallibility. Only God(s) are perfect. We determined that we also carried an obligation to the sites of significance we were representing to introduce deliberate flaws in our representations to preserve the sanctity and individual uniqueness of those stones in context with their original sites.

Regarding AI-driven tools for generating cultural output, access to these tools is currently uneven and heavily determined by one's level of education, socioeconomic status, and the economic development of one's country. There is also an iniquity in the distribution of influence over the development of these tools. Coders and those who harvest data en-masse for model training have great influence over the model's output by the design and selection choices that they make, whether deliberately or unconsciously. These can then reproduce existing societal biases, cf. the discussion of the New Jim Code in Prof. Ruha Benjamin's 2019 book "Race after Technology". The expanded reach of such tools into more aspects of our lives, combined with a historical lack of guidance and regulation of their development, has created a crisis of faith in the benevolence of AI's trajectory. Perhaps we will need something analogous to Rotary's Four-Way Test ("Is it the truth? Is it fair to all concerned? Will it build goodwill and better friendships? Will it be beneficial to all concerned?") to ensure that ethical considerations are embedded into the global culture of AI development. In this project however, we have attempted to move away from a model of mass data harvesting towards cultivating a relationship between the individual and technology.

Another area of overlap between the AI/ML community and the art world concerns the use of others' intellectual property. In the former domain content creators whose works are scraped by web crawling scripts rarely receive remuneration or give their consent to such use of their intellectual property. This echoes the practice of factories that mass-produce artworks with the esthetics of Indigenous art without consulting Indigenous artists on how their cultural patrimony is exploited. The commodification of cultural expression in this way reflects an enduring ars nullius mindset, even as the parallel concept of terra nullius has gradually been dismantled in places with settler-colonial histories (e.g. Australia and the United States). Such a mindset has provided a fig leaf for cultural institutions in the global North to justify their retention of cultural artefacts looted from the global South: just consider the patronizing, anachronistically colonial responses of the British Museum towards calls for repatriating the Benin Bronzes, the Parthenon Marbles and other looted antiquities, even as it can no longer be trusted to guarantee its own collections' security.

Hearteningly, recent developments in technology have reclaimed some power for cultural custodians. For example, in parallel with Greek efforts to repatriate the stolen Parthenon Marbles, activists recently attempted to conduct photogrammetry in the gallery housing the Marbles with sub-millimetre accuracy in order to create ultra-realistic reproductions. Tellingly, officials at the British Museum sought to shut down this work for fear of setting a precedent: Heaven forbid the rightful culture owners get their hands on a convincing replica. Similarly, the Digital Benin database brings together records of all the Benin Bronzes known to have been looted by the British, while negotiations with European and American collections continue for restituting the looted Bronzes to Nigeria.

In our project, we were mindful of the potential for imbalanced power dynamics in our collaborations from the outset and did not want to keep perpetuating a transactional and unidirectional mode of academic exchange. In sharing best practices for photogrammetrically documenting cultural heritage with our research partners, we have enabled our partners to use these skills as they see fit. We are indeed fortunate that they have chosen to entrust us with scanned copies of the monoliths with us, and that they continue to endorse the direction of our project.

Interstellar Flight Press: To return to the initial questions that drove the project, you mention in the conference video the current state of and potential for human/robot swarm interactions in public, such as in the workplace.

Your team has taken the research from the psychology lab to the art gallery. Art makes us pay attention and makes the familiar unfamiliar. Through art, we see the world differently.

And yet, we're also at a place where we'll need to see the normalcy and perhaps even some comfort in robot swarms. So why did you choose to display *SACRIFICE* as a performance art piece at a gallery? And do you plan to continue your research in such venues?

DW & JG: As Jaques stated in William Shakespeare's "As You Like It", all the world's a stage, especially when it comes to the social interactions that play out between us in daily life. To understand how these interactions will look in more holistic and naturalistic environments, we will increasingly need to leave the laboratory setting and go out into places where people may conceivably interact with autonomous robots. Inspired by the work of practitioners such as Prof. Dana Kulić, we believe that a gallery setting offers hitherto untapped opportunities for eliciting and studying spontaneous interactions between humans and robotic systems. We are planning on continuing our investigations in this context as the field continues to unfold.

IFP: Sacrifice is a name that creates tension with the idea of trust, as you mention in the conference video. I'm curious about how your audience at the 2022 exhibition of the work reacted to both the name of the piece as well as to the experience of it?

DW & JG: We found that our visitors were rather adept at articulating their impressions of the exhibit, so we will let their comments speak for themselves.

• "I did not become a stone however I did become a Stone. The stones at the edge of the room sat there as stones usually do. The Stones in the middle of the room (after a brief period of me exploring the space) surrounded and followed me at just under arms length, moving when I did and staying still while I was."

• "Unexpectedly I felt very moved by the swarm of moving rocks. I felt delighted by the strength of feeling"

• "A simulation of trusting or connecting with something out of our control or something we don't fully understand."

• "I joined a community. A swarm of creatures who were connected in their lives for a short moment."

• "This was a VERY interesting experience. The darkness disoriented me, but also made me present in the moment. I had no expectations, but was open to the experience. It was like co-ordinate dancing. I had no idea that I would so much part of the group."

• "I chose to be an observer, watching someone else interact with the stones. If I had been in the circle I might have hugged a stone—to see how warm or welcoming they were."

• "It was a ritualised, contemplative place, like a church so i acted respectful. The stones moved a bit like pets so it also felt a little bit playful and i didnt know what would happen."

• "I started to interact with them and while part of me wandered, I felt increasingly pulled to them and getting more connected to them. For some bizarre reason I spontaneously bowed to them.."

• "It felt like we were moving in concert—a 'rock concert' ha ha—as if taking cues from each other as dance partners. Through such synchronised non-verbal communication in a ritual space, a sense of familiarity and belonging developed. Overall a safe, fun and kind experience, beyond projections of robots as avatars."

• "rocks formations tricking my eyes my minds high anthropo energy despite zero human presence in the space except for myself Machine zuuurrring slightly distracted but the space was open for me to walk away"

IFP: Blurring of boundaries is also central to this project. There's the boundary between disciplines, and the boundaries between human and robot interactions. You note that you want academics to think about strict boundaries (for instance, Dr. Michałewicz asked in the conference video about whether *SACRIFICE* qualifies as archaeology). What do you want for the public to consider about these academic boundaries?

And since *SACRIFICE* was exhibited in an art gallery, what boundaries should we as the public consider between ourselves and the world in light of our need to interact with AI-based technologies more and more often in the future?

DW & JG: This project is a genuine exploration of antidisciplinarity and the practical challenges of implementing it. As a guiding philosophy, 'antidisciplinarity' allows us to adopt wholeheartedly a project-led, exploratory, and non-hierarchical approach to radical collaboration. It helps us to challenge traditional disciplinary boundaries while also testing institutional limits. We continue to investigate our own involvement in the processes of building up and breaking down disciplinary siloes and to what extent these boundaries remain relevant for contemporary research activities, if at all.

Likewise, through this experience, the public is invited to reflect on the categorical walls that we build in our own lives and to explore the liminal spaces of knowledge ordinarily closed off by the heuristics we all develop for quickly reading the world. Perhaps, by breaking down disciplinary barriers and collaborating effectively with the stones, they will be able to see a way to navigate their own challenges and capitalize on any unforeseen opportunities or unexpected interactions that arise.

IFP: I'd like to end by asking what's next for the team as a whole and as individual researchers? Has *SACRIFICE* opened up new questions and new spaces for inquiry for you?

DW & JG: At this point in time, most of us are continuing to distill insights from the November experience for forthcoming academic publications. On an individual level, two of us are finishing our doctoral theses, one is halfway there, one has just begun his PhD, and two are early-career postdoctoral researchers. With the project having generated such a richness of material, there is no doubt that reflections on Sacrifice will make appearances in several different formats over the coming months and years. We have stuck together because we have found this project stimulating for our other research efforts and felt that we have grown together. We hope to continue through to a second outing of the exhibit locally in February 2024, with further iterations of the experience to follow.

IFP: I'd also like to ask where this research into trust has taken your team since the 2021 presentation? And has that idea of trust shifted and deepened for you as researchers as well as members of the broader community?

DW & JG: Undoubtedly our understandings of trust have evolved over the intervening two years. Part of this evolution can be attributed to the volume of knowledge that we have come across since then, reflecting an ongoing maturation of the literature surrounding concepts of trust in our respective fields. There is also much to be said for getting a first iteration of the project into the public sphere and reading visitors' impressions of their experiences with the swarm. Having demonstrated the relevance of a concept of trust in such situations, we are now seeking to elaborate on several attributes of trust, including how it forms, how it is lost, and its interrelation with environmental factors and other performative parameters. These insights are particularly pertinent to Daniel and Elena's efforts to mathematically model trust-motivated human interventions and trust profiles respectively.

IFP: Also, are there plans to exhibit Sacrifice elsewhere, given that there are Science Gallery locations in other countries? Or will you exhibit further pieces farther afield?

DW & JG: We certainly intend to refine the experience so that it can travel as a self-contained exhibit suitable for installation in other galleries. To this end we have engaged interested partners both domestically and overseas through the Science Gallery network. We hope to share exciting developments in due course, however in the meantime your readers may keep up to date by visiting our website at https://robertwalton.net/project/sacrifice/.

About the Project: Sacrifice is an intimate ceremony performed with an autonomous swarm of stone-robots. Part performance, part experiment, Sacrifice is the product of a radical collaboration between University of Melbourne theatre, robotics, and archaeology specialists that invites you to interact with ancient and emerging technologies of contemplation. This performance artwork combines emerging swarm robotics and artificial intelligence technologies with globally significant ancient standing stones. It was created by artist Robert Walton, roboticists Elena Vella, Daniel Williams, Airlie Chapman and Eric Schoof, dramaturg Goran Đurić, archeologists Aleksandra Michalewicz and Tom Keep, master craftsman Justin Green, sound artists Madeleine Flynn and Tim Humphrey. The full team can be seen here: http://robertwalton.net/project/sacrifice/

IMMORTALITY, THE 1960S, AND THE POWER OF WOMEN'S VOICES: AN INTERVIEW WITH GWENDOLYN KISTE, AUTHOR OF RELUCTANT IMMORTALS

ANDREA BLYTHE

> "Women's voices have so often been silenced. That's true of real-life women as well as female characters. We tend to be seen as being less important to the world and less important to storytelling. You can see this throughout literature, and while it's been getting better over the last few years, we still have a long way to go."

Set in Haight-Ashbury during the Summer of Love, Gwendolyn Kiste's *Reluctant Immortals*, gives voice to two often forgotten women of literature—Lucy Westenra from *Dracula* and Bertha Mason from *Jane Eyre*. Having both been turned immortal against their will, the two women band together in the face of an eternity in which they must continually fight off the control of the men who changed them. When Dracula and Rochester make a sudden return, the two women draw on the strength of their sisterhood to make a stand and claim their own power and space in the world.

Interstellar Flight Press: Your novel expands on the stories of often overlooked women in classic literature—Lucy Westenra from *Dracula* and Bertha Mason from *Jane Eyre*. What drew you to these particular women? Why did you feel their story needed to be told?

Gwendolyn Kiste: Women's voices have so often been silenced. That's true of real-life women as well as female characters. We tend to be seen as being less important to the world and less important to storytelling. You can see this throughout literature, and while it's been getting better over the last few years, we still have a long way to go.

In that vein, I always wanted to know more about both Lucy Westenra and Bertha Antoinetta Mason. From the time I was a kid discovering *Dracula* and *Jane Eyre*, I desperately wanted to see the two of them survive their respective stories and get a chance to tell their side of things. In writing *Reluctant Immortals*, I was able to give them back their voices and hear everything from their perspective. Neither of them were treated well in the original tales, and this novel aims to deal with what it's like when your own personal story is erased. Especially right now, I feel like it's so important to prioritize women's stories. We're losing our voices and our rights at a terrifyingly rapid pace, so if there's any way that I can add to the discourse and center the narratives of women, then I feel like now is absolutely the time to do it.

IFP: As you were developing this world, how did you decide the powers and relationship to the rules of immortality? In particular, how did you decide upon Mr. Rochester's particular brand of immortality?

GK: I knew I wanted to explore and play with some of the traditional vampire lore. I also wanted to go back to the original source material and deal with how much our understanding of vampires and their immortality have changed over time. For example, Dracula can go out in the daylight in the original book; he just doesn't have any of his powers. That's a detail that's often forgotten because we have such a huge association with vampires turning to dust in the sun. So when it came to the vampires, developing the rules about them was a lot of fun, and felt like it came really naturally as I was plotting out the story.

That being said, Rochester's immortality—along with that of Bertha's and Jane's—was one of the biggest questions I had going into writing the novel. I had most of the plot mapped out, but I knew I wanted there to be a unique reason as to why they had lived for so long. As I was finishing up the first quarter of the novel, I realized that I needed to focus on what makes Bertha's character in *Jane Eyre* so horrifying and memorable: that attic where she's kept locked away. Once I decided to use that locale as the centerpiece of their immortality, the rest of it started to come together very quickly. I don't want to get too specific since that's part of the reveal midway through the book, but what I settled on definitely unnerved me, so I figure that's always a good sign as a horror writer—that you're even freaking out yourself!

IFP: Being immortal, Lucy and Bertha have a certain amount of power compared to the ordinary humans around them. However, they remain

locked in a centuries-long power struggle that makes them feel powerless. Can you talk about how power plays out in the story?

GK: I've always felt that power is such a strange thing. Often, even when people have it, they still feel powerless. That can manifest itself in a cycle of helplessness, as it does for Lucy and Bee. It can also play out as it does for Dracula and Rochester: no matter how much power they get, they still crave more. Whatever power you have, it usually never feels like it's enough. That's such a confusing and dangerous reality that affects the world around us all the time.

As the story progresses, however, Lucy and Bee ultimately come to realize that the only good expression of power is the sharing of power: with each other and with others who are trying to do the right thing. That, to me, is the only effective and empathetic use of power: not to hoard it, but to ensure that as many people as possible are given a voice. It's a bit of a utopic vision and maybe one that won't ever be possible, but it does seem like a much happier version of reality than the one we're currently living in.

IFP: One of the fantastic things about the novel is its 1960s setting, which evokes a sense of technicolor vibrancy to the tale. Why was this the right time period for these characters to live in?

GK: The 1960s were such a huge time for social change. Everything was shifting in America then, from politics to everyday culture. Up until the point where we meet Lucy and Bee, they've been trapped in a kind of stasis. They live day after day, stuck in a pattern. It's not until they're forced out into the world and really experience how much life is changing around them that they start to change themselves. That's what made the 1960s such a perfect and exciting time to tell this story: the era was changing, just like these characters needed to change in order to become who they really wanted to be.

This novel was also a chance for me to write in this particular setting, which I've always loved. Ever since I was a kid, I've been so fascinated by the 1960s, but I haven't had a lot of chances to write in that era before. It was so much fun to set an entire novel during the Summer of Love in California. In many ways, writing this book was such a dream come true as a writer.

IFP: In writing about the '60s, what kinds of research did you do? Were there any books or movies from that time period (or about that period) that were particularly inspiring to you?

GK: I watched a number of documentaries about the era, from a PBS film specifically about the Summer of Love to more general series about the 1960s in America. I also spent a lot of time poring over photography books that focused on that decade in California. There's so much great information and images from that decade, which really helped to bring it to life for me. Using different books and maps, I was able to determine the exact layout of the Haight-Ashbury District and even the specific locations of signs and graffiti that are no longer there. Obviously, very few readers might care about or even notice those things, but it was important to me to be as exact and authentic as I could be. There were literally stacks of books around the house for months, but a few of my very favorites were *Summer of Love: Art, Fashion, and Rock and Roll,* edited by Jill D'Alessandro and Colleen Terry and *The Haight: Love, Rock, and Revolution* by Joel Selvin and Jim Marshall, as well as a book about a now-defunct amusement park called *San Francisco's Playland at the Beach: The Golden Years* by James R. Smith. For the fashion and general feel of the era, I absolutely love *Sharon Tate: Recollection* by Debra Tate.

I also went back to the Hammer Dracula films, many of which were produced in the 1960s. That era of Technicolor horror which at once feels classic and modern was exactly the mood that I was going for in the book. I've described *Reluctant Immortals* as a super-feminist Hammer film, so it was definitely fun to watch those movies again. Such a wonderful dose of horror nostalgia.

IFP: What are you most proud of about this book? How do you think it has helped you grow as a writer?

GK: Honestly, I'm just so happy that I got the opportunity to write a book that gave voices to two characters I've loved for so long. Both Lucy and Bertha are so amazing, and I'm so glad that I got to put them together in *Reluctant Immortals* and explore their world and experiences.

As for how the book has helped me grow as a writer, I like to think that I'm getting better at plotting and planning my novels. This is only my third one, and the process of writing novels still feels mystical to me at times. Then again, the writing process so often feels mystical and strange, so maybe that feeling will never go away, and heck, maybe it shouldn't. That might be where the real magic of being a writer exists!

Gwendolyn Kiste is the three-time Bram Stoker Award-winning author of *The Rust Maidens, Reluctant Immortals, Boneset & Feathers, And Her Smile Will Untether the Universe, Pretty Marys All in a Row*, and *The Invention of Ghosts.* Her short fiction and nonfiction have appeared in *Nightmare Magazine, Best American Science Fiction and Fantasy, Lit Hub, Vastarien, Tor's Nightfire, Black Static, The Dark, Daily Science Fiction, Interzone*, and *LampLight*, among others. Originally from Ohio, she now resides on an abandoned horse farm outside of Pittsburgh with her husband, two cats, and not nearly enough ghosts. Find her online at gwendolynkiste.com.

D&D IN FULL COLOR: INTERVIEW WITH AJIT A. GEORGE, EDITOR OF JOURNEYS THROUGH THE RADIANT CITADEL

ARCHITA MITTRA

"Everywhere I turned, there was something terrible in the air. At the same time, so much media was grimdark–this idea that to fight the darkness, one needed to be darker still."

Journeys through the Radiant Citadel is a mesmerizing anthology of one-shot *Dungeons & Dragons* adventures, each written by an author of color, with Ajit A. George and F. Wesley Schneider serving as project leads. For Interstellar Flight Press, Archita Mittra sat down with Ajit to have a conversation about all that went into the making of this vibrant, multicultural, and astonishingly well-detailed book while also balancing his responsibilities as the Director of Operations for the non-profit the Shanti Bhavan Children's Project.

INTERSTELLAR FLIGHT PRESS: The Radiant Citadel is a haven of peace and restorative justice, offering help and sanctuary to lost travelers or fleeing wayfarers. Unlike other *D&D* settings often inhabited by monsters and other threats, the Citadel is a beacon of healing and hope. What inspired you to come up with such a setting?

Ajit A. George: The Radiant Citadel was both a response to the moment and time and to the prevalent media trends. I began working on it during the height of the Covid pandemic, the political strife that had engulfed America, the Syrian refugee crisis, the migrant detention centers in the U.S., and other tragedies. Simultaneously, during that suffering, a new billionaire was being minted nearly every day. It felt like this gross warping of society and our values.

Everywhere I turned, there was something terrible in the air. At the same time, so much media was grimdark–this idea that to fight the darkness, one needed to be darker still.

Something inside of me pushed back, and refuted that idea. Refuted the idea the world had to be like this. Out of that rejection, the Radiant Citadel was born. I believe art responds to the moment, and sometimes art tries to envision a different reality. That's what was churning inside of me as I created the Radiant Citadel.

IFP: As the Director of Operations of the Shanti Bhavan Children's Project, how do you divide your time between your nonprofit projects and game writing career? With the Radiant Citadel's focus on sustainability, inclusion, and helping those who are otherwise disadvantaged, do you find your communitarian interests blending and informing each other?

AG: It's a little bit of a juggling act, but my full-time position as Director of Operations for the Shanti Bhavan Children's Project is always my priority. I only infrequently write for games, usually after I've finished work for the day, and even then, I only rarely take projects.

The strange silver lining for me in the pandemic was because I wasn't able to travel to India or even within the U.S. like I normally do for my job, and because I wasn't seeing anyone or doing any of my normal things, I had a lot more time on my hands. It allowed me to lead, and write for the project, something I would never have been able to do under normal circumstances.

And yes, absolutely. My nonprofit work informs my game writing and vice versa. The two are intertwined in ways that are both obvious and subconscious. I think I am better at both for them being in my life.

IFP: Fantasy stories and games are often criticized for their escapism, yet at the same time, positive and uplifting narratives are needed to imagine a better world. The adventures in this book manage to be optimistic while also being rooted in real-world cultures and concerns (such as rebuilding a community or dealing with environmental/political threats). So, was that a conscious choice while conceiving this book? What are your views on escapist fiction?

AG: I think escapist fiction is okay in small doses if one is very aware that it's escapist and it isn't the only thing one is consuming. Too much of it, though, and I worry it destroys my ability to grasp the complexities of the world–I start seeing things from the absolutist point of view that escapist fiction often leans on. And that it also creates avoidist tendencies in me as I retreat into escapist fiction. So I take it in small doses.

As for the design choices, absolutely. I was very conscious of the direction I was taking the book–it was something that was part of the DNA of *Journeys through the Radiant Citadel* from Day 1 and part of my initial design and vision docs. It's a hard needle to thread, but I wanted the book grounded in the real world and complex problems while not being about war or conquest, and that there would always be hope in the face of adversity.

IFP: How has that journey from a player to a writer to a project lead on an official *D&D* book been so far? Tell us more about what it was like to conceptualize this *D&D* project and work with a team of culturally diverse writers.

AG: It's been a strange, beautiful surreal journey to go from player to project lead on an official *D&D* book, especially since I don't work for Wizards of the Coast. I'm one of only a couple of people who has led a book while not employed by the company. So it's been quite a privilege.

More importantly, I not only led the book but conceived of it, and to be able to dream of a project and then lead it–that's electrifying, especially since it's a project I've wanted to make real for years. To create a *D&D* book that was written entirely by Black and brown writers and more than fifty other people of color as artists, editors, designers, consultants, and other roles–that was amazing. The collaboration was magical, and we all knew we were doing something special, something dear to our own hearts. It will remain one of the proudest moments in my life.

IFP: I particularly enjoyed how each adventure in the game was structured —not just with plot hooks to contextualize the game in a wider setting, but also the pronunciation guides, prompts for further adventures, and in particular, the questions to aid in creating culturally diverse characters. Some of it, I suspect, was to ensure that players could avoid the trappings of cultural appropriation, but I think the guidelines can benefit writers or anyone looking to depict/approach other cultures respectfully. So, what were your (and the team's) thoughts while navigating such issues?

AG: You're right, we wanted to give a guide to players and help them navigate unfamiliar cultures thoughtfully. It can be daunting to approach a culture that one has no reference to, so giving as many aids as possible was important to us. It's part of why the new settings were paired with an adventure that took place in that setting. The best way to understand a new culture is by living in it, and the adventures were how we could get players to "live" in those cultures.

But also, we wrote the guidelines and supporting text so players would feel like they had permission to engage and play in what we had created. The last thing we wanted was the book to become a museum piece, something put on a shelf and admired from afar but never engaged with. That's how things wither and die–because people are afraid to do anything with it. And so our guidelines were a way of giving permission and encouragement.

IFP: Although the stories do not explicitly deal with colonialism or violence (well, except in fighting the monsters), the presence of diseased environments, wealth disparities, and even afflicted mythological beasts can easily function as metaphors for oppression and rebuilding a nation after a disaster. How did you (and your team) go about planning the central conflicts that the characters would solve or negotiate with?

AG: Yes, I was very intentional in a desire to avoid conquest, present-day colonialism, or gratuitous violence. I wanted to center the non-white, non-Western cultures and their people, not the colonizer. And I wanted to ensure that the conflict, where possible, was nuanced and that you could understand, if not agree, with the antagonists.

Still, we didn't shy away from the impact of colonization on non-Western cultures, and several pieces grapple with it in interesting and challenging ways. I'm proud of how we approached this because it focused on those who had been colonized, their stories, and the legacy of colonization.

I built out some specific vision documents to give directions to the writers, and then they took it and interpreted it through their own lens for the piece. I gave a lot of feedback, but I was impressed by how much they were in agreement with my desire to avoid familiar pitfalls and tropes.

IFP: *Journeys through the Radiant Citadel* introduces readers/players to new creatures and bosses. Do you have a favorite among those?

AG: It's hard to pick a favorite, but the **bakunawa** probably stands out in my mind, partially because of its complex and tragic story in the adventure. I really empathized with its plight, and it captured the horror of the legacy of colonization. But purely as a monster, maybe the **Soul Shaker.** I loved the art, and it's creepy as hell with all those hands! Too many hands!

IFP: As a graduate of the Clarion West Writers Workshop, how has that experience shaped you as a writer/ storyteller? Did you always want to write and work in the speculative genre/game writing?

AG: I think Clarion West left a mark on me through the rigor and the critical lens we used to examine any piece of writing. It made me both a more astute and observant reader and a sharper writer. It also opened my mind up to different perspectives and styles of writing, things I hadn't encountered or appreciated before.

And yes, I've always loved literature, particularly fantasy, and science-fiction. I never knew how it would manifest in my life, but I always knew I wanted to write in the field.

IFP: *D&D* has quite a large fanbase in urban India, and other tabletop role-playing games are slowly catching up. Do you have any advice for writers based in the homeland (as opposed to those living abroad and having access to more opportunities) who are interested in pursuing game writing/design as a career?

AG: I have a lot of empathy for those living in India who want to break into games writing because most of the jobs are in the U.S. But one place to start would be the **Desis & Dragons Discord channel**. It is a huge community of Indians who are talking about games, playing games, and even working on games together. Finding that community and building together can open doors.

Also, if they can afford it, trying to attend **Big Bad Con** in San Francisco is a great opportunity. There is a networking event there specifically for people of color trying to break into games and a lot of companies and other game professionals go there to mentor or hire. It's totally worth attending if your budget allows for it.

IFP: What are you currently working on? Are there any plans for a second volume for *Journeys through the Radiant Citadel*, or any exciting future projects that you'd like to talk about?

AG: I am taking a little break from my work in games because it's been very exhausting, and I want to get back to some personal projects. I'm working on a short story that I'm excited about, and I am doing some research and taking some notes on a novel. I hope to share something new with the world soon!

About the Editor

Ajit George is the Director of Operations for the international non-profit the Shanti Bhavan Children's Project. He has spoken at numerous events including TEDx, the International Monetary Fund, and NPR on the topics of education, gender equality, community development, and poverty alleviation. He is featured in the original Netflix Documentary Series, Daughters of Destiny. He is also on the board of the Indian Institute of Journalism and New Media.

In the field of games, he graduated from the Clarion West Writers' Workshop and has written for a variety of indie companies including Bully Pulpit, Thorny Games, and Monte Cook Games. He has organized international collaborative larp events and is an energetic diversity consultant, speaker, and activist. He has most recently written for Dungeons & Dragons' Van Richten's Guide to Ravenloft and is the creator, project lead, and writer for

D&D's Journeys Through the Radiant Citadel. He recently won the 2022 Diana Jones Award for Excellence in Gaming.

TOXIC RELATIONSHIPS AND GREEK MYTHOLOGY: INTERVIEW WITH JORDAN KURELLA, AUTHOR OF I NEVER LIKED YOU ANYWAY

J.Z. WESTON

Jordan Kurella's writing can be found in *Apex, Glitter + Ashes,* and *Strange Horizons*, and he was nominated for Best of the Net in 2018. His debut novella, *I Never Liked You Anyway*, re-imagines Orpheus and Eurydice as modern-day music students. It's short, sharp, and deliciously snarky. J.Z. Weston interviewed Kurella on Greek myths, tragedy, and music majors.

Interstellar Flight Press: I loved how you twisted the usual story of Orpheus and Eurydice on its head, turning a tragic love story into the tale of a toxic relationship. What made you look at this myth and say, "I bet Orpheus was a pretentious asshole?"

Jordan Kurella: Gosh, isn't he, though? The worst!

My 9th-grade English teacher never saw Orpheus as tragic. Ms. Lee called him a stalker. She said, "What kind of man has his boyfriend 'whoopsies' kill his girlfriend and then go to the Underworld to get said girlfriend only to make sure she's following him out." She said, "Girls, if your boyfriend comes to get you from somewhere and is making sure you're following him? Leave."

She had similar feelings about Penelope in The Odyssey, how she was robbed of having a good time. She felt a lot of things about the women in Greek Mythology. This book is mostly written from her passionate ideas.

That and also knowing how music majors in college operate. I might have hung out with too many of them, having been a musician in college. Perhaps too much of one.

IFP: Half of the story takes place in the Afterlife, with Eurydice learning to be a ghost and coming to terms with her life. Here, her best friend is Penelope, from The Odyssey. What inspired you to pair up Eurydice and Penelope as friends in the Afterlife?

JK: There's a line in the book, in the first chapter, that says how they both had problems with men beginning with "O," Orpheus, and Odysseus, respectively. Considering that Eurydice got tossed away for Aristaeus (in how Ms. Lee saw the original myth), and Penelope spent decades fending off suitors only to have Odysseus not pay attention to her when he got home (thanks PTSD!), it made sense for them to be friends in the Afterlife.

In my experience, people tend to come together in community due to similarities of circumstance, or experience, hobby, or just stuff that happened to them that is awful. Eurydice and Penelope are the latter. They can complain about these two men, and Penelope was a formidable woman, and a mother, and a ruler. She likes to feel useful in the Afterlife, and she's very much that woman to Eurydice, but Eurydice teaches her some things, too.

It's a great friendship. I love them both.

IFP: The story of Orpheus and Eurydice is quite popular. What was the hardest part of adapting such a well-known story?

JK: Hardest part, I think, was keeping as close to the myth as I could: especially with the thing that finally kills Eurydice. That is *not a spoiler*, she starts off in the first chapter dead. Anyway, with that thing, I spent probably four weeks searching for that thing. I needed it to be specifically what it was, but within the parameters of the myth. Gosh, I remember, I was starting to get mad—super frustrated, oh my gods—and then I found it! I was on Discord with my buddies when I found it, and I YELLED! They had no idea what I was yelling about. So that took a long time. More annoying was retrofitting it into the manuscript, lolsob. Making sure it was foreshadowed enough and solid enough to make sense.

Oh, also: between the two POVs, one was *way easier* to write than the other. Won't tell you whose.

IFP: In your book, both Eurydice and Orpheus are polyamorous, and Eurydice is also in a relationship with Andromeda (or Andi, as they prefer to be called). Their relationship serves as the healthy mirror that reflects just how bad Orpheus is for Eurydice, though the Andromeda of Greek myth had no connection with either of them. Why did you choose to include that particular figure in your story?

JK: Andromeda, in the Greek Myth, is basically fridged for the greatness of a man. So, honestly, Andi is put in there as something for people to immediately worry, "*oh no are they going to die*?" For those that know the myth.

And then does Andi die? Who knows? I do.

IFP: Other than your own, what is your favorite retelling or adaptation of a Greek myth?

JK: This book was heavily inspired by Margaret Atwood's *The Penelopiad*. That's probably one of my favorite retellings of Greek Myth. It's Atwood's re-envisioning of The Odyssey from Penelope's perspective, told in a gorgeous, lyrical style that sticks to the bones. It's beautiful and gorgeous and worth a read.

That's probably my favorite retelling of a Greek Myth, hands down.

Jordan's debut novella, I Never Liked You Anyway (Vernacular Books) has been called "beautifully queer" by Publisher's Weekly. Sarah Gailey called it "an irresistible read." Lauren Ring said it was "effortlessly flawless."For more from Jordan Kurella, check out his website: https://www.jordankurella.com/

HOPE, HORROR, AND QUEERNESS: AN INTERVIEW WITH LUCY HANNAH RYAN, AUTHOR OF YOU MAKE YOURSELF ANOTHER

J.Z. WESTON

"I feel like my queerness is almost inextricable from horror."

Horror has provided fertile ground for countless authors to explore queerness, bodily autonomy, and societal pressures. Among that list is up-and-coming author Lucy Hannah Ryan. Her work tends towards the literary and the lyrical, with a haunting quality that lingers. J.Z. Weston recently had the opportunity to ask them a few questions about their newly published collection, *You Make Yourself Another* (*Half Mystic,* April 2023).

Interstellar Flight Press: There is a long association of queerness and horror. Where do you see yourself within that tradition?

Lucy Hannah Ryan: I feel like my queerness is almost inextricable from horror—the first crush I had on a woman and fully understood what I was feeling, it was Star from perennial queer favorite vampire movie *The Lost Boys. Rocky Horror* is my mum's favorite film, so she took me to a sing-along for my fourteenth birthday. I cut my teeth, writing-wise, writing *Buffy the Vampire Slayer* fanfiction and spent most of my teen years begging my friends to watch *Jennifer's Body* with me because it's so funny. Trust me, there's definitely no other reason I would want to watch it over and over. Horror, and in a lot of ways, explicitly or implicitly queer horror, is all over my adolescence. It's kind of an integral part of me, so of course, it's all over my work. There's something kind of beautiful to me about how dominant queer voices are in horror; you call me a monster, fine, I'll be that monster. The way the LGBT community has historically taken gleeful ownership of the thing used to harm us, reclaiming it, is radical and incredible, and I think the horror tradition is merely an extension of that. I couldn't be prouder to make even a little splash in those well-traveled waters. I didn't become obsessed with *The Picture of Dorian Gray* when I was thirteen for nothing.

IFP: Several of these stories show characters transforming in order to protect themselves or perhaps enact revenge. I'm particularly thinking of "Carcass" and "In Bloom". Why do you think that stories of transformation lend themselves so readily to this theme?

LHR: It's almost a power fantasy, isn't it? That's what I was grappling with when I was writing "In Bloom" in particular. There's something very alluring about taking a situation where you feel powerless and turning the tables, being unconquerable. I think that's kind of at the root of a lot of both revenge fantasies and, weirdly enough, superhero stories. This is a very nerdy reference, but there's a moment I come back to a lot in a 1989 Catwoman run, where Selina tells her sister, Maggie, who is a nun, that being Catwoman makes her feel unassailable; nothing hurts her, she's fearless. Maggie asks, "Do you really feel so much safer in there?" And Selina, referring to Maggie's nun's habit, replies, "Do you?" What she's becoming might not be safe or healthy, but she's free for the first time, untouchable. I think a lot of people with trauma and pain can relate to that urge, I certainly can.

IFP: Many of these stories—particularly "Maybe It's Better When It's Burning" and "Satellite Child"—deal with experiences of pain and chronic illness. What do you think makes stories of the fantastic such a fitting lens for those themes?

LHR: I think there is an inherent body horror element to being chronically ill. It's awful and terrifying to be in a body that hurts you and affects you in ways you cannot control. It's like possession, sometimes, something other than you piloting the body as it shifts and aches and changes. And I think again it's an alluring fantasy that all this pain and change means something, that there's something kinder, or stronger, waiting at the end of it. I think there were a couple of times on the blog tour where I mentioned my lifelong fascination with faery changelings, folklore literally created to explain away children's illnesses and death with something more palatable. I spent my childhood with this overpowering, recurring fantasy of bursting free of my own skin and the pain being over, something else burning through. For me, there is no sickness without the fantastic glittering like a mirage just out of reach.

IFP: How did you decide how to organize this collection? What was the reasoning or vision behind putting these stories in this specific order?

LHR: I think there's a journey happening with the shape of the book. In some ways, the stories get darker, deeper, and more opaque the further into the collection you read, but not without symmetry. Actually, the reason the first and last stories are placed where they are is because their endings echo; a girl climbing a tree, one waiting for morning and the other already basking in the sun, a change having settled deep within them both. It gives the whole collection a sense of looping back to the beginning, I think.

IFP: Who do you consider your literary influences? What other works of queer literary horror would you recommend to Interstellar Flight Magazine's readers?

LHR: Oh, great question. I think the obvious answers are Carmen Maria Machado and Shirley Jackson, though I actually came to both after I started writing this book. It's almost like I found them because I was meant to, and I hope that my words can happily, hauntingly, walk on the ground they laid before me. Whilst she's not necessarily a horror author, there's definitely a touch of Ali Smith to my work, queer and surreal as it is. Again, not strictly horror and not always explicitly queer, but Megan Abbott's terrible and toxic women are always an inspiration. I read Virginia Woolf and Oscar Wilde at just the right time in my teens to be entirely too pretentious. I'm also inspired, maybe more so than novelists, by poets, who often marry queerness, horror, and bliss more succinctly and fearlessly than a novel or story can because poems tend to speak to baser emotions. Richard Siken, Sam Sax, Ocean Vuong, Chen Chen, Hanif Abdurraqib, Maria Howe, Louise Gluck, Natalie Diaz, Clementine von Radics, my friend, and editor Topaz Winters... more than I can possibly name, really, and I know I'm missing some out. Poetry has a reputation for being fluffy and flowery, pretentious, but to me, it's best when it's brutal, a little gory, sharpened like a knife, so of course, the fingerprints of all of those writers are ghosting over the pages of *You Make Yourself Another*.

IFP: What projects are you working on right now?

LHR: I'm a little bit in-between things now. I spent five years working on this book, which is a long time, so I'm trying to be okay with taking a little break, especially since I've had a lot of change going on in my life recently, but I always do, and always will have things going on in the background. I have a theme—and a title—for a second collection already, though it only has two complete stories so far, and I have been tentatively working on a novel for a couple of years, adding to it on fits and starts. I haven't spent a lot of time appeasing my inner poet for a while, though, so maybe that will be my next outlet. I guess I'm working on everything and nothing! That's a very writerly response, isn't it?

Lucy Hannah Ryan (she/they) is a poet, fiction writer, and essayist. Her work concerns gender, sexuality, and weird bodies, inspired by lifelong chronic illness. They have had the pleasure of being featured in various publications, including *Gay Times, Bullshit Lit*, and *Pink Plastic House.* Their chapbook *Death & the Maiden: Odes to the Dead Girls of Pop Culture* was released by *Alien Buddha Press* in August 2022, and they are a reader for *Sword and Kettle Press.* She lives in London with her cat, Nova.

OLD LEGENDS THROUGH THE VOICES OF THE "THINGS AND BEASTS" THEREIN: INTERVIEW WITH MELISSA RIDLEY ELMES, AUTHOR OF ARTHURIAN THINGS, A COLLECTION OF POEMS

T.D. WALKER

"The raw material of this collection comes from my decades-long critical and personal reading both of the scholarship on Arthuriana and of the literature itself, so I'm absolutely certain it's informed by the ideas I've already been preoccupied with and my views of the various iterations of the legend."

If we look closer at familiar worlds through the eyes of characters not often given voice, we see those worlds in deeper, richer ways than we had before. In this way, Melissa Ridley Elmes gives us a fresh view into the world of Arthurian legends in her poetry collection, *Arthurian Things* (Dark Myth Publications, 2020). Through her poems speak animals, objects, people, and the landscape around them, sharing with us novel insights into a world that becomes at once familiar to us and yet surprisingly new. T.D. Walker spoke with Melissa Ridley Elmes about the Arthurian world as presented in her book.

Interstellar Flight Press: In the foreword to *Arthurian Things*, you give us a wonderful background into your creation of the book, concluding that "Isn't it about time we gave the things and beasts of

the Arthurian world a chance to step into the limelight? After all, they have been there the whole time, waiting patiently for us to notice them."

Once you had the "things and beasts" assembled into poems, what shaped how you ordered the poems in the collection? And how did you want the order to guide the journey your readers take through Camelot via the book?

Melissa Ridley Elmes: This is such a great question, and it's one of the things I struggled with most when finally assembling the collection–I think any poet who's assembled a collection will acknowledge that it's not a straightforward affair! In the end, I took that time-honored approach of printing each poem out on its own page, laying those on the floor of my office, and just looking for threads of theme, recurring figures and ideas, and poem-types. This, of course, did eventually lead to the poet playing hopscotch, me jumping across rows of pages to relocate one poem, find another, and so on–so there's a mental image for your readers!

I knew there were a lot of cat poems, so I decided early on the cats would be the linking figures taking us through the collection, wandering through Camelot as cats are wont to do. The sonnet cycle clearly had to be kept together, and I knew I wanted those poems toward the end but not at the very end because the focus of the collection still needed to be ultimately on my animals and objects, which ending absolutely with those human poems would have undermined; as it stands, they're folded in with everything else, and I like that choice. I also wanted to make sure I showcased the variety of poem forms and styles by not placing unrelated poems of the same type together, to keep readers engaged. I kept those poems that were clearly paired or following the same idea together, with the exception of the lyre songs; I broke those apart to have music woven through the manuscript because I love musicals and flash mobs, and the idea of a spontaneous song and dance set interrupting the other poems appealed to me–although I doubt anyone not in my head would notice or think of that! I also wanted some poems to just kind of step out of nowhere and take us in a completely different direction, so we didn't get mired into one place or idea for too long, so I sorted the poems to showcase the expanse of the geographies of the Arthurian world, going for movement indoors and outdoors, into small and intimate spaces and back out to large and sweeping landscapes.

IFP: You're a scholar of medieval literature with a deep understanding of your subject, but as you wrote the poems for the collection, did your view of the stories surrounding Arthur change in some way because of this poetic exploration?

MRE: I don't think so. The raw material of this collection comes from my decades-long critical and personal reading both of the scholarship on Arthuriana and of the literature itself, so I'm absolutely certain it's informed by the ideas I've already been preoccupied with and my views of the various iterations of the legend. As a scholar of medieval Arthurian literature, it's absolutely not changed my views of the stories in any appreciable way–although what this project did give me the chance to do was to explore the lacunae, or blank spaces and unexamined corners and moments, and the transmission of ideas across time and place, which are topics I'm a little obsessed with from a theoretical stance, and that was deep fun for me. As a writer, what I notice has changed is my appreciation for how simultaneously easy and difficult it is to participate in the writing of Arthurian material.

If my collection showcases anything, it is that you can literally start anywhere and write about anything and have it still be recognizably Arthurian in the end if that's your goal–it truly is an absolutely malleable subject area and inspirational wellspring for writers. And that's both liberating–you can do whatever you want to!–and also challenging because readers do have certain expectations, so if you are writing for a popular audience determining how much to bend the rules and in what directions in service of your aims can be a tricky puzzle. I think it was easier for me to write this collection of poems that intentionally seeks to fracture the legend into a kaleidoscopic view of things from multiple vantage points than it is for, say, someone novelizing the Arthurian legend and thus requiring more unity throughout their work. It's easy to keep things fresh when you're looking through the eyes of cats and combs and swords and flies, but much harder from the steady perspective or point of view of well-known and well-explored human characters.

IFP: And did you want to shape the way your readers—who have at least a basic knowledge of the legends—see the people, things, and themes in the stories?

MRE: I did want to shape the way readers encountered the legend in this collection, in so far as I wanted them to consider it from nontraditional vantage points and perspectives and through the prism of theories of Arthurtime, erasure, literary transmission, and gender, rendered into poetry. I did not consciously have an agenda for what I wanted them to see or determine or think after reading the collection–I just hoped it would give them something to think with and to enjoy on a belletristic level.

IFP: One theme that recurs in the book is agency, or lack thereof. Tristan and Isolde fall in love not because of their own desires but because of a magical potion. A rose observes that Guinevere "had been harvested from her family." And even the eponymous weapon in "A Sword in the Armory" wishes to have been a horseshoe instead of an instrument of death.

So I was struck by the poem "The Skipping Stone's Adventure," which speaks to the idea of agency and what to do when what agency you have is denied you. At first, the stone, which has been thrown into the water by a youth:

But as I dove lower, lower still into the murky depths

I realized that the page had made choices for me that

I might not be quite okay with;

The stone accepts its fate and turns to the details of objects around it, including at the end, Excalibur. Was there something about that sense of agency—and our notion of it in relation to the Arthurian legend—that you want to challenge in your readers?

MRE: I love this question! I don't have an answer to this question!

(It's true, I really do not have an answer to this question!)

Honestly, that poem started out a little inspired by Bilbo Baggins–Stone, like Hobbit, finding itself on an unexpected journey through forces beyond its ken, and realizing after the initial hesitancy that hey, this is actually a great adventure! (In my mind's eye, I actually saw the stone, like Martin Freeman's Bilbo in the film adaptation, shouting joyfully, "I'm going on an adventure!")

But as I think about it–and I'm riffing, here–the question of agency looms large throughout the Arthurian legend, as it does throughout the medieval cultures that produced its earliest iterations. There is always a tension between the real and the ideal; one of the foundational preoccupations of the early narratives is the limitations of human beings, that even if you are a great man, there is always still that capacity for sin and failure because of human nature, innately flawed despite one's best intentions. It's a very Christocentric culture that produced the early tales, and the relationship of flawed mortal with/to perfect divinity is undeniably a thematic vein running through the tales–it's the central focus of the Grail quest, for instance. This worldview is also informed by the idea of Fortuna, the goddess of fate, whose turning wheel can bring men at the height of their fame and glory crashing down into ignominy–this was a central philosophical idea in medieval European culture, enshrined in Boethius's *Consolation of Philosophy* and, perhaps more recognizably for modern audiences, in the lyrics of "O Fortuna" from the *Carmina Burana,* a collection of thirteenth century "little songs" set to music by Carl Orff. There are multiple medieval manuscript illustrations of Fortune's wheel, and it appears in medieval Arthurian texts. The important thing about this wheel is to remember that everyone is susceptible to it, from the richest and most powerful king to the unknown man toiling in a field to the thief languishing in prison—no one can determine their fate or know what will come to pass. What matters is how you endure trials and tribulations when they come to you.

The whole Arthurian legend is predicated on the certainty that Arthur's kingdom will fall–not if, but when–and it falls because of the actions of the people who love him most, not at all stemming from malice on their part, but because they cannot stop themselves from loving one another and give in to temptation and desire. But arguably, and I think, more importantly, it also falls because Arthur refuses to act, until it is too late, in calling out and dealing with the behaviors that he is responsible as king for weighing and measuring–he fails to live up to his responsibilities as much as they do theirs. There's a lot of agency in all of that, but also a lot of perceived lack of agency, "I can't do anything about this" because of the web of relationships involved, so that, in the end, all that's left to these characters is their choice of how to handle it when their world comes crashing around them. That perceived lack of agency is an important illusion that ultimately turns the whole legend into a tragedy. A Boethian Tragedy.

And it's only just now, thinking through all of this trying to come up with an answer to your question about agency, that I realize I think my stone is a Boethian stone, anchoring the collection in this idea that the only agency we truly possess is how we handle what comes our way, but that's actually a lot of agency, if we pause to consider it, and considering it opens up whole new ways of engaging with the world that may be unfamiliar and even uncomfortable but are no less opportunities and possibilities. It's a hopeful poem as much as an unexpected adventure–I never realized that before now!

And, too, Tolkien, as a medievalist himself, would also have been influenced, consciously or not, by Boethian principles, so it's very possible Bilbo is also a Boethian hobbit—another thing I hadn't considered before now. Thanks for this question!

IFP: The Arthurian legends are ones that people keep returning to over and over, which we see yet again in "The Rosary of the Hermit in the Wood Reminds You of the Importance of Faith and Hope in Stories," in which the rosary exhorts us:

[...] do not criticize the faith and hope of anyone

Much less those who rely on them as the foundation

Of stories they hold dearest

Stories give us hope, and in turn, hope gives us stories to hold onto. Though the book came out months before the stretch of social isolation that began in March 2020, this idea of finding hope and faith in stories feels more urgent in the last couple of years than ever. In this time of pandemic and political turmoil, why might the Arthurian legends be

particularly useful to us as a society? And did the pandemic change the way you view the poems in your book?

MRE: The easy part of this question first–no, the pandemic has not changed how I view the poems in this book. It's quite removed from my pandemic experience, to be honest. My views on these poems change mostly through discussing them with other people–as happened in my answer to the question about the stone's agency earlier on. You've definitely shifted my view of that poem!

Now, to tackle the weightier part of the question.

The Arthurian legends have always been a vehicle for social, cultural, and political commentary; from their very inception, they were already preoccupied with ethical considerations—I co-edited a collection of scholarly essays that will be published in 2023 on that very subject of ethics in the Arthurian legend, and our contributors have done an excellent job of mapping the contours of Arthurian ethics to showcase the legend's various uses for cultural and political purpose.

Here in the United States, for example, of course, we have the idea of "Kennedy's Camelot," the tragedy of this "great leader cut short in his prime," that idealization of things; but even earlier in American history, we have the uses of "chivalry" including the Arthurian legend shaping the early U.S. South's ideas of itself as the natural inheritor of the White, Anglo-Saxon Protestant tradition they viewed as being codified in the Arthurian legend. Filtered through nineteenth-century British Romanticism and Tennyson's idealized view of Camelot, the Arthurian legend served as a vehicle for the transmission of ideas of "noble superiority" that framed the racism and patriarchy of American society. It was used as a didactic tool for children to instill ethics and manners commensurate with the dominant cultural ideals into them, and medieval literature and language more broadly was taught in American women's colleges, assuming those women would become the mothers teaching and guiding their children thus inculcating these ideals into each new generation and thus, perpetuating white nationalism.

The presence and development, and these uses of the Arthurian legend, in the US has been investigated by many scholars, among them Alan and Barbara Lupack in their 2001 book *King Arthur in America*. More recently and importantly, scholars have begun investigating more explicitly how the legend specifically and chivalry more broadly has served as a vehicle for the development of white nationalism and informed black culture in the US through that prism in the modern world, and important studies on this subject include Mary Dockray Miller's 2017 *Public Medievalists, Racism, and Suffrage in the American Women's College*, Matthew Vernon's 2018 *The Black Middle Ages*, Cord Whitaker's 2019 *Black Metaphors: How Modern Racism*

Emerged from Medieval Race-Thinking. Geraldine Heng's 2003 *Empire of Magic: Medieval Romance and the Politics of Fantasy* is essential for the understanding of medieval Arthurian literature as colonizing enterprise and to understand the binding of the term "Anglo-Saxon"—with which the Arthurian legend is also inextricably bound–with racism, the work of Mary Rambaran-Olm, particularly her 2021 *Smithsonian Magazine* article "The Many Myths of the Term 'Anglo-Saxon'"three-part series "History Bites: Resources on the Problematic term 'Anglo-Saxon'" on *Medium*, provides a good starting point.

It's unpleasant and uncomfortable but also objectively true that in modern society, the Arthurian legend as a whole is inextricably bound up in white supremacist and patriarchal ideologies. This is something everyone studying, writing, and reading Arthuriana has to come to terms with. Fortunately, because the legend has always had a critical and didactic aspect to it, we can change the lens of what is being investigated and written; what is being criticized, by whom, and how; and what lessons are being transmitted through Arthurian literature. The tradition is that *Arthur will return when there is most need of him*–"rex quondam, rexque futurus, the Once and Future King"—and our current cultural and political climate is actually quite ripe for an Arthurian Renaissance—we're already seeing it happen, as I discuss in my answer to your next question!

IFP: Are there contemporary speculative poetry collections that explore the same Arthurian legends as yours that you'd like to recommend to readers of *Interstellar Flight Magazine*? And are there past renderings of the tales you'd suggest we read?

MRE: The most recent Arthurian poetry collection that Interstellar readers would particularly enjoy is probably *Eye to the Telescope*'s 2018 Arthuriana issue, edited by Adele Gardner: https://eyetothetelescope.com/archives/027issue.html Truthfully, I didn't know about this collection when I developed my own, which I was writing around the time of its publication, but I love that Mary Soon Lee also wrote about Camelot's cats!

There are SO MANY new Arthurian works—television, film, and media, as well as literature. We're seeing a real fluorescing of the legend, and that tends to happen when things get a little shaky socially, culturally, and politically.

Recent Arthurian works I wholeheartedly recommend, though they are not poetry:

Drop everything right now, get yourself to a bookstore or library, and read Tracy Deonn's *Legendborn* and *Bloodmarked*. Just do it. Don't talk back, don't argue. You're welcome in advance. By far the single best modern Arthurian adaptation available today, and I do not make such a claim lightly. These books are everything you could ask for by way of both honoring the medieval origins and modernizing the Arthurian myth–just perfection.

I also recommend the *Once and Future* Arthurian duology by A.R. Capetta and Cory McArthy, Kieren Gillan's *Once and Future* graphic novels, and *The Story of Silence* by Alex Myers.

All of these works I've mentioned are doing that reimagining of the Arthurian legend through new avenues and exploring social, cultural, and political concerns.

There are many more recommendations in the notes in *Arthurian Things!*

Melissa Ridley Elmes is a Virginia native currently living in Missouri in an apartment that delightfully approximates a hobbit hole. Her speculative poetry and fiction have appeared in *Star*Line, Eye to the Telescope, Illumen, Spectral Realms, Haven, Liquid Imagination, World of Myth, Reunion: The Dallas Review Online,* and various other print and web venues, and her first collection of poems, *Arthurian Things*, was published by Dark Myth Publications in 2020 and nominated for the SFPA Elgin Award in 2022. Find out more at her website: https://melissaridleyelmes.wordpress.com/

APOCALYPSE AND PERSEVERANCE: COVID, SCIENCE FICTION, AND POETRY OF SURVIVAL: INTERVIEW WITH JEANNINE HALL GAILEY, AUTHOR OF FLARE, CORONA

T.D. WALKER

Much about the COVID pandemic seemed as if it could have been out of a science fiction story. And yet, for so many of us, the years since the pandemic began have been ones of deep personal reflection. Jeannine Hall Gailey explores the intersection of the personal and the dire possibilities science fiction gives us in her new poetry collection, *Flare, Corona* (*BOA Editions*, 2023). TD. Walker spoke with Jeannine Hall Gailey about apocalypse, the natural world, and the hope we see in the poems in this book.

Interstellar Flight Press: Given the title of the book, which to my ear echoes both the corona of the sun as well as the coronavirus, can you tell us about how this book took shape? Some of the poems were written and published before the pandemic, but it's difficult for me to read anything post-2020 outside that lens. When did the book come together for you as a project? And did the pandemic shift the way you ordered the poems?

Jeannine Hall Gailey: I started writing about the pandemic in late fall 2019 —when it first started hitting the news. I had a sense, a feeling, that something huge—and hugely bad—was about to happen. But most of the poems in the book were written from 2016–2019—before the pandemic, during the Trump years, when I was having all these multiple health crises at a time when it felt like the world might be teetering on the precipice of something critical. The book was originally called "Post-Life" after one of the earliest poems, when I was entertaining the idea that death was pretty imminent, and after my MS diagnosis, it changed to "Flare" when I started noticing the solar weather phenomenon and incorporating those poems in the book, along with my first tentative poems about living with MS. The title didn't become "Flare, Corona" until fairly late when I decided to incorporate some of the pandemic poems I'd been writing in the book. It seemed ridiculous to leave them out at that point—the pandemic was such a big part of everyone's life for the last three years. So it really became the collection it is now fairly recently. I was ecstatic when BOA called me about the book—I was starting to question if I was going in the right direction. And I probably wrote ten new poems after the book was accepted for publication.

IFP: "Irradiate" is such a compelling poem to begin the collection with: I read this as both the origin story of the poet as well as that of the landscape, the natural world you reference so often throughout the book. I'm particularly struck by the first line of the second stanza: "I knew what it meant to illuminate," which sets up the voice of the book as an authority. But in saying "I knew" and not "I know," that authority shifts into the past. Why did you choose this one as an introduction to the collection? And how did you want readers to view the rest of the book through this poem?

JHG: "Irradiate" is sort of an ominous poem, isn't it? I chose it to be paired with "Calamity"—a sort of funnier, if still ominous in tone, poem—in order for readers to be prepared to read about real personal crisis and environmental crisis (they are paired, in my mind) as well as be prepared to laugh at outlandish hyperbole.

There is no separation in this book between the personal and the environment —it's a semi-permeable membrane, as it were. Your body's health—cancer, neurological, and immunological problems—are directly linked to the things that poison our particular environment. I know the places I grew up were distinctly unsafe—from a radioactivity point of view—I knew that the chemical pollutants in our air, water, and soil do make their way into our bodies and have impacts. I took a class in college called "Environmental Toxicology," and another on "Environmental Law (for Engineers)," and those two classes have really impacted the way I think about the world. Nuclear power is not clean and safe. Plastics are not clean and safe. The things you've been promised were almost always compromised. (Environmental law ended up being a class about what companies could legally get away with and how little they have to pay for literally causing human death—very little—and we're seeing that exact thing play out in Ohio right now. It was a very scary class for me about the lack of ethics that engineers are taught and how they prioritize money and business over human life and definitely over the environment. Oh, and how all the Superfund money goes to lawyers and not to cleaning up the sites.) If we do not pay attention to our world and actively help heal us both, it could easily kill us—something humans don't seem to like to think about.

IFP: *Flare, Corona* is a book of its time, of these pandemic years as well as your personal history. Which makes the shifts into the speculative all the more intriguing. We hear mentions of alien invasions, atomic bombs dropping, apocalypse after apocalypse. And yet, you always bring us back to the personal, the human element continuing on after disaster.

Science fiction is often viewed as less personal than other genres, if only because the genre is not of the here and now in its context. So, I'd like to ask: why do you find science fiction so effective as a way into the present and, more significantly, into the personal?

JHG: Well, I'm the daughter of a robotics scientist who grew up coding computers and playing chess with robot arms, so my whole life is a little bit science-fiction-y. My awareness of a poison or threatened environment—which started living in Oak Ridge, Tennessee, where the soil, water, and food are often contaminated with radioactive cesium (though the government probably won't tell you how much) or living in Cincinnati, which had its own Superfund site at Fernald, or even here with Hanford a couple of hours away, looking like a martial landscape with desert and barbed wire and signs saying "Keep Out." For me, science fiction is real—and personal. I like working in persona because it allows poets to use the tools of fiction writers on a smaller scale. It allows us to think outside ourselves, and of course, mythological and fairy tale, and comic book characters often contain these universal Jungian archetypes that are easy to identify with and place yourself within the world with.

IFP: A number of the self-portrait poems in your book are also science poems or science fiction poems. As we see you, you're distanced from yourself by putting yourself in other worlds in the science fiction poems, but we're brought closer to your experience through our understanding of the characters and tropes, such as in "Self-Portrait as Radioactive Girl," "Mutant Sonnet: Self-Portrait as Bad 1950's Science Fiction Movie," and "Self-Portrait as Mutant."

While reading your poem "Self-Portrait as MRI," I paused at the lines " I don't know if I believe // in these science fictions, these certainties / of soul." This is a collection that is centered on uncertainty. There is something about science's ability to constantly question what we think we know that is made concrete in science fiction. Perhaps this

goes back to my previous question, but I'd also like to ask about that doubt.

JHG: Yes, science certainly doesn't have all the answers, any more than religion does—which is why people are attracted to both. People love certainty, and there's so little of it, especially when you are confronted with things like death and afterlife and what's the best way to live out your final days, and what has meaning. Questioning things is kind of my modus operandi as a poet—questioning the roles women play in pop culture, like in my first book, or questioning the limits of medicine right now, like in this book, or how the workings of the universe (solar flares, eclipses) impact our human bodies on earth.

IFP: And on the subject of science fiction, I also see this collection as a poetic guidebook for navigating apocalypse, whether personal or global. What would you like for your readers to question about their assumptions surrounding end-of-the-world scenarios after reading your book?

JHG: I'm naturally a person who thinks in worse-case scenarios, which is why I've read so much apocalypse literature—even during my childhood in the seventies, those were my favorite book topics—and there's something in those worst-case scenarios that engenders hope and a desire to survive. Survival is a very important topic to me. I'm a hopeful pessimist, or an optimistic realist, however, one wants to classify it. Even in the darkest days—say, right after a terminal cancer diagnosis, or an MS diagnosis, there are still things to appreciate—still beauty, still the people you love, still art and music. Essentially, crisis makes us more ourselves.

IFP: You return us in these poems to the landscape again and again, particularly in gardens, what can be cultivated. Planting that which promises to bloom becomes an act of resistance, as in "2020 Didn't Start," "In the Second Year of the Plague, I Plant a Fig Tree," and, of course, in "Planting Camellias as Act of Resistance."

And yet, "At the End of Two Years of the Plague, You are Tired of the Word Resilience" begins, " Even as you dig and plant, as you search / the skyline for something, anything better, / as you snap pictures of pink rhododendron and jonquils." There's a tension between these flowers and fruit which aren't resilient, or not for long, and your poems and photographs, which persist and carry their beauty and consolation.

Why bring the poems back to the landscape again and again? In particular, how do you want your reader to see the tangible, if fragile, flora against the science fictional elements you've layered in the book?

JHG: I had a weird fixation with trees and flowers when I first got my terminal cancer diagnosis—that's when I started up my photography habit (I had done a little in high school, but it had been a dormant practice) by taking pictures of trees, and while I've always done some minor gardening—planting bulbs and herbs and the occasional tree—the pandemic gave me the time and patience to try to learn more about gardening in this particular place, with our particular weird climate.

I think there is a consolation in nature that nothing else provides, and taking pictures (or writing poems) about those things can help them persist, even if climate change wipe them off the face of the earth. Birds, too, played a strong role in my mediating on nature during the pandemic. I've seen so many species that during the almost 20 years I've lived here, I've never seen before or didn't have time to notice. It's like getting to know a friend who's a little mysterious, figuring out the local flora and fauna.

IFP: One question the book raised for me is what the world will be like after COVID. Or, really, whether there can be a time after COVID when we're all returned to some sense of normalcy. Poetry shifts our attention to what we take for granted, and I see that in the penultimate poem of the book, "A Story for After the Pandemic." The poem lists what we will do after COVID is no longer the threat it had been, which is hopeful. And yet, primed by the language of disaster in the previous poems, I'm reminded that I'm not quite ready to think about engaging with the world as deeply as the poem promises we will.

The pandemic was a time of introspection for so many of us, a practice that parallels the deep attention poetry requires. After COVID, should we question the purposes and effects of poetry in light of the disaster that was—and is—the pandemic?

JHG: I hope that poetry about the pandemic will serve as a reminder to future generations of what can and will happen—pandemics, after all, have been happening on a regular basis since human history began—the last one, the 1918 flu, which lasted three years and killed one in every ten Americans, has barely any literary footprint. Americans like to stamp out unpleasant history, but history has lessons that can help us manage crises, so I hope it doesn't stamp out the literature this time around.

I think also people were reminded of their mortality and I hope that drove up reading and engaging with the literary arts. I don't know for sure that it did; that's just my optimist side, hoping.

IFP: I'd like to end with a question about disaster and hope. Throughout, there's a threat of power loss or an acknowledgment of the fragility of the grid, as in "When I Thought I Was Dying," "Self-Portrait as Murder Mystery," and "Lights Out." Of course, this loss of

electricity would be detrimental, especially on a wide scale. There's the literal loss of electricity, but looming larger is the idea of power loss in the sense of losing agency.

And yet, "Lights Out" ends by reminding us "Now we seek the unfamiliar silence, / the strange solace of perfect dark." The past few years have been strange, to say the least, but we can adapt. With that in mind, I wanted to ask how you have adapted to the pandemic as a poet "behind the scenes." Has it changed your process as a writer? And in this post-COVID era (which perhaps isn't truly so), what projects are you currently working on?

JHG: I've got another manuscript almost ready to go, and lately, I've been resurrecting mythological characters again, this time talking about climate change, virology, and the cyclical nature of disaster.

The pandemic definitely made me feel isolated (I'm an extrovert, but I have asthma, MS, and a primary immune deficiency, so I'm at high risk for bad outcomes with covid), and I'm hoping to return to at least partial normalcy as they come up with better protections and better antivirals to help us all control covid deaths, disability, etc. I wrote a LOT of poems about covid—over 100—and only a few made it into *Flare, Corona*. Also, during the pandemic, I started doing walks around the neighborhood, and made friends with local farm and winery workers, and ended up being invited to start a book club at a Woodinville winery, which was a great way to connect (in a small way) with my community again. I'm just now scheduling in-person readings for the first time in three years, which is going to be...interesting? challenging?

Jeannine Hall Gailey served as the second Poet Laureate of Redmond, Washington. She's the author of five other books of poetry: *Becoming the Villainess, She Returns to the Floating World, Unexplained Fevers, The Robot Scientist's Daughter*, and *Field Guide to the End of the World*, winner of the Moon City Press Book Prize and the SFPA's Elgin Award. She's also the author of *PR for Poets*, a non-fiction guide to help poets publicize their books. Her work has been featured on *The Writer's Almanac, Verse Daily*, and *The Best Horror of the Year*. She holds a B.S. in Biology and an M.A. in English from University of Cincinnati, and an MFA from Pacific University. Her poetry has appeared in *The American Poetry Review, Ploughshares*, and *Poetry*; her personal essays have appeared on *Salon.com* and *The Rumpus*. Find out more at her website: https://webbish6.com/

CAUGHT BETWEEN TWO WORLDS: FAMILY, FAR AWAY PLACES, AND FORMAL POETRY: INTERVIEW WITH LINDAANN LOSCHIAVO, AUTHOR OF APPRENTICED TO THE NIGHT

T.D. WALKER

> "My tangible world always contained elements of the supranormal, however, I never revealed this to outsiders—— and deliberately omitted it from my writing ——until the pandemic."

Although much of recent speculative poetry, like much of all contemporary poetry, is written in free verse—that is, the lines do not have a strict meter—many poets today work in traditional forms. Not only do these forms give us beautiful poems, they remind us of poetry's rich traditions, such as the work of early speculative poet Christina Rossetti. Such structure also calls to mind other frameworks in which we find meaning, particularly heritage and family. T.D. Walker spoke with LindaAnn LoSchiavo about the formal poems in her book, *Apprenticed to the Night* (*Beacon Books*, 2023).

Interstellar Flight Press: You begin the collection with the poem which shares its title with the book, a poem that invites us in through a quote from Christina Rossetti's "Goblin Market." In this poem, an otherworldly owl offers the speaker of the poem to explore the night,

though it rescinds the offer. Why did you choose to begin the collection with this poem? And how did you shape the rest of the book through the lens it offers, given what the owl refuses?

LindaAnn LoSchiavo: Christina Rossetti's father, Gabriele, born in Vesto (Abruzzi, Italy), was living in a foreign land (England) in exile, therefore, he had to adjust and learn a new language. Though my Neapolitan maternal grandparents were not exiled to the USA, they never adjusted to New York nor learned to speak English. They felt displaced, disrespected, and disappointed; their sad resignation affected me greatly since we lived with them until I was 4 ½ years old, and I adored them. I'd always daydreamed about a faraway sphere *Italia senzo tempo* [*timeless Italy*], where Dante would be writing poetry, and Puccini would be conjuring up grand operas, where my grandfather would still be a teenager studying art and painting, and my convent-bred grandmother would still be a girl mastering lacemaking, European refinements that seemed inaccessible to an American child like me.

I felt caught between two worlds, living in a dull one, always pining for the fantastic other.

My Catholic upbringing colored the way I read Rossetti's poem, too. Critics have analyzed "Goblin Market" as an allegory of temptation and salvation, or a comment on Victorian gender roles and female agency, or a work of erotic desire and social redemption.

I leaned toward seeing Lizzie and Laura as one individual, L, at different stages of development.

Pleasure-seeking Laura, heedless and eager for instant gratification, is L in her childish phase.

Cautious Lizzie, suspicious of satisfaction that comes easy, is L as a responsible adult.

In my title poem, instead of evading the quotidian and "indulging darkness" via enchanted goblin fruit, the narrator temporarily outwalks pain, thanks to an accommodating owl who pierces "a pinhole in the sky." When the owl realizes the narrator has opted for escapism and self-indulgence (i.e., arrested development), it withdraws access and implores her to manage reality's challenges and grow up.

"Its lunar eyes implored me to retrain

My gaze, accept mundanity, enjoy

Scant years allotted to my fading name...."

After this prelude, and its reference to Rossetti's "Goblin Market," the collection sets forth to chart the narrator's hurdles as she stumbles through childhood trauma and loss and gradually matures.

Deliberately, one of the last poems (placed third to the last) reprises the reference to close the loop, as it were.

IFP: How did the collection take shape? Where in the process did the speculative elements emerge? Did anything shift or surprise you as you wrote and ordered the poems in the book?

LL: Typically, with any new manuscript, my attention is divided between composing and researching potential publishers. However, since *Apprenticed to the Night* was written under contract, its final destination was pre-arranged, and this freedom was liberating. Since my proposal included a selection of core poems and I had gotten their feedback, these polished pieces became the skeleton. New poems added bones, internal organs, and flesh until I had a complete body of work arranged in a (somewhat) chronological order.

One of my new verses, the title poem, deliberatively speculative, prepares the reader for the elements of fantasy, alternate history, impossibility, and the supernatural.

One surprise as I wrote new material, always aware of my October 1st deadline, was how easily I could set aside a piece that did not fit. Then, in order to magnify key themes, fortify a suite of poems (i.e., the dying mother section), or to make a transition smoother, I kept writing Golden Shovels and Centos, whose reverb from other poets became a Greek chorus.

IFP: The poems in your book weave between the material and spiritual realms. You give us richly detailed portraits of the family in New York in poems such as "Merletto [Lace]" and "The Bones of the Hospital [Le ossa dell' ospedale]" before leading us into the spectral world of "The Poltergeists of President Street." In this poem, we see "Haunting memories must have gnawed at the apparition's loneliness, continuing a ferocious domestic drama, echoing long ago chaos."

Since the poems, like the ghosts, move between worlds, how did you want your readers to engage with the supernatural elements in your poems in light of the richness of the remembered tangible world? What do you hope to shift in the way they see both, particularly in poems such as "The Widow's Missing Necklace"?

LL: My tangible world always contained elements of the supranormal, however, I never revealed this to outsiders—— and deliberately omitted it from my writing ——until the pandemic. My stay-at-home Mom, for example, communicated telepathically with my Dad when he was at work. In our family, telepathing was not considered "extraordinary." It was taken for granted. One day when I was 11 years old, and my mother realized my father left important paperwork behind, she said, "Call Daddy. Make him come home." There were no further instructions. But I soon realized that I, too, could telepath a message successfully; my father returned a few minutes later, asking, "Why am I here? I'm supposed to be driving to New Jersey!"

Later on, as a teen, I volunteered to read the Tarot to help raise funds for scholarships —— with the condition that I would never touch nor accept money. In some cases, I did "read" the Tarot cards. But more often, as the querent approached my table and before the querent spoke, I "heard" the question —— and the answer, too.

The poem "The Dungeon Ghost" is based on my necromancy, telepathy, and psychic gifts.

In my own life, I move easily between the mundane and the spiritual realm; the spectral world is not "out of the norm," and I hope readers will be open-minded when reading these poems.

My Uncle Larry, who held poker games in a violently haunted house, is also the deceased husband who returns his widow's missing necklace, its clasp now repaired.

In my family, none of this was considered "extraordinary."

My paranormal collection, "Dark and Airy Spirits," features more of these experiences.

IFP: To return to Christina Rossetti, the poet appears in your collection, both before and in the body of your poems "Apprenticed to the Night," "Cento: Nightsong for Mother," and "Spellcasting on Samhain." In a poem not in this collection, you've written about her sister-in-law in "Elizabeth Siddal Rossetti, Cemetery Superstar."

What do you find about Christina Rossetti's poems that is so compelling even now, especially as a speculative poet? And since *Apprenticed to the Night* is a book about family, do you see the Rossetti family as part of the larger legacy of Rossetti's work?

LL: Her simple language can seem so artless and unaffected, yet there are gems to be mined in her oeuvre. Speculative poetry gave the never-married Christina Rossetti a vehicle to express her disappointment with the narrative of romantic love that invariably failed women. Ex: in "The Prince's Progress," she offered a second-person condemnation of a dawdling fairy-tale prince.

Like Poe, Rossetti used Gothic imagery to depict not only environments with typically barren wastelands but also doomed characters without hope of redemption or salvation —— as seen in "The Hour and the Ghost," "The Ghost's Petition," and elsewhere.

As a true Gothic writer, Rossetti devoted quite a number of speculative poems to restless ghosts, vengeful spirits, and death, using Gothic imagery to portray her views of life beyond the grave and how it affects those who are still alive.

In the poem I referenced in my cento, "A Chilly Night" by Rossetti, we follow a speaker who gets out of bed "at the dead of night" to walk to the "lattice alone" and watch for her mother's ghost in the moonlight.

Yes, the Rossetti family definitely fostered, funded, appreciated, and boosted Christina's work. Also, her famous brother Dante added his very popular artwork to her writing.

IFP: Many of the book's poems are in different forms. I'm especially curious about those with metered lines, as in "Golden Shovel: Night's Nemesis" and "My Mother's Ghost Dancing." For these formal poems, how do you approach composing the lines in meter, particularly in light of the full arc of the poem? What do you find appealing about writing in meter, especially since most speculative poems are not strictly metered?

LL: I identify as a formalist, and my "go to" mode, for years, has been blank verse composed in iambic pentameter, which you noticed even in my "Golden Shovel: Night's Nemesis" —— although most other poets will rely on free verse when tackling a Golden Shovel (i.e., the lazy way out).

"Night's Nemesis," the second poem in the collection, subtly echoes the first poem by using the owl again; here, it's "Owl-eyed determination not to sleep."

Whereas Sara Teasdale's very short poem was an ironic comment about tormented nights of writing poetry, verses that readers would assume was written in ease, in "Apprenticed to the Night," *night's nemesis* is insomnia. Its disruption and discomfort are echoed in the harsh plosive stop of P words: people, prayers, polish, apology, and pit, meant to poke the reader. Normally, I would not end a line with weak words such as *and*, *that*, or *like* —— but a Golden Shovel deals a poet a hand that cannot be changed.

Here's what I find appealing about formal verse: the meter and the subtle rhyming, which requires far more discipline, skill, and craft than free verse.

Poetry is created with a rhythm. By tuning my ears to iambs, trochees, and spondees, I feel I have a better sense of a line's rhythm.

Meter is especially significant when reading poetry aloud because it guides the desired voice fluctuations.

Yet much of the skill in formal verse is making the scaffolding disappear: the rhymes ought to seem quite natural, unforced.

You may have noticed even if a poem is in blank verse, I'll add rhyme to certain lines for emphasis.

Specifically, in "Merletto" (Lace), the repetition of rhyming words such as lace / face / place / embraced / trace / braced/ debased are there to mimic the redundant patterns of lacework.

In "My Dungeon Ghost," the ten-beats of each line are deliberately not iambic to convey the waywardness of this classmate's life and his self-destructive choices. Yet each stanza is tied off neatly with a couplet as a mighty exhale after the onrush of the madness.

In "My Mother's Ghost Dancing," the first stanzas focus on 3-syllable words that begin with M: minuet, mortality, metronome, marathon. The bilabial nasal repetition of M is also picked up in morphine, mother, mode. The second and third stanzas introduce D words, a stop consonant, to drum up a feeling of impending doom in the melody: Depression, endurance, dance, despite, defiant, deceiving. Then the fifth and sixth stanzas release a cluster of E words, a relaxed mid-front vowel, to lighten the tempo: energy, expressed, embrasures, freed, embrace, entertainment, erase, everyone's. These deliberate sound shifts create the full arc of this 24-line poem hand-in-hand with the iambic pentameter. Slant rhymes (dance / hand) tie the last two line together.

. . . But first she wants to dance.

A coldness sidles up to seize my hand.

IFP: On the topic of formal poems, you also include centos in the collection, such as "Cento: Benighted Night." What is your process for writing these poems that lace together lines from other poets? How do you choose the poets you borrow from, and what makes their poems work particularly well for this form?

LL: From the moment I started working on "Apprenticed to the Night," I began to write down titles of favorite poems about the night, for example, Robert Frost's "Acquainted with the Night" and other moody pieces that fit my themes.

The process starts with a practice of regularly reading poetry and keeping a journal. My vast wine cellar of verse is there to dip into. The same way an adult acquires knowledge about which wine to serve with fish, a poet acquires a mental database about which poets write movingly about mothers, or nightmares, or growing up as an Italian-American, or living in New York.

The next step is identifying why I need a cento. Will it magnify a theme? Will it make for a smoother transition? When I look over the lines I might repurpose, these must all maintain the same verb tense and POV. Most importantly, the cento must build its own interior narrative arc.

IFP: What are you currently working on? In October 2022, Audience Askew Chapbooks published *Messengers of the Macabre: Halloween Poems* which you wrote with David Davies. Are there other projects you have in the works as well?

LL: My works in progress are these three manuscripts:

* * "Always Haunted: Hallowe'en Poems"—24 speculative poems—completely written and illustrated. This is now with a publisher who requested it.

Summary: Haunting and harrowing visions of All Hallows' Eve here include horrific crimes committed on October 31st, a honeymoon homicide, mysterious witches, amorous vampires, dead serious poltergeists, along with a pageant of autumnal imagery sure to evoke goosebumps beyond the spooky season.

Essence: Wearing the cunning costume of a Hallowe'en poetry collection, 24 poems reimagine macabre true crimes and explore injustices.

* * "Dark and Airy Spirits"—60+ poems + illustrations. These poems are both speculative and paranormal.

Summary: The uncanny poems in "Dark and Airy Spirits," focused on the afterlife and netherworld, deftly weave a multifaceted tapestry of atmospheric nightscapes, poltergeist-plagued parlors, shapeshifting seducers, restless souls, graveyard reunions, along with the poet's poignant real-life encounters with spirits. In this hybrid mix of prose-poems and formal verse, the collection creates a portal for the passing of souls. To stand in the circle of their spell is to perform along with them a kind of blessing and valediction.

Essence: These eerie verses will haunt you the way art should, illuminating the way the living and the deceased sustain an intimate conversation which death alters but cannot silence.

"Apprenticed to the Night" has dramatically changed my thinking about a poetry book's narrative arc. I'm trying to bring that cohesiveness and tension to "Dark and Airy Spirits."

- * "Past Tense: Poems & Portraits of Suicides"—speculative poems and nearly finished artistic portraits. "Past Tense..." will be my follow-up to "Felones de Se: Poems about Suicide" [Ukiyoto, 2023].
- **Summary**: Spanning a period from 1902–2022, this collection employs a dynamic range of forms, arrow-shot elixirs in words that summon the shock of suicide. Tapping art's fundamental impulse to

preserve, these provocative poems speak to the human desire to fix in words what would otherwise slip our grasp.

- **Essence**: Slip into death's sidecar for a journey that promises to be honest, aching, and intimate.

Native New Yorker LindaAnn LoSchiavo, a four time nominee for The Pushcart Prize, has also been nominated for Best of the Net, the Rhysling Award, and Dwarf Stars. Elgin Award winner "A Route Obscure and Lonely," "Women Who Were Warned," Firecracker Award, Quill and Ink, and IPPY Award nominee "Messengers of the Macabre" [co-written with David Davies], "Apprenticed to the Night" [Beacon Books, 2023], and "Felones de Se: Poems about Suicide" [Ukiyoto Publishing, 2023] are her latest poetry titles. In 2023, her poetry placed as a finalist in Thirty West Publishing's "Fresh Start Contest" and in the 8th annual Stephen DiBiase contest. For more information about *Apprenticed to the Night*, see the publisher's website: https://universepress.net/product/apprenticed-to-the-night/

STEM, WOMEN SCIENTISTS, AND SEXISM: INTERVIEW WITH JESSY RANDALL, AUTHOR OF MATHEMATICS FOR LADIES: POEMS ON WOMEN IN SCIENCE

T.D. WALKER

"I felt furiously angry as I researched the scientists, and I was constantly tempted to basically set my notebook on fire out of rage and frustration."

One of the aims of science fiction that gives us hope about the future of humanity is to show equality in access to education and employment opportunities in the sciences. We as a society still struggle with that today in the field. Before we can move forward, though, we need to acknowledge the inequality of the past. T.D. Walker spoke with Jessy Randall about researching the lives and crafting the voices of the historical women scientists presented in her book about their struggles and triumphs.

INTERSTELLAR FLIGHT PRESS: You mention in the acknowledgments for your book, *Mathematics for Ladies*, that a lecture by Professor Barbara Whitten of the Colorado College physics department about Sarah Frances Whiting sparked both the poem about Whiting as well as the larger project. How did the project evolve out of that poem? And how did you choose the scientists you feature in the collection?

JESSY RANDALL: In her presentation, Dr. Whitten showed a slide of a star image, which to my eyes, was just a grayish smear. She said that Whiting's colleague Annie Jump Cannon was able to recognize these star images years after cataloging them—even though she cataloged thousands and thousands of stars. The name "Annie Jump Cannon" was so great that I wrote it down and then did some research on her. Her life and work were fascinating, and I ended up writing around twenty or thirty poems about her, thinking maybe I could do a little chapbook. That idea didn't go anywhere but instead led me to research other women scientists. I read several library books about women in STEM (I'm a librarian), in particular a series of "Biobibliographic Sourcebooks" edited by Grinstein et al., which led me to more and more women. I also received recommendations when I talked about the project to friends and family. I ended up with over a hundred poems, too many for a book. A friend of mine, poet Daniel M. Shapiro, helpfully advised me to cut the "I am so and so and I did such and such" poems and keep the ones that were more "I can break your heart or teach you something or be a metaphor that works perfectly." So I tried to do that and also to have a diverse group of scientists, women of different backgrounds working in a variety of fields.

IFP: Part of the power of the poems in the book is in the details you focus on that take your readers to the larger context the women were working in (and often against). For instance, we see Caroline Herschel making a mirror, Maria Mitchell decrying Vassar's curfew that kept her away from the night sky, Charlotte Angas Scott attending lectures behind a screen at Cambridge to prevent her from distracting the male students.

Since this is a book that takes us from historical details to the larger themes at work, I wanted to ask about your process for researching the lives and work of the scientists you focus on. How did you approach that research? Did your professional work as an archivist shape the way you sought and interpreted the materials you used?

JR: Yes, absolutely. The "biobibliographic" books brought me to most of the scientists—I wouldn't have known about them otherwise, as they aren't household names. From there, as a librarian, I knew how to find primary source materials for some of the scientists. I could track down published diaries and letters and memoirs and sometimes make use of digitized images of handwritten materials or original drawings. It's a bit circular, of course, because part of the reason I went into librarianship is that I love research and writing, so it's not so strange that I would start up a writing project that involves a lot of research.

IFP: One of the overarching themes of the book is the women's agency and how they struggle to achieve ownership of even their own ideas. We see Maria Sibylla Merian collecting caterpillars and that "she

decided / to leave [her husband] and to take back her maiden name." Later, Marie Germain contends, "I'll call myself *Leblanc*." In "Rebecca Lee Crumpler (1831– 1895)," you note about Dr. Crumpler that "She called herself *doctress*. / She called herself *businesswoman*. / She called herself *being*."

How do you see identity tied with this sense of agency denied to the women in the book? And did the way the women saw themselves shape the way you want your readers to see them through the poems?

JR: You can't escape issues around names when you research historical women in STEM fields. Women's names were frequently removed or buried. Historically, women scientists often used pseudonyms or published anonymously. If she married, a woman scientist had to think about her name in a way that her husband did not. If she'd established a reputation with her original name, did she start over with a new name? And what if she married another scientist, as many of the women in my book did? Did she take her husband's name and risk her work being confused with his? Or risk people assuming she rode his coattails? These issues, and the language around the issues, will seem, I hope, very old-fashioned to people now and in the future, but for the women in my book, they were immediate and real.

IFP: Moving back to the idea that the poems move from personal details to larger conclusions, I'd like to ask about your use of details from some of the scientists' childhoods. Susan La Flesche Picotte witnesses racism and resulting death during her childhood. Hertha Ayrton's views were shaped by her parents' work and her experience as one of their eight children. We see six-year-old Elizabeth Blackwell pushing herself to extremes, as your notes tell us: "As a child, she deliberately makes herself suffer to see what her body can withstand."

I'm curious about your process with these poems that take us back that far into your subjects' lives. I read these examples as pushing at time: if we're given a glimpse that far back in these women's personal histories, then we need to look even farther forward from them. How did you think about time in relation to the poems? And did that sense of time affect how you chose the details you used for the poems?

JR: I remember a writer (I can't remember who) saying the childhood part of a biography is always the most interesting. I didn't read full biographies of all the scientists in my book, but when I did, I often found wonderful stories in the childhood sections—stories that were different from the crushingly frequent "faced obstacles, was told no, was discouraged, suffered, was ignored, was left out" later part of their lives. I couldn't capture a full whole person in each poem—heck, even in a thousand-page biography, a person can't be fully captured. But I did want to include visions of these scientists in different parts of their lives.

IFP: One thing I appreciate about the collection is that among all the struggle, you also show us moments of joy. These women faced adversity, but they also found meaning and even happiness through their work. For example, in "Elizabeth Cabot Agassiz (1822– 1907)," we see her personal and professional fulfillment: "As I write these lines I remember / that day in the boat and how happy / we were." Alicia Boole Stott calls her work "My imagination on paper. / Heaven." And there's defiance and confidence wrapped up in the concluding lines of "Ynes Mexia (1870– 1938)": "I may // have started late but I'll finish strong."

Even though the women in your poems accomplished great things, the sexism they faced weighs that down. But these moments of contentment and of triumph counteract that. That said, there's a sense of determination throughout. How did you approach tone when you were writing the poems for the book? And did that shift as you were writing the poems throughout the project?

JR: I wrote a lot of furiously angry poems. Wait, that's not quite true. It's more that I felt furiously angry as I researched the scientists, and I was constantly tempted to basically set my notebook on fire out of rage and frustration. Some of the poems may have started out as, you know, "Goddammit! Sexism sucks! Let me tell you in detail how!!" because that's where the research took me. But, you know, no writer or reader wants to dwell in complaint for too long. And anyway, the scientists wouldn't have gotten any work done if all they did was wallow, and I followed their lead.

IFP: Many of the poems are in first person, though some are in third. What was behind this shift, giving us some of the women's voices directly and showing others' lives from a more distant vantage?

JR: Sometimes third person was required by the subject matter. For Nina Karlovna Bari, for example, I wanted to talk about her death, which may have been suicide. I couldn't do that very well in first person—I needed to leave some ambiguity. I also worried about speaking from the point of view of women of color. It seemed ... ugh, I've just googled synonyms for "arrogant," "obnoxious," "brash," ... none of them are quite right. For so long, in literature, writers—usually white men—have felt fully entitled to write from the point of view of people whose experience is far from their own. I'm not 100% against that, in theory, but I was uneasy with the idea that I could imagine the experience of all of these scientists in equal measure. So, sometimes I used third person because I didn't feel I had the right to speak for a scientist. Other times it was because I wanted to leave some mystery or unknowns that wouldn't make sense if the poem was in first person.

IFP: Another one of the aspects of the collection that I appreciated is the directness of the poetry: you give us the women's voices in language that doesn't obscure them, as they often had to obscure themselves. In that way, we're invited into the conversation to really listen, which makes the conclusions your poems lead us to all the more compelling. As a reader, I feel like I've heard from this wide-ranging set of women, and yet the effect is still that of a cohesive work. Can you take us through balancing your own poetic voice with the scientists' voices you inhabit to create the collection?

JR: Ah, what a wonderful thing to say. Thank you! Certainly, my idea with the book as a whole was to call attention to these amazing women scientists who are not as famous as they deserve to be. I'm not a Hollywood producer, someone who could really make a difference, you know? I can't throw millions of dollars into a film about Elizabeth Blackwell. The best I can do is to make a bite-size, intriguing, real-seeming (that's a funny expression!) glimpse into the life and work of these scientists. I'm afraid there is probably a through-line with the voice, though. Writing personae poems is a good excuse to experiment, but I think it's impossible to escape your own voice overall.

IFP: If we could end with a return to the idea of faith in self and work, I'd like to ask you about "Mary Treat (1830– 1923)." We see her as feminine, as a hostess, arranging the habitats of the spiders she studies "so guests don't startle." She looks at her subjects "like kids / stare at sweets." She inhabits the guise of a teacher: "I schooled Darwin on bugs."

What makes this poem so compelling for me is that you turn these feminine aspects of her life into what is most powerful about her: "I write / like a woman and invite readers in." She makes moves toward inclusiveness when the larger scientific community of the time must have worked toward excluding her and other women working in the sciences.

The women in your collection have all merited biographies and even fictional works about their lives. That said, what is it about poetry's ability in particular to "invite readers in" that made the genre work well for you as a way to explore their lives and achievements?

JR: Doing science as a woman is important and useful. I've just been reading about Fanny Hesse (1858–1934), who, because she did the "women's work" of cooking, was able to solve a problem with samples in Petri dishes. Gelatin melts, and specimens would be ruined, but Hesse suggested using agar, which has a higher melting point. HUGE innovation. Think of how much further ahead science would be if women hadn't been excluded! OK, but back to poetry and inviting people in. At some point in the project, I started picturing kids in school: young scientists being bored in English classes and young poets being bored in science classes. And I thought maybe these poems could help cross that divide. We still don't have gender parity in the sciences, and we know that girls are still getting steered away, one way or another (see https://www.aauw.org/resources/research/the-stem-gap/).

Now, conversely, I do understand that reading poems might be boring for almost EVERYONE—but at least they're short, right? And maybe, if young people learned about more than just Marie Curie, if they heard about the contributions women have made, maybe they wouldn't drop out of that higher-level math class or whatever. Representation matters, and short poems don't take long to read. This all sounds way more didactic and prescriptive than I ever wanted the poems to be, but wouldn't it be cool if all the seventh-grade kids had to become, for a day, experts on one woman scientist in the book?

Jessy Randall's poems and stories have appeared in Asimov's, Nature, Poetry, and Scientific American. Her most recent book is Mathematics for Ladies: Poems on Women in Science (MIT, 2022). She is a librarian at Colorado College and her website is http://personalwebs.coloradocollege.edu/~jrandall/.

SEASONS OF QUESTIONING: GRIEF, PARENTING, AND NAVIGATING ILLNESS: INTERVIEW WITH EMILY HOCKADAY, AUTHOR OF *NAMING THE GHOST*

T.D. WALKER

Grief opens us to ask questions of ourselves and of our world as a way of contending with deep loss. The poems in Emily Hockaday's *Naming the Ghost* carry us through that process of questioning and give us space to consider how we see losses through what can and cannot be answered. T.D. Walker spoke with Emily Hockaday about her 2022 collection, published by *Cornerstone Press.*

INTERSTELLAR FLIGHT PRESS: The poems in *Naming the Ghost* form a loose narrative as we follow the speaker as she grapples with the presence in her home that she understands as a ghost. How did the project begin? Did you change direction as you wrote the poems for the book?

EMILY HOCKADAY: So this project began when I was doing a poem-a-day month back in 2019. I actually did three back-to-back months of that, and these ghost poems were almost entirely produced during that time. You'll see the seasons change from winter to spring in the book, and that reflected the actual changing seasons that I was writing during.

This was a really weird time for me: a chronic illness began presenting with very unnerving symptoms around the anniversary of my father's death. My mind immediately went to the most dire places, even as doctors ruled out disease after disease. I felt haunted by these symptoms but more profoundly haunted by my own anxiety surrounding them. It took a while to get a diagnosis, which added to the anxiety.

IFP: The question arises again and again in the book: who is the ghost? Other questions arise, and for me, as a reader, I felt drawn into the process of questioning as much as the process of the speaker's world unfolding before me. As you wrote the poems in the book, how did this sense of questioning affect the structure within each poem? And within the collection as a whole?

EH: The questioning in these poems arose organically because as I was writing, I was questioning everything. My body, my health, my sanity, doctors, mortality—you name it. I did have to be careful with the questions in the poems because, as every workshop leader will tell you, putting questions into a poem can be really tricky. They break up the lyrical flow, and while I wanted the questions to do the work, I didn't want them to be obtrusive, repetitive, or gimmicky. There are definitely poems I held back from the manuscript and questions that were pruned out of poems because they were just too much.

IFP: One of the compelling aspects of the book is that you take us to an edge of otherworldliness but keep us firmly grounded in the world as we know it. Dreams give us that glimpse into the liminal space, the space of questioning.

We see the speaker's dreams, but also, as in "How the Ghost Got In," those of others as well: "In my dreams. / In my husband's dreams; my daughter's dreams." In "The Sound of the Ghost," the speaker asks, "Or is it only me / who wakes in the night, out of someone / else's dream?"

What drew you to using dreams as a thread throughout? And did you want to challenge your readers' ideas about what we can know about our world as they exist in dreams?

EH: I wanted the opportunity to use larger metaphor to explore the themes in the book or insert surreal moments (in the way that actual dreams sort and quantify what the brain is mulling over), and I felt like the ghost was kind of crowding those opportunities out in the waking moments. Or, in other words, when the speaker was awake, there wasn't room for any metaphor/surreal elements that weren't directly tied to the ghost. I also wanted to indicate that there wasn't any refuge in sleep—this current of anxiety followed the speaker even in her dreams.

IFP: While dreams are significant, the poems are very much grounded in the physical, which creates an intriguing tension between what we can ask of our senses, how we sense what we sense. In "The Amygdala Speaks for Me," the speaker asserts that "The ghost teaches me about

my brain." In "The Ghost Transcends," she asks, "What makes it so hard to love / the body I'm in?" And in "I Tell Friends:" "My body betrays me. / The fibromyalgia pain becomes something / more sinister: my father's ALS, cancer, terminal. / Surely this will end with my death."

And yet, the poem I returned to is "The Body I Had," which concludes, "I see through me / to the past-me to the body / I had before my daughter. / I am the only one / that thinks my body now / is more beautiful." There's hope in this, and there's a sense of endurance in this. In one of the last poems in the book, we see that "my edges are / becoming visible / again," that she is changing yet again, a body in space rather than a ghost herself.

In the poems, the cadence of the language feels like a question as much as the questions themselves raised about the body and its limits. And yet, there's the tension there, too: the short lines assert and attest. How did the process of crafting the structure of the poems work with the underlying questions you raise through them?

EH: Crafting the shape of the poems and the line breaks was totally different than any other book I've written. I mentioned already that I wrote these during poem-a-day challenges—well, at the time, I had almost no time to write, so I wrote these by using the voice-to-text feature on my phone while pushing my daughter in the stroller home from daycare. So, at the end of this writing period, I had a bunch of prose blocks that I had to chisel into poems.

I wanted the poems to look somewhat uniform, and I think that was actually a holdover from them all being little blocks of text to start with. So when breaking these, I looked for places that might give the lines new meaning if they were separated or add tension to the poem.

There were some poems where I was struggling to break the lines, and for those, I looked at syllabic line breaks, which again gave that feeling of uniformity.

IFP: Let's turn back to the ghost. In "The Ghost Is My Own," a therapist raises the question of whether the ghost is the speaker's recently deceased father, which is a question that remains with the reader.

There's also a strong focus on parenting throughout. The speaker's child is still quite young, and many of the details in the poems show the speaker in her daily tasks of caring for the baby. We also see the ghost engaging with the baby, such as through books in "The Ghost Has Started Reading."

The lines that conclude "Forget About the Ghost" drew me in: "It may be that she'll forget the ghost, / until one day she's perhaps a mother / herself, watching her own child, / feeling something just over her shoulder."

If the ghost is the speaker's father, then we can read this both as a literal ghost watching the now-baby and her future child. We can also read this as the ways in which parenting styles are passed down through generations. I'm curious about the layering here: because the identity of the ghost is so in question, and because those who have small children must be, by necessity, preoccupied with parenting, was there a further question here that you wanted to explore about the ways in which parenting styles are handed down and altered over generations?

EH: I think I wanted to explore passed-down anxiety or the anxiety associated with changing from the role of child to parent. After becoming a parent, I was suddenly very concerned with my own health—not just because I had an illness that I couldn't get a diagnosis for, but also because I now felt this responsibility to stick around. I had this new important job, which was parenting. I didn't want anything to come between me and that new role. And I remembered my mom telling me that when us kids were little, she had a period of being really concerned about her own health for that same reason.

And then, of course, there is the anxiety that comes with keeping a child safe.

IFP: One of the potential pitfalls of a "project book" is that by keeping your reader with the same narrative voice mulling over questions about the ghost throughout, you might lose your readers.

And yet, every poem in this book feels like a fresh look at the issues at hand, and we can see the narrator progressing through the questions even if she's not able to definitively answer them. We may look at the same things in subsequent poems, but we never see them the same way as in the previous ones. So I was absolutely compelled to move with her on that path through to the end of the book.

Was this question of retreading ideas in your mind as you wrote the poems? And how did you ensure that each poem is not only unique but also integral to the coherent whole the book makes?

EH: I'm so glad to hear that you felt the poems didn't get stale. I did worry about retreading the same topics too much! There are a lot of poems that didn't make it into the manuscript because I didn't feel they added anything to the conversation/story of the poems. I hoped that since the story progresses, and there's a kind of resolution at the end, that the poems leading there wouldn't feel too similar and would instead add something to the collection as a whole. And I did try looking at the ghost/situation from as many different angles as possible so that I would have poems to choose from rather than feel like I needed each poem just to get the manuscript thick enough.

IFP: In "Who Bends the Light," I loved the lines describing the baby learning words: "Language grows inside of her / like the roots of a garden."

Poetry gives us language for its subjects, and in this book, we see a language of mourning built from the words of a body, pained and enduring, and of the quiet dailiness of parenting a baby. So, I'd like to return to your process regarding the language of the poems. How do you see the language that you used both in the process of writing the poems and now after the book has been completed? And how do you want your readers to reassess how they engage in speaking both about ghosts as well as bodies after reading your book?

EH: As I mentioned, these poems kind of tumbled out of me. Once I wrote a couple of ghost poems, I realized that they were going to be a thing, so at that point, I took my time exploring and questioning this metaphor, using whatever language came to me.

It was later in the editing process that I thought more carefully about the language I was using. I went through and saw that I used the word "ghost" way too much, and one of my cherished beta readers mentioned that the ghost was less scary/impactful than what was literally happening to my body and my sanity. So then I went back through the manuscript with the word "ghost" highlighted, and I only kept it where I really wanted it. I replaced many instances with what I was literally trying to describe: pain, fear, fatigue—the symptoms I was experiencing and the paranoia it was causing me not to have a diagnosis. I wanted to replicate what was happening in my body and mind—without being too relentless.

IFP: I'd like to end by asking you what you're currently working on. Do your current projects have similar themes as *Naming the Ghost*, or are they more of a departure from this book?

The next project I'm excited about is *In a Body*, which, as the title indicates, also touches on the experience of being in a body with a chronic illness. This book is much different, though! These poems were all written after I received a diagnosis and treatment, so the poems don't come from a place of fear but rather a place of looking for peace.

This book is being published with Harbor Editions in October 2023, and the poems are stand-alone rather than a series like *Naming the Ghost*, and while there are still some poems that deal with grief, the main theme of *In a Body* is ecology and ecopoetry. These poems look at what it's like to be in an ill body and how other bodies in nature—plant, animal, fungal, geological—function and can function as metaphor.

Emily Hockaday is the author of NAMING THE GHOST (Cornerstone Press 2022), IN A BODY (Harbor Editions, October 2023), and six chapbooks. She is the recipient of grants from NYFA's Queens Art Fund, the DeGroot Foundation, Cafe Royal Cultural Foundation & NY City Artists Corps. She can be found tweeting @E_Hockaday and online at www.emilyhockaday.com.

SCHOLARSHIP, SONG, AND THE SUPERNATURAL: INTERVIEW WITH KENDRA PRESTON LEONARD, PHD, AUTHOR OF GRAB

T.D. WALKER

Poetry gives scholars a way to manifest their insights into their subjects in thought-provoking ways to audiences outside academia. T.D. Walker spoke with Kendra Preston Leonard about her poetry collection *Grab* and how her research shaped the poems in her book.

Interstellar Flight Press: *Grab* begins with "Gretchen at the Loom / Gretchen am Webstuhl," a poem in the voice of title character, a character in Goethe's *Faust* who is seduced and will die for drowning her child, born out of wedlock. The poem shifts between English and German, and we see Grab and the juxtaposition of the English meaning of forcibly taking with the German for grave.

The collection ends with "Smash und Grab," the concluding lines of which warn, "I will grab you / and smash until you are like me." Again, we see references to both the English and German meanings of Grab.

We first see Gretchen contemplating her grave, then we see the speaker of the final poem threatening revenge. Did you begin the collection with this framework in mind? Or did the structure come about later?

Kendra Preston Leonard: Beginning with "Gretchen" and ending with "Smash und Grab" was planned. I wanted to open and close with poems that played with the English and German meanings of "grab." Gretchen is weaving her lover back to life from the grave, but the revenant she creates is not what she expects, and her heart becomes her grave, the thing that undoes her. "Smash und Grab" seemed like low-hanging fruit, with its potential double meanings. It's a reversal of the point of view of "Gretchen," in which it's the revenant who speaks, who comes of its own accord, who visits those who do not expect it. These two poems, both in English and German, are mirrored bookends for the collection.

IFP: Many of the poems are about or refer to storytelling. The speaker assures us in "A Ukrainian Love Story" that "Of course, this is a true story!" In "A Masque to be Played Before the Queen," we see supernatural performers unfolding a story before the court. We're also given the voices or images of figures from literature: Gretchen, Othello and Desdemona, and Cassandra.

So I'm curious too about the idea of the library as a place of great spiritual power. In "Prairie Ghosts," we see "Ghosts come to the library, / and forever after whisper / recommendations in patrons' ears." And a harpy exercises her power in "At the Archive."

For me, these poems serve as reminders about how story serves as spirit: guiding spirits, warning spirits, and so on. How do you want your readers to experience story in light of the way the poems and their speakers and subjects engage and fight against their own stories?

KPL: It's true that for some of the poems in this collection, you might like them more if you know a little bit about the stories they reference: *Bell, Book, and Candle*, the myth of Cassandra, Shakespeare's Othello, Goethe's Gretchen, Bulgakov's *The Master and Margarita*, other things. Retellings and references like these are like fanfiction—they allow you to tell new stories about existing characters and explore new ways of thinking about plots. I don't know that any of the characters I reference here fight against their earlier written incarnations, but rather are liberated from myth, given agency, or take actions we don't read about in their origin stories. I hope readers come away from those poems thinking that for every story, there are countless possible tellings; for every story, we should ask who the narrator is and what their motivations are. Cassandra is a good example: the most common story told about her is that she promised to sleep with Apollo if he'd give her the gift of true prophecy. She agrees, he gives her the gift, and then she refuses to sleep with him, so he curses her, making it so her prophecies aren't believed. In my "Cassandra at the Bonfire," I use a different version of the myth, in which Cassandra's gift comes from letting snakes lick her ears. I make a Cassandra with a radically different source of power, a Cassandra who hints at powers we don't find in the classical myths, a Cassandra speaking for herself.

As for libraries—I've done a lot of archival research, and archives and libraries are places where we show what value we put on the life of the mind. They exist for the creation and use of knowledge and also for pleasure and hope. They're magical and utilitarian and bring people joy and save people's lives.

IFP: We also see dancing throughout the collection. There's the dance hall at the center of "Macalla / Echo." The speaker of "A Spell to Rest the Dead" will use dance as a way to ward off ghosts. Dead men are said to dance in the waters in "A Ukrainian Love Story."

So I'm curious about your use of dance in the context of the supernatural in this collection. What prompted your use of this thread throughout, and how do you see the language of movement in relation to the language of the supernatural?

KPL: Ritual movement is embedded in the idea of supernatural powers: in many stories and tales, practitioners use hand gestures as part of casting a spell or controlling someone or something. In some traditions, dance is used to call on supernatural beings or to communicate with them. Secular dance has its ritualized movements as well, from the way a dancer ties on pointe shoes to dancers lining up for a Texas two-step. I like the idea that moving in specific ways can communicate or bring about actions: in "A Masque to be Played Before the Queen," it's the patterns the dancers make that calls catastrophe to the court.

IFP: Although the collection starts in German language, we're soon given a wider view into the world. The first poem is grounded in Gretchen's experiences and shifts between German and English, but we're also given references to magical rivers around the world: "*jordan, styx, sanzu, yawar mayu*"

Through the collection, we're taken through England, Scotland and father on through Ukraine, Russia, and the American Midwest. There's also a sense of restlessness in the poems of *Grab*, which creates tension with the idea of the grave as a resting place. How did you choose the locations you'd focus on in the poems? And did you find the contrast between locations pushing the collection in a particular direction?

KPL: No matter where you are, there's something that can grab you.

IFP: Since you are a scholar, I wanted to ask about your work in musicology and your writing in other genres, such as plays and song lyrics. How did your academic work inform the poems in *Grab*?

KPL: In two ways: one, my academic background gave me the research tools I used in digging into folklore and mythologies and word origins and history; and two: a number of the poems are partially inspired by places where I've lived or done academic research, or ideas and works I came across while doing scholarly research. The harpy of "At the Archive" is based on a very real person at a very real place, and the musicians and the musicians' gallery of "A Masque" came from my scholarly work on music in depictions of Elizabeth I on film.

IFP: To continue with the idea of your work outside poetry, I also wanted to ask about your other creative writing. I read the spacing in your lines as pauses for breath or contemplation, silences that give the speaker room to build to the next revelation. In "Kappa tankas" and "Trí Púcai," indentations open this space for me, and the first and final poems give room for language shifts in this way too.

Which leads me to ask how you see the poems on the page in light of your work written for performance. Does your writing for theater and music parallel or diverge from your poetry?

KPL: My song lyrics are often very similar to my poetry, but I don't use the more dramatic spacing like I do in "Gretchen"—everything is left-justified for ease of reading. In my libretti, I use line breaks and spaces very deliberately, but, again, everything is left-justified—and the line breaks and spaces are there to communicate the flow of thought, emphasis, emotion, and character to the composer and the performers. I also include notes like "with resignation" or "breathlessly" to indicate a character's mood or the way I want the text to be sung. With libretti, I'm also creating multiple voices and personalities within a single work, so I use different kinds of patterns and language to distinguish them.

IFP: What are your current and forthcoming projects? Are they in the same mode as your poems in *Grab*, or are they going in a different direction?

KPL: I've just finished an opera libretto for composer Steven Sérpa and Opera Queens in Austin, TX, and it has a strong and beautiful queer supernatural component. I'm currently working on the libretto for the opera adaptation of my novella *Protectress*, which is a sequel to the Medusa myth and is being set by composer Jessica Rudman. It's workshopped by Opera Contempo in Utah later this year.

Kendra Preston Leonard writes about music, movies, gorgons, werewolves, Shakespeare, feminism, nature, ghosts, disability, drama, race, paleontologists, and much more. Her first chapbook, *Making Mythology*, was published in 2020 by Louisiana Literature Press. Her novella in verse, *Protectress*, a sequel to the Medusa myth, was published by Unsolicited Press in 2022. Also a musicologist and music theorist, she has written numerous scholarly books in addition to poetry, plays, lyrics, and libretti.

SHORT SFF, DAY JOBS, & LATE NIGHT TV: AN INTERVIEW WITH WILLIAM LEDBETTER, AUTHOR OF THE LONG FALL UP: AND OTHER STORIES

HOLLY LYN WALRATH

Interstellar Flight Press is lucky to have acquired the print versions of William Ledbetter's bestselling audiobook series, *The Killday Series*. In November of 2024, we published Bill's latest collection of short stories, named after the Nebula Award winning short story, "The Long Fall Up". The collection is full of stories that meld high-concept science fiction with the character-based, emotional storytelling any reader will love. Managing Editor Holly Lyn Walrath interviewed Bill about his love of sci-fi, writing short fiction, and of course, pets!

INTERSTELLAR FLIGHT PRESS: Why science fiction? What about the genre is it that you love? How did you get into SFF?

WILLIAM LEDBETTER: I guess I started writing science fiction because I've always loved it. I grew up watching Lost In Space, Star Trek, Voyage to the Bottom of the Sea and those old late night, black and white movies like The Day the Earth Stood Still, Them, Creature from the Black Lagoon, and Earth vs the Flying Saucers. When I started reading books for pleasure, I seemed to immediately gravitate toward science fiction as well. So much so, that when assigned the task of writing a short story for homework in high school, it was of course science fiction, and it received a lot of praise from my teacher and even a few classmates. I think I was kind of hooked on the idea of writing SF after that.

IFP: We know you've got a pretty science-heavy day job. Does your day job impact your writing, and if so, how?

WL: Most of my day job career has been in the aerospace industry, where I worked on interesting projects like the radiator system for the International Space Station, a new rocket launch system, and aircraft turbine engines. I learned a lot about the nuts and bolts engineering side of that industry and what was required to get big clumps of metal to fly in the sky and space. I've always been excited by that, so once I started trying to write science fiction for publication, I tried to make it as realistic as possible in order to make my fiction seem like something that was possible.

IFP: You've been writing short fiction in the SFF fields for a while now. What are your thoughts on the current state of SFF short fiction?

WL: I think SFF short fiction is in a good place. With the addition of online magazines that require only an internet connection to read and online submission systems that enable stories to be sent from anywhere in the world, we are seeing new and interesting voices emerge, telling stories from unusual and original perspectives. It's an exciting time and I'm so glad to be a part of it.

IFP: All your stories are heavy on the tech AND the emotion of the characters. How do you balance the "hard" and the "soft" sides of science fiction when you're writing?

WL: I try to make my stories about people, so I think the emotional core is the most important part, and it should drive the story, but I also think those hard and soft aspects are often complimentary. Cold, uncaring machines or those unassailable laws of physics are often the antagonists in real life and in fiction, can be used to make human problems all the more human. I think the best science fiction is really about how some future situation like an apocalypse or space travel, AIs, or alien invasion affects the protagonist in the story.

IFP: We know you love pets (and so does IFP)—can you tell us about your furry friends?

WL: We have three cats and a dog. All rescues. Two of the cats, Molly Murder Mittens and Princess Buttercup are sisters from a litter of five that we fostered (this is why we don't often foster kittens.) They pretty much own the humans in the house. The other cat, Trixie, was a hungry, skinny stray that wandered up into my mother-in-law's backyard during a family gathering about fourteen years ago. She is not a fan of the younger sisters, who pick on her all the time. Annie is our black lab mix who came home with us after a stop at PetSmart to pick up cat food. She believes she is a princess and expects to be treated as such.

. . .

IFP: Your novelette "The Long Fall Up" won the 2016 Nebula Award. What was it like winning the award? Did you have any idea your story was a contender before it was nominated?

WL: I have to say winning a Nebula Award is definitely one of the highlights of my writing career. Seeing my name on that long list of amazing writers who also won a Nebula is stunning and still amazes me. But yes, there were early indicators. "The Long Fall Up" received a lot of really good reviews. It did well in the SFWA recommended reading list for that year. One of my friends sent a text message cursing me for making her cry, and someone even asked my permission to use it as an example in a writer's workshop. I ended up on the shortlist with some amazing writers in my category, including my long-time friend Bonnie Jo Stufflebeam. This was both good and bad. I was pumped that people in the SFWA writing community felt my story was of high enough quality to be in that group, but also, upon reading those stories, I felt I had little actual chance of winning. So, when I did win, I was truly gob-smacked.

IFP: Can you share any advice for new writers, maybe specifically those interested in getting into short fiction?

WL: Even now, after having written multiple novels, short fiction is still my preferred form. It enables writers to stretch their wings and try new things without the huge time, dedication, and risk of trying them in a novel. I think it is also a perfect medium for new writers to hone their skill set and find their voice. Once you start selling short fiction to professional markets, that's a good indicator that your novel can succeed. I also think short fiction has become a rather uniquely speculative fiction thing. Short fiction used to be popular across all genres and literary forms but seems to have dropped out of the mainstream consciousness in the past 10–20 years. If you tell someone you are a writer, they don't ask where they can find your stories; they ask about your books. But shorts are still a strong storytelling vehicle in speculative fiction. Short stories are even picked up by Hollywood from time to time. Check out the story origins in the animated series Love, Death & Robots or the movie Arrival, etc.

IFP: What are you working on right now?

WL: I've recently sent my agent the synopsis and first three chapters for a new standalone novel. If he can find it a home, the story will be told entirely from the POV of an alien race as they try to save their planet. No humans at all in this tale. I'm also working on a few other short pieces I haven't sent out to publishers yet. "Level Seven," the third novel in my Killday series, will be published in audio on December 7 (then in print next year), and I have a new short story called "Enough," about a graffiti artist taking on an illegitimate fascist government, coming out in the March/April edition of Analog magazine.

William Ledbetter is a Nebula Award winning author with two novels and more than seventy speculative fiction short stories and non-fiction articles published in five languages, in markets such as Asimov's, Fantasy & Science Fiction, Analog, Escape Pod and the SFWA blog. He's been a space and technology geek since childhood and spent most of his non-writing career in the aerospace and defense industry. He is a member of SFWA, the National Space Society of North Texas, and a Launch Pad Astronomy workshop graduate. He lives near Dallas with his wife, a needy dog and three spoiled cats.

Grab a copy of THE LONG FALL UP today!

OUT OF THE EARTH, OUT OF THE CLOSET: MYTHMAKING AND QUEERNESS: AN INTERVIEW WITH MAXWELL I. GOLD, AUTHOR OF ANOTHER MYTHOLOGY

R. THURSDAY

With *anOther Mythology*, Maxwell I. Gold utilizes the structures of mythmaking—most noticeably, Hesiod's Theogony—to explore and construct narratives around queerness, belonging, self-conception, and our place in the world (or above it, or under it, or...) in these rich, lyrical prose poems. R. Thursday interviews Maxwell I. Gold on his latest poetry collection, out this week from Interstellar Flight Press.

INTERSTELLAR FLIGHT PRESS: I thought we might start with something easy (this is a joke). Your book is made up of prose poems. What do you see as the defining characteristics of a prose poem, and what made you choose that form for this work?

MAXWELL I. GOLD: Frankly, a prose poem is a prose composed in a poetic form. There's not a story component, and it is sometimes confused [with] a flash piece, but it's not. Perhaps prose poetry accurately conveys my longwindedness as a person and my love for words in ways I am sometimes unable to expound verbally.

IFP: You said in your author's note that you drew on several mythologies, though obviously, Greek was the main frame you were working from. I wondered, for example, while reading of the 'leathery

serpent-boy,' how often did other belief systems influence the visuals and conceptions of these poems?

MG: While the main body was taken with a more Theogony-type structure that involved similar themes, names, gods we're all familiar with, I wanted this to be a book that rolled traditional conceptions of Western and non-Western myths on their heads. I researched various mythologies and belief systems from Māori, Okinawan, West African cultures, Egyptian, Mesopotamian myths, and the usual suspects, which include Greek and Norse cultures.

Additionally, I had also considered new myths, new names, and new gods and goddesses as I was writing this book. Deconstructing the old world and re-inventing new myths for those who might want to see themselves in them.

IFP: Many of the poems center on Chthonic gods and settings. What do you see as the appeal of death/psychopomp/underworld deities, especially for queer people?

MG: I think confinement and spaces beneath, below, and away from what was to be considered normal relate to many in the queer community because they are words that describe places that are othered; and they have been reclaimed. They're not places to be locked away like Tartarus or the Void, but spaces that we embrace as our own, or something that has always been ours.

IFP: The poems involve multiple characters (it seemed to me), but all are written in first person. Was it difficult to differentiate between them, either in style or conception? Did you see it more like speaking to an element in these figures that you identified with into something more like a collage?

MG: I did see them as different characters, though there was an element of myself speaking through them which made it easier to write the poems in first person. I typically write my poems in first person. Sometimes, I will write in third person, but I feel the experience is more immersive for the reader to remain in first person. At times, I felt it was both speaking to a particular moment and as the character.

For example, in Post-Eros, I was attempting to speak to the primordial god Eros, and the poem became a reaction to that idea, or rather Eros' reaction itself.

IFP: Another thing that struck me was the similarities in theme and style to classic cosmic horror. I'd never really considered classic myths through that lens before, but it totally made sense. Was that connection intentional? What do you see as the differences and overlap between these types of stories?

MG: I write most of my poetry with a cosmic horror flare, so perhaps there wasn't intention at first, but upon further reflection, I do consider the concept of mythology and, in particular, mythology from this lens fitting for cosmic horror. Classic myths were beautiful in their poetic structures, but the stories were dark, ugly, and exposed much of the indifference often exhibited in cosmic horror.

IFP: My two favorite poems were 'The Moth' and 'I Am Yawn,' both of which seem to involve almost mundane concepts/objects expanded to monstrous proportions. Can you talk a bit about the interplay between recognizable elements and fantastical reconfigurations?

MG: I really enjoyed writing both of these. *I am Yawn, The Moth, Below, the Pit,* and technically *Post-Eros* were poems inspired by the primordial gods as described in Hesiod's Theogony. The only exception being *The Moth,* which draws from Mesopotamian and Abrahamic belief systems on the myth of the Behemoth. Chaos, love, void, and monsters are some of the most common and terrifying aspects of every mythology and belief system in humanity. They are at the core of it all. These poems had to have something simple and powerful within them that set them apart from the other poems in the chapbook.

I am Yawn was my attempt at trying to capture Chaos' unending desire and contempt for existence as well as its destruction within a single gasp. Or our feeble perception of what that might possibly never be.

Maxwell I. Gold is a Jewish American multiple award nominated author who writes prose poetry and short stories in cosmic horror and weird fiction with half a decade of writing experience. Some of his books include Oblivion in Flux: A Coection of Cyber Prose from Crystal Lake Publishing and Bleeding Rainbows and Other Broken Spectrums from Hex Publishers. Five-time Rhysling Award nominee, and two-time Pushcart Award nominee, find him at www.thewellsoftheweird.com.

DISABILITY, QUEERNESS, & POETRY AS COMMUNITY: INTERVIEW WITH ENNIS ROOK BASHE, AUTHOR OF BEAUTIFUL MALADY

JULIE REESER

> "I think that people caring about each other is one of the most beautiful things that can exist."

The twenty-five poems in ennis rook bashe's B*eautiful Malady: Poems (Interstellar Flight Press, 2023)* chapbook bring the reader to a world of love and loneliness, strength and frailty. Julie Reeser interviewed ennis rook bashe about their poetry as community, and finding empowerment through the creative life.

INTERSTELLAR FLIGHT PRESS: This chapbook resonated with me as a disabled and chronically ill person. That's not a common experience, despite the hard and persistent work for representation. I don't believe inclusivity is happening rapidly enough, especially with the sudden influx of millions of long-covid patients. And while the disabled community is huge, connecting can be difficult. That's one of the functions of poetry: connecting and communicating concepts and mutual experiences. Can you talk a little bit about using your voice in poetry as a queer and disabled person, and how that creates a wider dialogue?

ENNIS ROOK BASHE: Creating work through which readers can feel seen is incredibly important to me as an author, and I'm always awed by the knowledge that my work can touch others. It feels like magic—I'm just tapping out some fun little ideas on my phone, and BOOM, another human person is experiencing a feeling.

In many of the persona poems that make up this chapbook, I view a lot of my process as communicating not only my viewpoints, but also the viewpoints of others. Fictional villains. Characters given short shrift by their original authors. People who maybe only exist in my head. And, encompassing all that, an expression of the collective voice of the community. I like how poets can use "I" to mean "we."

IFP: One of the more subtle and harrowing experiences a disabled and/or chronically ill person can experience is medical trauma. You touch on this in your poems and the Author's Note at the back of the book. You mention disbelief as one form of abuse that we experience—how does speculative poetry as a genre lend itself to healing and re-empowering the reader?

ERB: An experience that's common to many disabled people is being silenced or going unheard:

"No, you're not really experiencing that."

"No, you couldn't possibly need all that."

"No, you don't understand your body, you don't know your own mind."

Poetry inherently runs counter to silence because, ultimately, it's about the expression of truth. Even when I'm writing a piece from the perspective of a wizard or a cyborg, I am speaking the truth of that character and channeling the free expression of that voice. It's a way for readers to vicariously experience being validated and perceived. I hope that by sharing truths, I can help others to feel less alone.

IFP: The chapbook has a romance running through it in eight poems about a person named Rose. The story has a gothic feel, and my favorite part is that despite Rose being disabled and ill, she's the heroine. As someone whose lover and best friend is also their caregiver, reading this relationship flipped around felt fresh and welcome. Can you talk a little bit about this romance element and what it means to you?

ERB: I'm a romance novelist in addition to being a poet. It's very aligned with my interests as a trauma-informed mental health professional: we are wired for community. Our brains are built to be around other people who can help us feel safe. Romance novels, and love stories with happy endings in general, can speak to those parts of the brain. As writers, we can create a better world for our readers in their imaginations.

When I was first revising this chapbook, Interstellar Flight Press gave me extensive notes about expanding it and linking the work's themes. I wanted to create a long narrative poem (which is a form I'm immensely interested in coming from a prose background) that touched on the larger idea of sickness as something that could be beautiful and even romanticized. And I think that people caring about each other is one of the most beautiful things that can exist.

IFP: "Death is a Lesbian and She Can Pick Me Up" might be the best poem title I've ever encountered. One idea in it, along with "Trauma is for People Who Fear Death" is that death isn't the worst thing that can happen to a body. "I realized the grief I leave behind / will belong to other people" is such a piercing and perceptive line. It pairs nicely with the line, "pain is the fairytale stepmother forcing me to sift lentils" from rose ghost v. But nowhere are you saying to give up. The poems in the chapbook remain hopeful and active—"What I love most about Death is that she understands / how busy I am"—will you talk about this?

ERB: Abled people in my life often comment about how optimistic I am and how great it is that I try to keep busy, even on days when I have to crawl around my apartment. And I've never understood any of those compliments. What am I supposed to do, sit around feeling sorry for myself? I'd get bored!

I would say that my philosophy—not only as a writer, but as a person—can be described by this one quote from a favorite classic writer of mine, Frances Hodgson Burnett.

"There is no time for fear!" he cried out in the field. "Let us go on with our work."

When life feels overwhelming, I focus on doing the work that's just in front of me. Climate apocalypse? No time to doomscroll, I have a volunteer shift running a support group. Big election? I'm going to phone bank for three hours and then take a bath. One of the scholars who wrote the Talmud said—and this is just one translation—"You are not obligated to complete the work, but neither are you free to abandon it."

The quote is talking about what I think of as the Great Work, the task of fighting evil and making the world a better place for future generations. Ultimately, I think that's what we as humans are here to do, and I'm glad my ideals come through in my writing.

I experienced the presence of my grandfather's spirit when he died, before I even got the phone call saying that he had passed from his body. All my fear and grief over losing him was replaced by the unshakeable feeling that he would be able to do what he loved again (he was a professor of Psychology) and that everything was going to be all right.

Everything. Absolutely everything in the entire world.

Death, I think, is like that.

But there's so much to do *here* first.

Ennis Rook Bashe is a queer romance novelist and poet whose work has appeared in Strange Horizons, Cricket, and Liminality Magazine. Their debut chapbook, Glitter Blood, was an Elgin Award nominee. If you enjoyed the disability-related themes in this chapbook, you may also enjoy their fantasy romance series Hunters of the Cairn, set in a world where only disabled and chronically ill people can become monster hunters. Find more Ennis at https://linktr.ee/ennisrookbashe.

CONTRIBUTOR BIOGRAPHIES

Patrick Barb is an author of weird, dark, and horrifying tales, currently living (and trying not to freeze to death) in Saint Paul, Minnesota. His published works include the dark fiction collections *The Children's Horror* and *Pre-Approved for Haunting*, the novellas *Gargantuana's Ghost* and *Turn*, as well as the novelette *Helicopter Parenting in the Age of Drone Warfare*. His forthcoming works include his debut sci-fi/horror novel *Abducted* from Dark Matter Ink. His 2023 short story "The Scare Groom" was selected for *Best Horror of the Year Volume 16*. Visit him at patrickbarb.com.

Andrea Blythe is an author, poet, and game writer, who loves exploring the fantastical, horrifying, and weird. She is the author of three poetry chapbooks, the most recent being *Twelve: Poems Inspired by the Brothers Grimm Fairy Tale* (*Interstellar Flight Press*, 2020). Her fourth poetry collection, *Necessary Poisons*, is forthcoming from Interstellar Flight Press in 2024. Her fiction and poetry has also appeared in various anthologies and journals, including *Corvid Queen, Luna Station Quarterly, Enchanted Conversation, Quail Bell*, and more. She is a member of the Science Fiction and Fantasy Poetry Association and the Horror Writers Association. Find her online at andreablythe.com.

Grant Butler is the author of the novel *The Heroin Heiress*. His short fiction has been published in *Sick Cruising, Close to the Bone, Mardi Gras Mysteries, Punk Noir Magazine*, and *The Siren's Call*, and his nonfiction has been featured in *Interstellar Flight Magazine, Hear Us Scream, Certified Forgotten*, and *The Best New True Crime Stories*

Salena Casha's work has appeared in over 100 publications in the last decade. She survives New England winters on good beer and black coffee. Subscribe to her substack at salenacasha.substack.com

Tanvi Chowdhary is a researcher based in New Delhi; currently pursuing her PhD in English Literature. Popculture enthusiast and professional hot-chocolate maker.

Ryan Fay is the editor at *Enfrightened Press*, which focuses on academic discussions of the horror genre. His expertise is in examining social justice issues in horror films and literature.

J. V. Gachs is a Spanish ESL writer. Her work has been featured in anthologies like Scott J. Moses' *What One Wouldn't Do* and Chelsea Pumpkins' *AHH! That's What I Call Horror!* Her debut novel, *Epiphany*, was published by *Off Limits Press* in 2023, and in Spanish by *Dolmen Editorial* in June 2024. As a self-translating author, her second novella *Spooky Lovers* will be published in English by *Interstellar Flight Press* and in Spanish by *Dimensiones Ocultas* in 2024. Next year, *Mad Axe Media* will publish her novella *Unholy*. Obsessed with sudden death, ghosts, and bisexual characters, she always writes with a cat (or two) in her lap.

Brishti Guha has a PhD from Princeton and is an associate professor of economics at the Jawaharlal Nehru University, New Delhi. Apart from publishing academic papers in international journals, she enjoys writing on science fiction and ancient India and translating Sanskrit literature. Her pieces have appeared in *Analog Science Fiction and Fact, Samovar, New Myths, Sci Phi Journal, Eye to the Telescope, the Dr TJ Eckleburg Review, Mercurian, Chrome Baby, Jaggery, Empty Mirror, Ezra,* and *Newfound*.

Indrani Guha is a Harvard alumnus and a psychotherapist.

Taylor Jones writes fiction and poetry about the possible future and the impossible present. Her work is often inspired by her background in and love of biology. Her writing and art have appeared in *Reckoning, Spit Poet Zine, Smoky Quartz, South Broadway Ghost Society, Interstellar Flight Press,* and *Barren Magazine*. She lives in Denver, Colorado, in a house full of plants. Links to her work can be found here: https://linktr.ee/trjonesartwork.

Alex Kingsley (they/them) is a writer, comedian, game designer, and playwright. They are a co-founder of the new media company Strong Branch Productions, where they write and direct sci-fi comedy podcast *The Stench of Adventure* and other shows. Their short fiction has appeared in *Translunar Travelers Lounge, Radon Journal, The Storage Papers,* and more. In 2023 they published their short story collection, *The Strange Garden and Other Weird Tales*. Their debut novel *Empress of Dus*t will be published by S*pace Wizard Science Fantasy* in Fall 2024. Alex's sci-fi plays have been produced in LA, Philadelphia, and Chicago. Alex's writers SFF-related non-fiction for *Ancillary Review of Books*. Their games can be downloaded pay-what-you-will at alexyquest.itch.io.

Born and raised in Southampton, UK, **Hesper Leveret** studied Ancient History at Oxford and now lives in Liverpool with her family and chronic pain. She writes speculative fiction about beauty and heartbreak, magic and imagined mythology. Her stories appear in venues including *Fireside, Interzone, Cosmic Roots and Eldritch Shores,* and *Luna Station Quarterly*. Her interests include reading books and escaping rooms.

Vanessa Maki is a queer Blerd, freelance writer, and artist. She has written for a variety of publications including *Pink Advocate, Dread Central, The Mary Sue,* and many more. She's a former regular contributor for *Pink Advocate* and *The Mary Sue*. You can find her on Twitter and Instagram @theblackbuffy.

Archita Mittra is a writer, critic, editor and artist from Kolkata, India. Her work has appeared in *Lightspeed, Locus Magazine, Reactor, Strange Horizons*, and elsewhere. She is an Ignyte finalist for the Critic's Award while her fiction and poetry have been nominated for the Pushcart and best of the net prizes and longlisted for the Toto Award. You can find her haunting Twitter and Instagram @architamittra.

Mahailey Oliver holds an English MA from Stephen F. Austin State University in Nacogdoches, Texas. Her work has recently appeared in *Spark to Flame, Forget Me Not Press,* and *The Afterpast Review.* She teaches sophomore English at a Title 1 school in Texas, and enjoys stargazing, hammocking, and manifesting autumnal vibes.

Robert P. Ottone is the Bram Stoker Award-winning author of *The Triangle* and is also the best-selling author of *Curse of the Cob Man, The Sleepy Hollow Gang, The Vile Thing We Created*, and *Nocturnal Creatures*. His short fiction has been collected in *Wrapped in Plastic and Other Sweet Nothings* as well as *Her Infernal Name and Other Nightmares.* He holds two master's degrees in Education, as well as an MFA in Children's Literature. A bagel-loving fabulist of spooky absurdity, Ottone enjoys cigars, cocktails and time with his wife.

Julie Reeser is the author of the novella, *Language of the Spirit.* Her short fiction can be found in *Beneath Ceaseless Skies, Bourbon Penn, Factor Four,* and others. There's a cool carousel of stories you can ride on her website: persephoneknits.com. She is disabled, but not done.

Gretchen Rockwell is a queer poet who can frequently be found writing about gender, science, space, and unusual connections. Xe is the author of the Elgin Award-nominated chapbooks *body in motion* (*perhappened press*) and *Lexicon of Future Selves* (*VA Press*) as well as two microchapbooks; xer work has appeared in *AGNI, Cotton Xenomorph, Whale Road Review, Palette Poetry*, and elsewhere. Find xer at gretchenrockwell.com or on Instagram at @daft_rockwell.

Chloe Smith is a physically disabled and autistic writer and poet from the UK. She is a fan of movies, TV shows, and books, and has articles on all three published in a variety of online and print publications, including *Interstellar Magazine.* For more of her work, please check out her website: chloesmithwrites.wordpress.com.

Christina Sng is the three-time Bram Stoker Award-winning author of *A Collection of Nightmares, A Collection of Dreamscapes,* and *Tortured Willows.* Her poetry, fiction, essays, and art appear in numerous venues worldwide, including *Interstellar Flight Magazine, New Myths, Penumbric, Southwest Review,* and T*he Washington Post.* She currently serves as Vice President of the Science Fiction & Fantasy Poetry Association.

A 2016 MBA graduate and published author, **Priya Sridhar** has been writing fantasy and science fiction for fifteen years, and counting. *Capstone* published the *Powered* series. Priya lives in Miami, Florida with her family.

R. Thursday is a queer educator, historian, writer, and all-around nerd. Lives with the world's most copacetic cat in South King County, Washington.

Megan Wegenke is a writer and a lifelong devotee of sci-fi, fantasy, and weird fiction in all their myriad forms. Her long list of interests includes cooking, bookbinding, theatre, roller derby, bad puns, historical fashion, and vampire fiction with lesbian subtext. She has an MA in fiction writing from the University of Wisconsin-Milwaukee, where she got a SCUBA certification in the process of doing research for a novel manuscript. Megan lives in Chicago with her partner and three incorrigible cats.

Lisa Timpf is a retired HR and communications professional who lives in Simcoe, Ontario. Her poetry, fiction, creative non-fiction, and book reviews have appeared in *New Myths, Star*Line, The Future Fire,* and other venues. Lisa's speculative haibun collection, *In Days to Come*, is available from *Hiraeth Publishing*. You can find out more about Lisa's writing and artwork at lisatimpf.blogspot.com.

T.D. Walker is the author of the poetry collections S*mall Waiting Objects* (*CW Books*, 2019), *Maps of a Hollowed World* (*Another New Calligraphy*, 2020), and *Doubt & Circuitry* (*Southern Arizona Press*, 2023). She hosts and curates poetry programs for shortwave radio, most recently *Line Break*. Find out more at https://www.tdwalker.net

Holly Lyn Walrath is a freelance editor and author based out of Houston, Texas. She holds a B.A. in English from The University of Texas and a Master's in Creative Writing from the University of Denver. Her poetry and short fiction has appeared in *Strange Horizons, Fireside Fiction, Daily Science Fiction, Luna Station Quarterly, Liminality*, and elsewhere. She is the author of three books of poetry: *Glimmerglass Girl, The Smallest of Bones,* and *Numinous Stones.* Find her online at hlwalrath.com.

J.Z. Weston writes short stories and reviews. They have a soft spot for contemporary and urban fantasy and are particularly fascinated by how stories teach us to be human. You can find more of their work at jzwestonauthor.com.

INTERSTELLAR FLIGHT PRESS

Interstellar Flight Press is an indie speculative publishing house. We feature innovative works from the best new writers in science fiction and fantasy. In the words of Ursula K. Le Guin, we need "writers who can see alternatives to how we live now, can see through our fear-stricken society and its obsessive technologies to other ways of being, and even imagine real grounds for hope."

Find us online at www.interstellarflightpress.com.

facebook.com/interstellarflightpress
x.com/intflightpress
instagram.com/interstellarflightpress
patreon.com/interstellarflightpress

www.ingramcontent.com/pod-product-compliance
Lightning Source LLC
Chambersburg PA
CBHW060655190726
48289CB00002B/420
* 9 7 8 1 9 5 3 7 3 6 4 2 0 *